"Miss Greentree! You are truly the bravest woman of my acquaintance!"

"Lord Montegomery?" Her hazel eyes widened. "What can you mean?"

"I mean that you have come to my house. All alone. I congratulate you."

Vivianna wondered if he was trying to be amusing. She had come here to leave her card, but instead had been allowed into his inner sanctum. She had not expected to see him, but when the opportunity was given to her she had not been able to resist.

But now that she was actually standing before him, seeing the gleam in his eye, noting the way his dark hair fell forward over his brow . . . Her breath hitched; her fingers tightened on her bag. This was Oliver Montegomery at his most dangerous.

Vivianna did her best to pretend she was unaffected. "I do not think I have anything to be afraid of, my lord," she said evenly. "You are a gentleman, are you not?"

He smiled and gently shook his finger at her. "I was born

but I am afraid

earn the right to

Other **AVON ROMANCES**

Her Scandalous Affair *by Candice Hern*
In The Night *by Kathryn Smith*
A Kiss in the Dark *by Kimberly Logan*
Must Have Been The Moonlight *by Melody Thomas*
Seducing a Princess *by Lois Greiman*
Stealing Sophie *by Sarah Gabriel*
What an Earl Wants *by Shirley Karr*

Coming Soon

Alas, My Love *by Edith Layton*
A Woman's Innocence *by Gayle Callen*

And Don't Miss These
ROMANTIC TREASURES
from Avon Books

Just One Touch *by Debra Mullins*
Sin and Sensibility *by Suzanne Enoch*
Something About Emmaline *by Elizabeth Boyle*

SARA BENNETT

LESSONS IN SEDUCTION

AVON BOOKS
An Imprint of HarperCollins*Publishers*

This is a work of fiction. Names, characters, places, and incidents are products of the author's imagination or are used fictitiously and are not to be construed as real. Any resemblance to actual events, locales, organizations, or persons, living or dead, is entirely coincidental.

AVON BOOKS
An Imprint of HarperCollins*Publishers*
10 East 53rd Street
New York, New York 10022-5299

ISBN: 0-06-058438-6
www.avonromance.com

First Avon Books paperback printing: March 2005

Printed in the U.S.A.

10 9 8 7 6 5 4 3 2 1

Prologue

The Greentree Estate
Yorkshire, England
1826

Vivianna put a finger to her lips, her hazel eyes wide in her oval-shaped, grubby face, her curly chestnut hair in desperate need of a wash and a good comb. Her two little sisters, their faces as smeared with tears and dirt as her own, huddled close together, eyes big, and held their breath.

Voices, outside the cottage, were drawing closer.

Vivianna recognized one of them as the whiskered man who had been here earlier, peering at them through the window, trying to coax them outside.

The whiskered man frightened her.

When he had gone, stomping off and shaking his head, the three girls remained hidden in a dark corner of the bedroom. To amuse them, Vivianna had told her sisters a story about three little girls who had been stolen from their mother and taken far away by a woman with a thin, narrow face and her evil husband, and then abandoned.

It closely resembled their own story, but in Vivianna's version the three little girls had been reunited with their mother and all had been well. A nice happy ending.

"Hungry," two-year-old Marietta had declared when the story was finished, her blue eyes wide, her fair curls dancing about her face.

"I know you're hungry, 'Etta," six-year-old Vivianna had replied softly, "but we ate the last bit of the loaf this morning. I'll try and find some food outside. When it's dark." She had no idea how she was going to accomplish this, but she knew that as the eldest it was her job to look after her two younger sisters.

Marietta had smiled with complete trust. Francesca had simply whimpered and clung closer to Vivianna's skirts. Dark-haired and dark-eyed, she was like a little pixie, and at one year old she wasn't able to understand what was happening. Only that they were no longer safe in their warm and comfortable home with their friendly servants. Francesca had been asleep when the man had come and bundled them into the coach with Mrs. Slater and sent them away.

Far away.

Vivianna did not know how much time had passed since that night—days and weeks had become confused in her mind. She was even beginning to forget how everything at home had looked and felt. Mrs. Slater had not been cruel to them, but neither had she been particularly kind. And once the man she said was her husband turned up, she was even more ambivalent. The couple had spent most of their nights and days locked in their bedroom, and fed the children only if they felt like it. It had fallen to Vivianna, a child herself, to calm her youngest sisters and to try and look after them all as best she could.

When the man had grown angry, she had told them stories until they slept. And then Vivianna lay with her eyes wide open, trying to think of a way to get home. Her sense of helplessness and weakness made her stomach ache. She longed desperately for her home and her mother, but the awful thing was she did not know where they were.

Oh, she knew that her home was in the countryside, but she didn't know what it was called or the village it stood near—she never *had* to know—she had always been kept away from anyone who might ask too many questions.

Somehow Vivianna understood, even as a tiny child, that her existence was a secret.

As for her mother . . . she had been "Mama," and Vivianna had no idea of the names others called her and where in London she went when she was not with her children.

The Slaters kept them prisoners in the cottage, and then one morning, a few days ago, the girls awoke to find the couple gone. Alone in the cottage, the children waited. And waited. Vivianna had been certain Mrs. Slater would return, but she didn't. The three young sisters had been effectively abandoned in that dark, sagging cottage.

Once more Vivianna did her best to look after her sisters—even at the age of six her sense of responsibility was highly developed. She was mature for her years; her hazel eyes held a determined expression that should have belonged to a much older person.

The voices came again now, drifting into Vivianna's consciousness. She blinked and shook off her dreamy thoughts. By now she was so tired and hungry that she tended to imagine things. Once she had seen a lion prowling through the overgrown garden, only to realize a moment later it was nothing more dangerous than a scrawny tabby cat.

But she could definitely hear the whiskered man. And then a woman's voice. There was something achingly familiar in the soft, educated tones.

"Mama?" Vivianna whispered. She knew it wasn't her mother, and yet the voice drew her. "Stay here," she instructed her sisters. Very carefully, she crept out of the damp, pungent bedroom and into the front room. A small-paned, dirty window looked out to the garden, where weeds had strangled anything useful or pretty. Now she could see the whiskered man and, standing beside him, a tall and elegant lady, her honey-colored hair piled neatly on her head. Her gown was black, and beneath the ankle-length hem were a pair of elegant black slippers with a small heel. Vivianna knew that the wearing of black garments meant that someone close to the lady had died.

"Boastin', she was, in the village," the man was saying.

"Who was boasting, Rawlings?" asked the lady, following him up the narrow path between the weeds to the front door. "Such a mess," she added to herself, frowning at the garden. "I had not realized how much things had deteriorated since Edward . . ." Suddenly she looked very sad.

Rawlings had not heard her. "The Slater woman, ma'am. Saying the three girls were the daughters of some high-class London tart. Boastin' how much money she'd been making by keeping them hidden away here on the estate."

The lady gave the cottage a doubtful look. "Are you quite certain the children are still here, Rawlings?"

Rawlings met the lady's pale eyes. "They are, my lady. Won't come out. That oldest one, shaking like a leaf she were, but brave! She stood in front of the others as if she meant to fight me."

"I can hardly believe it," the lady said, again more to herself than Rawlings. "It is bad enough for those two to run off without a word, but to abandon three young children in their care! 'Tis monstrous."

"There was a rumor that the Slater woman was a baby farmer, my lady. She was paid to care for unwanted children—children born out of wedlock or the children of soiled doves. She'd brought these three with her from down south, but no one knows exactly where they come from. I expect their mother, whoever she is, was glad to be rid of them."

"They are children, Rawlings, and they are in desperate need of a home, and I intend to find them one."

Vivianna felt shaky. There was something fierce and yet at the same time gentle about this lady that struck a chord deep within her. Instinctively she knew that here was someone she could believe in. Someone to whom she could entrust the care of her two little sisters.

The cottage door was opening. "Hello there?" called the lady in black. Then, in a quieter voice, turning to Rawlings, "What are their names? What are the children's names?"

"The eldest one is Vivianna, my lady. I heard that, once, in the village, Mrs. Slater called her Annie, but the girl didn't like it and wouldn't obey her till she called her by her rightful name."

The lady smiled. "Vivianna. And the others?"

"They're just little 'uns—I don't know their names, my lady."

"Very well. Vivianna? Vivianna, are you there?"

Vivianna froze in the shadows. The lady entered the

cottage and stood, accustoming herself to the gloom. The three of them could probably still escape, if she was quick. But Vivianna had liked the way the lady had called her by her proper name, and she didn't want to run away. Besides, where would they go? Here in the cottage she had been able to keep her sisters safe, but beyond it was another matter. She felt alone and afraid, and very, very tired. Again she sensed that there was something about this lady that made her trustworthy. That she was someone who could help.

"Vivianna?" The lady called again, softly, urgently. Her black skirts brushed against the filthy wall. She did not bother to exclaim and move away or to brush the dirt off; finding the children seemed to be her most important—her *only*—consideration.

"Here I am."

The lady started and turned. Rawlings made as if to rush and grab Vivianna, but the lady held up a hand, her attention wholly on the little girl. Vivianna saw that her eyes were light blue and kind. They kindled a warm fire in Vivianna's weary and frightened heart.

"Who are you?" Vivianna asked. She did not mean to be rude—during these months with Mrs. Slater she had begun to forget her manners—but she needed to know.

"I am Lady Greentree, my dear. I own your cottage and the land upon which it stands. This is my estate."

There was a rustle in the doorway on the far side of the room and two little figures scurried toward Vivianna. Vivianna saw that her sisters' faces were freshly tear-streaked and that Marietta was clutching her beloved rag doll that she had brought with her from home. She pulled her sisters close, holding them safe against her grubby skirts.

For a moment Lady Greentree looked as if she

might cry, too, and then she asked gently, "What is your full name, Vivianna? Can you tell me from where you have come?"

"Mrs. Slater brought us here," Vivianna said slowly, and her eyes threatened to shut. It was the hunger, she supposed. "We came from the country, but I don't know where. There was a village, but I don't know what it was called. Our house was big and full of fine things, and there were servants. . . . No one ever called me anything other than Miss Vivianna, not until Mrs. Slater started calling me Annie."

Vivianna wished there was something she could say or remember that would magically allow them to go home. She had a horrible feeling that now that they had been taken away, they would never find their way back again.

Marietta had been gazing intently at Lady Greentree, and now she lisped, "Mama?"

Lady Greentree's eyes filled with tears. "Oh, you poor little dears!" She took a shaking breath and held out her hand. "I have no children of my own, and it has always been my sorrow and regret that I was not so blessed. My husband Edward was an officer in the army, in India, but now he is dead and I am a widow. I am alone, just as you are alone. Will you all come home with me and allow me to look after you?"

Vivianna looked longingly at the soft white hand held out to her. The hand that reminded her achingly of her own mother.

Rawlings drew in a sharp breath. "My lady, you don't even know whose spawn they be!"

Lady Greentree gave him such a look that his face flamed red. Vivianna liked that, and she liked the way the lady's hand remained held out toward them, steady and waiting. A promise. She took a step forward, and then another, despite being hampered by her sisters' clutching fists. Vivianna put her own hand, cold and faintly sticky, into that of Lady Greentree's. Warmth enfolded her fingers.

And her heart.

Lady Greentree smiled down upon her as if it were Vivianna who had offered her sanctuary, and not the other way around. "Come, my dears," she said softly. "Let us all leave this awful place."

Chapter 1

Berkeley Square
London
1840
Fourteen years later

Inside the tall, elegant London townhouse, Lord Montegomery was impatiently allowing his valet to put the finishing touches to his evening ensemble. Fitted black coat and tapered black trousers and a fine white linen shirt with a high collar and white cravat. The only splash of color came from his waistcoat; bottle-blue velvet with gold embroidery and large gold buttons.

There was a time when Oliver never would have worn such an item, when black and white were the only accepted colors for evening dress. The waistcoat was unforgivably vulgar and tasteless, but he thought it appropriate; it represented to him the present state of his life. Tonight he was planning to spend a pleasant few hours at Aphrodite's, before moving on to a drinking house affectionately called the Bucket of Blood, where he hoped to see some bare-knuckle fighting and lay a bet or two. In the past, a night like that would occur every month or so, but now it was close to every night. Drinking, gambling, carousing; his standards had slipped. To all intents and purposes he was on a downward slide—everybody said so.

And that was just as he wanted it.

"My lord?"

A glance at the door showed him his butler, looking troubled.

"What is it, Hodge?"

"The young *person* who called earlier is outside in the square. I can see her lurking by the garden railings. Should I call the constables?"

"Do you mean Miss Vivianna Greentree?"

"Correct, my lord."

Oliver frowned at his own reflection. Here was a complication he had not expected. Miss Greentree from Yorkshire, come to ring a peal over him.

"My lord? Shall it be the constables?"

Oliver picked up his ebony-handled cane. "Efficient as the members of Sir Robert Peel's Metropolitan Police Force are, Hodge, I do not think they are required just yet. Let her be. If she tries to follow me, she will find she has bitten off more than she can chew. Send the carriage around. I am ready."

Hodge bowed and went to do his bidding, while Oliver followed at a more leisurely pace. Miss Greentree might be an unexpected complication, but he did not think she was a particularly dangerous one. In fact, her presence in London might well enhance his wicked reputation even more. Time would tell what part Miss Vivianna Greentree from Yorkshire had to play in this story.

* * *

Miss Vivianna Greentree stood outside the tall, elegant London house, its windows ablaze with light, and felt very small. Beneath the thin soles of her leather half-boots she could feel every bump in the square, and the cold crisp air made her shiver despite her sensible wool gown and her warm cloak with its fur-trimmed collar.

Impotent anger stirred inside her, a dark, smothering sense of frustration that had been building since she left the Greentree estate all those days ago in response to a frantic letter from the Beatty sisters concerning the fate of the Shelter for Poor Orphans.

Before her, on the west side of Berkeley Square, the elegant Queen Anne home of Lord Montegomery rose up like an accusation. The Montegomerys were an old, proud, and aristocratic family, and Oliver was the last of them. What would a gentleman of his privileged background know of poverty and abandonment? Vivianna's fingers tightened upon the riding crop she held in one hand—protection, in case she needed to go into streets that were less than suitable for a woman of her class and refinement.

Vivianna had already been up to Lord Montegomery's door to ask that he speak with her on a matter of urgency. The supercilious-looking butler who answered her brisk use of the knocker had informed her that Lord Montegomery was about to go out to his club, and besides, he did not allow unaccompanied *female persons* into his dwelling.

As if, Vivianna thought furiously, it was *her* reputation in doubt rather than *his*!

Again her gloved fingers tightened upon the riding crop. Well, he would soon realize that Miss Vivianna Greentree from Yorkshire was not so easily thrown off the scent. She was determined that the Shelter for Poor Orphans would not close down because of one selfish gentleman.

A rattle of wheels and clatter of hooves heralded the approach of a carriage from the far end of the square. It drew to a halt outside Montegomery's house. His lordship, it appeared, was preparing to go out to his club just as his butler had said.

This was the moment Vivianna had been waiting for. Even she, country bumpkin that she was, knew that fashionable London gentlemen were wont to go out in the evening. And from what she had learned of Lord Montegomery, he was a very fashionable gentleman indeed.

Quickly, she moved into the shadows by the iron railings that protected the garden and the plane trees in the middle of the square. One of the passengers on the mail coach, with whom she had shared the long journey south, had been very informative when it came to London gentlemen of Lord Montegomery's ilk, and with an eye to the future, Vivianna had encouraged him to talk of such creatures in general.

"Gaming and drinking clubs, night houses, and disorderly women! My goodness, miss, you mind yourself in London, a sweet innocent little thing like yourself."

Vivianna did not consider herself "sweet," and although she was "innocent" in the physical sense, she was very well read and informed. Nor did she believe herself to be in any danger from Montegomery. A man like that would prefer all the superficial womanly virtues—sweet and biddable, and certainly beautiful, in a wan and helpless sort of way. Vivianna knew herself to be none of these things; certainly she was not beautiful in the current fashion. To be like Queen Victoria was now the aim of every girl—short and pretty and plump.

Vivianna's eyes were large and hazel, and her hair was chestnut, thick and glossy when she allowed it its freedom. She was tall and buxom—Junoesque—with a voice both clear and precise. And she had a way of looking at men that tended to make them squirm nervously. A gentleman of her acquaintance had once said of her that when she turned her gaze upon him, he felt as if she were making judgment, and that in summing up she had found him lacking.

No, Vivianna thought, she was in no danger from a known rake and scoundrel—she was well able to protect herself—and she doubted she would need the riding crop to drive him off. Her aim was to confront Montegomery, make her appeal to him, and persuade him to her point of view.

And Vivianna knew she could be very persuasive indeed.

The front door had opened. She could see the gleam of mirrors and marble within, and the bright splash of flowers. No doubt Lord Montegomery's house was very beautiful, and Vivianna admired beauty, but she did not envy him. Her mother came from a family, the Tremaines, who had made their money by "trade"—Lady Greentree's grandfather had been a seller of meats. The Tremaines were not at all blue-blooded, and Vivianna's mother had gained her title from her husband, Sir Edward Greentree. She had also gained a beautiful, if isolated, home in Yorkshire and, more importantly, a family who loved her.

Surely that was the point, wasn't it? That everyone should have someone to love them? Even a man like Lord Montegomery would understand an appeal put to him in those terms.

Wouldn't he?

Suddenly there he was, the gentleman himself: Lord Montegomery. Vivianna's eyes narrowed, and she leaned forward to see him better.

Obligingly, he paused a moment on the doorstep, the light falling upon him. He was tall, with broad shoulders shown to best advantage by his well-made coat, and a lithe, physically fit body. He swung a cane in one hand and held his top hat in the other, as he turned his head toward the approaching vehicle. His hair was dark and glossy, combed back at the front and longer, curling over his high white collar, at the back. He glanced nonchalantly in her direction, seemingly enjoying the clear, crisp evening air, and Vivianna was presented with a face that was angular—a straight nose and high cheekbones with dark side-whiskers and a square jaw—and handsome. And yet more than that. There were plenty of handsome men in London. This man, for all his fine clothes, looked like a pirate. Someone of whom to beware.

A shiver of awareness made her draw her cloak closer about her.

Had she really expected him to be a kindly old gentleman? Besides, Vivianna told herself, she had faced more hopeless tasks in her twenty years. Persuading a rich and selfish gentleman to change his mind, to do some good for others less fortunate, should be a simple matter. She had no reason to be afraid of him—for surely it was fear that had brought that heaviness to her chest, and anxiety that made her skin tingle and her breath quicken?

With another shiver, Vivianna moved closer to the garden railings.

Lord Montegomery had left his doorstep for the street, swinging his cane as if he hadn't a care in the world. Vivianna supposed he hadn't. Well, *that* was about to change. As she watched, he climbed into his carriage, and soon the vehicle rattled around the square and out in a southerly direction.

Vivianna picked up her skirts and ran. Her hackney cab was waiting for her on the other side of Berkeley Square, hidden by the central gardens.

She wrenched open the door and sprang inside.

"Follow the black carriage!" she called, and was flung back against the worn squabs as the driver enthusiastically obliged.

Are you certain this is appropriate behavior for a young lady? Would it not be more sensible if you came back in the morning and left your visiting card? Lady Greentree's softly modulated voice sounded in her head.

Perhaps, she acknowledged, under other circumstances her actions would be considered impetuous and a little improper, but these were desperate times. She must speak with this man, convince him to change his mind and save the Shelter for Poor Orphans. She could not see the hard work of so many, the happiness of so many more, come to nothing because of the spoiled and rich Lord Montegomery.

Yes, my dear, that is all very well and fine, but are you sure you are not enjoying your adventure just a little bit more than necessary?

Vivianna thought it better to ignore that question.

The hackney was rattling along nicely to wherever they were going. Her righteous anger gave way to a new spurt of anxiety. She hoped his destination was not Seven Dials or St. Giles's, or one of the other dangerous areas of London. Even though she had been in the city for such a brief time, she had seen the overcrowding and smelled the horrid odors.

She hoped that Lord Montegomery really was going to one of his clubs, or even to one of the gentlemen's gaming houses or rowdy drinking dens to be found in the capital. A respectable lady like herself may not be exactly welcome in the last two, but with a crowd about her she would feel safe enough, and if she kept her mouth closed and her eyes down, surely she should not attract too much unwanted attention.

The hackney's wheels rumbled over a cobbled section and turned another corner. An omnibus, full of passengers even at this time of night, groaned by and the two drivers exchanged shouts she found incomprehensible. Just as well, perhaps. Vivianna's thoughts turned inward once again, settling on Miss Susan and Miss Greta Beatty and their frantic letter. The words seemed literally burned into her brain.

Dearest Miss Greentree,

As our most respected and beloved friend, and our supporter from the very beginning, we write once more to beg for your assistance. Awful news! We have just heard that in nine weeks our Shelter for Poor Orphans is to be taken from us. Demolished! Please, Miss Greentree, there is no time to be lost! Come to London as soon as you may. Do make haste if you would see this dreadful wrong made right before it is too late. . . .

The rest of the letter had been almost illegible. That the gentle and practical Miss Susan and Miss Greta should be driven to write such wild prose could only mean that the matter was very serious indeed. It was impossible for Vivianna to deny them her help and support, despite the fact that she could hardly credit what she was reading. The Shelter for Poor Orphans to be torn down in nine weeks?

She *would* not allow it.

The hackney rattled again, turning into a broader and certainly more sober street, lit by soft gaslights. Vivianna closed her eyes. The Shelter for Poor Orphans had been her triumph, a dream she had long held close to her heart, and which had finally been brought to fruition by hard work and much stubborn determination.

The shelter was a place for abandoned children, those poor mites who had not been lucky enough to have a darling Lady Greentree come to their aid. It was a place where they could be cared for, fed, and given an education. It had been Vivianna's dream alone, until Miss Susan and Miss Greta had come to Yorkshire to contribute to a group of lectures at the annual Hungry Children's Dinner. The talk given by the two sisters had riveted her. They had spoken so passionately, they had been so heartfelt in their determination to help these orphaned and abandoned children. Vivianna realized at that moment that their dream was also hers.

The following day they met over tea at a respectable hotel and found that they did indeed share a desire to save those children unable to save themselves. The two sisters had inherited a bequest from a rich uncle, and they meant to put it to good use. Vivianna had no money in her own right, but Lady Greentree was comfortably wealthy, and generous, and she had entrée into some of northern England's most influential families.

Their partnership was born.

The Beatty sisters and Vivianna had decided upon London as the best place for their Shelter for Poor Orphans. "London," said Susan Beatty, "is where there is the most desperate need." Vivianna had never been to London, but she saw the less salubrious parts of the city starkly through the eyes of her new friends.

The Shelter for Poor Orphans took shape.

They found a building, and though in poor condition, it had far exceeded their hopes. Called Candlewood, it was part of an old estate, falling down from lack of funds, and stood some miles to the north of the city. Indeed, it was almost in the country, and there was plenty of room for a garden to grow vegetables, and for long walks in the adjoining woods. In no time at all it was the home to twenty-five needy children, and the women had plans to take in many, many more.

And then that unfeeling wretch threatened to ruin everything.

Vivianna had known as soon as she read the letter that she could not let that happen. She was not the sort of woman to stand by and watch her dream be destroyed. She would come to London to take whatever action was necessary.

Lady Greentree, though worried and concerned at her going, had learned long ago that once Vivianna committed herself to something this passionately, there was little anyone could say or do to stop her. Or even to slow her down. Vivianna did not care for the strictures that society tried to place upon her, a young spinster. She believed there were more important things to life than adhering to so many—to her mind—pointless rules.

"I will not be made helpless just because I am a woman," she had told Lady Greentree. "I am going to London to save the shelter."

Her sister Marietta had begged to be allowed to

come, too, but for less noble reasons—"To see the sights and the shops, Vivianna!"—while Francesca, the youngest, had declared that nothing, not even the sights of London, would ever entice her away from her beloved moors. Vivianna promised to write to them when she reached London, to tell them how long she was staying.

So she and Lil, her maid, took the mail coach for the Great Northern Road, and London.

Before they left, Lady Greentree spoke frankly to her.

"You will of course be staying with your Aunt Helen in Bloomsbury. I have put a letter for her in your trunk explaining, but I am certain she will not mind your impromptu visit, Vivianna. You will be company for her, poor Helen." For a moment Lady Greentree's face clouded as she thought of her sister, married to the disreputable Toby Russell, and then she rallied. "I have also written a letter for Hoare's Private Bank in Fleet Street, so that you can draw on my account there. You will have expenses, and who knows, you may want to buy a new dress or two!" She smiled fondly at her eldest daughter, as if she didn't really think it likely. "Now, have you everything, my dear?"

"Yes, Mama, I have everything. Don't fret. I will be perfectly all right."

Lady Greentree had sighed, then nodded. "You have always been a headstrong girl, Vivianna. I knew it when you brought home that tinker's child when you were ten and informed me he needed a new pair of shoes. In some ways, Vivianna, it is a blessing to be so sure of your direction in life. In others . . . I fear for you. Do not be too impetuous. I beg you to think first, or you may find yourself in a great deal of trouble."

Seated now in the hackney cab, Vivianna wondered

if Lady Greentree's prediction was about to come true. Because not only had she gone rushing off to London, but upon her arrival at her aunt's home, Vivianna had pretended to have a bad headache and had promptly retired to her room. Once there, she paused only to change her clothing, snatch up her riding crop, and creep out.

Lil, her maid, had been her unwilling accomplice, as she was in many of Vivianna's schemes. Lil found her a hackney cab, and sent her on her way with the admonishment to come back "in one piece, miss, for Gawd's sake!" And as for poor Aunt Helen, if she were to discover her gone . . . She was already quite mad with worry concerning her rackety husband, and Vivianna knew it was wrong of her to add to the woman's burden.

But somehow all of that paled to insignificance when she thought of the children.

The carriage containing Lord Montegomery drew to a halt in front of a long, three-story building. A doorman, who had been standing at attention dressed in a red coat with a military cut, strode down to meet Montegomery like a soldier marching proudly into battle.

Vivianna's hackney had also come to a halt. She peered out at the bland, respectable façade. The place looked mundane, but she supposed exclusive gentlemen's clubs did not need to advertise their wares on the outside. As she sat, hesitating, Montegomery vanished inside and his carriage moved off. It was time to make her own decision. If she did not do something now, she may as well go back to Yorkshire.

Vivianna was not a woman to retreat easily; she was a fighter. She climbed down out of the hackney and paid off the driver. His fingers closed over the shilling coins. "Here, miss?" he asked her, a strange expression on his face. "Are you sure? Right here?"

"I am perfectly sure, thank you."

"But it's an academy, miss. Run by an abbess. An' I can see you is a laced-woman . . . eh, that is, a lady."

Vivianna only understood a few words of what he said, and even then they made no sense. Her chance of following Montegomery inside was dwindling. "I will be quite safe, driver, thank you," she said coolly.

The man opened his mouth, then closed it again, and with a flick of his wrists turned the hackney back into the sparse stream of evening traffic. Just as Vivianna drew the hood of her cloak up to hide her face, another vehicle pulled up outside the sober building, and another gentleman alighted. Ignoring Vivianna's cloaked figure standing irresolute upon the footway, he strode briskly toward the open door.

Here was her chance.

Vivianna fell into step behind the gentleman, hurrying to keep up, as if she had every right to be there. The red-coated doorman was bowing him inside. Breath held, head lowered, her cloak wrapped tightly about her, Vivianna moved to slip by him and within.

The air whooshed out of her lungs. She had run straight into a muscular arm, stretched out at waist height and barring her way. Gasping, Vivianna looked up and found the doorman, a sun-browned individual with a broken nose, staring down at her with hard gray eyes.

" 'Round the back, girl," he barked, his demeanor disapproving.

Vivianna hesitated, while behind her on the street another coach was drawing up.

" 'Round the back!" he ordered again, giving her a little shove, and brushed by her to attend the new arrival.

The doorman seemed to have made an assumption as to who or what she was—just as the hackney driver had done, she remembered now. What that assumption was, Vivianna did not know, but it did not really matter. This was maybe her only opportunity to get inside and confront Montegomery.

Vivianna hurried back down the steps and in the direction that the doorman was impatiently pointing out to her. There was, she saw now, a narrow lane running down one side of the building. As she stood peering into the shadows, a cart rumbled up behind her, and she quickened her steps and found herself in a courtyard behind the house.

The door into the back of the house had been left open and Vivianna darted inside as if she had every right to do so.

The air was full of the smells of cooking and starch. A small room to her left looked to be a scullery. She kept walking down a long corridor of closed doors, leaving the kitchen and the laundry behind her. It wasn't very well lit, and she felt her way by running one hand along the wall. Ahead, sounds of merriment grew louder. Another door, and a shorter corridor, and Vivianna blinked.

Light, shining through a beaded curtain, and with it the movement of chattering people and the clink of glasses. Vivianna clutched the riding crop tightly in her hand, hidden by her cloak. She doubted she would need it now, but something made her loath to put it aside. The heaviness in her chest had increased, and she felt as if her corsets were too tight.

"Montegomery can't be far," she murmured to herself, to keep up her courage.

Vivianna lifted her chin, like Boudicca going into

battle, and made her entrance through the beaded curtain.

Immediately a warning note rang in her head. *This* was a gentlemen's club? Vivianna gazed about in surprise. It was very elegant, done up in the French Rococo style, with pale walls and much curling gold decoration. Mirrors were everywhere, and the reflections of dozens of candles gleamed like stars. The furnishings were elegant and uncomfortable-looking—definitely not the overstuffed chairs and sofas that were currently in vogue.

It was not as Vivianna had expected. She had been imagining sober gentlemen sitting about in leather chairs, reading books and newspapers, and discussing the unruly House of Commons over glasses of brandy. There were plenty of gentlemen in this large, elegant room, but there were also many ladies. She also saw an enormous table spread lavishly with plates of prepared food and glasses of champagne.

Were ladies permitted into the hallowed halls of a gentlemen's club? Vivianna had not thought that was the case, but she was an innocent in such matters, and if necessary that was her defense. Perhaps this was a special evening, a gala evening, and ladies had been invited to attend? Vivianna blinked and looked more closely at the ladies in question. They were certainly very beautiful, and very richly dressed in brightly colored muslins and silks, reminiscent of an earlier age—Rome, perhaps, or Troy. Richly *and* scantily dressed.

Her cheeks warmed. If Lady Greentree walked into such a place, she would turn and walk straight out of it again. What had that hackney driver said to her before she sent him away? Something about this being an "academy" run by an "abbess"? The warning note in Vivianna's head became an entire orchestra. Again she ignored it. There was no time to change her plans now. Glimpses of women's limbs through gossamer-thin silks was irrelevant to her right now. Perhaps, she thought doubtfully, London society was more liberal when it came to female attire than that in Yorkshire.

Anyway, the fact that there were women present suited her plans; it enabled her to move about far more easily in search of her prey. With a quick glance left to right, to assure herself that no one was taking any particular notice of her, Vivianna began her journey across the room, keeping close to the wall and using draperies and green leafy plants for cover. If anyone did notice her, she thought with beating heart, they would believe her to be a gentleman's shy spinster sister, or a maiden aunt, come down from the country to partake of the pleasures of the capital, and unused to company.

Hovering near an aspidistra, Vivianna peered about the room, seeking Montegomery's dark and handsome visage. What if he wasn't here in this room? This was a large house and there must be other rooms. What if she had to search them all? Again Vivianna stilled her fears. If she had to examine every inch of the place, then she would!

But she was in luck. In the next moment she spotted him, standing in a doorway off the main room. There was a woman before him, her gown constructed of some shimmering silken stuff Vivianna had never seen before, the draped bodice disclosing a great deal of bosom and the skirt cut in such a way that her lower limbs were almost completely visible. Shocked, Vivianna raised her eyes abruptly.

The pair of them were laughing, and the woman ran a finger lightly down his chest in a gesture that was teasing and yet surprisingly intimate. They drew closer, spoke briefly, and then Montegomery stepped back into the room out of sight. The woman smiled over her shoulder in that same teasing, intimate way, as she moved toward the table where champagne sat cooling in ice.

Was she fetching him a glass of champagne? As Vivianna hesitated, the woman was approached by another, older gentleman with blossoming side-whiskers, who began to engage her in conversation. She glanced back toward the doorway apologetically, and then turned a brilliant smile and her full attention upon the new arrival. Vivianna knew a chance when she saw it: a chance to beard the lion in his den.

Swiftly, Vivianna moved in a direct line toward the doorway through which Montegomery had disappeared. No time now to play at being invisible. No time to play it safe. No time . . . She brushed by an attractive older woman, her dark hair streaked with gray, wearing a sumptuously beaded black gown and a great number of diamonds. The woman's startled glance was echoed by others. Vivianna's shoulders ached with tension, and any moment she expected someone to stop her, to ask her what she thought she was doing.

It did not happen.

She reached the open door and stepped inside, closing it quickly behind her. *Now I have you!* Her trembling fingers found the key and turned, locking them both in.

Chapter 2

First things first: Make quite sure he cannot escape.

Vivianna removed the key from the lock and slipped it into the pocket sewn into her skirt. Only then, with a deep, sustaining breath, did she turn to face the room. It was just as elegant as the one she had left, but far more intimate. A fire crackled in a fireplace, ornaments gleamed on small, polished tables, and a very large chaise lounge was draped in scarlet silk and dotted with crimson cushions. Upon the wall was a framed painting—a Botticelli Venus—all golden hair and pink flesh.

His back to her, Lord Montegomery was standing by the uncovered windows. A tall, dark, broad-shouldered figure against the night. There was something distant about him, as if he were a man who was all alone. For a moment she hesitated, uncertain, feeling like the intruder she was.

As if sensing her gaze upon him, he turned, a half smile of welcome curving his mouth. His smile turned quizzical. He blinked deep-set eyes that were of a blue so intense and so dark they almost appeared to be black.

"I thought this was the Venus Room," he said in a deep, deceptively sleepy voice. "You look more like Diana the Huntress." His gaze slid over her in a leisurely fashion. "Although with far too many clothes on . . ."

The meaning of his words barely touched her. If she thought of them at all, Vivianna believed he was trying to be witty at her expense. There was nothing wrong with her good Yorkshire cloth. She took a step forward, hands clasped around the riding crop, her voice ringing out. "Lord Montegomery?"

His intense gaze sharpened. "Do I know you, madam?"

"No, my lord, but you will. My name is Miss Vivianna Greentree, and I am here to restore your conscience to you."

His dark brows rose, and something shifted in his expression—as though he recognized her name. But, as that was impossible, Vivianna did not allow herself to be distracted. He took a step closer across the splendid Aubusson carpet. "My conscience?" he repeated. "Do I have one to restore? And if I did, would I want the bother of it?" His gaze flicked down to her hands and the riding crop. His lips thinned. "I am sorry, Miss Vivianna Greentree, but there seems to have been a misunderstanding. I prefer *not* to be beaten. Not by you or anyone else. I am a man who likes his pleasure *without* a sting in it."

That was when Vivianna's single-minded purpose began to unravel. What on earth did he mean? Who did he think she was? She blinked, opened her mouth, then closed it again. She mustn't be sidetracked. They may be interrupted at any moment; she must present her argument while she had the chance.

She drew breath again. "My lord, I am here about the—"

"You're new."

"I . . . that is, no, I—"

There was a gleam in those dark blue eyes as once more they swept over her, taking in her cloak, and her plain wool dress with the neat lace collar. He looked at her for all the world as if she were wearing something as transparent as the women out in the other room. He walked around her—*prowled* around her, rather—and his mouth tilted at the corners. Warily, Vivianna turned with him, keeping him in her sight at all times—which wasn't difficult, she told herself, when he was wearing such a garish waistcoat. Now he was considering her hair, which she knew full well was windblown and wild from the wait in Berkeley Square, and her face, flushed with righteous indignation.

And—how bizarre!—she could tell he liked the look of her. Of Vivianna Greentree, who had never sought the attentions of any man. She felt his interest like a warm wave, washing over her, as his gaze took a leisurely journey from the top of her chestnut head to the tips of her leather half-boots. His smile grew, making him appear even more like a pirate, and even more dangerous. But what amazed her most of all was her own reaction. She was unprepared for it, had never expected it, and so it took her completely by surprise.

There was confusion and anxiety, of course there was, but underneath . . . Vivianna felt a shiver deep inside her. It was as if Montegomery had touched her in a place no man had ever touched her before. A secret womanly place she had never known existed. Until now. Realization swept over her. *Good Lord, this won't do!*

And still he prowled with an elegant grace. Like Krispen, Lady Greentree's beloved tomcat, he had that wonderful litheness mixed with a certain smug self-assurance. Unfortunately, she did not expect Montegomery to be quite as easy to manage as Krispen.

"Hmm, perhaps we can come to some arrangement after all," he said.

They were clearly at cross-purposes, and Vivianna could not let it continue. "There is only one arrangement you and I can come to," she said sharply, her voice a little strained. "You will change your mind about—"

"You're very . . . firm, Miss Vivianna Greentree. I can tell you will be a hit here at Aphrodite's." His eyes gleamed at her, as if he had made a joke. She felt beguiled, bewitched, and totally out of her depth. "I'm extremely flattered you've come to me first, but I don't want the crop. I do want you, however. Even though your appearance reminds me of one of those tedious do-gooders who bleat about the poor."

Tedious do-gooders! Shocked, Vivianna froze, and he took the opportunity to circle around behind her.

"I'd like to change your bleats to sighs," he murmured, so close that his breath stirred her hair, and then his fingers brushed over the sensitive skin of her nape.

Vivianna jumped and spun to face him again, her heart beating fast, her body alive with conflicting signals. "My lord—"

"My name is Oliver, and I prefer it to all this 'my lording.' Say it."

"Oliver—"

"Better. Now, I am sure we can both benefit from

what I have in mind." His dark brows lifted at her lack of perception. "Pleasure, Miss Greentree! I want to take pleasure from you, and give pleasure to you, and I am willing to pay more than the standard fee if it will buy your full cooperation."

Pay? Sighs? Pleasure? *You're new.*

With a series of horrid clicks, everything fell into place. Vivianna stared into his handsome face and knew she had made a terrible, terrible mistake, and that Lord Montegomery was about to make a worse one. "Sir, I fear you are under a misapprehension—" she croaked, but he thought it was all part of the game. The game he had believed her to be playing from the moment she entered the room.

"There is an earnest wholesomeness that shines from your eyes, Miss Greentree. Do you know, the thought of corrupting you has shaken off my boredom completely."

"Oh, has it!" she declared. "Has it really!" She felt light-headed. Finally she understood what the hackney driver had been trying to tell her and she had failed to comprehend. She had inveigled her way not into a gentlemen's club, but into a high-class brothel!

"Let me divest you of your cloak."

He flicked open the fastening at her throat and the cloak promptly slid from her shoulders to the floor. Vivianna's eyes widened, and he smiled into them. He was taller than her by a head—a surprising occurrence for a woman who was usually looking down on the men around her.

"You seem to have forgotten what you were going to say," he said, and lifted his hand to brush one long finger down her cheek. Brief, light as the contact was, it raced through her body like one of the new railway engines.

"I know perfectly well what I am going to say," she told him in an oddly breathless voice.

"Do you? Your eyes are telling me things, too, did you know that? Your pupils have become large and dark, and there is a flush on your cheeks. Here . . . and here . . ." He touched her again, and this time she gasped. "Your lips are soft and open, just a little. As if you want me to kiss them."

"No, they are not! I do not—"

"Yes, they are. Soft and open."

Vivianna felt her lips tingle, felt her heart redouble its efforts. He was so close to her now that his breath warmed her. His eyes were holding hers as if there were no one else in the world but her and him. And that was how it felt, as if they were together on a small, brilliantly lit stage and all about them was the darkness of an empty theater.

Why, this is the strangest thing! I am humming. Every part of me is so alive. Has he done this to me?

Vivianna was focused on her own feelings, but the growing ardor in Montegomery's handsome face could not help but flatter her. Just as she had never felt this before, no man had ever before looked at her in such a way—as if he would gobble her up. She was finding it difficult to move, to breathe, to think. Her reasons for being here were blurring, while his presence had sharpened. And despite being very aware of it, she could not seem to do anything about it.

Good Lord! He is leaning in against me.

And he was. The entire length of his body was pressed to hers, from chest to hip and thigh. And he wasn't like her at all. He was hard, his muscles so taut there was no softness to them whatsoever. His arm curled about her waist, holding her there against him, and there was power and strength in the sheer effortlessness of it. Her breasts were crushed to his chest, and it hurt a little, and yet the pain was also very pleasurable indeed. So much so that she wanted to be held tighter, closer, nearer.

Vivianna's breath left her lips in a soft whoosh, just as he bent his head and trailed a kiss along her temple, down over her cheek. "Be assured, Miss Vivianna Greentree," he whispered. "I am a man who knows how to satisfy a woman."

"I'm sure you've had plenty of practice!" Her voice was husky and small—a mouse's squeak—and he rightly ignored it.

He smiled as his lips brushed across hers, light as air, and then back again, more forcefully. He ran the tip of his tongue around her own lips, as if to imprint the shape of them. Her head spun as if she had partaken of some of the champagne on the lavish table outside. And then, most shockingly of all, very slowly and very gently, he drew her bottom lip into his mouth and sucked upon it.

Vivianna felt her toes curl in her half-boots. Heat rushed into parts of her body where it had never been before, parts that she had hardly known existed. Her breasts swelled and ached, the place between her legs melted. She heard herself moan, and couldn't help it. Didn't want to. It occurred to her that it would be so easy, so very easy, to forget everything but the here and now. This pleasure he had spoken of was dangerous. *He* was dangerous.

There was heat in his eyes, making the blue burn. Did he feel this dangerous passion unfurling in him, too? As she tried to focus beyond the heat to the man within, he smiled at her with a rake's arrogance that told her he had conquered many women, and she was just one more.

Instantly Vivianna was shocked back into sanity.

Her spine turned to steel; her head cleared. In the confined space she struggled to lift her hands and place them flat against his chest. His dreadful waistcoat felt warm from his body, and momentarily she was distracted again by the hard muscle within, and then one of the gold buttons scratched her thumb and she was sobered.

"Come, Miss Greentree," he drawled, his voice vibrating in her skull, "come lie with me on that chaise lounge over there. Flesh to flesh, skin to skin. I have the urge to lick you all over."

The image flared across her mind like a summer storm. Hot and heavy and breathless. She rebelled against it. His muscular arms tightened, but she pushed him. Hard. Unfortunately, it was Vivianna who stumbled backward, and half sprawled across a mahogany side table, sending a marble bust into a dangerous dance. It occurred to her fevered imagination that they resembled an illustration she had seen once on the cover of a novelette that Marietta had smuggled into her room. The woman reeling, in fear for her life—or virtue, Vivianna had not been sure of which—and the man leering at her villainously. It was the sort of thing Marietta enjoyed, but Vivianna had dismissed as foolishness. Villains just didn't loom over defenseless women like that; not when Vivianna was around they didn't, anyway.

Now melodrama had suddenly become real life, and it was too much for her.

"No, you won't have me." She sounded hysterical and completely unlike herself, but somehow the words felt appropriate to her situation. "You'll never have me!"

He choked on laughter. Then, composing himself,

he gave her a long look from under dark lashes, as close to a leer as he could manage. "Ah, but I will have you, my lovely innocent," he avowed dramatically, and then spoiled it by tucking his hands into the pockets of his trousers and grinning. "Is this part of the game? I am enjoying it very much. I can't wait to ravish you. Or are *you* going to ravish *me,* Miss Vivianna Greentree? I promise not to struggle too much."

The look in his eyes . . . the response from her own treacherous body . . . Vivianna knew it was time to put a stop to this before it really went too far.

"My lord," she managed, and held up a hand to halt him, although he had made no new moves toward her. "I am not one of the . . . the women of this establishment. I see now that it is not what I thought but a . . ." She took a breath and calmed herself. "I have come to speak with you, that is all. I attempted to see you at your house in Berkeley Square but your butler refused me entry. I have traveled all the way from Yorkshire to ask you, no, to *implore* you to reconsider your decision to demolish the Shelter for Poor Orphans."

The warmth left his eyes. There was a glitter in them, like, Vivianna thought wistfully, distant lightning—the storm was receding. Oddly, he did not seem very surprised.

"The Shelter for Poor Orphans. I see. How disappointing."

She straightened, pushing away from the safety of the table. The seriousness of her situation was sobering, but Vivianna was not a woman to be intimidated. "My name is Miss Vivianna Greentree. I am one of the founders of the Shelter for Poor Orphans. It is administered by Miss Susan and Miss Greta Beatty, and they wrote to me, informing me of your plans. I have come to London to add my pleas to theirs."

Silence. It seemed, to Vivianna, to last for a painfully long time.

He was watching her, and his expression was quite closed to her, whereas before she had believed she could read him rather well. She had no doubt that behind that handsome mask his brain was assimilating her words with ease. There was nothing foolish about Lord Montegomery—well, apart from the buttons on his waistcoat.

"Miss Vivianna Greentree."

"That is my name, my lord."

All warmth and desire had vanished from his eyes. He was cool now, and perhaps more than a little irritated by her spoiling his evening. "You followed me from Berkeley Square, Miss Greentree. How did you get into this place? I very much doubt Dobson would have let you through the front door."

Under his speculative look her face colored. "I entered through the back door," she replied, refusing to admit she had done anything wrong. *The end justifies the means,* she reminded herself.

"I see." He said it slowly. "You crept into the back of this house like a thief, and now we are locked in this room together, you and I. What did you mean to do with the riding crop? Beat me into submission?"

Vivianna found it difficult to keep her gaze on his. "I brought it for protection. I have never been to London before, and I did not know what sort of people I might encounter."

"Well, that explains it." His voice was very dry.

"I believed this place to be a gentlemen's club. I did not realize it was a house of ill repute," she went on, her face even redder than before.

"A house of very fine repute, I would say. Gentlemen such as myself come here to enjoy themselves and have their senses titillated by ladies such as yourself. Well, not quite such as *yourself,* Miss Greentree." His mouth quirked up, but his eyes remained cool. "It is not my practice to seduce reformers. I find that unless I keep their mouths constantly occupied they bore me with their lecturing."

Vivianna's face burned, but it was anger that made her voice tremble as she replied, "Then I count myself fortunate, my lord, that I am not to your taste."

"Oh, I wouldn't say that," he murmured, and gave her another of those long, assessing, and blatantly lecherous glances from beneath half-closed lids.

"You are insufferable," she began, clutching the crop with shaking hands. Perhaps she would use it on him after all.

And perhaps he realized it, for he smiled. And then all trace of humor left his face and he said, rather coldly, "Do you always behave so rashly, Miss Greentree? No doubt where you live everyone knows you and you are safe. This is London. You cannot do as you wish here, and if you venture into some of the more lawless districts, a riding crop will not save you. Do you understand me?"

Vivianna did not lower her gaze. How dare *he* lecture *her*! "I understand you perfectly, my lord," she said through stiff lips.

He stared at her a moment more, and then he shook his head. "But you'd do it again without hesitation, wouldn't you? You're one of those crusading women who believe they know best."

"I prefer to think of myself as committed," Vivianna said through her teeth.

"Then be warned, Miss Greentree, I do not permit interference in my affairs. Not by you or anyone else. I do not take kindly to it."

Vivianna was angry; very angry. Interference! If he imagined she would turn about and go meekly back to Yorkshire, then he was even more arrogant and deluded and . . . and misguided than he seemed. Vivianna was used to getting her own way, and when she felt as strongly about something as she did the shelter . . .

"Don't do it, Miss Greentree."

He wagged a warning finger in her face. He was closer to her than she had thought. Vivianna managed not to flinch.

"Don't do what?"

"Whatever plot you are formulating behind those big, beautiful eyes. Don't do it. I might have developed a sudden fascination for lovely, bossy women, but you are treading on dangerous ground. Take my advice, Miss Greentree, and go home while you still can."

Vivianna felt her jaw drop a little. Lovely? Bossy? She swallowed. *Keep to the point!* "I cannot allow you to tear down the shelter," she said. "Believe me when I say that I will do anything to stop you."

He was closer still, although she had not seen him move. His breath was warm against her skin. His gaze dropped to her lips. He smiled. He did not say anything; he did not need to. Her own words repeated in her head like an echo. *Anything. I will do anything to stop you.*

"My lord—"

"Oliver. Say it."

"Oliver," she repeated like an obedient child, and then couldn't think of anything else to say.

He dropped his head until his brow was resting against hers, and closed his eyes. His lashes were thick and dark, like his hair, and his skin was warm and smelled of sandalwood and brandy and man. So near. She could turn a little and kiss him, if she wanted to.

And she did. Oh yes, she did. . . .

And then, as she trembled on the brink of something momentous, he straightened and turned away, and just like that he left her standing flushed and hot and confused. His voice was tight, as though he spoke through his teeth.

"I will have a hansom cab called for you. Go home, Miss Greentree, before it is too late."

Angry with him and herself, Vivianna followed him. "I will not be threatened by you! And I will not go anywhere until you promise me you will not touch the shelter!"

He laughed without humor. "I will promise nothing of the sort. And even if I did, I wouldn't keep my promise. The shelter is an eyesore and I am going to have it pulled down, Miss Greentree, and I am going to build something much nicer in its place. In a year, the railway will pass by Candlewood, and many respectable middle-class families will be seeking respectable middle-class homes outside the bustle of the city. It is my belief, Miss Greentree, that this is the way of the future."

Vivianna felt her breath catch in her throat, but somehow she managed to get the necessary words out. "My lord . . . eh, Oliver . . . *my lord,* the shelter provides a home for children who have nowhere else to—"

"I would have thought a dwelling in the city would be more convenient," he continued with a studied indifference, as if he didn't care a jot, and went to stare out of the window.

"But don't you see? Candlewood is perfect! They are safe there, and the country air is healthy for them, the water is clean, and they have a garden. . . ."

Frustrated tears filled her eyes as she gazed at his implacable back. *Don't cry,* she thought, *don't cry!* "Where will the children go if you demolish their home? What will become of them?"

"That is not my concern." He turned to face her, his expression blank, his gaze indifferent. "Frankly, Miss Greentree, *none* of this is my concern. My man of business leased the place to your friends for one year, and now that year is ended. I am under no obligation to extend it."

"But we believed—"

"What you believed is nothing to do with me. If I must be blunt, then I shall. I need the money; I must demolish."

"So you can spend it on places like this," she said, rage tearing through her, and the longing to smash something.

He grinned. "That's it. Whores and brandy and gaming. My three greatest passions. I believe the money I make from Candlewood will keep me in the lifestyle to which I've grown accustomed for at least two more years. That is all that matters to me."

Vivianna swallowed her fury and frustration, and tried one last time. "The fate of these children is the concern of us all, Lord Montegomery. We are all responsible. Please reconsider."

He yawned. "Miss Greentree, you're starting to bore me. I came here to enjoy myself, not to be lectured. My patience is now at an end. If you continue to harangue me I will have to take action. I wonder if your reputation is pristine enough to withstand the story of your being arrested by the Metropolitan Police at Aphrodite's? What would your family and friends say then, I wonder?"

Shock made her speechless, but only for a moment. "You are a monster!"

"Good, you realize it at last. Now, I will go and find Dobson and he will call a cab for you, and you will get inside it and you will leave. And I will never see you again. Do you understand me, Miss Greentree?"

Vivianna's mouth set in a mulish line, and just for a moment, as she met those surprisingly watchful eyes above his smirking mouth, she wondered if he was deliberately trying to frighten her away. But whatever his intention, she was beaten. This time. Although, if Montegomery thought this was the last of the matter, then he was a fool as well as a rake. Except that he wasn't a fool. She had learned that much.

"What is your address?" he said now. "And do not lie—I will be able to tell if you are not honest with me."

"Queen's Square, Bloomsbury," she replied sullenly, not looking at him.

"Very good," he declared, as if he were a tutor giving her a lesson. "Now, one last thing . . ."

She looked up at the pause. He was holding out his hand steadily toward her. An ebony and silver ring winked on his little finger. "The door key, Miss Greentree, if you please. I have a feeling you have it hidden about your person somewhere.

What would he do if she were to withhold it? But once again he seemed to read her thoughts and that smile touched his mouth—oh yes, he would relish the opportunity to wrestle with her for possession! Vivianna fumbled in her pocket and all but threw the key at him. He caught it, gave her a brief bow, and strolled to the door. Vivianna stood, outraged, as the key turned in the lock and the door opened and closed behind him.

She was alone.

Had he bested her? Had she squandered her chance? Perhaps she should have waited until the morning, presented herself properly, spoken to him with cool and calm logic. . . .

It would have made no difference.

Oliver Montegomery was a rake, the type of man who cared little for others and everything for himself. He would not have answered her any differently, no matter how prettily she wrapped up the facts for him.

And yet he must. Somehow, she must ensure that he did.

Behind her the door opened again. There was a rustle of stiff skirts and a strong, sweet perfume. Vivianna turned sharply and found herself being surveyed by a dark intelligent gaze in the face of an elegant woman. It was the same woman she remembered seeing out in the other room with the beaded black gown and diamonds about her throat. She was older than the other "ladies," but still beautiful, the lines upon her face giving it interest despite her air of aloofness. It was a face that had laughed and lived, but it was a face that had also suffered.

"You should not be here," the woman said in a rich, educated voice with a light French accent.

"So I have already been told," Vivianna replied, ignoring Montegomery, who had also reentered the room.

A flash of something lit the woman's large, dark eyes—amusement, perhaps—before she became serious once more.

"This is no place for a respectable young lady, and I can see that that is what you are, Miss . . . ?"

"Greentree," Vivianna supplied, darting a fulminating look at the "gentleman." He had moved to a table with a decanter and was pouring himself a glass of brandy.

"Miss Greentree," he added with emphasis, "is a founder of the Shelter for Poor Orphans."

Vivianna felt the woman's stare upon her. There was something almost familiar in it, and yet she was certain she had never met her before. Then the woman gave a sophisticated, very French shrug. "I do not understand."

Vivianna threw off her own momentary inertia and took charge. "I do not know your name."

Another smile. "I am called Madame, Miss Greentree. That will do for now."

"Very well, 'Madame.' I have traveled from Yorkshire to speak with Lord Montegomery. I am, as he has said, a founder of the Shelter for Poor Orphans. The Shelter is presently housed at Candlewood, a house which belongs to Lord Montegomery and is leased to us. We were told the lease would be indefinite and the house would be available to purchase, but now it appears that Lord Montegomery wishes to demolish the house and . . ." She took a breath. "I wanted to ask him not to. But I fear he isn't a man who thinks much of anything but himself."

Madame gave a brittle little laugh. "But all gentlemen are so, Miss Greentree. Oliver is neither better nor worse than the rest of his kind."

Vivianna felt her tension ease. She glanced sideways at Oliver, to see how he was reacting to his hostess's summation of his character. He was standing against the darkness of the windows, looking elegant and yet with that air of danger and aloneness she had felt surrounded him from the first. He had narrowed his eyes at them over his brandy.

"You think so?" he asked in deceptively soft tones.

"I could have ruined her, Madame. I could have forced her, although she seemed to be enjoying herself so much I don't think it would have been force. But I was a perfect gentleman. Don't I deserve some credit for that?"

Outrage had stolen Vivianna's voice, but Madame answered for her. "Of course you do, Oliver," she soothed him. "You are not quite as despicable as you pretend to be—I do know that, *mon chéri.*"

He returned her smile, as if he couldn't help himself. "I am whatever you want me to be, Madame," he replied with smooth good manners.

Madame laughed again, and then she wrapped fingers heavy with rings about Vivianna's arm. "Come, Miss Greentree. I will make certain you reach your cab safely. You were fortunate tonight, as Oliver has reminded us. Please, do not risk yourself again."

Briefly, Vivianna thought of refusing, but there was no point. Lord Montegomery had won this round. But Vivianna would never give up—the orphans were relying upon her—and once she had set her mind upon winning, she did not do it by half measures.

"Goodbye, Miss Greentree. Do not forget your whip." Oliver had raised his glass to her. Mocking her, daring her. Gloating. The last thing she saw as the door closed on them were his dark eyes and his victorious smile.

"You are headstrong." Madame's tones were clipped, as she half led, half tugged Vivianna toward the door. The room's inhabitants turned to stare—someone laughed. The doorman in his red coat was waiting, his battered face stern. Suddenly Vivianna was glad she still had her riding crop.

Madame drew Vivianna's attention back to herself. "You must learn to rein in your impetuosity, *mon chou.* To give some thought to your actions. To come here was a grave mistake, Miss Greentree, because you have given him the upper hand now. Remember, a man like Oliver Montegomery cannot be bullied, he can only be led. *Persuaded.*"

Vivianna, about to object to being called "my cabbage," turned her head to stare. "What *can* you mean?"

Madame met her eyes thoughtfully. "You are not a fool," she said, "and neither do I think you are a prude. Most ladies would have fallen into a faint as soon as they set foot in here. You did not. Indeed, I think, Miss Greentree, it would take a good deal to make you faint! And you understand very well what I mean. Oliver is no more selfish than any other gentleman, and he can be got around. He finds you amusing and refreshing. Play upon that. Maybe he even desires you—it is clear that his tastes are jaded and he is looking for something new and different. Play upon *that,* if you dare. If you are skillful enough you can achieve your aim."

Vivianna's face had begun to burn long before Madame had finished. She pulled away from the older woman.

No matter how fascinating I find lovely, bossy women.

Oliver Montegomery's voice mocked her.

She ignored it.

"I would rather give myself to a snake than try and please that man," she said furiously, and strode past the doorman and out into the chilly night.

Behind her she heard Madame give a rich laugh, as if she could tell bluster from truth, and then the door closed with a thud. As promised, there was a hansom cab awaiting her.

"You for Queen's Square?" the cabbie asked her.

"Yes, I am." Vivianna climbed in.

"You just come from inside there?" She felt the driver's eyes assessing her from his seat behind and above her compartment.

"Of course not," Vivianna retorted, although he must have seen her hasty exit.

He gave as much credence to her answer as she had expected. "That's Aphrodite's, ain't it? Best academy in London!"

Vivianna was suddenly very tired, too tired even to care that she had left her cloak behind. She leaned her head back against the squabs, ignored the talkative hansom driver, and closed her eyes.

Persuade Lord Montegomery? Use her feminine wiles on him? Her mouth quirked. That was assuming she had any wiles, which she had not. Vivianna told herself she was not the sort of woman to flirt, or to speak in other than a plain and direct fashion. She had never had the time or inclination to ponder the mysteries of desire and physical passion.

It was true she had once perused a booklet called *Mr. and Mrs. England,* which dealt with the ways in which married couples could consummate that passion without conceiving. Books on such matters were illegal in England, although there were those, like Vivianna, who thought that in the right hands they were important and necessary. At the time, *Mr. and Mrs. England* had not pertained to her; it had fallen into her hands by chance and she had read it through curiosity. But now the images in it came back to her with surprising and disturbing clarity.

Persuade him.

"No!" Her voice was unnaturally loud in the compartment. She would use reason and logic. That was what was needed in this situation—reason and logic had worked before, and it would work this time.

Feminine wiles indeed!

But as the cab rocked her gently through London's dark streets, Vivianna could not help but remember the intimate feel of his lips brushing against hers, the warm and expert touch of his long fingers on her skin, and the expression of unwilling fascination in his dark blue eyes.

Chapter 3

Oliver didn't stay at Aphrodite's Club after all. Not long after Miss Vivianna Greentree left, he discovered that the desire to spend a few hours with one of Madame's lovely protégées had fled. Their beautiful faces and scantily clad bodies were suddenly stale. Dull. Miss Vivianna Greentree, with her passionate belief in her cause and her honest hazel eyes and her soft sinful lips, had taken the shine off them.

He didn't like to admit it, and he certainly didn't understand it. He had realized who she was almost at once, but had pretended to mistake her for one of Madame's girls. He had set out to embarrass her, to frighten her with his attentions into catching the very next stagecoach northward. The last thing he needed now was this added complication. But he had seriously misread her character. Instead of putting her off with his mauling, it seemed he had lain down a gauntlet, and he had little doubt that she would eagerly pick it up. In hindsight, he should have allowed Hodge to send for the constables.

The encounter had left him feeling baffled and irritable. Not least because what had begun as an attempt to frighten her had turned into something else entirely. One moment he had been playing the rake, and the next he had forgotten everything in the need to have her beneath him on Aphrodite's chaise lounge. That loss of control wasn't something that had happened to him recently, in fact not since he was a randy lad first discovering how different girls could be.

He sent his carriage on ahead of him and waved off the offer of a link boy to light his way. Tonight he preferred to walk through the quiet streets of London, alone with his own thoughts. For the last year it seemed to Oliver that he had been on a journey to nowhere—a hellfire journey through the stews of London. He had let it be known that his life had ceased to matter, that he did not care what happened to him, and that he was a threat to no one.

The truth was, since his brother Anthony's death, he had stopped feeling anything much, apart from the single-minded determination that drove him toward a goal that was yet to be achieved. Pleasure, well yes, sometimes there was that, and sometimes it helped. The heat of passion in a woman's arms, the rush of gratification when he won at cards, the sharp excitement when his horse came first in a race. There was some pleasure to be found in those things, but it never lasted long. Strangely, before Anthony died, he had believed the life of a rake might be quite nice, but now he longed to draw a halt to the charade. Perhaps he was growing old, because he found himself dreaming of quieter, more mundane pursuits.

But for now Oliver must carry on existing in this barren winter landscape.

"So, what did you expect?" he asked himself savagely. "That this would be easy?"

Of course not, but he hadn't thought he would feel so alone.

Although that wasn't quite true; he wasn't entirely alone. Lady Marsh, his only living relative, was aware of the plot. Oliver had a feeling that she would have stood by him whatever he did.

Lady Marsh, widowed and with no children of her own, had never made a secret of the fact that she wanted Oliver to marry and create an heir as soon as possible. Without an heir there would be no one left to carry on the Montegomery name, and no one to whom to leave her considerable fortune. Lady Marsh, with her stern eyes and ramrod-straight back, believed a young man of birth and breeding should make his mark upon the world in ways other than drinking and gambling and pleasuring himself on unsuitable women.

She wanted Oliver to marry and have a son and to make a proper life for himself. It was a rare month that passed by without her reminding him of it, and lately it had been twice or thrice a month that she had harangued him. The last time remained fresh in his mind.

"Your father, my brother, was a rascal, Oliver," she had said, her eyes so like his, boring into him. "And yet for all that he had a brain. He could have used that brain to make something of himself, to do *something*. He didn't. Such a waste. He was dead at forty, killed when his horse took a jump and he didn't. And for what? For a ridiculous wager. Don't let the same thing happen to you."

"Anthony was the one who grew up expecting to

marry and produce an heir," he had reminded her. "Anthony was groomed to head the family from the day he was born. They are rather large shoes to step into, Aunt. I'm not certain they fit me at all well."

"Oliver, you are not your brother, of course not. You are not Anthony; he was solid rock and you are quicksilver. The two cannot be compared. That does not mean you will not fit his shoes admirably." Then, her eyes still delving into his, she had said, "When do you think this business with Lawson will all be over?"

"I don't know."

"I know I said I would support you, but it has been a year now and nothing has come of it." She had waved her hand with all the arrogance of her age, position in society, and wealth. "Let it go."

"No."

Lady Marsh had sighed. "You are a very stubborn young man. I don't know why I bother with you."

"I don't know why you bother with me either, Aunt."

Oliver had never imagined Anthony would die before him—it was as unthinkable as the sun failing to rise each morning. Fifteen years older than Oliver, Anthony was a man who took his responsibilities to his family, class, and country very seriously. He was a little dull and occasionally pompous, something which Oliver delighted in pointing out to him. But Anthony was a good and honest man, and until he set his heart and mind upon Celia Maclean, his only interest had been in the family and the Tory party. Once Anthony met Celia, however, his thoughts turned to marriage and fatherhood, and Oliver had been relieved to think that soon there would be lots of little Montegomeries to carry on the family name. That would leave Oliver free to continue in his role as the disreputable younger brother, with no responsibilities but to please himself.

Instead, tragedy had stuck. A little over a year ago Anthony had died, and the fate of the Montegomery family now rested upon Oliver's unprepared shoulders.

Lady Marsh did not, nor ever would, blame him for his brother's death. Others did. Oliver certainly blamed himself. In the still darkness of the night, Oliver often lay awake, sick with regrets. There were ways of sending a man to his end that did not involve a bullet or a blade, and he knew that although he had not fired the fatal shot, he had been an unwitting accessory to Anthony's death.

The guilt weighed heavily upon him tonight, and the determination to have revenge on the one who had held the gun to his brother's head—the man Anthony had loved and trusted and believed to be his friend. Perhaps Miss Vivianna Greentree had caused his black mood. She had been so very enthusiastic and sure of herself and her damned cause. She had shimmered with life, and she had wrung emotions from him he had thought firmly tamped down. Indeed, if he had been a sulky fire she would have had him burst into roaring flames in no time at all.

Oliver snorted at the image—she had made parts of him hot, that was certain!—and swung his cane. But it was true, the woman had stirred sensations in him he had almost forgotten. When had he last felt so alive? Probably not since long before Anthony's death. His brother had often chastised him for wasting his youth and vigor on less admirable pursuits. Of drifting without any real goals.

Oliver's reaction to Vivianna Greentree puzzled him. She wasn't beautiful in the classical sense. Her hair had russet tones, and although it was knotted quite severely at her nape, there was a thickness to it, a sensual richness, that made him want to slip his fingers through the strands and press his face into it. Her skin was so fine that he wanted to smooth it with his hands and taste it with his tongue. Her lips were full and when he had kissed her, they had reddened, grown swollen, while her hazel eyes, so passionate and bright, had grown sleepy and dark. She had let him touch her, kiss her, as if she could not help herself.

If he was really the unprincipled rake he was playing, he would have had her instead of wasting his breath arguing with her. He remembered now the manner in which she had responded to his kisses. Not fainting or wailing or running for her life. No, she had relished wholeheartedly his every attention—at least at first.

Oliver's steps slowed. He found himself wondering how she would look beneath him as he plundered her in his bed. All creamy limbs and heaving breasts. Would she cry out his name as she climaxed, or demand he hand over Candlewood in payment for her virginity? He shook his head in disgust at his own thoughts. If he had been lusting after only her body he could understand himself—beneath her dull and sensible clothing she was curved and soft in all the right places, with breasts just the size he liked them. But her hair? Her skin? Her *eyes*?

Oliver realized then he had stopped and was standing in the dimly lit street. As if he were lost. With an impatient sound, he began to walk again. She was a certain type of gentlewoman, he reminded himself, whom he particularly despised. A narrow-minded, crusading do-gooder. From Yorkshire, of all godforsaken places! And she wanted to prevent him from doing something he had every intention of doing. Did she imagine she could instill him with a social conscience by earnestly coming all this way to see him? Oliver shuddered.

But remembering now her fervent expression when she spoke of Candlewood, and then her pain as he deliberately destroyed her hopes, Oliver grimaced. He did not like hurting things smaller and more feeble than himself, although he was dubious that label applied to Vivianna Greentree. Well, it had had to be done. Pointless letting her believe she could persuade him to change his mind. And yet he couldn't say he had enjoyed that part of their encounter.

Damn the woman!

What would she think if she knew the full extent of his sins? Would a determined social reformer such as herself rise to the challenge? Or would she consider him beyond redemption? He hoped it was the latter, for her own sake he really did. He had been playing the rake for so long now that the role came easily to him, too easily. And Miss Vivianna Greentree was such a sweet armful. . . . With any luck he had frightened her off, and she was even now on her way back to Yorkshire.

With any luck.

Mrs. Helen Russell was waiting for Vivianna, and she was in a state. Lil, hovering anxiously behind her, grimaced a warning.

"You went out alone, Vivianna! I've been worried sick! What would I have told your mother if something had happened to you? Oh, I feel quite ill."

Vivianna and Lil between them supported her to a chair against the wall. Mrs. Russell waved a hand in front of her face, looking even more ravaged and exhausted than usual. She turned big blue accusing eyes upon Vivianna and shook her head.

"I had thought better of you, Vivianna, really I had. I did not know where you had gone, and neither did your maid here. We thought you had been kidnapped by some foul persons seeking ransom."

Lil caught Vivianna's eye and bit her lip.

"Not that I expect we would have been able to pay it," Mrs. Russell went on, setting aside her attack of the vapors as other, more practical concerns took root. "We can barely pay Cook or the grocer, so I imagine a ransom is out of the question. And Toby wagers so much on the cards that I sometimes wonder—" She stopped, sighed, and attempted a smile. "Well, I suppose my sister would pay it anyway. Amy is quite well off, is she not? Yes, if there was a ransom, then Amy would pay it."

"Of course she would," Vivianna soothed. "But there is no ransom, Aunt. I am sorry if worried you, but I simply had to speak with . . . a person about the shelter. I did not expect to be so long. Forgive me."

Mrs. Russell eyed her a moment more and then rose to her feet. "Very well, dear, I will put this down to your unfamiliarity with London and the stricter code of behavior here, but don't do it again. Or if you do go out, take Lil with you. A young lady does not go about London on her own, and she certainly does not go about alone at night!"

"Yes, Aunt, I'm sorry. I will know better in the future."

"What's this, what's this?" A deep, attractive voice drifted from the direction of the front door.

Vivianna only just managed not to groan aloud as Toby Russell strolled toward them. He was decked out in a coat severely pinched in at the waist and grossly padded at the shoulders—she was certain he was wearing a corset—and his waistcoat was even more garish than Oliver's had been. Toby's face was still handsome, though deeply lined about the mouth, and his eyes were as watchful of opportunity as always. Vivianna had never liked him, and she knew from Lady Greentree that Helen had lived a miserable life with him. If there was the perfect example of a charming wastrel, then it was Toby Russell. He treated Helen abominably, he was vicious when cornered, and he was never, never to be trusted.

He served as her caution, Vivianna thought, if she were ever tempted to marry a handsome rake herself.

Toby strolled by Lil, and the little maid stepped back abruptly.

"Vivianna has been very naughty," Helen said, "but I have spoken to her and she has promised not to do it again."

"Sounds intriguing," Toby said, with a leer masquerading as a smile. "Do tell, Niece."

"Actually, Uncle Toby, I am rather tired. If you don't mind, I think I will retire now. Come, Lil."

Vivianna preceded her maid up the stairs to her room, trying not to listen as Helen asked her husband, in a plaintive voice, why he had not come home to supper.

"That Mr. Russell tried to pinch my bum," Lil said furiously when the bedroom door closed.

Vivianna's gaze narrowed. "Did he? Lil, I'm so sorry. Stay well clear of him, he's not a nice man."

Lil cast up her eyes at Vivianna's words. "You don't have to tell me *that,* miss. I can see it at a glance. Don't worry, I can handle meself."

Vivianna smiled. Lil was small and skinny and fair, with brown eyes; a lively girl. Vivianna had found her, starving, in York, when she was little more than a child. The young girl had touched her heart with her plight, and Vivianna had persuaded Lady Greentree to employ her. Her loyalty and intelligence were beyond dispute, and Vivianna had never once regretted her impetuous action.

"I know you can, Lil," she said gently. "I'm sorry I put you in such a difficult position with Mrs. Russell, but I had to see Lord Montegomery."

"I understand, miss. The shelter means the world to you." Lil began to help Vivianna to undress. "But all the same," she went on quietly, "you need to take care. This Lord Montegomery could have done anything he wanted to you, and me and Mrs. Russell would have been none the wiser."

He *had* done what he wanted to her, Vivianna thought, trying not to blush before Lil's sharp eyes. He had touched her, and kissed her, and held her against his body. And she hadn't struggled, not one bit. She had pressed back against him, and sighed, and moaned when he kissed her. She had enjoyed it. She had wanted more.

"Miss?"

Vivianna shut out the images. "I thought he would be sympathetic, if only I explained properly, but . . ." She shook her head in despair. "He doesn't care, Lil. He doesn't care what happens to the orphans."

Lil touched her arm gently. "They reckon you can't change a sow's ear into a silk purse, but if anyone can teach him the error of his ways, miss, then it's you."

An unwilling smile curled Vivianna's mouth. "Thank you, Lil."

"Now come and get warm by the fire, miss. You're cold and damp, and you need some hot milk."

Vivianna allowed herself to be fussed over, sinking

back into the chair and lifting her feet toward the flames.

Persuade him.

Her smile vanished. That was what the woman had said tonight, the beautiful older woman with intelligent dark eyes called Madame. Vivianna did not pretend she did not understand how that persuasion was to be affected—to kiss him and let him kiss her, to touch him and let him touch her. Employ her feminine wiles.

Except that Vivianna had never used her feminine wiles before. She did not even know whether or not she had any. She had always considered herself a bookish, serious girl, and that feminine wiles were for pretty little creatures who knew nothing about poverty and abandonment, and cared less. And yet Oliver Montegomery had looked at her as if he saw something in her that she had not known was there. Until now.

Persuade him.

Was it possible?

Vivianna had once heard a lecture on women and their imprisonment by society. The speaker put forward the idea that society expected women to appear pure, fragile, helpless, and always defer to the greater knowledge of their menfolk. And if they dared to be different, or worse, if they lived the sort of life a man might lead, then their reputations would be destroyed and they would be cast out. Out into the darkness that forever circled the bright light of polite society and was inhabited by the fallen women and the adulteresses and those who were too willful to be borne.

She did not believe it at the time—*she* was different and *she* had not been cast out. But now she realized that she was just as bound up in the rules as all the other women of her class and situation. Seeing those girls at Aphrodite's had given her a glimpse into another world. Not that she wanted to be an . . . "abbess." Was that what the hackney driver had called Madame? No, she didn't want that. But neither did she want to marry a man like Oliver, just so that she could have him kiss her whenever she wanted him to. *Men* did not marry to gain such experience. There was an entire area of womanhood that she had never really thought about before, never imagined it was possible for her to enter unless she married.

It was all very intriguing. . . .

But *that* would have to wait, Vivianna told herself, coming back to earth with a thump. Tomorrow she must call upon the Beatty sisters, to hear their grievances and discuss what they could do to save the shelter. Or, if worse came to worst, where they could shift the orphans temporarily. It was possible her friends had come up with a new plan, something that did not involve the use of "feminine wiles."

A sharp pang of disappointment stung her, but before she could question it, the sound of raised voices elsewhere in the house interrupted her thoughts. It was Helen and Toby. Vivianna shivered. In haste, Helen had married a charming, handsome rake, thinking she could change him, and now she repented at leisure. Under no circumstances would she ever allow herself to fall under the spell of such a man.

Vivianna was up bright and early the next morning, despite her long journey south and her late and eventful evening. She had promised to go to Candlewood as soon as possible and see the Beatty sisters, and she knew they would be waiting for her. Poor Miss Greta and Miss Susan, they must be beside themselves with worry.

She had dressed in another of her plain, practical gowns and was sitting impatiently while Lil tended to her hair, when one of her aunt's maids came tapping upon her door.

"Miss, there is a gentleman to see you downstairs in the sitting room. Lord"—and she glanced at the card in her hand—"Oliver Montegomery."

Vivianna felt herself go cold, and then hot. With a brilliance that had only previously been reserved for dreams, she recalled last night in the room at Aphrodite's, and the feel of his body against hers, the warmth of his breath on her face, the brush of his mouth against her lips. *I have an urge to lick you all over*. Her breath caught and then resumed with a soft gasp.

Lil was staring at her accusingly.

"I . . . very well, thank you. I will be down in a moment."

The girl bobbed a curtsy and retreated. For a moment Vivianna refused to meet Lil's eyes, but Lil was better at this than she. "You told me nothing 'appened," she said, and pinned the final piece of Vivianna's hair in place. "I can see that's not true, miss. You're on fire, you are. What did that beast do to you?"

"He's not a beast," Vivianna retorted primly. "At least, not the ravening kind of beast. More a smiling, charming, very handsome kind of beast. He kissed me, that's all. I didn't struggle. It was nice, and I had never been kissed before, at least not by someone like Lord Montegomery."

Lil shook her head. "You're going to get hurt."

"No, I'm not. I know what I'm doing, Lil. Believe me, if for one moment I thought I was going to fall in love with the man, then I would have a long look at Uncle Toby and Aunt Helen—that would cool my passion."

Lil's wry smile was agreement enough. "Do you want me to come down with you, just for company?"

"No, I will be perfectly all right. He can hardly ravish me in my aunt's sitting room, can he?"

Lil's look was ambivalent, but Vivianna laughed and, checking her appearance once more, made her way downstairs. Her steps slowed. She began to wonder what he wanted. They had parted as enemies last night. Had he come to apologize? To beg her pardon and tell her he would be only too pleased to cede to her request?

Somehow she did not think so. There had been nothing of capitulation in his face when she closed the door behind her last night, only that irritating and victorious smile.

Well, there was only one way to find out.

Vivianna smoothed her skirts, took a breath, and went into the sitting room.

He was standing with his back to her, peering out of the window. The second time she had come upon him in that stance—evidently it was habitual for him.

"My lord?"

He turned, a smile on his lips, and bowed in a negligent and yet elegant manner that Vivianna was certain could only be achieved if you were from one of the oldest aristocratic families in England.

She had thought that she must have imagined the effect he had had upon her, but now, seeing him again, she knew that she had exaggerated nothing. It was the strangest thing, but she could feel her blood slowing, like a warm, languid river, gliding through her body and under her skin. And yet her heart was racing like a railway carriage down a long, straight track. Most peculiar. Oliver Montegomery might be the type of man she had always sworn to stay clear of, but her body had plans of its own.

"I came to make certain you had reached your home safely—" Oliver began.

"How . . . how kind of you," she said.

"—and to wish you safe journey back to Yorkshire."

Vivianna's eyes narrowed. "I am not returning to Yorkshire just yet."

"Pity," he retorted.

"In fact, I am planning on an extended stay."

"Best stay away from me, then," he said, his eyes fixed meaningfully on hers, "or you'll spend it in places a lady usually avoids—for instance, on your back."

Vivianna straightened her already straight spine. "I know you think to intimidate me by speaking in this caddish manner, my lord, but you can't, so you may as well desist. Besides, I believe that lying upon one's back is only one of the ways in which . . . Well, I am sure you don't need instruction from me."

No hysterics, no fainting, no cries of maidenly distress, and certainly no promises to leave London and never return. Vivianna Greentree simply reminded him that there were other ways of making love than on one's back. Oliver laughed—he couldn't help it.

He must have been insane, coming here. There she was, staring him down with those brilliant hazel eyes, shining a light into his soul. He felt like he should shield himself from her, protect himself with bell, book, and candle, and at the same time he recklessly didn't want to.

"You're wasting your time," he managed, and propped himself against the back of an armchair, as if he were still too intoxicated to stand.

"Well, it is my time to waste." Her brow wrinkled faintly and she took a step nearer. "How did you know where I was staying?"

He smiled in triumph. "You gave me your address for the hansom cab, remember?"

"Of course!" Her frown cleared. She looked about her as if the room were new to her. "Can I offer you some refreshment, my lord? My aunt is not yet risen, nor my uncle, but as you have been thoughtful enough to call, I am sure they would not object."

She was offering him refreshment? After what he had just said to her? Oliver shook his head in bewilderment. "No, I will not stay. I am in need of something stronger than tea, Miss Greentree. You have that effect upon me."

Isn't it a little early for strong drink? He could see the question in her eyes, but she did not speak it aloud. In a moment she would be lecturing him on the joys to be found in abstinence.

He had hardly slept at all last night, but still the dawn had found him wide-eyed and alert. His mind had been full to overflowing with the unusual, the interesting, the delectable Miss Vivianna Greentree. He had found himself going over their encounter again and again; he had found himself remembering the passion and the determination in her eyes.

This, he had realized, as the street sweepers got to work outside his window, was a woman who felt deeply. Who would not give up her mission without a long and protracted battle. In short, she was going to be a right pain in the arse. Why then did he find that trait so admirable and so fascinating?

And yet he did, and more than that. He wanted to hold her in his arms and kiss the life out of her. Put his hands all over her and make her moan, make her cry out for more. One moment his thoughts were on a higher, intellectual plain, and the next he had become completely carnal.

God help him, was he going mad?

"Miss Vivianna Greentree," he drawled, and it was nectar in his mouth. "I do like your name."

"Oh, do you, my lord?" She looked startled, as well she might, but pleased, too. And suspicious, as if she knew very well he was playing a devious game with her.

"Call me Oliver, I beg of you," he said, and his irritation was genuine. Having come to the title of "my lord" late in life, after many years spent simply as Mr. Oliver Montegomery, he had never gotten used to it.

"I am sure that for me to call you 'Oliver' is most improper," she replied, and her lips pursed prettily.

"I feel improper," he murmured, and stepped closer, and was secretly amused by her obvious determination not to step back. "I like your face, too. Particularly your mouth, oh yes, I like your mouth. And I like your—"

"I . . . have you had second thoughts, my lord . . . Oliver? About Candlewood? I thought perhaps you had had time to reconsider. Overnight. I am to see the two Miss Beattys today and it would be a great relief if I could offer them some hope."

He gave up.

"No, Miss Greentree, I have not had second thoughts."

"If only you would—"

"Damnation, don't lecture me, woman!"

She stopped, her mouth open, her breath coming fast. He had startled her, he saw, but not frightened her. He doubted even a charging elephant would frighten Miss Vivianna Greentree.

"I am trying to make you understand that—"

He groaned. "There's only one way to stop you, isn't there?"

She blinked. "Is there?"

Her skin was like cream, her pupils were dark, her lips soft and sinful. Oliver took her shoulders firmly in his hands, leaned in, and kissed her. Desire reared up, struggling to break free, but he held it on a firm rein. "This is why I came," he said, plundering her mouth again. "And this. . . ."

After her initial surprise, Vivianna kissed him back. She even went so far as to wrap her arms about his neck and cling on.

"I don't trust you," he ranted. "Not for a minute."

"Then why—"

"Stop talking." He sent his tongue exploring the warm depths of her mouth. And damn her if she didn't return the favor, mimicking him, unashamedly enjoying herself. Just to be sure he wasn't imagining it, Oliver drew her tongue into his mouth and sucked on it. She did the same with his, turning his body to hot, rigid steel.

He clasped her bottom through the thickness of skirt and petticoats and drew her up on her toes, then pressed her hard against the place that most needed it. He could imagine making love to her and doubted he would survive the experience.

Oliver groaned into her mouth and then almost wept as she arched herself against him, a living candle in his arms. That was when Oliver knew he couldn't hold on to that rein much longer; in another heartbeat the horse would have bolted.

Someone cleared her throat.

Vivianna took a breath, and then another. Every part of her protested, but she pulled away and stood, dazed, looking about her. It was as if she were waking from a dream.

"Miss!"

Lil was standing, shocked, in the doorway. Vivianna realized then how dangerously close she had come once more to allowing Oliver to have his way with her. She could feel the blood in her face, and the beginnings of panic, but she held herself in check. Her voice, when she spoke, was as close to normal as she could manage under the circumstances.

"Lil, Lord Montegomery is just leaving. Can you show him to the door?"

"Yes, miss." Lil sounded flat and cold.

"My hat and cane." Oliver was watching her, his eyes full of the wry humor that was pulling at his lips. As if it were all a jest to him. But was it? Was she just another conquest? The idea should have appalled her, but it did not—instead Oliver intrigued her. When he had kissed her so thoroughly, there had been a moment when she could have pulled away and slapped his face, but she hadn't. Instead she'd kissed him back, because she was curious and because it was what she wanted to do.

"Goodbye, my lord," she said, and stayed exactly where she was.

Vivianna straightened her shoulders and waited for Lil's return like a soldier who has been found wanting and is about to face a commanding officer. The comparison made her smile.

"I'm glad you're amused, miss," Lil said, and Vivianna could see the anger jumping under her skin, making her eyes water. "I'm glad you think it's funny. That man . . . I warned you, I did. He's after you, miss. He had his hands all over you and I—I could see it in his face. He's after you, and he'll not stop. Not until he has what he wants."

Vivianna let her finish. "Lil, I know you are concerned for me, but really, I can look after myself."

Lil shook her head back and forth several times. "Oh, miss, you know nothing about men like that. He'll hurt you, he'll destroy you. He can make it so that no decent person in England will be in the same room as you! Do you want your name ruined?"

"I don't see why—"

"Course you do, you just don't want to admit it. You think you won't care, but you will. Oh, you will. Miss, please, stay away from him."

Vivianna walked past her to the door. "I will take care, Lil, I promise, but I will not stay away from Lord Montegomery. He is the key to saving the shelter, and I will not be frightened off just because he kissed me . . . once or twice."

Lil groaned.

"Actually"—and Vivianna turned and met her stare defiantly—"I enjoyed it."

And she marched back upstairs, leaving a muttering Lil to follow.

Chapter 4

Miss Greta and Miss Susan Beatty were like a pair of cage birds, fluffy and petite, with bright eyes and gentle voices—but they had characters of pure steel. When Vivianna had first met them in York, she had been aware of an unconscious urge to smile at their seemingly sweet naïveté—what could two middle-aged, middle-class spinsters know of the world, after all?

She soon realized she had foolishly underestimated them.

The Beattys weren't birds, they were terriers. Determined and pugnacious little women who, once they had decided upon a course of action, followed it through to the very end.

The idea for a home for abandoned children had long been their goal, as it had been Vivianna's. If Vivianna had supplied the passion for the project, then the Beatty sisters had supplied the sheer grit and determination to secure a building where the children could be housed.

Greta and Susan Beatty really were an indomitable pair, and Vivianna had never thought to see them defeated by anything or anyone.

Until now.

Seated across from them in their small and shabby parlor—"I hope you don't mind, Miss Greentree, but it's easier to heat than the drawing room"—she wondered if she was witness to the unthinkable.

"We believed the lease would be perfectly secure." Miss Susan clasped and unclasped her hands. "Lord Montegomery's man of business explained that the one year was all he could offer us—that the estate had belonged to Lord Montegomery's brother and there was a delay with the transfer of the property. He assured us that Candlewood was not part of the entail and that after one year the lease could be extended, or we could buy it. We were told that Lord Montegomery wanted nothing more to do with it, and that he certainly had no intention of ever living here. Everything was settled . . . we thought. And then, as the end of our lease drew near and we went to make arrangements to extend it, we learned . . ." She shook her head, unable to continue.

Miss Greta took up the story. "How could we know he would change his mind? A gentleman should abide by his word, should he not, Miss Greentree?"

"Perhaps he is not a gentleman," Vivianna replied.

"But such an old, distinguished family!" Miss Susan exclaimed. "I believe they are very proud, too. Several times the reigning monarch has offered the Montegomery of the day a peerage, only to be turned down. Their family motto states: 'It is enough to be a Montegomery.' They finally accepted the title of baron from King George, the lowest grade of peerage, but nothing more."

Miss Greta was frowning at her. Miss Susan returned to the point.

"We wrote to Lord Montegomery to ask if he would reconsider our lease, but his reply was brusque to say the least. He suggested an alternative place, a former lodging house in Bethnal Green. But how can we accept such an offer? Candlewood is everything we promised we would give our orphans; if we moved them to Bethnal Green it would feel like a betrayal. Of our principles and the children!"

The more practical Miss Greta added, "We planned to repair the roof and the drains, and to expand into the rooms that are presently unoccupied. So much potential, Miss Greentree! We had such hopes!"

"Candlewood is perfect and now it is to be demolished and smaller houses built in its place." Miss Susan blinked back tears. "He stands to make a lot of money, evidently, and that is all that matters to him. But what about our orphans, Miss Greentree?"

"We have written several times, imploring him to change his mind, but the only reply we had was to tell us we have nine weeks to evacuate Candlewood. It is almost as if, for him, we have ceased to exist."

"Oh, he knows you exist," Vivianna assured them with a smug little smile. "At least, he does now. And don't worry, my friends, I will do everything in my power to see that he changes his mind."

The two sisters leaned forward, their bright eyes fastened upon her. "You are very good, Miss Greentree," Miss Greta said, while Miss Susan nodded wildly. "To come all this way to help us. The orphans do appreciate it. *We* appreciate it."

Vivianna responded in what she hoped was a confident manner, but inside her head her thoughts were chaotic. Earlier, when she had arrived at Candlewood, the Beattys had lined the orphans up before her in the hall, and the children had given her three cheers.

The sisters knew all the children's names and so did Vivianna—she had been kept informed by their many letters. The children were not strangers to her; she felt as if she recognized and loved them all. Perhaps that sense of familiarity was what made the difference in these matters. Perhaps if Oliver were to meet them, if he were to see them, even a man with a heart as hard and uncaring as his would be swayed . . .

"Miss Greentree?" Miss Greta was watching her expectantly over the fruitcake, and Vivianna realized she had missed part of the conversation.

"More tea?" Miss Susan was holding the teapot aloft in one hand and the milk jug in the other.

"Thank you."

"I was telling you a little about the history of Candlewood," Miss Greta said. "It may help you, when you tackle Lord Montegomery, to know the family story."

"What is the family story?"

Miss Greta settled herself to explain. "Candlewood was built by Lord Montegomery's grandfather. A folly, in hindsight. It was supposed to be a monument to the family, but instead it ruined him. He squandered most of his wealth on it, and even then he did not have enough to finish it. The Montegomery family has a house in London, as well as an estate in Derbyshire, so they have no use for Candlewood. They have always considered it inconvenient and uncomfortable. However, Anthony Montegomery, the elder brother, was very fond of Candlewood and often stayed here, especially overnight when he was on his way to Derbyshire. The house and grounds were left to him by his grandfather, but unfortunately there was never enough money for the upkeep, it was literally crumbling away. And now Anthony is dead, too, and the house belongs to Oliver Montegomery."

Had Oliver mentioned a brother? Vivianna did not think so. "I did not realize Lord Montegomery had a brother."

Miss Susan gave a sad smile. "Yes, and his is a strange and unfortunate story. He spoke briefly of his brother when he was last here."

"Oliver . . . that is, Lord Montegomery was here?" Vivianna raised her eyebrows in surprise. "I did not realize you had met him in person. I thought you conducted the matter of the lease through his man of business and by correspondence."

"At the time we first leased Candlewood we had not met him, no, but since then he has been here twice, or is it three times?"

"But why so many? I do not understand."

"Neither do we." The two sisters exchanged glances. "When he visited he would spend a great deal of time walking about the house, just looking, and once he brought a man with him who took measurements and hammered on the walls."

"How odd."

"It was, rather. We have also had Lord Lawson here once, shortly after we moved in, but that was to welcome us. In Anthony's stead, was what he said."

The two sisters watched her expectantly.

"Lord Lawson?"

Miss Susan was eager to enlighten her. "He is a member of Sir Robert Peel's Tory party, and some say he will be the next prime minister. He may have been so now if Lord Melbourne had not inveigled his way back into government because the queen is so fond of him."

The Beatty sisters did not appear to be impressed with Lord Melbourne, and Vivianna did not blame them. The prime minister was deeply conservative and seemed not to believe in reform of any kind. He had lost office in 1839 to Sir Robert Peel, but due to Queen Victoria's refusal to dismiss her current ladies-in-waiting and allow Sir Robert to install new ladies of his own party's persuasion—as was the custom—and Sir Robert's subsequent stubborn stance on the matter, Lord Melbourne had been asked to return as prime minister. But it was, Vivianna felt sure, only a matter of time before Lord Melbourne was once more ousted—he was very unpopular with all but the queen, and now that she was enraptured by her new husband, Prince Albert, he had lost even her wholehearted support.

"Why would Lord Lawson welcome you in Anthony's stead?" Vivianna asked, puzzled.

"Lord Lawson was Anthony's very good friend."

"Lord Lawson has written to us since his visit," Miss Susan added. "He sent a note in response to our news that Candlewood was to be demolished, saying he would do all in his power to prevent it, but that as the property now belonged to Lord Montegomery, it may be a difficult matter."

"Still, it cannot harm us to have a champion of his standing," her sister added. "Lord Lawson is very well thought of. A great man."

Vivianna agreed it would do them no harm to have a possible future PM on their side. "But I still don't see why Lord Montegomery would visit Candlewood when he has said he wants nothing more than to see it turned to dust. It is odd."

"Very odd."

Vivianna sipped her tea. "It may be helpful," she

said carefully, "if I knew the strange and unfortunate circumstances of Anthony's death."

"It is mostly gossip," Miss Susan replied with a grimace, "but if it will help . . ."

"Anthony had been to a dinner at his club in the city," Miss Greta took up the story. "Afterwards, he walked to Candlewood—he often did that, he said it cleared his head. He was planning to sleep here overnight before traveling on to his home in Derbyshire in the morning. His brother was to collect him by coach and they would travel together. You see, Miss Greentree, at that time there were no permanent staff at Candlewood—only those who came once a week to do some cleaning."

"So Anthony Montegomery was here on his own?"

"Yes, all on his own. When his brother arrived in the morning, he found him lying in the hall, quite dead. He had been shot in the head. It was put about that someone had broken into the house, a thief perhaps, and finding Anthony here alone, had shot him to escape. The odd thing is, the pistol that did the deed was Anthony's own, and it was found beside his body. Gossip would have it that he took his own life, but the full facts of the matter have never come out because no one ever came forward, and of course the family rejected suicide. Oliver took his brother's death very hard. I have heard he was quite changed by it."

The story *was* a tragic one, Vivianna thought. To lose one's brother in such circumstances made her heart ache for him. But did Oliver's loss excuse his selfishness in removing the orphans from their home? No, it did not.

"After Anthony's death, Oliver inherited the Montegomery estate, the house in London, and Candlewood." Miss Greta's eyes flashed. "You know the rest."

"Why do the gossips believe Anthony killed himself? Was he an unhappy man?"

Miss Susan leaned closer. "There *was* a reason he may have killed himself, Miss Greentree. Evidently he was about to become engaged to a girl, a girl he loved very much, but the night he died he had come upon his brother and the girl . . . embracing. I suppose, if he thought his heart was broken and all his happiness destroyed, he might contemplate suicide."

"I see that he might," Vivianna murmured. Anger seared through her, turning any lingering pity to steam. "How terrible. And why am I not surprised?"

"The Montegomeries were once a great family," Miss Greta added fuel to the fire. "They had wealth and position. But now they are on the wane. If Anthony had lived, perhaps they may have risen again. Everyone says he had promise, and with a friend like Lord Lawson . . . But his brother . . ." She shook her head. "He is handsome and charming, I grant you, at least superficially so, but I believe he spends all his time in the pursuit of his own pleasure."

"And he is so lacking in any sort of honor and proper feeling that he stole his brother's fiancée. And his brother discovered it!" Miss Susan declared.

There was a silence while Vivianna picked over the ruin they had made of Oliver's character. Could this unsavory fellow really be Oliver, with his dark lock of hair falling over his brow, his intense eyes, and his charming smile? No doubt Oliver had also fascinated his brother's lady-love—Vivianna did not hesitate to put the entire blame on him. What chance did the lady have against such odds? He was her Uncle Toby all over again; a wicked and hard-hearted rascal who would stop at nothing to indulge his own appetite.

This morning he had kissed her as if he could not

help himself. If Lil had not interrupted, how far would matters have gone? She hadn't felt under threat when he kissed her and held her—just strangely excited and curious—but she admitted now that she was an innocent when it came to men like Oliver Montegomery. He could not have become such a famous rake if he were not very good at what he did.

"Is there hope, do you think, Miss Greentree?"

Vivianna began to pull on her gloves with brisk, determined tugs, her eyes alight in anticipation of the battle ahead. "I believe so, ladies. I will let you know as soon as I have any news. Goodbye for now, and do not worry!"

The two sisters seemed cheered, some of the strain clearing from their faces. Vivianna kept the brave smile plastered to her own face until the coach set off, rumbling down the driveway to join the London road.

The Beatty sisters had given her much to think on. Not that she had the solution to their problems, not yet, but at least she felt she knew more about Oliver Montegomery, the man, than she had before. Perhaps she could turn it to her own advantage. Then again, she doubted he would be so easily overcome. For all his lazy smiles and indolent charm, there was a sense of strength and purpose about him that she was yet to fully understand.

Oh yes, there was far more to Oliver Montegomery than met the eye.

And what about Anthony's fiancée and the rumors that Oliver had stolen the lady's affections and his brother had seen them? Hardly admirable. But would a man seemingly without scruples be so changed by what he had done that he spent his days and nights in a drunken stupor? Surely they were more likely to be the actions of a man suffering excessively from guilt and regret. A troubled soul.

Might there be hope for him? *Redemption.*

Vivianna knew she was just the woman to lead him there. And at the same time complete her own mission in regard to Candlewood. A memory of his mouth on hers intruded briefly, but Vivianna pushed it aside. She must concentrate on her purpose and not be distracted by this unlikely attraction she felt for him.

She would visit Berkeley Square tomorrow—she had no expectations of being allowed in or of Oliver being home, but she would leave her card for him, with a handwritten message upon the back of it. Something simple like . . .

I can help you.

Yes, let him make of that what he wished. Vivianna shivered, and thought that one way or another it would not be long before Oliver called upon her again . . .

Lady Marsh lived in Eaton Square, Belgravia, and she greeted Oliver with an unassumed pleasure that made him wonder, as he always wondered, why she continued to ally herself to him. After Anthony died, any sensible woman would have wiped her hands of him, but she hadn't, and he was grateful.

They spoke generally for a time, of this and that, some of it gossip. Although she did not go into society much anymore, Lady Marsh liked to keep herself abreast of the latest news. Her arthritis kept her housebound and often bedridden, although today Oliver thought she seemed spry enough.

"Oliver," she said at last, and her eyes, the same dark blue as his own, the same dark blue as all the Montegomeries had, fastened upon him. "I do not want to repeat myself, but it is time you found a wife and settled down and gave the Montegomeries an heir."

He laughed despite himself. "No, please don't repeat yourself, Aunt!"

"Oliver, be serious, this is very important. You need to think to the future."

"Do I?"

"Oliver, I loved your brother dearly, and yes he was very dependable and solid, but he had neither your brilliance of mind nor your practical clearheadedness."

Oliver smiled and sipped his wine. Clearheadedness? Let his aunt have her illusions if she wished. If she could have seen him this morning in Queen's Square, kissing Miss Vivianna Greentree in front of the servants, she would know that was something he singularly lacked. Perhaps he *had* lost his mind. That was it: Vivianna's lecturing had sent him insane.

Evidently Lady Marsh took his smile for encouragement, for she continued on.

"Oliver, you do not have a partiality for Celia, do you?"

He blinked. "Celia Maclean? Of course not, Aunt."

"I see. It is just that . . ."

"It is just that she was Anthony's fiancée . . . almost," he said grimly, "and she and I were together the night he died. I know, I was there."

"So you were," she replied, and waited.

"It was a mistake," he said with uncharacteristic awkwardness. "Just a stupid mistake. If Anthony hadn't seen us, no one would have known . . . *he* wouldn't have known. I never wanted to marry Celia, and I'm very sure she didn't want to marry me. I betrayed his trust, but not from any ill will towards him. It was a simple, stupid misstep."

Lady Marsh nodded. "Thank you, Oliver. I thought perhaps you were nursing a secret broken heart for the girl. I am glad to hear you are not. Well, as you yourself admit that you have no partialities, I have taken the liberty of drawing up a list of suitable young ladies." She ignored his cynical grin. "I am sure, if you cast your eye over it, you will find someone to your liking. While I do not expect any of these young ladies to be as exotic as some of your current . . . friends, they are far more suitable as wives. Someone to grace your table, and on whom to hang the family emeralds. And, most important of all, someone to produce an heir to carry on the Montegomery name. To be blunt, Oliver, we need a filly of good breeding and bloodline if you are to have a strong colt off her."

Again Oliver laughed. That was one thing he liked about his aunt, she was not mealymouthed. His smile faded. He supposed he would do it, even though he had seen enough arranged marriages for the idea to leave him cold. But it was his duty now, wasn't it? He would marry a dull and suitable girl and father a child on her, and she would be prepared to put up with his indifference to her, his failure to love her, for the sake of belonging to one of England's oldest families. Not to mention Lady Marsh's fortune.

Lady Marsh was watching him, trying to read him.

"Very well, Aunt, I will examine your list. Although these days my reputation is not quite what a prospective father-in-law might want for his daughter."

It was Lady Marsh's turn to laugh. "I think you would find he would be too dazzled by my fortune to take any notice of your reputation, Oliver."

She was right; he knew it. He was the bitter pill that must be swallowed for the sake of Lady Marsh's fortune—not Montegomery money, which was a mere trickle these days, but that of her late husband. And yet, as he followed her into the dining room to partake of luncheon, Oliver suddenly found himself wondering what he would do if—unlikely as it seemed—Vivianna Greentree was on his aunt's list of prospective brides. Would he be disinterested then? The thought was so deliciously tantalizing he wanted to stop and savor it.

What was it about her? Putting aside her obsession with Candlewood, wasn't she the epitome of the sort of woman he had always avoided? Or perhaps it was just that he was tired of being pleased; perhaps he needed someone like Vivianna, someone who would stand up to him and look him in the eye.

Damnation, don't lecture me, woman, he had said to her this morning, and she had looked straight through him. No, not through, *inside* him. And then he had kissed her. And he had known, wrap it up in whatever lies he liked, at that moment, with his lips touching hers, that *that* was the true reason he had come to see her.

"Oliver." Lady Marsh was looking ahead, not meeting his eyes, and suddenly he felt the tension in the twisted fingers resting upon his arm.

"Yes, Aunt?"

"I had a visit from Lord Lawson a day or two ago."

Oliver felt his face go blank. "Oh?"

"He had come, he said, because he had heard disturbing news about Candlewood. That you meant to tear it down. He was very . . . well, you know what he is, he was very authoritative, as if he were giving one of his speeches to Parliament. He asked me if I could change your mind, and that it would not reflect well upon the family if you went ahead. That sort of thing."

"What did you tell him?"

"I said you were your own man and I had little influence over you."

"Good."

"Actually, I had the feeling he was rather glad you were demolishing the place, but he thought he should pretend the opposite. That man is so devious I sometimes wonder if he himself knows what he's thinking."

Oliver smiled. "While Candlewood is standing his reputation is in danger. He thinks when it is dust he will be safe. But soon he will learn that matters are not quite as simple as that. . . ."

"Oliver . . . he mentioned Anthony. He said Anthony would not have liked the person you have become. He said that Anthony would have felt let down by you."

For a moment Oliver felt sick with fury, but he swallowed it down. Made himself calm again before he spoke. "I see." He allowed the thud of her cane to fill the silence as they reached the dining room.

"Oliver, I have been thinking. . . . I do not know if you should go on with this plan of yours, to avenge Anthony. I know I gave approval, and at the time I quite saw the point you were making, but now . . . well, I have been wondering of late whether we have been looking for a culprit to blame when there is none. Perhaps Anthony did kill himself, Oliver. I know it is not what you want to hear, but we must face the fact that as levelheaded as Anthony seemed, he may have decided, in a foolish moment, to take his own life."

Oliver knew he must choose his words carefully, and yet he felt hot and dizzy, as though he had been out in the sun too long. Had Lord Lawson caused this, his aunt's doubt? Now, when it was almost over? Perhaps, he thought bleakly, she had always doubted him, but had played along for his own sake, to salve his conscience.

"Anthony would never have killed himself," he said, and only the tremor of his voice showed the pressure he had to bring to bear upon himself. "His heart was stouter than that. He was murdered and we both know by whom. Be patient, Aunt, that is all I ask. It will be over soon."

"Oliver, are you positive that—"

"Yes. You think I want to close my eyes to the possibility that Anthony killed himself, because then I would have to accept the blame? I *do* accept the blame. If I had not been with Celia, then Anthony would have told me what it was that was bothering him. He had spoken before, but only bits and pieces, nothing that had made much sense at the time. That night he had finally come to me to explain the whole story, to ask me for my advice. Despite the difference in our ages, despite what people thought about our differing characters, he sometimes did ask my advice, you know. But that night Celia was there, and . . . He walked out, he walked all the way to Candlewood, and took his secret with him to the grave."

Lady Marsh's cane thudded on the floor, muffled by the carpet. "You will not listen to me, Oliver, so I may as well save my breath. Only let me say this one more thing."

They had reached her chair at the head of the table. "You may say whatever you wish, Aunt."

Lady Marsh struggled into her seat. Settled at last, she looked up at Oliver, and her hard, proud face was pleading. She looked her age, and she looked worried.

"Oliver, you must find a wife and marry. There is solace in making a family of your own. You are too much alone these days. Oh, I know, you are always with people, but a man can stand in a crowded room and still be alone. Look at my list of brides and choose one. Please."

Oliver forced himself to smile, forced the anger from him. She meant well. She loved him, in her way.

"Very well, I will look at your list, Aunt."

Pointless, brother! Miss Vivianna Greentree will not be on it.

Anthony's voice in his head took him by surprise, and Oliver gave a more genuine smile. Anthony would say such a thing, cut straight to the heart of the matter. That was something he missed a great deal now that his brother was gone—someone to tell him exactly what he thought without skirting the issue, or pandering to his sensibilities.

And at that moment he realized what it was about Vivianna that intrigued him so. She, like Anthony, did not scruple to tell him exactly what she thought.

Not that she would ever change his mind, he told himself hastily, for she couldn't. Candlewood had to be torn down, and he had offered the orphans an alternate shelter. That they had rejected his offer was not his problem; he had no desire to become a champion of the poor and homeless.

No, Vivianna would never persuade him to do anything he didn't want to do, but it would be . . . *interesting* letting her try.

Chapter 5

"Miss Greentree is here, my lord. She wants to leave her card. There is a message written on the back of it."

Oliver looked up at his blank-faced butler, wondering whether he was hearing things. His gaze dropped to the card upon the silver salver held in Hodge's gloved hand. The white square was plain and unadorned, apart from the simple words, *Miss Vivianna Greentree, Greentree Manor, Yorkshire.*

The fact that he had been in the library, sitting and brooding over a glass of brandy and thinking of her, seemed to have conjured her up.

"What does the message on the back say, Hodge?"

The butler turned the card over and pursed his lips. "It says: 'I can help you,' my lord."

Oliver considered this. *I can help you.* So many possibilities. It intrigued him, as it was no doubt meant to. "Show her in, Hodge."

Hodge quickly wiped the surprise from his face. Ever since the incident of Celia Maclean, Oliver had a rule that no unaccompanied females were allowed into his home unless he gave prior instruction. He had now set a precedent, for Hodge, himself, *and* Miss Greentree.

"In *here,* my lord?"

Hodge did not look about at the library; he did not have to. The dark tones, the heavy furniture, the leathery smell of the books, all spoke of this being very much a masculine province. It was not a room that a lady had been asked to share recently, certainly not to sit and chat or, in Vivianna's case, lecture. Too bad, thought Oliver. If she wished to help him, she would have to do so on *his* terms.

Hodge had departed, and soon returned with Miss Greentree. The door closed heavily behind her.

She was dressed in another of her plain dresses. This one was dark green, gathered at her waist, the full skirt hiding numerous petticoats and almost brushing the ground—he saw a hint of black shoe. The bodice was very tightly fitted, with no adornment other than a high lace collar, and the sleeves also fitted to her arms, tight to the wrist, where they were trimmed by a white lace cuff to match the collar. Her chestnut hair was bundled into a heavy knot at her nape—no braids or ringlets—and pinned in place beneath a modest straw hat tied with black ribbons. She carried a practical-looking drawstring bag in her gloved hands.

Oliver's *second* thought on seeing her was that he would like to throw the bag out of the window, followed by her hat, pull out all her hairpins, and let her hair tumble down around her.

His *first* thought: Her dress might be plain and unadorned, but that, and its fittedness, only made it more obvious that the body beneath was rounded and very womanly. He wanted to peel it off her, throw it in the fire, and then dress her anew. Red silk. Yes, Miss Vivianna Greentree would look very fine in red silk. Perhaps a red silk shawl, with a fringe to dangle tantalizingly over her breasts and her thighs as she lay on his sofa before the fire, her eyes half closed beneath her long dark lashes, her hair shimmering about her shoulders, and her smile all for him.

It was a delightful fantasy.

Abruptly Oliver stood up, his glass still in his hand. Vivianna was watching him with ill-concealed dismay, and, with her gaze lingering on the glass, a good deal of censure. He realized then that she thought he was drunk—she had already made her case against him and pronounced sentence. She had judged him a useless, worthless creature. He could hardly blame her for that; he had taken pains to portray himself as exactly such a man for the past year. Besides, her lips were pursed so disapprovingly and yet so appealingly that he thought he may as well go ahead and help her to think the worst.

He wanted to shock her, didn't he? He wanted to drive her away?

Oliver gave her his best drunken smile, managing to sway a little at the same time, as if he were having difficulty keeping his balance. "Miss Greentree! You are truly the bravest woman of my acquaintance."

"Lord Montegomery?" Her hazel eyes widened, her fine skin flushed. "What can you mean?"

"I mean that you have come to my house. All alone. I congratulate you."

Vivianna wondered, watching him execute a wobbly bow, if he was trying to be amusing. He was obviously the worse for drink, although it was hard to tell how worse for it he actually was. She had come here to leave her card with its message, and instead had been allowed into his inner sanctum. She had not expected to see him, but when the opportunity was given to her, she had not been able to resist. But now that she was actually standing before him, seeing the gleam in his eye, noting the way his dark hair fell forward over his brow . . . Her breath hitched; her fingers tightened on her bag. This was Oliver Montegomery at his most dangerous.

She should not have come here alone. Again.

Vivianna watched him watching her, and did her best to pretend she was unaffected. "I do not think I have anything to be afraid of, my lord," she said evenly. "You *are* a gentleman, are you not?"

He smiled, and gently shook his finger at her. "I was born a gentleman, Miss Greentree, but I am afraid I have long since ceased to earn the right to be called one."

He went to the decanter and poured himself another glass of brandy, although she was quite certain he had had more than enough.

"What did you mean, Miss Greentree, when you wrote, 'I can help you'? Have you come to offer me solace? I am a man in great need of solace, as you can see. Or do you think you are the woman to set me back on the . . . the straight and narrow? I am sure you have *whipped* many a man into shape."

She colored at his hint of the episode at Aphrodite's, but did not look away. Strange, but drunk as he obviously was, his eyes were clear and watchful still, the blue untainted by spirits or vice.

"I have come to offer my help, my lord, because yesterday I visited Candlewood, and I heard from my friends there of your brother's death. I realize now that you are a man suffering grievously, and that you may simply need someone to talk to, to guide you. That is what I meant when I wrote upon the card."

He set the decanter down with a rattle. "If you mean I have a guilty conscience, then nothing could be further from the truth. I have no conscience."

Seeing him with the refilled glass in his hand, his dark hair tousled, his neckcloth askew, his stance indolent, Vivianna could well believe he was exactly the type of man he said he was. And yet . . . there was a tiny voice in her head that told her that within the scoundrel was a man worth saving.

She rallied. "I do not believe that. Any man can change for the better, if he wants to."

He laughed angrily. "And you are an authority on that, are you? Perhaps you want me to become one of your disciples, one of your creatures, forever grateful for your charity and interest. People would point me out, as I followed you about to . . . to *meetings*, carrying your papers and your bag, listening to your every word with humble amazement. 'There is old Montegomery,' they would say, 'brought back from the brink by Miss Greentree. What a woman she must be to have wrought such a miracle!' You want me to be your slave, Miss Greentree. You want me to hand Candlewood over to you, and my soul with it. *That* is what you want, isn't it?"

He seemed suddenly very animated. She swallowed. "Not at all," she said quietly.

"You know nothing about me," he went on, those intense eyes fixed on hers, such pain and anger in their depths that she felt her own heart contract.

"Your brother died at Candlewood, and his death was connected to you. I know you feel guilt and sorrow. Perhaps that is why you want to demolish Candlewood, to wipe it from your memory, but that will not help, my lord, truly it will not. Pain cannot be so easily dismissed; it carries on, inside, like an unhealed wound. Sometimes your only chance of healing, of making amends, comes through thinking of the greater good rather than of yourself. Give Candlewood to the children."

He stared at her. She truly amazed him. The passion in her eyes was something to behold, and the trouble was, she meant it. She thought she was doing him a good turn, and herself at the same time. Make amends for his brother's death by helping others.

He shook his head. "You speak with such authority on pain and suffering, Miss Greentree"—his voice was harsh—"but you only know what you have seen secondhand. You are too young to have suffered, and your background is obviously privileged. A fine house, a loving family, friends who have your best interests at heart. You are a sham."

Hurt flared in her brilliant eyes, and then died away. She looked older, suddenly, the bones of her face beneath that fine skin more accentuated. Ah, there *was* something . . . Vivianna had her secrets, too.

"You do not know me."

He smiled. "My point exactly. I do not know you, and *you* do not know *me*."

She looked away, her back and shoulders rigid. Had he struck her a mortal blow? More likely she was just regrouping, deciding on her next line of attack. He did not dare to hope he had put a stop to her onward charge. Not surrender, not yet.

"Do you know, Miss Greentree, that my aunt has drawn me up a list of prospective brides?"

The words came out of nowhere, startling even himself. She looked at him, her lips slightly parted, a frown wrinkling her brow beneath the hideous hat. Perhaps she, like him, felt that the situation was slipping out of control. And yet he could not seem to stop himself.

Vivianna's eyes delved into his. "Has she?"

"Yes, she has. A list of young ladies of birth and breeding, those she considers suitable recipients of my proposal of marriage. What do you think of that, Miss Greentree?"

He gestured for her to be seated, as if his choice of bride were a subject she would find fascinating. In fact she did appear fascinated. Her cheeks were flushed, her eyes shining. Or was she just humoring him? Handling the lunatic gently.

"Why does your aunt want you to marry?" Vivianna sat down upon a sofa by the gently burning fire and stripped off her gloves in a businesslike manner.

"My elder brother is dead and I am the last of my line. What was his responsibility now falls to me."

"I see."

"So you think it is perfectly acceptable for my aunt to choose my wife?"

Vivianna thought it was appalling, but she didn't want to say so just yet. Why did he want her answer, anyway? Surely he did not want a matrimonial adviser, and if he did, he certainly would not choose her! Would he . . . ?

To give herself time, she looked about her at the room. It was rich in color and smelled of books. Her favorite sort of place, she thought with a hidden smile. If he had asked her into his library because he thought to discomfort her, he could not have been further from the mark.

"I am waiting, Miss Greentree."

"I think it is a pity that you cannot find a wife for

yourself," she said bluntly. "After all, your aunt's choices cannot be yours. Although she may sift through their pedigrees and tally their dowries, she cannot know what it is about a woman that truly fires your heart."

The brandy glass was warming between his palms, but he wasn't drinking from it. In fact he seemed to have forgotten about it, as he leaned forward in his chair, his gaze upon hers. "Fires my heart? Very poetic, Miss Greentree, but my aunt despises poetry. She wants me to father some poor infant, to continue on the Montegomery bloodline, and then I can sink into obscurity and he can rise above me. To be blunt, she wants a woman I can breed with, nothing more."

Vivianna felt her cheeks flush. This was not the sort of conversation a spinster should be having with a rake, but there were lots of things she had done lately that she was not supposed to do—most of them with Oliver. "Then surely if that is the case any female would do? The kitchen maid or the girl selling flowers on the corner!"

He was still leaning forward in his chair. There wasn't much space between them at all. His eyes were so dark and mesmerizing, she thought if she were not careful, she would fall into them. He may be bad—*he was very bad*—but unlike Toby he was not a man to dismiss lightly. Vivianna knew that despite what she had learned about him, despite his callousness toward the fate of the shelter, there was something about this man that attracted and captivated her.

She may well be a silly virgin, eager to embrace her fate, but it was too late to go back now; she could only go forward.

"I doubt my aunt would approve of a flower girl sitting at my table as my wife, Miss Greentree, worthy though you will no doubt tell me she is. The Montegomery family is an old and proud one. We prefer to marry like."

"Anyway," Vivianna said, ignoring the hint of a smile on his mouth and the way his eyes teased, "despite what your aunt says and wants, I think it must be *you* who makes the final decision. Remember, my lord, the woman you decide upon will be your wife. You will be bound to her, for better or worse, and even though it seems to me that you intend to ignore her as much as possible, there will be times when you may find it necessary to be on reasonable terms with her. You should at least find someone you can converse with without starting an argument."

She was thinking of Aunt Helen and Toby.

"You are very practical." He leaned back in his chair, and for a moment he looked bleak, as if what had begun as a joke had lost its ability to make him smile. Then his gaze lifted once more to hers, and she saw the dangerous spark in those depths.

"Would you like to throw your rather ugly hat into the ring, Miss Greentree? Would you like to supply the heir to the Montegomery name? Just think, you could turn all my properties into Shelters for Poor Orphans."

He was not serious, of course. He was teasing her, and he had been drinking. And yet, even though it was a cruel jest, sensation washed over her. The idea of being his, and he being hers, was suddenly, blazingly wonderful.

Vivianna swallowed nervously. To escape his watchful eyes, she looked down at her hands clasped in her lap. There was her wool gown, sensible and unflattering, and beneath it her three petticoats. There were the tips of her shoes, plain and practical, and her stockings, thick and warm and made to withstand the Yorkshire moors. Again, all very sensible and practical. Because, she reminded herself, that was what she was.

Sensible and practical.

She might dream about stepping outside society's boundaries with Oliver, but she could never be his wife. Nor would she wish to be. Being in the power of such a man had never been one of her dreams—quite the opposite, actually. She wanted to retain her freedom, to do as she wished, to help others. And yet . . . since she had met Oliver Montegomery she had begun to wonder whether that freedom of the mind and the spirit might also encompass freedom of her physical needs and passions. Men indulged themselves in affairs, why shouldn't she?

Vivianna looked up at him again and discovered him still watching her, as if he found her features as endlessly fascinating as she found his. Now there was a touch of amusement creasing the skin about his eyes—or was it arrogance? Doubts began to gather. Maybe he hadn't been seeking her help at all? Maybe he just wanted to embarrass her, to drive her from his life, to rid himself of her troublesome presence. Well, Vivianna would not be driven!

"I am afraid the Greentrees are neither an old nor an aristocratic family, so your aunt would not approve. But if I married you I would have to make a condition," she said, and gave him a sweetly false smile.

He blinked; she *had* surprised him. Good! "Condition?"

"I would make you promise never to demolish Candlewood, and to pay for its upkeep and repairs into perpetuity."

"Ah, I see. Unfortunately, that is not a condition I can agree to, Miss Greentree."

"My lord, can you not see that Candlewood is perfect for the orphans? They are safe there, and there is room for them to run about and play. They can be children. Some of them have never been allowed to be, simply, children."

He was watching her with a blank face and Vivianna heard her own passionate tones fade into silence. She was wasting her time, and suddenly to her despair she knew it. He wasn't touched or moved; he simply did not care. And nothing she was going to say to him in regard to the orphans, no appeal she could make to him, would make the slightest difference.

Vivianna stood up. Her disappointment was a bitter taste in her mouth, but she did not let him see it. She made her voice cool and uncaring. "Perhaps, when you have chosen your bride, you can furnish me with her name? She may prove to be more amenable than yourself."

He laughed softly and also rose to his feet. "I don't know why I want you, Vivianna," he said, and he did not sound drunk. He simply sounded cross. "There is something about you, something that makes me wonder what it would be like to undo your hair and take off your dress and your shoes, and lie you down upon my bed and make love to you over and over again. You are a distraction, and one I could well do without."

Her face flamed, her voice was choked. "You seem to delight in trying to embarrass and humiliate me."

"I do, don't I?" He no longer sounded drunk, not at all.

"I had better go now."

"Vivianna."

He should not call her that—they were near-strangers—and yet her name sounded like a promise in his mouth. She looked down and saw that he was holding out her glove toward her. She had dropped it as she stood up, in her haste to leave. Vivianna eyed it warily, as if his hand were a viper ready to strike. He knew it, too, and again was amused by it.

"I can keep it if you like," he drawled. "A keepsake."

Vivianna snatched the glove from him, but not quickly enough. His fingers closed on hers, cool and strong and remarkably steady. As she had known she would be, she found herself drawn closer to him, though her feet were unwilling and her heart beating hard.

"Oliver, please . . ."

"I won't hurt you," he whispered. "Your lips are so soft and sweet, Vivianna, that I simply must . . . Ah," a sound of deep relief, as his mouth brushed upon hers. And now the touch of him against her made Vivianna feel as if it had been she who had drunk the brandy, for her head was light and her skin felt too tight to fit her.

One arm came about her waist and with his other hand he cupped her jaw, holding her face still for his examination. His eyes were so close to hers it was like drowning in the deepest part of the ocean.

"Oh yes, there is passion in you," he murmured. "It spills from your soul and makes sparks in your eyes and brings color to your cheeks. I can taste it"—he kissed her again—"on your lips. I would like to have you, Miss Greentree, all of you. I want to be the first to make you feel the hunger that lovemaking can bring—and I think I would be the first."

She pushed her hands against his chest, but there was no movement. She had the mad notion that he meant to ravish her right here in his library, and she would put up no resistance. Because, in her secret heart, she wanted him to.

His mouth pressed to hers, his warm breath mingling with her own. His kiss deepened, and she tasted him, and the fire of desire caught light inside her. Was this the hunger he had spoken of? Because already she felt famished. Vivianna's hands slid over his shoulders and clung there. Her eyes were closed, too heavy to open, but that only added to the experience, for now touch and feel, smell and hearing, were everything. The texture of his fine jacket, the moist heat of his mouth, the clean scent of his skin, the beat of his heart against her body, heavy and hard.

He pressed his thigh between hers, crushing her petticoats and skirts, until she could feel him through the layers of cloth. Intimate. He bent his head and kissed her, little nibbling kisses, down her throat. She arched her neck and tried to breathe, clinging to his shoulders as if she would spin away if she let go. He held her firm, one arm about her narrow waist, and pressed his face to her bosom, his breath hot through her wool dress and boned corset and linen chemise. Her skin was afire.

"You are wrapped up like a gift," he said, and when she forced her lids to open, his face was in front of hers again, his eyes blazing. "Hooks and buttons and laces."

She could hardly breathe; her voice was shaky. "There is safety in hooks and buttons and laces. There is time for ardor to turn to good sense."

His hand molded to her breast. "I can feel your stays," he said, "but I can feel you, too."

"I can feel you," she managed. And she could feel the warmth and the gentle strength of his hand.

"I want to put my mouth on you. Have you ever had a man's mouth on your breast?"

"No!" she gasped in protest, but already the image

of it was sending tremors of delight through her, almost too much to bear.

He bowed his head, as if he, too, were struggling with control. And then, with a groan, he kissed her again, his tongue in her mouth, and she found it was a simple matter to return the favor, to feel him and explore him and want him . . . good Lord, she *wanted* him. . . .

And that was the problem, wasn't it? He knew how to make her want him, and in a moment she would be beyond thought or control. The plain fact was he was experienced and she was an innocent. If she did not learn better, she would never be able to do as she willed with him. He would use her and discard her.

Vivianna would not save the shelter; she would not even be able to save herself.

It took all her effort to pull away, to put distance between them. When all she wanted to do was sink back into his embrace.

He looked as beyond thought as her, but even as she stood, trying to breathe, watching him, his eyes regained their cool composure, his mouth its lazy smile.

"Should I apologize?" he asked her. "I did warn you."

Vivianna pushed at her hair, found it loose and tangled about her shoulders. "Yes, you did," she said. Her voice was growing stronger and calmer, as gradually the turmoil inside her ebbed. She picked up her hat from the sofa and, tucking her hair beneath it, tied it firmly under her chin. Probably not as neat as when she had set out, but it would do.

"Vivianna," he said, and there was that note in his voice again, half pleading and half demand. She felt her own treacherous senses respond and did the only thing she could. Reached out to the bellpull, and gave it a sharp tug.

"Go on. Run away," he mocked. "Go back to Yorkshire. That's the only way you'll escape me now. You'd be wise to heed the warning."

"You're trying to frighten me into leaving," she said firmly.

He laughed angrily. "I wish I could."

The door opened and Hodge stood there, his servant's face without expression. Vivianna moved toward him. From somewhere she found a normal voice, and used it.

"Thank you for seeing me, Lord Montegomery. I hope you will consider what I have said."

The outer door closed on Hodge's disapproving face, and Vivianna went down the steps feeling as if she had been buffeted by a great wind. Except that the storm was inside her.

Her aunt's coach was waiting, and Vivianna climbed within. It was then that her body seemed to collapse, and she gave a soft groan of relief. But as she drove out of Berkeley Square, Vivianna had to fight to stop herself from turning around, to not give in to the urge to go right back to him.

To Oliver.

It was then that the plan unfolded before her, the audacious plan that had been formulating in her head ever since her visit to Aphrodite's. All this time she had been pushing it away, telling herself logic and good sense were enough, and all the time the solution to her problem was right there, waiting for her to catch its eye. Vivianna needed to save the shelter by persuading Oliver to change his mind, but she could not bully him—Madame had been right. Madame had also been right when she said that Oliver found her amusing and refreshing.

His tastes are jaded and he is looking for something new and different. Play upon that, if you dare. If you are skillful enough you can achieve your aim.

In short, he wanted her, sexually. It was true; he had told her so on numerous occasions. Oh yes, partially it had been an attempt to send her wailing back to Yorkshire—Vivianna may be innocent, but she was not a fool—but the way in which he had kissed her, touched her, looked at her showed he had not been playacting all of the time. Oliver Montegomery lusted after her. She was in possession of something he very much wanted—her body.

It was true Vivianna could not bully him into submission, but she could *lead* him. . . .

Such a daring and exciting plan must also include some danger, and yet Vivianna asked herself what it was she was really risking. She had already declared her intention to thumb her nose at society, to live to enjoy her own freedom. And she had already begun to experience the pleasure that freedom could give her, the pleasure of being with a man who may not be suitable in other ways but who was physically attractive to her. Oliver appeared to be that man. So she would be risking nothing that she was not already prepared to risk.

But Vivianna knew her own limitations. She could not seduce Oliver Montegomery. The idea was ludicrous. She needed help. Vivianna needed to learn the ways of women whose bodies were their trade. She needed to tease him, cajole him, outrake the rake.

Vivianna needed to find herself a teacher in seduction.

Chapter 6

At Queen's Square, Lil was waiting for Vivianna.

"I was about to come and fetch you, miss," she said, her narrowed gaze inspecting Vivianna. Checking for signs of debauchery? Vivianna wished she could laugh at the idea, but debauchery was no longer as unlikely an outcome as it had once seemed. "Is everything all right, miss?"

"The Beatty sisters seem to believe I can make everything right," Vivianna said bleakly.

Lil's pretty face was compassionate. "Poor miss. Is there anything more you can do?"

"Murder him," Vivianna murmured, but shook her head when Lil's eyes grew big and round. "It was a joke. Don't worry, I will think of something."

"I'm certain you will," Lil agreed. "You've a kind heart, miss, and a good one."

"Thank you, Lil," Vivianna said, touched, and yet there was a trace of guilt in her heart right now. For her aim in besting Lord Oliver Montegomery was not entirely altruistic, not this time.

"Everyone at Greentree Manor knows that Miss Vivianna always has her way when it comes to her orphans."

Lil made her sound rather bossy, Vivianna thought. The truth was, Vivianna had never fully recovered from her abandonment as a child, and she had set herself the lifelong task of trying to make things right for other children not so fortunate as herself. She could never find her own mother, she knew that now and had long ago accepted it—it was quite likely that her mother was dead—but that did not mean she could not give others a happy ending.

Suddenly she felt terribly homesick for Greentree Manor, for Yorkshire and the moors. She wanted Lady Greentree, and her two sisters—Marietta with her fair hair and blue eyes and irrepressible smile, and Francesca, dark-eyed and wild-haired, a law unto herself. They were her family, and she missed them. London was vast and uncaring, and her errand appeared hopeless. It seemed that Oliver wanted to destroy the shelter, and his brother's memory with it, to fund his profligate lifestyle.

There was nothing she could do to stop him.

Apart, that is, from throwing herself into his arms and allowing him to make love to her, "over and over again." This was the time to strike, while his passion was still hot, while she had a good chance of persuading him to do as she wanted. The fact that she wished to experience physical passion with Oliver Montegomery was a secondary matter, but it would help her to approach her new task with a certain . . . enthusiasm.

"Lil," she said, looking up.

"Yes, miss?"

"Would you know how to . . ."

Lil waited expectantly, her face turned to her mistress, her brown eyes fixed trustingly upon Vivianna's. And Vivianna knew she could not ask Lil to teach her the finer arts of ensnaring and enslaving Oliver Montegomery. Lil probably knew a great deal more than her mistress about such matters—her past was colorful and worldly—but Lil had tried to put it behind her. She considered herself "respectable" now, and the word meant a great deal to her. It would be unfair to place her in such a position. No, Vivianna must ask someone who was more pragmatic about such things, someone whose profession it was to understand the ways of men.

"Miss?"

"Never mind. Is Aunt Helen in her sitting room? I will join her in a moment."

Aunt Helen was resting her eyes—her euphemism for taking a nap—but she sat up as Vivianna entered. She looked wan and tired. Vivianna had heard her aunt and Toby arguing long into the night, and afterward the sound of her aunt weeping had gone on even longer.

Vivianna found it difficult to believe that once Helen Tremaine had been the belle of the Tremaine family. "My sister could have taken her pick," Lady Greentree had told her sadly, "but she chose Toby Russell. He was a rake even then, and not to be trusted, but she believed she could change him for the better. Poor Helen."

"Could your family not have forbidden the banns, Mama?"

Amy Greentree had sighed. "My brother Thomas was in India, in the army—he and my dear husband were friends and brothers-in-arms. My younger brother, William, did make some effort, but Helen promptly ran off with Toby, and William let them wed to hush up the scandal." Lady Greentree had bitten her lip. "He lost his temper and said if she was determined to marry a cad, then he wished her well of it."

"I had thought Uncle William more forbearing," Vivianna had said. She did not know her uncle very well, but he had always seemed a bluff, kindly sort of man. Her Uncle Thomas—the elder brother—had died before she came to Greentree Manor, so she had never known him. It was Uncle William who was now head of the Tremaine family.

"William?" Lady Greentree had laughed. "He is not forbearing at all, my dear. He likes to have his own way, does my brother William. Let us just say that I am eternally glad that my dear husband took me to live in Yorkshire, and William lives in London."

"Vivianna? I was asking you how you are faring with Lord Montegomery and the shelter."

Helen was clasping her hand, and Vivianna shook off her abstraction and squeezed her aunt's trembling fingers. "Not very well, I'm afraid. Never mind, I mean to persist. You know me."

Helen sighed. "I think you are very brave, my dear. Toby says there are rumors about Lord Montegomery, and not very nice ones. He says . . . well, perhaps I should not repeat it, but then again if it will help you . . . he says that rumor has it that Lord Montegomery stole his brother's fiancée, and his brother killed himself."

Vivianna made a face. "I have heard that rumor."

"The girl was Celia Maclean. A tragic tale. Evidently they were . . . well, it was more than a kiss. She has never married and, of course, her reputation is quite ruined."

"But *he* continues to go about in society," Vivianna said.

"Well, dear, he is a Montegomery, one of the *best* families, and a man. It is different for a man."

It was grossly unfair, in Vivianna's view, but Helen did not seem able to see that, or if she did, she accepted it as the natural order of things.

"My brother William may call in the next day or so, if time permits," she went on. "Of course he is very busy, but as head of the family, he likes to keep an eye on us all."

"I'm sure he does, Aunt Helen."

Vivianna planned to visit Aphrodite's in the next day or two, but she would not tell Helen that.

"I trust William," Helen added, and her once-lovely face looked old and bleak. "These days, he is the only man I do trust."

The evening shadows were long as Oliver, in his disguise of scuffed trousers and plain jacket, strolled out into the London streets. As usual he was thinking of Vivianna Greentree. The woman seemed to have a knack of wearing the ugliest clothing and of bundling her hair up so tightly it could not possibly do her any good. And yet, despite that, and her preaching ways, Oliver found himself thinking about her almost constantly. It was doing his peace of mind, and his concentration, no good at all.

He turned into a narrower, darker street. Why had Vivianna really come to his house? He had begun to wonder if Miss Vivianna was suffering the same ache of the flesh as he, but of course that could not be. Probably he was imagining the blurred look in her eyes and her enthusiastic responses—a case of wistful thinking. It was the shelter that motivated Vivianna. Everything she did was for the sake of her orphans. He could not trust her—these days there were few people he could trust—but that did not mean he could not enjoy himself with her.

For a long time after Anthony's death, the future had ceased to exist. Now there was a sense of life-to-be-lived stirring inside him. As if there may be a future for him, after all. And little though he may trust her, it had begun with the arrival of Vivianna.

He saw again her face, dreamy after he kissed her, and felt again her fine skin and soft mouth, smelled her sweet, wholesome scent. She was a meddlesome nuisance, interfering with his plans—Candlewood must be demolished, that was the crux upon which everything else revolved. His strong attraction to her was an added complication and had taken him by surprise. Did she realize how dangerous their association had become? He had always prided himself upon his ability to control his desire, had always despised those men who believed it their right to force a woman against her will, but he was finding it increasingly difficult to stop.

Oliver passed a lane so narrow a man would have to turn sideways to walk down it—eyes watched from the darkness—and finally reached the place he had set out for. Torches flared at the front door, and there was noise and the smell of ale issuing from within. He strolled inside.

It was not the best of places, but neither was it the worst. Once a respectable inn, it had degenerated, the customers coming from the miserable lodging houses in the area to escape the crowding, at least for a while. Because it was mediocre and forgettable, few gentlemen frequented it, and that was as he liked it. Oliver found his way to a quiet table in a shadowy corner and sipped his ale, prepared to wait as long as he had to.

He had only been there some ten minutes when the familiar figure slipped into the chair opposite him.

"Sergeant Ackroyd."

Dark eyes and hair, a ferrety face that had never been handsome.

"Yer lordship," Sergeant Ackroyd said, and glanced about nervously. He, like Oliver, was wearing plain clothing that had seen better days.

"What news do you have for me?"

The policeman's gaze met his and flicked away as quickly. "Not a lot to report, yer lordship. The gentleman in question ain't been about much. Stuck indoors on government business, so I hear."

Oliver thought, *He thinks he's safe; he thinks he's won. I want him to feel like that. It will make the shock even greater when he learns that he hasn't.*

"No one has called on him, then?" he asked aloud.

"No one as shouldn't, yer lordship."

Oliver had asked Sergeant Ackroyd not to call him that, but the man had ignored him. He seemed to gain some sort of pleasure from saying it, or maybe it was just the fact he was hobnobbing with a peer of the realm.

"Well, keep watching. I am about to set a small test for our friend. I want to see how he reacts."

"I'll keep me eyes peeled, yer lordship, don't worry."

Oliver nodded, and left him there. Sergeant Ackroyd would do his job, now Oliver had to do his.

Aphrodite's was sober by daylight; more like a boy's grammar school than a disorderly house. Vivianna tucked a strand of hair behind her ear and considered her options. The hackney cab had gone—she had sent it away, afraid that if she didn't she would change her mind and turn craven at the last moment.

This was no time for second thoughts and doubts. If she was to sway Oliver to her will, she must use every weapon she possessed, but she must understand the game first.

With a deep breath, Vivianna climbed the steps to the door beneath the portico and gave it a resounding rat-a-tat-tat. The echo reverberated within, and in moments heavy footsteps approached.

The doorman peered out at her. His battered face looked tired, his graying hair was not so neat, the neckcloth at his throat was untied and dangling, and his coat was plain black. But his gray eyes were sharp, and they narrowed in recognition.

"Oh, 'tis you," he said, and swung open the door, though he remained in the way, blocking her entrance with his broad-shouldered form. "What do you want now?"

"I want to see Madame."

"You want to see Madame?" He appeared amused rather than surprised. "What do you want to see her for? She don't take no respectable women here, only the unrespectable ones." And he smirked at his own wit.

Vivianna refused to be intimidated. "I don't want to work here," she retorted, "I just want to speak with her. Now let me in."

He eyed her a moment more, his eyes sparkling with humor, and then with a shrug he stepped back. Pretending that her nerves were not stretched to their very limit, Vivianna followed him inside.

Polished wood shone richly; there was a strong scent of roses from a Chinese vase upon a pedestal. The sound of a piano being played drifted down the staircase. The doorman continued to observe her, as if her reactions were a source of fascination to him. He was beginning to annoy her.

"This ain't any old academy," he informed her with an air of pride. "Miss Aphrodite runs a superior establishment. Not any old riffraff are allowed in here, only gentlemen, and only those who got the class and the blunt. Plenty so-called 'gentlemen' call themselves gentlemen and ain't. Miss Aphrodite, she's a real lady herself, and she knows what makes a real gentleman. She were famous in her day, she were. A famous *courtesan.*" He drew it out as if it were three words. "She had earls and dukes visiting her every day of the week, she did. A Frenchie, a prince it was, gave her a chateau just for spending one night with him. Miss Aphrodite, she's a great lady."

"Dobson!"

He froze, his battered face comical in dismay, and turned around. Vivianna also turned toward the voice.

Madame—or Miss Aphrodite, as Dobson had called her—was standing in the gallery above, dressed in another simple but very elegant black gown, her hair arranged in soft ringlets about her face and drawn into an intricate knot on top. Jewelry—a gold and emerald and topaz necklace—circled her throat, and her fingers flashed with precious stones. As she descended the stairs with a rustle of silken petticoats, Vivianna wondered whether the display of wealth upon her person was a reminder of her past glory.

"Miss Greentree? I did not expect to see you here again. Have you come for your cloak? Surely you could have sent a servant for such a trifling task?"

In truth, Vivianna had forgotten all about her cloak, but she used the excuse now. Better to tread carefully, she thought. If she blurted out her real reason for being here, she might find herself once more out in the street and the door to Aphrodite's closed firmly behind her.

"I hope you do not mind me coming, Madame?"

The woman smiled, and there was something in it at once comforting and yet startling. As if a beautiful and inanimate painting had suddenly come to life. The floor rocked beneath her feet, and then steadied. Vivianna took a sharp breath, wondering if the London air was beginning to disagree with her.

"You may call me Aphrodite, if you like, Miss Greentree. It is my real name, though rather a mouthful, don't you think?" Her accent was faint but attractive. She must be in her late forties. Perhaps she came to England after the Revolution, as a child, with so many of the other escapees of the Republic. A blue-blooded émigré turned courtesan? Vivianna supposed it was not beyond the realms of possibility.

"She insisted on seeing you," Dobson said. "She looked harmless enough."

Aphrodite gave him a bewitching smile. She was still beautiful now, but in her youth Aphrodite must have been breathtakingly so. Surely, if anyone could help her to bring Oliver to heel, then it was she.

"My faithful Dobson has been with me for many years," Aphrodite said, and her gaze warmed as it rested on the doorman. "When he was young he fought with the 12th Light Dragoons at Waterloo. He is a hero. That is very good, is it not, for a boy from the Seven Dials?"

Dobson rolled his eyes, but he had turned pink with pleasure at her praise. "Them days is long gone, Miss Aphrodite, as you well know. Besides, I prefer the peaceful life in me old age."

"You are not old, my friend. Young enough, at least,

to keep order in this house. Sometimes the 'gentlemen' are unruly, are they not? There are fistfights."

"Very unruly, but they're still gentlemen. They don't know what a real fistfight is."

"*Non,* they don't."

Vivianna had the strangest feeling that although the two of them were speaking in words she understood, there was an undercurrent of something more. And then Aphrodite's dark gaze drifted back to her and grew curious.

"I do not think you even remember your cloak until I mention it, Miss Greentree. Perhaps you would enlighten me as to why you really came to see me?"

It was now or never.

"I want to speak to you about Lord Montegomery," Vivianna said in a rush.

Aphrodite and Dobson glanced at each other, and a secret exchange was made between them.

"Very well," Aphrodite said. "Come with me. Dobson, will you see that those lobsters have been delivered? I am tired of chasing after that fishmonger. Frighten him, *mon ami,* with your snarl."

"You leave it to me, Miss Aphrodite."

He strode off toward the back of the house, and Aphrodite turned and led Vivianna into a room off the hall. It was as elegant as the rest of the house. A tapestry covered part of the wall, the pastoral scene intricate and breathtaking. A bowl of flowers sat on a table, and the chairs and sofa were covered in delicate, hand-painted fabric. The windows overlooked a small side garden, where a tree was blooming, its petals scattered on the ground like snowflakes.

Aphrodite gestured toward a decanter, but Vivianna shook her head. The other woman then seated herself upon a chair and Vivianna sat down to face her.

"I don't know what Oliver has done, Miss Greentree, but I am a little surprised you find it necessary to complain to me."

Vivianna shook her head. "I have no complaint. That is not why I have come. And, you were correct, neither was I thinking of my cloak. I came to ask you something. I . . . it is probably an imposition, and you may refuse—in fact, I am sure you will—but first will you listen to me? Please?"

Aphrodite's expression was aloof, but Vivianna had no doubt that behind that polite mask her mind was turning. "Very well, Miss Greentree. What did you wish to say to me that has caused you to brave family displeasure and public censure, by coming to my house?"

Vivianna hesitated. She had meant to tell Aphrodite as little as possible, and to simply ask for the benefit of her expertise. But now she sensed that Aphrodite would refuse her if she did not explain more fully her reasons for wanting such help.

Aphrodite was watching her, the polite smile fixed to her lips. "Come, Miss Greentree," she said with the slightest note of impatience. "It cannot be so bad. I have been called many names, believe me. If you have come to berate me or abuse me, I will hear you out. Say what you will, and put us both out of our misery."

Vivianna's eyes widened. "Oh no! I have not come to berate you, nor abuse you. Nothing like that, I promise you. It is a favor I would ask of you. I . . . But first I think I must tell you why I would need such a favor. Will you be patient just a little longer?"

Aphrodite had been watching her with quizzical eyes, and now she bowed her head, relaxing slightly.

"I believe I have already explained to you that Lord Montegomery owns a property called Candlewood. It is leased to some friends of mine, and we are using it as a home for orphans—the Shelter for Poor Orphans. Lord Montegomery now wishes to demolish the building and build houses, and he is evicting the orphans. Oh, he has offered alternate accommodation, but it isn't the same. Candlewood is ideal, the perfect place for these children. It is their home. I came to London to try and prevent him from going ahead with his plan, to make him understand. But he will not listen to me."

Aphrodite had been sitting quite still, but now she looked up with another polite smile. "Yes, you explained to me when you were here before." She waved a beringed hand. The emeralds and pink topaz about her throat flashed in the light from the windows. "Orphans. Abandoned children. You feel an empathy towards them, Miss Greentree?"

It was clear from her tone that Aphrodite felt little. Vivianna tried not to let it upset her. "Yes, I do."

Aphrodite raised elegant brows. "Why?"

Vivianna was taken aback. "My reasons are personal."

"Very well"—with another meaningless smile. "But you must realize that Oliver will no more listen to me than he will to you. Less so, I should imagine. At least you are his social equal. I am . . . *psht!* Nothing." She snapped her fingers.

Vivianna frowned. "Nothing? But you are clearly an aristocrat, Madame! A French émigré, perhaps? An escapee from the Bastille—or rather, the daughter of one."

Aphrodite gave her little smile. "You are too kind, Miss Greentree," she said, but she did not explain her antecedents, and it was clear she had no intention of doing so.

But Vivianna was curious. "Was it true? The things your doorman said about you? That you were a great courtesan with many rich and famous lovers?"

Aphrodite lowered her lashes, hiding whatever feelings may have shone in her eyes. "I was famous once, *oui.* Like Madame du Barry, like Madame de Pompadour." She smiled. "Do you understand, Miss Greentree, what a courtesan is? She is a woman trained to play a part, and yet she is *a*part. Often she comes from poverty, or maybe she is of the bourgeois and has fallen upon hard times, or been ruined by some man, *psht!* The courtesan, she can drift in and out of so-called polite society; sometimes she can be accepted by it, just as she is accepted by the *demimonde.* There are many courtesans who have married well and put on the cloak of respectability. Others, like me, prefer to remain free of such bindings."

"Oh." Vivianna blinked.

"A courtesan gives more than just her body, *mon chou.* She gives her charm, her intellect, her ability to amuse and please. She is a companion and a lover. Sometimes she is wife, mother, and child, all in one. A successful courtesan is sought after by many men, and she cannot stay with a single one, not for long. Unless she falls in love"—and now she looked up, and her eyes glittered—"and that would be a very grave mistake if she wants to continue being a courtesan."

"I can see it would."

"Now, Miss Greentree, what is it you wish to ask me?"

Fascinating as the conversation was, she had been told, politely, to hurry up. "Madame . . . Aphrodite, the other night, you said that there were ways of persuading a man. Of leading him. I want you to teach me about those ways. I want to use them on Oliver."

There was a surprised silence. "You want to learn to be one of the *demimonde*?"

Vivianna's face flushed bright red. "No," she gasped. "No, I don't want that. I simply need some advice on how to capture his interest, and to keep it, so that I can persuade him to change his mind."

"It seems to me, Miss Greentree, that you have already captured his interest."

"But I don't know how to use that interest to my best advantage. How to . . . to . . . make him stop!"

Aphrodite laughed. "You mean how to keep him at arm's length until you are ready to submit to him?"

"Yes. And once I do submit, I need to know how to hold on to his interest. To hold on to it, Madame, until he agrees to my terms." She sighed. "You see, I am very ignorant of such things."

"Naturally you are, *mon chou*. Respectable society does not teach its daughters the perils of desire. They prefer them to be naïve and pure and dependent, and so they must be ignorant."

Vivianna watched her, considering her words. It was something she had often thought about herself, but to hear Aphrodite say it was a revelation. Had she more in common with a famous courtesan than her own peers?

Aphrodite fiddled with the gold mesh bracelet that circled her wrist, turning the catch around and around. "You must care very much about your orphans, Miss Greentree, to sacrifice yourself like this. Or perhaps it is not such a sacrifice?"

Her glance was arch, and Vivianna supposed she should act the part of the indignant virgin, but she was too honest to prevaricate. When Oliver looked at her, when he touched her, she felt pleasure she had never known before. Why should she pretend she did not?

It was as if Aphrodite read her thoughts in her face. "You realize that if you are discovered you will be ruined in the eyes of the world you live in? Gentlemen may enjoy visiting my house, but they would not like the thought of a prospective wife visiting it also, for whatever reason. And if they knew you were planning to use your body to ensnare Lord Montegomery, they would close their doors to you forever."

"I know this. I will not be discovered. Besides, I want to know what it is like to . . . to be with a man like Oliver, and I do not want to marry him. I have seen enough of marriage to know it is often not the best life for a woman. I am content to remain a spinster."

"Marriage is a comfortable jail cell, *oui*? It can be so. It can also be very happy, Miss Greentree. You are young. Do not close all those doors just yet, not until you are certain of the direction you wish to take." Aphrodite waited a moment, and then she smiled. "Yes, I will help you, but only if you will do me a favor in return."

Vivianna's eyes widened in surprise. "Yes?"

"Tell me . . . why do you feel so passionately about your home for orphans? I do not believe it is simply the wish that gentlewomen often have to help those less fortunate than themselves. Charity, *psht!* This is something more, something close to your heart. It shines in your eyes, *mon chou*."

Vivianna had not intended to become so intimate with the courtesan, but she realized that to keep such a distance now would be insulting to Aphrodite, and unrealistic. Besides, how could the tragic story of Vivianna's childhood matter to Aphrodite?

"Very well—it is no secret, although it is so long

ago I think most of the Greentree family and their friends have forgotten it. I am one of them now, and I am happy to be so." But she settled herself on the edge of her seat and prepared her words.

"The truth is, I do not know who I am. I and my two sisters were abandoned as children and Lady Greentree found us and took us in. She was a widow with no children of her own, and I could not have asked for a kinder, dearer mother. But despite my good luck, or perhaps because of it, I have always felt a closeness to children like myself. Abandoned. Alone. I want to help them, and the Shelter for Poor Orphans is my way of doing so. It is my passion, you are right, and I would do *anything* to save it."

And to make Oliver yours, just a little, a voice inside her head mocked. *You would like him to look at you as if you were the only thing in the world worth having. Wouldn't you?*

Vivianna cleared her throat and thrust her thoughts away, back into the shadows where they belonged. She felt as if she were on the verge of making new discoveries about herself, and she wasn't sure if she would like them, or the person she may well become.

Aphrodite was sitting with her head bowed, turning her gold mesh bracelet. After a moment she rose to her feet, moving gracefully to the table which held the decanter and glasses. She poured herself a drink, the lip of the decanter rattling against the crystal glass. *Her hands are shaking,* Vivianna thought.

"I can see why you are drawn to help others, Miss Greentree," Aphrodite said, her back to Vivianna. "Tell me, how old were you when you were abandoned?"

"I was six years old, I think."

A clock on the mantelpiece ticked off the seconds; outside in the garden a sparrow flitted from branch to branch, finding insects. Time stretched on, and Vivianna became uneasy. Still, Aphrodite did not turn.

"Will you help me to persuade Oliver?" she finally asked. "I understand it is an imposition, and yet . . . I think you *will* help me."

At last Aphrodite faced her, her dark eyes were shining with what could be tears. Clearly the story had moved her far more than Vivianna had thought it would, and relief swelled within her. For all her cool sophistication Aphrodite had a tender heart, or perhaps there was something similar in the other woman's past. Perhaps as a child she, too, had been left, or her parents killed by the Revolution.

"Yes," Aphrodite said, her voice husky with emotion, "I will help you, Miss Greentree. It is not an imposition, and although I have no scruples about such things, I have another condition. I will not send you to Oliver Montegomery to have your heart broken. Do you understand that? If you are ever in danger of falling in love with him, of losing sight of your true aim in all of this, then you must desist. Is that understood?"

Vivianna nodded with what she hoped was more certainty than she felt. "Of course. You may be sure I will never fall in love with a man like Oliver Montegomery."

The words seemed to hang in the air between them—tempting fate, Vivianna thought, with a shiver.

"Return tomorrow morning at eleven, *mon chou,* and we will see what can be done."

"Thank you." Vivianna rose to her feet.

"I cannot promise miracles, but I think you will find it is not so painful as you expect, nor so complicated. You may even enjoy it."

"I am most grateful."

Aphrodite showed her out into the hall and accompanied her to the front door. "Tell me, Miss Greentree . . ." Her voice sounded a little husky now, as though she were tired. "Will you satisfy my curiosity a little further?"

Vivianna smiled. "If I can. What is it you wish to know?"

"Have you ever tried to discover who your mother was? Have you ever made attempts to contact her?"

Vivianna shook her head sadly. "My past is so shadowy now. With time memories have faded, and unfortunately I knew none of the necessarily details it would have taken to trace my family. Her name, or her home . . . I decided it was best to forget the past and make the most of what I had. My sister, Marietta, is more determined. She says she will find our mother one day. My younger sister, Francesca, says she has forgotten the past. For myself, when I decided to help other children, I realized how very fortunate I was in comparison to so many of them. I knew then that it would be selfish of me to continue to mourn my past. Who I am is no longer important to me; it is what I do with my life now that has meaning."

Aphrodite was staring at her, and her face was completely white. She reached out a hand and clung to the bellpull. Far away, Vivianna heard it jangling for the servant.

"Are you unwell?" she asked, shaken by the blank, blind look in the woman's eyes, the visible trembling of her lips in that chalky face. All her beauty had gone, and she was old.

Aphrodite shook her head—a ringlet fell lose against her shoulder. "What shall I call you?" she whispered. "Tell me, tell me, what is your name?"

There was an urgency in her voice that had not been there before. The careful French had faded. Suddenly Vivianna could hear the woman's true origins clearly, a brash London accent fighting through the Parisian one. It seemed that this famous courtesan had come from humble beginnings, just like so many others.

Startled by this new knowledge, and by Aphrodite's strangeness, she said, "My name is Vivianna."

Aphrodite trembled violently. "Oh," she whispered. "Oh."

Just then Dobson came running and, seeing his mistress so fragile and close to collapse, he caught her up against him, just as she began to crumple to the floor. Vivianna, who was holding her arm to support her, now stood uncertain.

Dobson gave her a furious look. "What have you done?"

Aphrodite swallowed, shaking her head. "No, no, she's done nothing. I need to lie down. I am unwell, that is all. I am unwell. Help me upstairs."

"You have let yourself get overtired. You know the doctor said you have to take better care of yourself." Dobson cast Vivianna another searing look, but his attention was all for Aphrodite. Concern filled his eyes, but also something warmer, deeper. Vivianna realized then that Dobson was not just Aphrodite's servant. He loved her.

Still holding her in his arms, he strode quickly toward the staircase. Aphrodite rallied, lifting her head to look at Vivianna over his shoulder, where she stood irresolute by the door.

"Come tomorrow. Eleven. Do not fail, *mon chou*!"

"I will come, Madame, I promise. If you are well enough—"

"I will be. I will be. Do not fail!"

Vivianna watched as they reached the top of the stairs and vanished into the shadows there. Was she ill, and, as Dobson seemed to suggest, Vivianna had tired her? "Maybe I have made a mistake in coming here," she murmured to herself. But no, despite what had happened, she did not think so. Aphrodite still wanted to help her, and Vivianna had found, as they spoke together, a trust in the other woman that was surprising. In many ways they were poles apart, and yet there was a similarity, too. As if, once, Aphrodite may have had the same questioning, passionate qualities as Vivianna.

Chapter 7

"Oliver? Have you had a chance yet to look over the names on the list?" Lady Marsh asked, and fanned herself leisurely. The early roses were blooming in her garden and she was enjoying being seated among them on this fine afternoon. Oliver had taken a turn about the lawn and had stood, gazing at nothing, until her question broke his reverie.

"I have, Aunt. I must say that none of them strikes me as a particularly riveting prospect. Maybe I could bear to stand up with them at a dance, but as for spending the rest of my life with any of them . . ." He shuddered dramatically.

"The rest of your life won't be very long if you continue on as you are," Lady Marsh said acerbically.

Oliver gave her his reckless smile. "Touché."

"Besides, no discerning woman would marry a man who wears a waistcoat like yours, Oliver."

Oliver glanced down at the offending item. A yellow waistcoat embroidered in a particularly repellent green, with red embellishments. The buttons were turquoise and large and shiny, their brass surrounds catching the sun. He smiled wickedly at his aunt. "What's wrong with it? You won't see many of these about London."

Lady Marsh shuddered. "I'm pleased to hear it."

Bentling, Lady Marsh's butler, was picking his stately way across the grounds toward them, a silver salver in one hand.

"Are you expecting visitors?" Oliver asked.

Lady Marsh snapped shut her fan. "No, I am not. How annoying! I wanted to go through the list with you. There are some quite lovely girls from whom to choose."

"Aunt . . ."

Bentling had reached them. "My lady, there is a young person asking to see you."

Lady Marsh took the card from the salver and read it. Her face remained impassive. "Very well, Bentling. Show the young person out here to me."

Bentling bowed and made his stately way back toward the house. Oliver threw himself carelessly into a chair, staring moodily.

A flash of color caught his eye on the edge of the lawn. Oliver looked up and felt his heart give a hard, painful jolt. Miss Vivianna Greentree was standing there in the sunlight, dazzling in a white muslin dress with patterned sprays of yellow and green. And she was holding in her hand a yellow silk parasol with a long, elegant handle and a green silk fringe. It was completely frivolous—one word Oliver had never thought to associate with Vivianna.

As the shock receded, his eyes narrowed. What had she done to herself? Her gown was still extremely respectable, but it was undoubtedly more fashionable, softer, more feminine, and with the tight sleeves and neckline shaped into a low V over her breasts, far more tantalizing. Her hair, too, was softer, with curls looped either side of her face, and the remainder fixed into a knot atop her head. Miss Vivianna Greentree had, like a butterfly, undergone a metamorphosis.

She stepped forward and his gaze slid down over her wide, gathered skirts and stopped, astonished. She had lifted her hem slightly, to assist her progress across the lawn, and he saw now that she was wearing yellow half-boots with ribbons tied at her narrow ankles, accentuating their delicacy.

His mouth actually watered.

A vivid image came to him of Vivianna, naked apart from her yellow half-boots. He thought he might instantly combust.

"Oliver?"

Lady Marsh was calling him impatiently. When he turned to her at last, blinking to clear his mind, she was frowning.

"Whatever is the matter, Oliver? Do you know this girl?"

"I do," he said, and to his relief his voice was its usual lazy drawl. "Prepare yourself, Aunt. You are about to make the acquaintance of Miss Vivianna Greentree."

"And *who* is *she*?"

"My nemesis," he replied dryly, and rose to his feet as Vivianna reached them.

"Lady Marsh?" Vivianna's voice was as firm as ever, but the restless flicker of her eyes told him she was nervous. And well she might be; if anyone could rout Vivianna, then it was Lady Marsh. Oliver prepared to enjoy himself.

"Lady Marsh, I do hope you don't mind me calling upon you unannounced, and without a proper invitation."

"It depends on what you are calling for, Miss Greentree."

Vivianna cleared her throat and glanced at Oliver. Her eyes widened at the sight of his waistcoat, and then shifted to his face. For some reason her gaze appeared to stick there, and she let it linger, perusing each feature one at a time. When she reached his mouth, Oliver grinned, and watched her face turn fiery beneath the parasol.

Lady Marsh sent Oliver a stern look, and then raised her brows at Vivianna. "Well, Miss Greentree? I am waiting. What is it you want?"

"Perhaps your nephew has mentioned my name, Lady Marsh?"

"No, I cannot say he has."

Lady Marsh was giving her no leeway, and Oliver grew even more amused. Had Vivianna met her match? He almost felt a little sorry for her—almost.

"Oh." Vivianna made as if to glance at Oliver again and then thought better of it, stiffening her back and staring directly at Lady Marsh. The creamy slope of her naked shoulders, and the swell of her breasts beneath the white muslin, were presented for Oliver's inspection. Not to mention her delightful profile. He prepared to admire her without, for once, being the object of one of her lectures.

"Lady Marsh, I am one of the founders of the Shelter for Poor Orphans, a private charitable organization which assists abandoned children. The shelter is located at Candlewood, and there my friends and colleagues are caring for some twenty-five orphans."

Lady Marsh looked a little startled. "Indeed."

"Your nephew wishes to demolish Candlewood, which will leave us with nowhere suitable to house the children. I have asked him to change his mind, but thus far I don't seem to have made much impression upon him."

"Oh, but you have," Oliver murmured, and smiled as another wave of warmth crept into her cheeks. He wanted to bend her over his arm and kiss her senseless.

The fantasy had its inevitable affect. Oliver shifted uncomfortably and wished he had not allowed his imagination to run riot.

"Oliver, please stop disconcerting Miss Greentree," Lady Marsh said, but she sounded mild, almost as if her thoughts were elsewhere.

"Miss Greentree knows I will not change my mind, Aunt. She should concentrate on finding other lodgings for her orphans, if she is not satisfied with the building I have offered her in Bethnal Green."

"I do not want another building," Vivianna cried, and he saw the wonderful passion in her face. Her eyes were alight, too, as her determination to have her way caught fire within her. "Candlewood is home to those twenty-five children. How can you ask them to leave their *home*?"

Oliver made an impatient sound. "You see?" he asked, turning to his aunt. "Miss Greentree will not accept that she cannot prevail."

But Lady Marsh jabbed her fan at him. "I think Miss Greentree has a very good point, Oliver. I do not pretend to know all the finer details of her argument, but I think you need to discuss it further with her."

"Aunt!"

Vivianna gave Lady Marsh a beatific smile. "Thank you so much, ma'am! I think . . . oh, if only he would come with me to Candlewood, to speak with the Beatty sisters and the orphans, I am sure—"

"Good God, no!"

"Why not, Oliver?" Another jab of the fan. "Surely it can do you no harm to meet these people."

Oliver began to feel seriously hunted. His aunt was wearing a look with which he was well acquainted. She was plotting something, and it did not bode well for him. While Vivianna was smiling as if she were a cat with a bowl of cream.

"Aunt, you are aware I cannot change my plans," he said quietly. "There is no point in talking."

"Oh, I don't know. I think talking is an excellent pastime," Lady Marsh replied, a wicked gleam in her blue eyes. "Go and talk with these Beatty women and their children and see what you can do, Oliver. Surely you're not afraid of a bunch of children, are you?"

Now both women gave him a suspicious look, except that there was a hint of laughter in Vivianna's sparkling eyes. Oliver cursed his aunt for turning against him like this. And Vivianna for appearing so suddenly, without warning, and sending his day into upheaval.

Warning? Do I need warning?

Yes, he thought grimly, he did! Where Vivianna Greentree was concerned he most definitely needed warning. He had a most unfortunate habit of losing control when she was near.

"Of course I am not afraid. It is just that I choose not to waste my time—"

"Come, come, Oliver, let Miss Greentree show you what wonders she has wrought at Candlewood. As your only living relative, I insist upon it."

He felt as if he were sliding down a slippery tunnel. The two women were closing in on him, figuratively speaking. His aunt had her own agenda, but Vivianna . . . if he continued to refuse, she would think him weak. A coward. For some reason Oliver did not want her to think him a coward, despite the fact that he had been playing a cowardly part now for over a year.

"Very well," he said in a long-suffering voice. "Very well, I will go with you to Candlewood, Miss Greentree. But we will go in my coach, and together. Or perhaps you would prefer not to spend so much time in my company?"

He made it sound like a threat, but although she cast him a quick, sideways glance, her reply was breezy. "I am not concerned," she said, and smiled. The smile was enchanting. He could forgive her the calculating eyes for the sake of the smile. And then she had turned back to Lady Marsh and was thanking her, apologizing for taking up her time, and saying goodbye.

Oliver sat down and watched her leave through slitted eyes, one leg crossed over the other, his foot swinging in agitation.

"What an interesting young lady," Lady Marsh said.

"Would you call her that? Annoying, infuriating . . . I think these are better words to describe Miss Greentree."

"Oh yes, very interesting. She is not in the usual way at all, is she? I suppose it would be too much to hope she has been presented at court?"

Oliver laughed in genuine amusement. "I very much doubt it, Aunt. She is more interested in slums than royal palaces."

"She is a reformer, Oliver. Is that what you are telling me in your own sardonic way?"

"Yes, Aunt, she is."

"And she is from . . . ?"

"Yorkshire, I believe. Greentree Manor. Her mother is a Lady Greentree, and she is staying in London with her aunt, Mrs. Helen Russell. I think there was some scandal there, but it escapes me."

"Toby Russell, a horrid man, yes, I remember. He eloped with Helen, a beauty, for her family's money, and the silly girl thought it was love. The brother, William Tremaine, was too terrified of scandal to hold out. Of course, Toby Russell soon ran through the girl's dowry. I wonder if she thinks it was worth it? All for love, eh, Oliver?"

Oliver gave a mocking smile. "If you imagine for a moment I am contemplating Miss Vivianna Greentree as a possible bride, then you are very much mistaken, Aunt. She would drive me to Bedlam in a month. Besides, you know that matters are coming to a head. I do not need any further complications. Please don't meddle."

"Who said anything about meddling?" Lady Marsh made her eyes suspiciously wide and innocent.

Oliver moved to take her hand and touch it to his lips. "I mean it, Aunt. Do not think to saddle me with Miss Greentree. I will peruse your list again. Maybe there is someone on it I can stomach after all."

Lady Marsh watched him, a little smile of satisfaction on her lips, which Oliver found very disturbing.

Vivianna leaned back in the coach and took several deep breaths. She could hardly believe she had been so successful. It was, she was sure, thanks to Aphrodite. She had called upon the other woman at eleven, as requested, only to find Aphrodite still unwell and unable to meet with her. But Aphrodite had left detailed instructions with a poker-faced modiste called Elena, who was awaiting her in the same elegant room.

The modiste had explained that it was she who made the clothing for Madame Aphrodite's protégées—

and Madame Aphrodite herself, she added, with a reverence that told Vivianna more about the modiste than Aphrodite. "I have a shop in Regent Street," she said proudly. Elena seemed to believe that Vivianna was one of the protégées, and Vivianna had thought it best to pretend it was so. Besides, new clothing was something Lady Greentree had instructed her about, and she had the letter allowing her to draw upon Lady Greentree's account at Hoare's Private Bank on Fleet Street.

In no time, Elena and her assistant had Vivianna down to her undergarments. Elena had then set about measuring her, discreetly murmuring numbers to her minion to be written down in a little book. The modiste had brought with her samples of cloth, pattern books, and some dresses that were already made up to a near-finished state. "Madame Aphrodite explained your size to me," she had said, when a surprised Vivianna had asked how they knew what would fit her. Aphrodite was clearly very observant, for with a few adjustments here and there, the garments had been complete. One of them was the white muslin dress with the yellow and green pattern that she had on now, and the matching half-boots, which pinched a little. Vivianna had never worn anything so frivolous, and had been quite sure it would not suit her.

She had been wrong. The dress had brought out the coquette in her, a part of her personality that she had not known existed. She felt attractive and playful, and she found she was enjoying herself.

The frivolous yellow silk parasol with the fringe and ivory-tipped handle had been added at the last moment. It had come with instructions from Aphrodite that, to her certain knowledge, Oliver was presently visiting Lady Marsh's house in Eaton

Square, Belgravia, and that Vivianna should call upon him there. There had been a note, too:

> *One thing I learned during my days in the demimonde was that a man can be held enthralled by a woman. If she continually surprises him, if he finds her mysterious, if she is different, then he will want her. The man we discussed is already attracted to you. He will not expect you to dress in such clothing. Keep him intrigued,* mon chou, *and soon he will give you anything you want.*

"But I know nothing yet!" Vivianna had wailed to Dobson, who had come to the room to deliver the message and the parasol. "I need to understand more, to learn . . . oh, just to know what to do!"

"What's to know?" Dobson had retorted. "I think you're a lovely girl, Miss Greentree, and if Lord Montegomery don't know that already, then he's a fool and not worth bothering with."

Vivianna hadn't been able to help smiling at his simplistic view of things, even as the fact that he knew her secret caused her some consternation. "When can I see Miss Aphrodite, Dobson?"

Dobson had avoided her eyes. "Don't you worry, she's just a little under the weather. It happens sometimes. She'll be all right soon. Call back in a day or two, miss."

"Dobson, it wasn't anything I said, was it? That made her ill?"

Dobson's gray eyes had met her worried ones. "No, miss," he assured her, his battered face turning gentle. "It wasn't nothing you said. She's a strong lady, but she's had tragedy in her life, and sometimes it all gets too much for her. She'll be right as rain soon, you'll see."

"I hope so."

"That umbrella there," he had added, nodding at the parasol and giving her a wink. "Used that on a French count, she did. He fell in love with her as soon as he saw her with it. Can't go wrong with that, miss."

So, reassured, Vivianna had left, clutching her new belongings and the parasol as if they were her ticket to win a lottery. The softer hairstyle had been her own idea, with Lil's help, and modeled on Aphrodite.

Now, as the cab rattled along, Vivianna remembered the look on Oliver's face when he had first set eyes on her across the lawn. He might have been struck by lightning. Oh yes, she recognized the expression in his eyes; she knew it well. It was very similar to the sensation that she, too, had felt when she set eyes upon him.

At least she had managed to persuade him to come with her to Candlewood. Or rather, Lady Marsh had done the persuading. Perhaps Lady Marsh would turn out to be an unexpected ally. Vivianna did not really understand why, but did it matter? As long as she won in the end, did anything else matter at all?

Vivianna reached the Russell house in Queen's Square, still full of her triumph. She couldn't keep the smile off her face as she stripped off her gloves, until she realized that Toby was standing near the door to the dining room, watching her with that detestable smirk on his face.

Vivianna didn't trust him an inch.

"And where has my niece been? And looking absolutely scrumptious, I must say!"

"Visiting friends," she said shortly, and moved toward the stairs.

"Don't run off, my dear." He moved quickly, his hand upon her arm. Vivianna would have liked to wrench it off, but that would be rude; this was her aunt's husband, after all. So she straightened and looked him in the eye, as if daring him to insult her.

Toby smiled. He had always been a handsome man and still was, but the depredations of drink and hard living were taking their toll. There were small veins reddening his cheeks and nose, and pouches under his eyes, which were particularly noticeable if he had been out very late the night before.

Vivianna could not help but wonder, as she did every time she saw him, how Helen could have married such a man. Love had much to answer for!

And yet, Vivianna knew how tempting a handsome smile could be. She should not pretend she was any more high and mighty than Helen, she thought bleakly. Not when she herself was moving nearer and nearer to the edge of that same precipice.

"I must get on, Uncle Toby, please excuse me."

"Of course, of course. Things to do, eh?"

Vivianna hurried past him and up the stairs, but she could feel his eyes on her all the way. Lil was waiting for her at the entrance to her bedchamber.

"I heard you come in, miss, but I didn't come down. That Mr. Toby likes to touch maids in places he's got no right to."

"If he is a danger to you, you must tell me so, and I will put a stop to it. I do not like him any more than you."

"He's no danger," Lil replied scornfully. "More a bloomin' nuisance. Don't worry, I can handle meself all right, miss."

Vivianna knew she was right. Lil had seen the seamier side of life, and no doubt had handled many

Toby Russells. Still, she did not like to think of Lil being under siege. Perhaps when she took Oliver to Candlewood he would have an epiphany, and she and Lil could go home, as unlikely as that seemed.

And then you will never see him again.

Vivianna stilled, overcome by the realization that that wasn't what she wanted. It wasn't what she wanted at all.

Oliver ran up the steps to White's and entered the club, tossing his hat and cane to the doorman. The dining room was crowded, waiters in starched shirts hurrying about, diners chatting with each other across linen tablecloths. Oliver swept his gaze over the room, searching for, and finding, Lord Lawson.

Tall, with graying side-whiskers and an exuberant mane of salt-and-pepper hair, Lawson was in his fifties and looked every bit the important man in Sir Robert Peel's Tory party. He was to be the next prime minister, if gossip could be believed, despite the fact that Peel had been tipped for the job—the thing was, the queen did not like Peel and she did like Lawson. She said she found Sir Robert too reticent, whereas Lord Lawson was a man she could talk to.

Of course, Lord Melbourne had to be got rid of first, but going by his present showing in the House that would not take long. The queen had been very much influenced by Melbourne in her youth, just as her mother, the Duchess of Kent, had been influenced by her comptroller of the household, the debonair and power-hungry Sir John Conroy. Although Victoria would not have thanked anyone for drawing comparisons. She hated Sir John Conroy with a passion bordering on mania—whisperers had it that when she was a child, she had come upon him and her mother in a very compromising position.

Lord Lawson had made a public speech of support last year when the queen had been embroiled in a scandal concerning Sir John and one of her ladies-in-waiting. The queen had come out of it badly—the lady was not pregnant with Sir John's child at all, but suffering from a terminal growth, and the public had turned nasty, booing the queen and calling her "Mrs. Melbourne."

Lawson's vocal support had pleased Her Majesty greatly, and the Tory party were beginning to see him as their answer to Lord Melbourne. Only a matter of time, then, before his star shone bright.

Oliver's hand clenched at his side. *Not if I can help it. . . .*

As if sensing his gaze, Lawson looked up. Those famous ice-blue eyes narrowed, and he leaned over to say something to his dining companion before making his way through the crowded room toward Oliver.

Oliver waited, leaning against a chair back as though he were weary. Or half drunk. He blinked at Lawson and returned his bow casually, his gaze wandering past the older man as if he didn't quite know where he was.

"Oliver." Lord Lawson eyed him with thinly disguised disgust. "I haven't seen you about for weeks. Been out of town?"

"Have I?" Oliver blinked. "I don't think so, Lawson, but you might be right. The days seem to blur into each other. Sometimes I sleep right through them—saves confusion."

Lawson smiled, but there was no humor in it. Oliver knew the other man thought him a wastrel and a nuisance—someone going from bad to worse through his own lack of backbone. Lawson was a great believer in backbone, according to Anthony.

"Your aunt, Lady Marsh, must despair of you, Oliver. Hasn't she tried to talk you 'round? You are her heir, aren't you?"

"My aunt is a most forbearing woman."

"She must be."

Oliver gave him another vacant and unthreatening smile. Lawson shifted impatiently, his gaze also skimming the room, or perhaps he was just checking to see who was within earshot and whether their presence mattered to him. He waited until a waiter circled them with a steaming plate.

"I believe you are selling Candlewood, Oliver."

"That's right. It's a monstrosity, always was, and it's falling down."

Lawson frowned. "Your brother was very fond of that house."

"Yes. He died in it."

Lawson's gaze sharpened, but when Oliver affected a yawn and leaned even harder against the chair, he relaxed again. Over the past year, as he had watched Oliver slowly slipping into the void, he had treated him with more and more contempt. He no longer thought Oliver capable of duplicity, and that made it so much easier to dismiss him. It was also probably the only reason Oliver was still alive.

"It's an amusing thing," Oliver went on disingenuously, "but there was talk that my grandfather built a secret chamber into the house. Rumor had it that he kept his fortune hidden there."

"A secret chamber?" Lord Lawson seemed to have solidified—rather like a dried frog Oliver had once found when he was a boy.

"Not that I believe it," Oliver drawled.

"So there is no secret chamber?" Lawson said sharply.

"Oh yes!" Oliver raised his brows. "Yes, there is a secret chamber. I meant I don't believe he had a fortune. If he had, he'd have spent it on Candlewood. Maybe, though, there are a few bits and pieces left. Jewelry and the like. I'll know soon enough."

"How will you know?" Lawson's voice was a hiss, his eyes blazing.

"Well . . ." Oliver blinked sleepily, pretending his heart wasn't thudding in his chest as if he were going into battle. "When the place is torn down, I thought I'd instruct the men doing the job to keep an eye out, eh? Do it a brick at a time, you see, and if they notice anything odd they can tell me."

"If you're sober," Lawson snarled, but he looked sick. As if he had just sustained a nasty shock.

Oliver smiled. "Oh, I'll make certain of it. Anything they find at Candlewood, I want to see it."

Lawson made a jerky movement, smoothing his waistcoat and then taking out his silver pocket watch to stare blindly at its face. Oliver watched him without comment, completely relaxed.

"Hmm, I must go. I have an appointment with Sir Robert." He snapped the cover of his watch closed and looked at Oliver under beetling brows. "When are you planning to begin the demolition?"

"Soon." Oliver yawned again. "Have to get those pesky women and children out first. Once they're gone, I'll have it down in a trice." He leaned closer, and smiled inwardly as Lawson edged away. "Need the blunt, you see."

Lawson gave him a cold, scornful glare. "You're a disgrace, Oliver. Your brother was worth a dozen of you." And then, without another word, he walked away.

Oliver watched him. It had all gone very well, no doubt about it. He had smashed Lawson's smug self-assurance to bits, so much so that he had been reading his watch upside down and didn't even notice it. Oh yes, Lord Lawson was a worried man. A very worried man.

With a smile he ordered a brandy—to celebrate. Anything that upset Lawson was worth celebrating. Now it was just a matter of waiting. What would Lawson's next move be? His lordship had been counting the days until Candlewood was demolished, but now he would be dreading the moment. He would be wondering whether or not there really was a secret chamber, and if so, whether it would be discovered. And if it was discovered, what would be found inside it. He must be beginning to feel a real sense of panic; Lawson had a lot to lose, after all.

Murderer.

Oliver bared his teeth in a wolfish smile, and it was far removed from the vacant one he had assumed for Lawson's benefit. Lawson would pay, by God he would, and soon. . . .

Chapter 8

The Montegomery coach seemed very luxurious after the hackneys, or the Russells' hired vehicle, which Vivianna had been using to take her about. She supposed that to own something like this was an extravagance, but the feel of the padded leather was sheer heaven, and the well-sprung body was far easier on her stomach.

Maybe there was some point to being a member of an old and aristocratic family after all.

Vivianna glanced across at Oliver.

Just as she feared—and hoped—he was watching her. Aphrodite had sent her another message with her newest gown, and although Lil's suspicious, hovering presence had prevented her from reading it all—she had finally stuffed the letter into her bag—she had read enough. Aphrodite predicted that Oliver would look at her, but warned that she must not be self-conscious about it. That she should feel secure in the knowledge of her own beauty. The list of instructions was burned into her brain.

Smile at him and look away.
Pretend to enjoy the scenery.
Pretend not to notice his attention.
Be unconscious of your effect on him.
Stay at arm's length.
Tease him with the movements of your body. . . .

Easier said than done, Vivianna thought. She was not secure in the knowledge of her own beauty. She was not the slightest bit interested in the scenery. And the fact that he was watching her with such unwavering intensity made the nerves in her stomach jump like crickets.

Vivianna was not usually so edgy around men—even handsome gentlemen like Oliver. What was it about him that was so different? From the first moment she had seen him standing upon the steps outside his house in Berkeley Square, she had felt he was unlike anyone she had ever known before. How could she pretend indifference to him when he seemed to possess the dangerous ability to unsettle her so?

"I did not know if you would come," she said, just to say something, and rearranged her skirts, smoothing the cloth. The dress was cream silk with a mauve stripe, and had been sent around that morning from Elena, Aphrodite's modiste. Very flattering, with full upper sleeves and a boned, closely fitting, low-cut bodice, as well as a tightly fitted, slightly pointed waist—a new fashion. The addition of a straw bonnet with red ribbons, and Vivianna felt quite giddy—like the frivolous girl she had never been . . . never *allowed* herself to be.

"I said I would. I am not in the habit of changing my mind." He was watching her hands, his eyes half closed as he settled back in his corner, so elegantly fluid. And yet the relaxed pose was a sham. His jacket might be tailored to fit his broad shoulders without padding or a single crease, and his glossy hair might be slightly disordered by the removal of his hat. But Oliver was alert and watching her. *Waiting to pounce?*

Vivianna shivered and drew her red Norwich shawl closer about her shoulders. She was watching him. Again.

She turned to the window and stared hard at the view.

"I am hoping that isn't true; I am hoping you will change your mind with regard to the shelter," she said evenly.

"Ah, but as I said, I am not in the habit of changing my mind, Miss Greentree. Candlewood must be taken down, brick by brick, stone by stone, until there is nothing left of it."

"And you can live upon the proceeds like some despicable potentate?" She shot him an accusing look.

The corners of his mouth curled. "Careful, Miss Greentree, your claws are showing. And you were doing so well, too."

Did he know what she planned? No, how could he, he was just being his usual obnoxious self. Vivianna turned to stare blindly out of the window once more, wishing she could scream and fling herself at him, and shake him until . . . Well, such thoughts were useless, of course. She may as well be a moth beating against a windowpane, for all the good it would do her.

After a moment, when she felt sufficiently calm again, she said, "I don't care what you think of me, my lord. Your opinion means nothing. *You* are nothing to me. You are like a bleak wind blowing across the moors at Greentree Manor—something to be endured but hopefully of short duration."

He laughed in genuine amusement. "I have never been likened to a bleak wind before. I don't know whether to be insulted or flattered. You have made me as important and fundamental as the weather. Perhaps"—and his voice dropped teasingly—"that is why I make you shiver, Miss Greentree."

"You do not make me shiver."

She turned and glared at him long enough to let him know she was very indifferent to him indeed, *very indifferent,* and then for good measure she yawned beneath her gloved hand and turned back to the scenery as she had been instructed by Aphrodite. There, she thought, let him see she did not care in the least for him. Aphrodite was right—men like Oliver needed to be treated with indifference to put them in their place. Under no circumstances must he ever guess just how disconcerting to her mind and body he could be.

Oliver grinned to himself. Just when he was trying to convince himself Miss Vivianna Greentree was a preaching crusader for good causes, who would have him falling asleep after ten minutes in her company she blew his argument to bits.

Of course, the fact that she was looking quite delightful this morning may have had something to do with it. Her cheeks glowed with temper, her eyes shone with emotion, and he wanted to take advantage of her. In every way. Not a gentlemanly thing to admit, perhaps, but Oliver had been playing a wastrel and a complete scoundrel for a year now. He had begun to wonder if, in some ways, it was more fun than being a gentleman.

He reached out and touched her wrist, where a strip of bare flesh lay between the hem of her sleeve and the fastening of her glove. Her skin was warm and soft, and a tingle ran all the way up his arm. Vivianna seemed to feel it, too. She gasped and turned to him with wide, startled eyes.

"What are you doing?" she whispered.

"Making you shiver."

He lifted her wrist—she did not resist. Bending his head, he placed a light kiss upon the inside of it, where the blue veins ran close to the skin, and appeared so fragile. He smiled to think that Vivianna should seem fragile, and his mouth opened against her flesh, tasting her.

"Oh."

He looked up at her through his lashes, and now there was more than just a tingle between them. Her eyes had darkened, her lips were parted, and there was a faint flush along her cheekbones.

"Stop it," she said in a strangled whisper.

"Why? You are enjoying it, aren't you?"

"That isn't the point—"

Oliver tried to see past her hazel eyes. As well as the green and brown there were flecks of gold. Her pupils were large and black, and he could see his own reflection there. She blinked, her lashes sweeping down.

"There are more important matters to discuss," she said primly.

Were women all so irrational, or was it just her? One moment she didn't seem to care how far he went, and the next she was untouchable. Oliver shrugged and slumped back into his corner. She could please herself, he didn't want to be here anyway, and once he had visited the bloody shelter he could go home to his own "more important matters." Lord Lawson, for instance. What would his brother's murderer do next? Lawson could never be underestimated. No, Oliver really didn't have time for Vivianna Greentree and her orphans. . . .

Gradually he became aware of a rustling sound coming from Vivianna's side of the coach. He glanced curiously in her direction and saw that she had taken a piece of correspondence from her bag and was reading it, holding it close to her eyes in the swaying vehicle. His gaze slid over her, observing her tense shoulders and the pulse jumping under the fragile skin at her neck, and he wondered what it was she was reading that made her so edgy. She was delightful, but he couldn't let her know he felt that way. She was insufferable enough as it was.

"A note from some grateful and worthy charity?" he drawled sardonically.

She sniffed, and stuffed the paper back into her bag, not caring if she creased it. But she did not seem herself, and the tension had not left her shoulders. Oliver's gaze sharpened. She knew he was watching her, but she did not return his gaze. Her breasts rose and fell on a deep, quiet breath, and the red shawl slipped from her shoulders and pooled about her on the seat.

"Have I displeased you in some way, Vivianna?" he mocked, trying to invoke her temper. "I can't help it if I have a weakness for beautiful, bossy reformers. Perhaps if you were to let me kiss you more often I might begin to recover from this most worrying malady."

He was enjoying teasing her. At any moment he expected her to give him a look from those brilliant eyes, or unleash her tongue on him, and he was looking forward to it. Instead she did something utterly astounding.

Vivianna glanced down and smiled a small, secretive smile, and smoothed her hands down over her skirts.

But it wasn't the same as when she had smoothed

her skirts a moment ago. This was different, so different that it made his heart rate double. She ran her hands over the silk in a manner so sensual that he forgot to breathe. Her gloves glided over the shiny cloth slowly, and he could tell she was thinking about her body underneath. One hand rested momentarily at her waist, and then brushed upward, her fingers barely touching the tight boned bodice, brushing across the full curve of one breast, and lingering there. Almost, but not quite, cupping herself.

He felt light-headed. Her fingers began stroking idly against her skin, as if she were enjoying it too much to stop, and his imagination went wild, and then she lifted her hand to her face and fiddled with a curl of hair that had freed itself from beneath the straw hat.

She was watching him, her hazel eyes fixed on his. Could she see the state he was in? Probably. If she dropped her gaze to his groin she'd realize he was almost beyond thought, unless she was too innocent to know what the heavy swelling pressing to his trouser buttons meant.

Oliver let out a relieved breath. But of course. She *was* an innocent—a spinster and a virgin. She did not know what she was doing, she did not understand how he was . . .

Vivianna licked her lips. Just a brief flick of that delectable little tongue, and then again, as if she had some particularly sticky toffee adhering to the plump, sleek surface.

It was amazingly erotic. He almost groaned aloud, and he was certain that his cock grew another inch. Two, maybe.

"Oliver," she said, her voice low, and leaned forward slightly. His eyes slid to the shadow of her cleavage, and he was so busy enjoying the curves of her breasts swelling over the top of her dress that when her hand pressed his knee he swore and nearly leapt through the window.

Vivianna jerked back, blushing. "I—I'm sorry," she managed stiffly. "I didn't mean to startle you. I wanted to say how grateful I—I was that you had agreed to come with me to Candlewood. How much I—I appreciate it."

Oliver wondered if he had heard right. It crossed his mind to puzzle what had had this amazing effect upon her, but then she was licking her lips again and he found he couldn't think straight anymore, and he really didn't care anyway.

"You appreciate it?" he asked, watching her through narrowed eyes. His blood was pulsing through his veins and he had the urge to loosen his cravat so that he could breathe properly again.

"Oh, I do. I do." She smiled, her mouth curved in a pink bow, her eyes slanted and mysterious, promising him . . . things.

Bloody hell!

She wriggled a little in her seat, and he felt a bead of sweat gather on his temple, picturing that curvaceous bottom beneath her petticoats, and then she pouted as if she could not get comfortable. Vivianna reached up and began to undo the red satin ribbons that held her straw bonnet in place. It slid down from her chestnut hair, slowly over her back, the ribbons trailing across her breasts. She placed her bonnet on the seat beside her.

"That's better," she said.

Today she had coiled those thick, wavy locks into braids and wound them around her head. His fingers itched to unwind her hair and rub his face against the silky strands. To take in her womanly scent.

He was watching her, he realized, with a mixture of fascination and suspicion. She could be a viper ready to strike, but although somewhere deep in his brain he knew the danger, he lusted after her too much to care.

Oliver watched, his body rigid, his throat dry, as she leaned forward again and slowly, carefully, began to remove her gloves in front of his unblinking gaze. She peeled them down and eased out each finger with exquisite care. Such a simple procedure—he had seen it hundreds of times—and yet she turned it into something so sensual, so stimulating he was nearly panting.

Vivianna had placed the gloves upon her straw hat, smoothing them, petting them, as if they were alive.

"Ah, that's better," she said again.

He cleared his throat. "Much better," he drawled, but she wasn't fooled. There was a glitter in her eyes now that told him she knew she had him in the palm of one of her soft, white hands.

"I believe that when you are not playing the black sheep you are a very nice man. I believe that, deep in your heart, you really want to give me Candlewood. Don't you?"

He laughed; he couldn't help it.

Chagrin filled her face and she turned away, but this time he wasn't having it. His hands snaked out and he grasped her fingers and held them tightly.

"I am not a nice man at all," he said in a low, husky voice. "I am a very bad man, and I give you fair warning."

"If you were a 'very bad man' you wouldn't give me a warning, fair or otherwise," she retorted, her hazel eyes a little bright as she tugged against his grip. "Let me go!"

"I don't think so."

And Oliver did what he had been wanting to do ever since she climbed into his coach. Claimed her mouth.

For a moment she was still, too surprised to protest, and then her lips seemed to melt against his, all trembling and soft and eager. He refused to let reason enter his head, and deepened the kiss.

Her mouth was sweet, warm, and willing. She was heavy against him, and he realized that she had tumbled forward into his arms, and all he had to do was hold on to her as he moved back, and she would be in his lap. He burrowed his nose into her neck, breathing in the scent of her, feeling that pulse, and then gently tugged her earlobe with his teeth. She gave a little shriek, and then groaned as his mouth nibbled its way across her cheek to her mouth again. Her hands clung to his shoulders, gripping the dark cloth as if she would never let him go.

He slid his arm around the curve of her waist and cupped her breast in his palm, or what he could feel of her breast beneath her undergarments. Often he found the lacings and fastenings of such garments tantalizing and erotic, but not today. Today they were simply in the way of what he really wanted.

His skin against hers.

She wriggled against him, and he wondered if she was thinking the same thing as he. He paused a moment in his kisses to lean back and gaze into her face. Her mouth was reddened and swollen, her eyes glittering and half closed, and she was breathing quickly. Whatever game she had been playing with him a moment ago, he did not believe she was pretending now. There was true passion in Vivianna, and not just for her orphans. This was passion for the pleasure to be had between him and her.

He wanted to claim her, to possess her body with

his. But more than that—he wanted her heart and soul. He wanted the essence that was Vivianna Greentree, although he didn't know what he would do once he had it. The realization was so strange and dangerous that a voice in his head spoke a warning.

Oliver knew he should stop—Anthony would have told him to stop. A true gentleman would stop. But, just as he had almost convinced himself that he was still a gentleman and here was his chance to show his better side, Vivianna spoiled it.

She licked her lips again.

With a groan, Oliver bent again to kiss her, pulling her against his chest so that as much of her was touching him as was possible. He didn't care she might feel how aroused he was, the hard length of him straining against his trousers. He wanted her to know. Oliver reached down and caught the folds of her skirts, drawing them up until his hand touched her petticoats and then, blissfully, the stuff of her stocking. Fingers sliding up, he found ribbons, and then the plain calico of her drawers. He edged his fingers beneath the loose cloth and, at last, touched bare flesh. Soft and warm. Trembling, he caressed the curve of her knee.

In Oliver's experience this was often the moment when women drew back. They might kiss and touch, but if a man put his hand beneath their skirts, on bare flesh, the game was up.

He waited for Vivianna to pull away.

She was combing her fingers through his hair. Her mouth was against his jaw, his throat, nibbling above his cravat.

His fingers slid higher, caressing, enjoying the tender flesh of her thigh. Now she would tell him to stop, he thought, panting. Now she would slap him, and berate him, and . . .

Vivianna gasped and her head dropped back, her throat stretched out to his mouth, as if her strength had deserted her. He made her a necklace of kisses, and then pressed his face into the swell of her breasts through the cloth of her bodice. She held his head and kept him there, her chest rising and falling violently, as if she couldn't find enough air in the close confines of the coach, or her corset.

His hand stroked against her hip, beneath her skirts, and then he pressed his palm to her soft belly. She didn't stop him, and his head was light as air. There was an opening running from the front to the back of the drawers, between her legs. Oliver took advantage of it now. His fingers slipped within and found warm, soft curls.

Vivianna went still.

Oh God, please don't let her stop me now . . . not now. . . .

Shaking, his fingers tentatively trailed through her silky hair, and found that warm, female opening. She was hot and moist—just like her mouth after all. He stroked her.

Vivianna moaned, a soft sound of absolute surprise and absolute pleasure. It was then that Oliver realized she wasn't going to stop him. In fact, she had stilled because she was concentrating so hard on what he was doing to her. Lost in the touch and feel of him, as he was in her.

Boldly, lovingly, he stroked her again, trembling as much as she. She moved against him, opening to him. He felt her warm breath against his temple, and lifted his face blindly for her mouth. She found him, her tongue hot against his. Somehow his seduction of her had become something far more. He felt, almost, as if she were seducing him.

"Don't stop," she gasped.

He laughed.

"Is this what women are meant to feel?" she asked. "All women?"

"Yes. Although sometimes they deny it, or deny themselves. . . ."

"You mean because they are respectable wives and daughters? I do not believe it is only courtesans who feel this way. All women are made equally, surely, and—"

He groaned, and kissed her to stop her damned talking. Her hands were fastened upon his shoulders, and she moved against his fingers, without shame, without embarrassment, completely lost in sensation. Oliver could feel her weeping against his hand, her body urging him on. He needed no urging. He had never felt anything more exquisite. Her breath was coming quickly now, and he stroked harder, leaning back so that he could watch her face. There was something very erotic in watching Vivianna come to her peak. Or perhaps it was the arrogant conquering male in him that made him want to celebrate his victory.

Her eyelids fluttered shut, her lips were slightly parted, her cheeks bloomed with the flush of sexual desire. She rocked against him, faster and faster, until finally she let out a sweet, soft cry. Her whole body arched, her braids tumbling down her back, her hands clutching at his jacket, and then she went limp in his arms.

Reluctantly Oliver withdrew his hand from beneath her skirts. His cock was hard and aching and he wanted nothing more than to push inside her and give himself release. But now was not the time. A quick glance toward the window showed him that they were well on their way to Candlewood. At any moment they would be turning through the ornate gateposts.

Gently, with particular care and attention, he rearranged her petticoats and skirts back over her stockinged legs and, shifting her into the crook of his arm, he smoothed and straightened the remainder of her clothing. She lay complacent against him, as trusting as a child. When he was done, he lifted her, both hands firm around her waist, and placed her back on to her seat on the opposite side of the coach.

Vivianna sat there and stared at him with an expression of growing and absolute horror.

Oliver was tempted to laugh, but he guessed she would not appreciate levity. Instead, he said, "We are nearly there. If we had half an hour more, Vivianna, I would not stop. I would take you right here, right now. And I *will* have you. I have just marked you as mine."

His voice was so low and fierce, he thought he had frightened her, until he saw the flash of anger in her eyes.

"How can you say such a thing?" she managed. "Have you no sense of what is proper?"

He grinned. *Proper?* After what they had just done? "I have your scent," he said. "You're mine."

She opened her mouth as if to retaliate, but it seemed she could find nothing to say, and she closed it again. She picked up her bonnet and put it on, tying the ribbons with fingers that trembled violently.

Oliver did his best not to remember the feel of her in his arms, the scent of her on his fingers, and squeezed his eyes tightly shut as his body throbbed and burned. But he promised himself that he *would* have her, and if he was any judge of women he did not think she would put up much resistance.

Chapter 9

Vivianna could not believe what had just happened.

After ignoring him seemed to have run its course, after he had put his warm mouth against her wrist and made her feel dizzy and strange, she had taken out Aphrodite's letter and read the last part of it. The final instructions.

> *When you have his attention then you must put it to good use. Lick your lips and imagine kissing him. Remove your hat and gloves slowly, as though you are undressing just for his pleasure. Brush your hands over your clothing as though you are naked. Rest your hand upon his knee and flatter him. Be assured, he will respond, but it is important that you keep him at arm's length.* You *are in charge,* mon chou, *remember that.*

She was in charge? Well, she had been for a time. As she smoothed her skirts and licked her lips, Vivianna had found she was enjoying herself. It might be wicked, it might be shocking, but it was also the most exciting and daring thing she had ever done.

And, astoundingly, Oliver had responded, watching her as though she were the most fascinating creature in London. Were men really such simple creatures? she had asked herself with a new and growing awareness. She had him in her power. She really, really did.

And then it had gone wrong. Suddenly he was kissing her and touching her, and she had forgotten the instructions and everything else but the sensation of his hands on her body.

She had failed.

If she wasn't so terribly embarrassed—and so terribly aware of him—she would have asked to be set down. She would rather have walked along the roadside like a journeyman than be seated here with him. Her body tingled and ached—especially the place he had touched and rubbed and plucked like a violin string, until . . . good Lord, he had made something happen to her! A great wave of heat and pleasure had rippled through her and she had cried out. Her skin felt as if the top layer had been taken off; so sensitive that even the still air in the coach abraided it.

Of course she knew she should have stopped. But she hadn't been able to. She hadn't *wanted* to, she corrected herself. She had been so caught up in the experience, in the pleasure, in being held in his arms like that, that she hadn't wanted to stop at all. It was what she had wanted from the beginning—to experience physical passion with the man of her choice without ties. To place herself into the hands of an expert.

Did that make her a fallen woman? An immoral woman? Vivianna did not believe that. She did not accept that. She could not! But, sadly, however much she had enjoyed herself, she was no closer to gaining her promise of Candlewood from Oliver Montegomery.

"Vivianna."

She didn't want to look at him. Not yet.

"Vivianna," he said, his voice low and caressing. "There is nothing to be ashamed of. Nothing to fear."

"I am not ashamed, and I do not fear you," she said in a jerky little voice she hardly recognized. No, she didn't fear Oliver.

Vivianna feared herself.

She had completely forgotten all of Aphrodite's instructions, and she had forgotten the shelter. How could she have forgotten the shelter? She had fallen into the arms of a rake and allowed him to pleasure her, and forgotten her real reason for being here.

"Vivianna?"

Slowly, unwillingly, she turned to him. She knew her face was scarlet, but she kept her eyes steady on his. He did not look like a monster. He did not look like a man who was about to wrestle her to the floor and have his way with her, although after what had just happened he probably thought she would welcome it. He looked like Oliver, and although his eyes were still dark with desire, and his mouth red from hers, there was a teaspoonful of doubt behind his usual indolent self-confidence.

"You enjoyed what we did, Vivianna. There's no reason to feel guilty."

She didn't feel guilty in the way he imagined, but she wasn't going to tell him that. "I did enjoy it, but it wasn't . . . that is, you didn't put your . . . your . . . inside me . . ." The right words escaped her and her voice trailed off. The *Mr. and Mrs. England* instruction pamphlet was vivid in her mind, with its clear and rather crude illustrations.

"No, I didn't come inside you," he said softly, and

smiled his wicked smile. She felt her senses fizzing and popping like champagne. "I'm going to, though. Soon."

Vivianna shivered.

The coach slowed and began to turn. She looked to the window and saw the crumbling gateposts of Candlewood, a worn lion atop each one, and the long driveway ahead. Vivianna didn't know whether to be relieved or disappointed, until she remembered that they still had to make the journey home.

Suddenly she couldn't wait to be free of him.

Oliver felt the coach draw to a halt. In the center of the circular carriageway was an old fountain, long since run dry, flanked by an untidy but colorful flower garden. Before them loomed Candlewood, his grandfather's monstrous obsession.

Thoughts of Vivianna and his lingering desire for her were put aside as Oliver remembered the morning he had come to find Anthony. It had been early, just after dawn. He had been supposed to collect his brother so that they could then travel on to the Derbyshire estate together, but in the awfulness of the scene of the night before he had almost forgotten that. Celia crying and Anthony's white, shocked face . . . No, Oliver had come here to Candlewood that morning to explain. Explain! Now, there was a Herculean task. Actually, he had just wanted to apologize. To somehow turn those dreadful hours back and start again.

Instead he had found his brother dead.

Now, as then, Oliver felt himself begin to seize up with a combination of horror, grief, and guilt. But he had not come to Candlewood to wallow in the past. There would be time enough for that when he had captured Anthony's killer and exposed him for the savage and pitiless creature he was. . . .

Oliver stepped briskly from the coach and turned to offer Vivianna his hand. She took it, but her fingers were unwilling and she quickly removed them, edging away from him as if she did not feel quite safe.

He gave her a proprietal glance. *Safe* was not a word he would use of himself, not when he was around Vivianna. He was like gunpowder, very unstable and likely to explode. At least he had regained control over his lust for her. For now. God help him on the journey home.

His thoughts scattered as a dozen or more children, wearing clothing made of all colors and patterns, like a flock of exotic birds, came running from the house and down the steps toward them. Behind the children, alternating between a quick trot and a sedate walk, were two dainty middle-aged women with fair ringlets.

"Miss Greentree!" the children cried, as if Vivianna had come to save them from some awful fate. "Miss Greentree!"

Oliver swore under his breath.

This was going to be worse than he had thought. Much worse.

Vivianna cast him a glance, but whether it was a look of warning to behave or to check whether or not he was about to pounce on her, he couldn't tell. Then the children were upon them, circling them and chattering, clutching at Vivianna's skirts and grinning up at her. In another moment the women had reached them, too, clapping their hands at the children as if they were ducklings to be shooed back to their pen.

"Give Miss Greentree a little room, children, please! That's better. Now give her a curtsy, girls, and a bow, boys. Excellent, Eddie and Jim! Beautiful, Ellen!"

Vivianna gave them all her brilliant smile. Despite what had happened in the coach, which must be deeply troubling to her, she had set aside her own concerns for the children. That smile was so real and unassumed—her entire heart was in it. Just as she put her heart into everything she did.

"I think you have met Lord Montegomery." Vivianna was busy organizing them. "My lord, you know my friends Miss Susan Beatty and Miss Greta Beatty."

"Yes, we have met. The last time you came to Candlewood you brought a carpenter." Miss Susan Beatty gave him a cool smile.

"You kept the children waiting outside in the cold while you and your man inspected the house." Miss Greta Beatty was also chilly.

Oliver hadn't realized that at the time. All he had wanted to do was find his grandfather's secret chamber, and discover what it was Anthony had hidden within it. He hadn't found a thing, and he could still taste the disappointment.

"Better a sniffle than the roof falling down on them, surely, Miss Beatty?" he said offhandedly, playing his part.

Their looks were glacial. Vivianna cleared her throat and regained her hold on the situation. "Well, that's in the past, and I am sure Lord Montegomery means to allow us all to stay inside today. We must make the most of his visit to Candlewood to show him what we have achieved here."

The Beatty sisters exchanged glances and smiled, and then their gazes returned to Vivianna with expressions of total love and trust. Oliver hid his exasperation with difficulty—the woman was incredible.

"We do thank you for coming, Lord Montegomery. We appreciate it. The *children* appreciate it." The two sisters were sincere—at least in their desire to please Vivianna.

"Do they?" Oliver raised his eyebrows and looked at the ring of curious faces that had gathered about him. One little boy with a freckled nose said, with all the confidence of the London streets, "Are they your 'orses, mister?"

"They are."

"Did they cost an awful lot?"

"Yes, they cost a great deal."

"Can I ride 'em?"

"What, all at once?"

The boy crowed in delight.

"You ever seen a lion, mister? A real one, I mean, not one o' them stone ones."

"I believe there is one in the zoo. Surely you don't intend to ride a lion as well as my horses?"

"Naw! I can ride a stone one, though. There's one inside Candlewood. I'll show you if you like."

"Thank you, but I prefer to ride horses. Very unadventurous of me, I know."

The boy chuckled, his eyes dancing. "You're funny, mister."

"Eddie! Have you been visiting the forbidden part of the house? You know it is dangerous in there."

Seeing the look of disapproval on the Beatty sisters' faces, Eddie bowed his head. But Oliver noticed that his smile was still there, and he thought that was a good sign both for the character of the boy and the child-rearing skills of the Beattys. He had grown up without a great many restrictions, almost an orphan himself, although his rackety father had still been alive then. Aunt Marsh and his grandfather had been his real parents, and Anthony the older brother, watching over him.

Who had been there to watch over Anthony, the night he died?

"Lord Montegomery, will you take tea?" Miss Susan was giving him an apprehensive smile.

Vivianna answered with, "Of course he will, won't you, my lord?" She didn't quite look him in the eye.

"Only if there is gingerbread with it," he said, pretending not to notice how the children were hanging on his every word. Eddie in particular was standing very close to him, and Oliver resisted an urge to check to see if his pocket watch was still tucked safely into his waistcoat pocket. Some of the little boys and girls were as old as ten, and others no more than toddlers. One little girl of five or six clung to a rag doll and peered at him under her too-big mobcap. He smiled at her, and had the satisfaction of seeing a shy gleam in her eyes.

"That is Ellen," Miss Susan murmured, nodding at the little girl with the shy eyes. She leaned closer, so that the child could not overhear. "Her mother sold her to a brothel. Some people believe that the use of an unsullied child will cure syphilis."

Oliver blinked, and knew his face had gone pale. This was not new to him; he knew such things happened. But to see the girl before him . . . it made him uneasy. It made a difference.

"She is unhurt," Miss Susan went on, as if she were discussing something quite normal to her world—Oliver supposed that such stories *were* normal to this respectable, middle-aged spinster. "One of the other girls in the brothel was kind enough to smuggle the child out to us. I have nothing against such places,

Lord Montegomery, if both parties wish to participate in them, but the selling of children . . . I cannot allow that."

"What about the boy . . . Eddie?"

Miss Susan smiled. "He's a scamp, isn't he? Eddie's father left him to be looked after by a lady friend. She treated him unkindly, and he ran away and lived on the streets, fending for himself. He's a good little thief, is Eddie, but we're hoping to find something more rewarding for him to do."

Miss Greta was on his other side, and attached herself to his arm—to keep him from escaping?—as they walked toward the house.

"Did you know, Lord Montegomery, that there are no schools for the poor, other than those funded by the church or charity? The government does not consider it necessary to educate children like these."

"Surely the 1834 Poor Law—"

"Yes, the Poor Law." Miss Greta's mouth pursed. "People without means were once supported in their own parishes. Now they are herded into workhouses, or else they starve. Families, my lord, are split asunder."

"I did not realize—"

"Workhouses are machines, Lord Montegomery. They are factories. All the inmates wear the same clothing and eat at the same time every day. Their days are structured. There is no place for individuality. Here at the shelter we celebrate individuality!"

"So I see—"

"The children at our shelter learn reading, writing, arithmetic, and spelling; these subjects are all important. But we also aim to teach them more than the basics. There is music—we have a pianoforte and hope to purchase some other instruments—a little French, and dancing. And of course cooking and needlework for the girls. We have found that some of the more respectable men in the village are willing to teach the boys the rudimentary skills of their trades. I do think boys benefit from a more masculine approach. It is a pity that we do not have horses here. I have heard there is a great demand for grooms, stable lads, coach drivers, and the like. Eddie, in particular, is very fond of horses."

Both sisters were eyeing Oliver expectantly, as if he should instantly agree to offer classes in horse riding. No wonder they had so many people helping them—no one dared tell them no!

"I am amazed," Oliver said, and was.

Vivianna watched him suspiciously. "Of course, the main thing we supply to the children, apart from education and good food and a safe place to live, is affection. Some of them have never been loved in all their lives, my lord. Can you imagine how that must feel? To be lacking in something so simple and yet so important as love?"

"Well . . ." He could not remember his father paying him any particular attention. He had been pushed off onto nannies and tutors until he went to school. Had he suffered particularly? He didn't think so—he hadn't expected any differently—or perhaps he had been a resilient child. But he had a feeling if he explained all that to Vivianna she would see it differently.

"We only have a small number of children at the moment, but we hope that as time goes on we will gather in more. Of course, we will need many generous donations from people who feel as we do. For now a roof over their heads is the most important thing."

Oliver supposed that he was meant to say that, naturally, they could keep Candlewood, and with his goodwill. But he didn't. He couldn't. Candlewood needed to come down—Lord Lawson had to believe it was so. The demolition of Candlewood was pivotal to his plan to trap Anthony's killer. He had offered to rehouse the orphans in Bethnal Green. Why couldn't they accept that his position was nonnegotiable?

As he stepped through the doorway, his gaze fell upon the place where his brother's body had lain, lifeless, at the bottom of the stairs. And for a moment Oliver could not breathe.

It hadn't bothered him so much when he visited the other times. He hadn't allowed it to. He had steeled himself and gotten through it. But today, perhaps because of Vivianna, he felt vulnerable and unprepared, and it struck him with the force of a sledgehammer.

When he had first seen Anthony lying there, he had believed that, in his despair, Anthony had shot himself with his own gun. It was only later, as shock and grief began to wane, that the doubts crept in. He began to remember the hints that Anthony had let drop about Lord Lawson, his great friend Lawson, and piece them together.

It went something like this: Anthony had accidentally come into the possession of letters that, if made public, would cause a scandal that would destroy Lawson's grand political career. Anthony had been torn as to what to do with these letters, and it had been this dilemma that he had come to discuss with Oliver the night he found Celia there. The night Anthony had died.

At first Oliver did not think it could be murder. His mind was too full of the scene with Celia and Anthony, and all the things he should have said and done. He had sunk into a gloom so deep he had wondered if he would ever escape it. And then, a couple of months after Anthony's death, Lawson had come to see him. They had sat in the library with a bottle of brandy, long into the night.

Of course, Lawson was full of condolences and spoke of his own sorrow, and they repeated stories about Anthony, and shed a tear or two for Anthony, and then . . . Then Lawson had began to talk about some personal papers Anthony had been keeping for him.

"Nothing very important, just some old letters," he'd said indifferently, his ice-blue gaze on Oliver. "Have you seen them?"

Oliver had felt the gloom in his heart shiver like lifting fog.

"Have another brandy, Oliver. That's it. Did Anthony ever mention the letters to you, by the way?"

Lawson was smiling, but there was something in his face that struck Oliver like a steel blade on bone. After a moment Oliver had forced himself to look away, to pretend he was drunker than he really was, and when he had lain his head in his arms and pretended to pass out, he had heard Lawson searching methodically through the drawers of the desk. Searching for the old letters that meant nothing to him. . . .

When Lawson had gone, Oliver had sat and stared into the fire and felt his brain working properly for the first time since Anthony had died. He remembered Anthony's hints and comments about Lawson, the worry line between his brows those last weeks before he died. Everything clicked together and the picture that formed was sickeningly clear. And the odd thing was that if Lawson had said nothing, Oliver probably would never have put it all together.

A few nights later, when Lawson asked him about the "old letters" again, he pretended not to know what Lawson was talking about. Of course, Oliver had realized by then that he, too, was in danger. If Lawson believed for a moment that Oliver was a threat to him, then he would kill him. Oliver had decided he must play a part—he would be a drunken and worthless gentleman who was swiftly running through his fortune. A fool who was of no harm to anyone but himself. And thus Oliver could keep an eye upon Lawson, without Lawson being aware of it.

During the weeks that followed, Oliver searched in every place he could think of for Lawson's papers. He looked everywhere, but found nothing. Because, of course, if Anthony had been in the possession of letters important to Lord Lawson, then he would have brought them with him to Oliver's house the night he found him with Celia. After that dreadful scene, he would have forgotten all about the letters, and when he had set out alone on his long walk to Candlewood, he would have taken them with him, tucked securely into the inner pocket of his jacket.

Candlewood was where those letters would be now. In the hidden chamber his grandfather had always hinted at and whose secret he had passed on to Anthony, the grandson who shared his obsession.

But by the time Oliver had worked all of this out in his head, Candlewood was already occupied by the Shelter for Poor Orphans. Oliver had tried searching the house a number of times, the last one with the help of a carpenter, but to no avail. The only way he could find the secret chamber was to dismantle Candlewood stone by stone.

And he'd do it, too.

That is, if Vivianna, blast her, would let him get on with it!

"Lord Montegomery?"

They were waiting for him, the two fair-haired sisters with their earnest smiles, and Vivianna, beautiful and good and not to be trusted.

Oliver said, "Lead the way," as if he had not been standing there in the doorway staring at nothing, and followed them into his grandfather's house.

Vivianna was of the opinion that the visit went downhill after that.

The Beatty sisters had laid out tea in the same small, shabby parlor as on her previous visit. Oliver did not seem to notice, nor care. Vivianna had seen the way he stared at the place where his brother had died—she was certain that was what he had been looking at. For a long moment it was as if he had gone away, and then, when he came back and rejoined them, he was . . . locked up. His feelings were hidden, deep inside him.

The Beatty sisters spoke to him at length about their hopes and ambitions for the shelter. No one could doubt their dedication and sincerity. Oliver listened to them without interrupting, and he seemed to understand and to care. Vivianna was certain he cared—she had seen the expression on his face when Miss Susan spoke to him about Ellen and Eddie. Oh, he cared, all right . . . just not enough.

When the two sisters were done, he sat back and fixed them with his dark blue eyes. His tone was measured and reasonable.

"I understand, ladies, that you are seeking to make better lives for these children. I have never said I disagreed with your work, nor failed to comprehend the importance of it. All I have ever said is that you cannot continue to carry it on here, at Candlewood. I have offered you premises elsewhere. I offer them again now."

Miss Susan shook her head, tears starting to her

eyes. "You don't see at all!" she burst out. "This is their home. We have a garden, we have woods to walk in. Fresh air! Where can we find air to breathe in London?"

"I breathe in London." Oliver's face was implacable, his mouth had turned mulish, and Vivianna knew with despair that he had not changed his mind. And he would not. They were wasting their time.

She rose to her feet. "I think we should leave," she said, trying to stem her anger. "Perhaps Lord Montegomery would benefit from time to think—"

"I do not need time to think," he retorted, also standing. "You have a little over seven weeks to evacuate these premises and find another. My offer still stands."

No one said a word.

Outside, Vivianna climbed numbly into the coach where not so long ago she had felt wildly alive. The children were now busy at their lessons, but there were plenty of faces at the windows, and plenty of hands waving. Oliver waved back, but he had lost his spontaneity. It was his attitude toward the children that Vivianna had found most surprising. Instead of merely tolerating them, or ignoring them, or treating them with disdain as for some reason she had expected him to do, he had smiled at them and made them laugh, and treated them as if they were interesting and pleasant company.

She had not expected to see that side of him, and now her heart was aching. Just a little. But then again, she reminded herself angrily, some men had the knack of making others feel special. That did not make them paragons of virtue. In his younger days, Toby Russell had been known for his charm, and look at him now. No, she could not trust Oliver Montegomery further than she could throw him.

She dared not.

The coach lurched forward, and soon Candlewood was behind them.

"I am very disappointed," she said quietly. "Despite your assertions, I had thought you might finally see the error of your ways."

Oliver gave an exasperated bark of laughter. "Vivianna, I would like to please you, but in this matter I must say no."

"But—"

"I must have Candlewood back. I must demolish it. There is no other option."

He looked grim. The lazy indolence was gone from his blue eyes. She knew then that there was something more to this than he had told her.

"No other option?" she repeated, narrowing her gaze at him. "You sound as if you are on a mission, Oliver. Surely the guilt you feel for your brother's death cannot be extricated by demolishing his house?"

"You do not know anything about the guilt I feel," Oliver said bleakly. "And you are wrong if you think I hope to cleanse my soul by removing the house," he went on, bitter self-mockery in his smile. "I hope to avenge my brother, Vivianna, not placate his restless spirit."

"Avenge him?" Vivianna frowned.

Oliver shot her a cold look full of Montegomery arrogance. "Enough. I have said too much. You have that effect on me, Vivianna. The matter is closed."

As if to prove his point, he shut his eyes and pretended to go to sleep.

Vivianna glared at him, fuming, as the coach made its way home. As if that would stop her! She was not in awe of him, and that tone of voice would not prevent her from doing what she must. She clutched her bag in her hands and heard the rustle of Aphrodite's letter. The sound was not exactly comforting, but it helped to remind her that she was not beaten, not yet. Not by a long way.

As the coach dwindled into the distance, Eddie watched from the window, rested his chin on his hands, and sighed. He had hoped to show the gentleman the stone lion. The gentleman had seemed interested and Eddie needed to tell someone. He couldn't tell the two old ladies. Oh, they were nice enough, and he liked them, really, but they would flap about and say it was dangerous. Miss Greentree would scold, too, but in a kind way because she was a kind lady.

Eddie didn't want them to stop him exploring.

He had a feeling the gentleman would understand, and that he might even do a bit of exploring, too. For several weeks now Eddie had gazed down into the black hole beneath the stone lion, noting how the stairs vanished into the darkness. There were things down there, interesting things, he was certain of it. The next chance he got, he'd creep down those stairs and see what he could see.

At least he would if he wasn't so afraid of the dark.

On second thought, maybe he'd take Ellen with him. For a girl, she wasn't too bad. He could hold her hand and pretend he was looking after her.

Eddie smiled, already feeling braver.

Chapter 10

"It's nice to see you again, Miss Greentree. Miss Aphrodite is expectin' you."

Vivianna smiled at Dobson a little nervously. "I received her message this morning. Is she recovered?"

Dobson winked. "I told you she'd be right as rain in no time, miss. She's waiting for you, if you'll come this way."

Again, in the upper reaches of the house, Vivianna could hear the tinkle of a piano and a woman singing. Did Aphrodite's protégées live here? Were they just biding their time until the men who enjoyed their favors provided them with cozy establishments of their own? It seemed an idle sort of existence, and not one that she envied them.

Dobson opened the door to the room with the pastoral tapestry, and Aphrodite rose with a rustle of black silk skirts. Her face was a little thinner and paler, her dark eyes a little larger, but otherwise she was unchanged.

Or was she?

Vivianna thought she sensed a new tension in the courtesan that she had not been aware of before, as if she were holding her feelings even more in check. But a moment later Aphrodite had taken her hand with her usual aloof and beautiful smile and asked her to be seated. Perhaps she had been imagining the difference, thought Vivianna. Besides, her mind was just too full of Oliver to concentrate much on anything else.

Last night she had dreamed about him. Her body had arched beneath his hands and his mouth had kissed and sucked upon hers, while his fingers brought her again to pleasure. It had swept through her, throbbing heated waves that made her moan aloud, and pulled her out of her sleep. As she lay in her bed, the ripples receding, a warm glow suffusing her, she could not pretend it hadn't happened. Even in her dreams Oliver made love to her, and she responded.

"I want to thank you for introducing me to Elena, and for your advice, Madame," Vivianna said, trying to keep the hint of desperation from her voice.

Aphrodite was watching her from a chair, and at the same time fiddling with a jet bracelet. Rings flashed on her fingers and her slender neck should have been bowed down with the weight of her precious necklaces. If her jewelry was any indication, then Aphrodite was indeed a fabulously wealthy woman.

"So I did help?"

Vivianna prayed Aphrodite could not read minds. "Yes, thank you, you did."

"Does Lord Montegomery still see you as the respectable Miss Greentree?"

Vivianna hesitated. "I—I'm not sure. I do not think he ever believed me to be entirely respectable. But then, *he* is not respectable, is he?"

A frown marred Aphrodite's brow. "Oliver does

not need to be as careful of his reputation as you do, Vivianna."

"Because he is a gentleman," Vivianna said darkly.

Aphrodite smiled. "Yes, there is that. However, it is my experience that when an English gentleman looks at a woman, he sees her in either of two ways. Either she is respectable or she is corrupted. The former he will place upon a pedestal and marry; the latter he will not."

"I do not wish to marry him!"

"Perhaps not, but you may wish to marry a gentleman someday. It would be a pity if your reputation was ruined and the choice taken from you."

Vivianna shifted impatiently. "I have told you before, I do not care what society thinks of me. The shelter is my main concern, and what I can do to save Candlewood. Why are you worrying about my reputation, Madame? Surely that is my concern?"

Aphrodite's dark eyes were so compelling, it really was as if she were reading Vivianna's mind. "The life of a courtesan is an honorable one, *mon chou*. She may share herself with many men, but she gives much in return. I have been the companion of many men, some of them I have been very fond of indeed, but only one have I loved. When I was young, I was very poor. I saw this life as my way out of poverty, and I took it, but in doing so I forsook love. Now that I am older I want that love again. I understand that it is *love* that is the most important element of all in our lives."

"Why are you—"

"I am telling you that you must not burn your bridges, Vivianna. I do not want to see you forced into a life you will end up regretting, because of one selfish man's desire."

Aphrodite was worried for her. Perhaps she sensed

that there was more to Vivianna's feelings for Oliver than a business transaction. Vivianna felt her heart soften. She leaned forward and held out her hand. After a moment, Aphrodite reached out her own cool fingers and clasped Vivianna's.

"You are very generous and very kind," Vivianna said firmly. "Thank you for your care of me. But I will manage very well, you will see. I cannot deny that I . . . I am curious in these matters. I have enjoyed Oliver's attentions—they are new and pleasurable—but I am fully aware of what I am doing. He is not coercing me in any way, I promise you. What I do, I do willingly."

Aphrodite squeezed her fingers. "That is what worries me, *mon chou*! Tell me, do you think Oliver is a man who will marry for love, or will he marry for duty, while enjoying himself elsewhere?"

Vivianna already knew the answer to that question. "Duty, but that has nothing to do—"

"Then that is how *you* must look upon this situation. You are doing your duty, you are trying to save your shelter. You must not love him, or believe he loves you. If you do, he will hurt you."

It was clear Aphrodite was speaking from a vast experience, and Vivianna could not dismiss her words. But instead she found her thoughts straying to the trembling of her body and the ache he made wherever he touched her; his hot blind kisses, as if he were as much enthrall as she, and the way in which he had looked at her afterward.

Surely if Vivianna was drowning in him, then Oliver was also lost at sea?

Aphrodite was watching her, and there was sadness in the line of her mouth. She shook her head impatiently. "You do not listen to me!" she declared.

"I do, really I do. But I am not the sort of girl who can stand back. My feelings are too close to the surface, and when I feel, I feel with every part of me. I can never play the part of indifference."

"Vivianna, at all costs you must protect your heart!"

This time Aphrodite was adamant, her dark eyes echoing Vivianna's passion.

After a moment Vivianna nodded, suddenly deflated. The advice was good, but it was also unaccountably depressing. She had been so looking forward to her next encounter with him. Since Oliver Montegomery had come into her life, everything had become brighter and warmer and a great deal more colorful. Now the world appeared monochrome once more.

"Yes, I see. I understand. Thank you, Aphrodite."

"Good."

The other woman finally seemed satisfied with the seriousness of Vivianna's response. "Now, what happened? And do not play games with me, for I will know if you are. Tell me, from the moment you said good morning, what happened between Oliver and yourself."

Vivianna shifted nervously in her seat.

"Come, *mon chou*, think of me as a very old relative who has seen everything and is shocked by nothing!"

Vivianna smiled. She supposed it was silly to be self-conscious; Aphrodite must have seen and experienced a great deal and she would not be shocked by anything that Vivianna said. This was business, she reminded herself, and she must treat it so.

"I did as you said, Madame. While we were riding in the coach I played at ignoring him, and soon I had drawn his attention to me. And then I touched myself and I leaned towards him and I—I licked my lips. It was quite simple, really; I enjoyed it. But then he . . . well, he began to kiss me—kiss me and touch me—and I forgot what I was doing. I'm sorry. . . ."

"Touch you where?"

Vivianna felt her face heat, but the fact that Aphrodite was so matter-of-fact about it helped her to be so, too. "He put his hand under my—my petticoats and touched me . . . in an intimate manner. I felt . . . it was very nice. And then I . . . it was . . . I felt as if I had died and gone to heaven," she finished in a rush. It was the only way in which she could explain the sensation Oliver had caused within her.

"You experienced the *petite mort,*" Aphrodite said quietly into the silence. "The little death. The climax to your love play." She tapped one finger on her chair arm and Vivianna noticed with dazed eyes that the rests were shaped like Egyptian sphinxes. With her dark hair and eyes, Aphrodite could well pass for Cleopatra.

"That he could bring an innocent to such a point so quickly and in such a situation says much for his skill. I did not realize. . . ." Aphrodite tapped the sphinx's head once more. "To be blunt, he has your scent now, Vivianna. He will be difficult to control."

I have your scent. You're mine.

Vivianna felt her eyes grow wider, and yet something inside her thrilled to the thought that Oliver wanted her like that.

"So, he believes himself to be the seducer, he thinks he is in charge of the situation. You must not let that happen. *You, mon chou,* must become *his* seducer."

"Yes," she breathed. "I want to do it." She looked into Aphrodite's carefully expressionless face. "Tell me what I must do."

Aphrodite smiled. "Your lessons grow more interesting, Vivianna. We are playing for high stakes now, but if you are willing to play deep then so am I."

Vivianna nodded. "I am willing. Tell me, Madame. Please."

"Very well, but it may not be what you expect to hear. The secret to seducing Oliver is inside yourself, Vivianna. Ah, *non,* quiet now, and listen to me," as Vivianna tried to protest. "The seductress you seek is within your own body, it is just that you have never sought her out, you have ignored her. Now she has been aroused, and if you are brave enough you must allow her to take command."

"I don't think—" Vivianna began doubtfully.

"That is your trouble, *mon chou.* You *think* too much. Your mind is your enemy when it comes to seducing Oliver. You allow that little voice in your head to talk you out of what you should be doing. Do not listen to your mind. It is your body you must heed. It is the seductress inside you, inside your body, who will help you most now."

Vivianna did not entirely understand—had she been listening to the seductress within when she had been in the coach with Oliver? She had enjoyed herself, until she lost control of the situation, and even then she had enjoyed it. But she had agreed to be tutored by the courtesan and so she must listen.

"Now that he has had so much, he will want more of you," Aphrodite said bluntly. "You must make certain that he is grateful for each new favor, grateful enough to give a little bit of himself into your keeping. He will think he is the master, that he is taking what he wants, but in truth, each time he takes, you will own him a little more, and a little more, until he is yours entirely."

"It sounds simple, Madame, and I understand what you are saying, but can't you tell me something more . . . more practical? Something I can do next time we are together?"

"Of course," Aphrodite said quite gently. "I go too fast and you are new to this. I think, next time you are together and he holds you and kisses you, you must tell him what you would like him to do. What pleases you. Say to him, 'I like it when your tongue touches mine.' Or, 'I like it when you kiss me there, or there, or there!' Set him to do your bidding. I am not telling you to speak like a coquette; he does not want that. He is attracted to you because you are not of the *demimonde*. Men like Oliver want to be the first to awaken the woman of their choice to passion. He is like a hunter seeking his prey, but at the same time he will be very pleased to know that you are enjoying his attentions."

"Should I touch him?" Vivianna asked, trying to sound as practical as the courtesan, but still feeling rather light-headed.

"Do you want to?"

Vivianna blushed. "Yes."

Aphrodite smiled. "Good, then I think you should touch him. Rest your hand upon his arm, let your fingers trail across his sleeve. Brush them against his chest, lightly, innocently. Lean in close to him when you speak, so that he has your scent. When he touches the peak of your breast, touch his. Watch his face, learn what he likes best. Believe me, his brain will soon be boiling like a turnip in a pot."

Vivianna laughed.

"And if he touches you again intimately, make him feel as if he has given you a most wonderful gift. Make him feel strong and important, Vivianna. Play upon his ego. Although it is you who will be controlling the moment, he must believe it is he."

Then, as if they had been discussing nothing more scandalous than the weather, Aphrodite rose and rang the bell for a servant, and they took tea and macaroons. Vivianna sipped and nibbled, but could not help but wonder what her family would think if they could see her now, taking tea in the home of a famous courtesan. Her mother would be shocked and appalled, probably, although her sisters would understand, particularly Marietta. Marietta was quite as daring as any young lady Vivianna knew.

"Tell me a little of your family, Vivianna." Aphrodite looked genuinely interested.

"What will I tell you?"

"Whatever you wish, *mon chou.*"

Vivianna wondered whether she could tell Aphrodite not to call her "my cabbage," but she supposed that would be impolite. Besides, she was growing used to it.

So Vivianna spoke about Lady Greentree and their home, and the moors, and how Marietta was beautiful and daring but rather lacking in foresight—"Impulsive," sighed Aphrodite—and how Francesca preferred the company of her dog and the moors and liked to see herself as a heroine of old—"Dramatic," murmured Aphrodite.

"While you, my dear Vivianna, you are passionate."

Vivianna laughed. "I fear so!"

"All the more reason to protect your heart. When a heart like yours is broken, it will not mend so easily."

Vivianna nodded, accepting the warning and the kindness that went with it. Who would have thought she could feel such empathy with a courtesan? A woman who stood outside the ranks of respectable society? And yet, in light of how Vivianna herself felt, it made perfect sense.

"Have you always lived in this house?" she asked suddenly, and then was embarrassed by her own curiosity. "I'm sorry, it is nothing to do with me."

"You may ask whatever you wish, Vivianna. No, I have not always lived here. I have lived in many places. Once I became famous"—with a smile—"I lived in Paris on the Boulevard de la Madeleine, and I lived in a house in Mayfair for many years, and there was another house in the country, which was very fine. All gone now. I was . . . ill for a time, and I did not want to please my friends anymore. I lost rather a lot of my wealth, but I retained enough to set myself up in this house. Now many gentlemen come to see my protégées."

"And they do not come to see you? I find that difficult to believe, Madame."

Aphrodite laughed in genuine amusement. "Well, maybe they come to talk to me and laugh with me and remember old times. I can still make a man look at me, even if I do not want him to share my bed. Ah, now I have been too frank with you, *mon chou,* I am sorry."

"No, no," Vivianna insisted, though her cheeks were warm. "I like frankness. I prefer it. What did you do in Paris, apart from . . . from . . ."

Aphrodite smiled at her clumsiness, but she answered readily enough. "I went to the opera and the theater and many, many saloons. I entertained the rich and famous, the artists and the writers, in my house on the Boulevard de la Madeleine. Once I held a dinner party there for ten special friends. There were many dishes, and when it came to dessert, I left the table and went myself to the kitchen to prepare it."

"It was special, then? A special dessert for your special friends?"

"Yes, very special. It was me." She laughed aloud at Vivianna's expression. "Oh, *mon chou,* your face! No, no, they did not gobble me up. I had my chef cover me in flowers and rosettes made of cream, all in different colors, and decorate me like a pretty cake. Then I was placed on a very large platter and covered with a very large silver lid, and they carried me into the dining room and placed me upon the table. And then the lid was lifted and . . . *voilà*!"

Vivianna knew her eyes were popping. "What did they do?"

"They applauded a great deal, and then they . . ." Her eyes grew sly, and her smile more so. "Well, that is enough for now, Vivianna. Later, perhaps."

"I'd like to hear of it," Vivianna retorted, and meant it.

Aphrodite laughed, delighted, and then her face grew solemn, almost sad. She spoke again, this time in French, and so softly Vivianna hardly heard her. But it sounded as if she had said, "I knew I would love you, but I did not expect to like you. . . ."

"Madame?"

Aphrodite waved her hand impatiently. "It was nothing. Nothing. Now, one more thing before you go. I have much spare time these days and I am writing the story of my life. Many courtesans write their life stories, you know. Respectable English people love to read about courtesans, even though they do not like to have them in their drawing rooms. I wondered if you would read what I have written, Vivianna, and give me your opinion."

"Oh, that would be . . . it would be a privilege, Madame."

Aphrodite smiled, as if Vivianna's wholehearted sentiments amused her. She went to an armoire on the other side of the room and took from it something rather like a diary, bound in red leather. She placed it in Vivianna's hands.

"There is no hurry," she said. "Take your time. And read it when you are alone."

"Thank you."

Aphrodite waved a hand again, dismissively. "I will send you word when you can come and see me next time."

"Thank you, I have very much enjoyed—"

But it seemed that Aphrodite was bored with her now, for she cut through her words quite abruptly. "Dobson will show you out, *mon chou*. Do not forget what I have said."

"No, I won't forget. Goodbye, Madame."

Dobson was waiting in the hall, dressed in his red coat and ready for the evening trade.

"I'm to see you safely into a cab," he said with a wink. "Miss Aphrodite's instructions. She is very particular where your safety is concerned, miss."

Vivianna had sensed that, too, and it puzzled her. Just as many other things about Aphrodite puzzled her. Perhaps the red leather book she now held in her hands would answer some of those questions.

"Have you been long in her employ?" she asked Dobson as they waited for one of the street errand boys to fetch a hansom cab from the stand.

"Nearly eight years now, miss. I knew her afore all this, but I did not find her again until eight years ago." He looked at Vivianna, suddenly solemn, and she saw the love in his eyes. Love and devotion, the giving of one's heart. All the things that Aphrodite had warned her against just now, over tea and macaroons.

"Ah, here comes the cab, miss." He handed the errand boy a copper and opened the cab door for Vivianna. "Take care, now."

"Thank you, Dobson."

Her throat was unaccountably tight, and her eyes unaccountably full, as Vivianna left Aphrodite's behind her.

Sergeant Ackroyd fell into step with Oliver as he was strolling home from an evening of drinking and gambling and visiting loose women. Well, not the latter. Loose women did not seem to attract him since he had met Vivianna. He kept hearing her voice in his head, telling him to behave himself. Unfortunately, she then spoiled it all by kissing him and sitting on his lap.

Nice fantasy, though.

"I 'eard our friend has been makin' inquiries about Candlewood. Whether tearin' it down is legal."

Oliver turned to look at Sergeant Ackroyd's profile, but could hardly make him out. The alley was very dark, and probably unsafe, but the policeman seemed to blend into it.

"He'll find it is entirely legal," he said.

Sergeant Ackroyd nodded. "So 'e was told.

"There was somethin' else, yer lordship, you might 'ave an interest in. Yer know the name Celia Maclean?"

Oliver stiffened. Sergeant Ackroyd obviously knew every sordid detail of his life. "Yes?"

Celia had been ruined because of him. Oliver had spoken to her after Anthony died, he had offered to marry her, but she had refused. She had told him then that she hadn't wanted to marry Anthony, either. Celia wasn't the usual sort of girl. Her loss of reputation hadn't seemed to bother her much. She had once told Anthony that her father kept trying to marry her to men she didn't love—but Anthony being Anthony, he hadn't thought the comment applied to him.

"Word is 'er Italian teacher made 'er an offer, and 'er father, thinking 'e'd never get 'er off 'is hands, said yes."

"Good God." Oliver tried to think. Did that mean Celia had been plotting to marry the Italian all along? Poor Anthony. He had loved the girl, and she hadn't loved him. She had wanted to be ruined—he should have known it at the time, but she had caught him at a weak moment. He'd arrived home, the worse for drink, and she had taken him by surprise. Oliver wasn't making excuses for himself—he would always blame himself for what happened—but this new piece of information at least relieved him of the guilt for Celia's ruined reputation.

"Looks like yer off the hook, then, yer lordship," Sergeant Ackroyd said, looking pleased.

"Yes, I suppose I am."

He thought again of Vivianna. She wasn't like Celia, not really, but there were similarities. That same unconcern with society's rules, that infernal curiosity, that determination to have her own way. But whereas Celia seemed to have landed on her feet very nicely, would Vivianna?

Of course, there was the question of her real motives. She had been more than willing in the coach, but now, in the chill of evening, he had to ask himself if she was just a very good actress. She certainly wanted Candlewood. Would she give herself to him, bargain with her body, to have it?

The idea was unpleasant, but he must consider it. Oliver might want her—but he should not trust her, no matter how much he was tempted.

Chapter 11

The meeting was held at the Mayfair home of the widowed Lady Chapman, an advocate for the London poor who had, according to the Beatty sisters, done much good in that area. Vivianna had promised to attend on their behalf, and although it was exciting to meet Lady Chapman and many other London reformers, she sat through the first part of the evening—which consisted of a lecture by a worthy gentleman on the workings of the workhouse—with her mind on other things.

Ever since her "lesson" with Aphrodite she had felt as if there really was a seductive stranger inside her, looking out on the world through her eyes. Her body had been more alive, more receptive to sensation than ever before. Tonight, when Lil had helped her to dress, she had felt the slip and slide of her clothing as if for the first time, and the hairbrush against her scalp had made her want to wriggle in her chair.

Her body appeared to be more attuned, on the brink of new experiences, and it frightened her, but at the same time she found herself tingling with anticipation.

She had sent Oliver an invitation, with Lady Chapman's permission. It had been a spur-of-the-moment decision, but she told herself it was the good and sensible thing to do. Possibly his implacable heart might be softened by being surrounded by people who put the welfare of children, such as those at the shelter, to the forefront. He would not come, of course not, but simply receiving the invitation might sway him a little bit, force him to rethink his position.

"Wasn't it Lord Montegomery who wished to demolish Candlewood," Lady Chapman had asked quizzically.

"Yes, but I hope to change his mind."

Lady Chapman had surveyed her with a cool, curious stare, and then she had smiled. "I think," she said, "that you could do anything you put your mind to, Miss Greentree."

Now Vivianna hoped she was right.

The gentleman finished his lecture on workhouses. As he bowed in response to the polite applause, Vivianna had the oddest sensation. As if someone behind her were watching her. For a moment she did nothing, telling herself she was imagining it, but the feeling persisted, and at last, unable to resist it, she turned her head to look.

Her breath caught, her heart began to pound.

Oliver Montegomery, elegant in a black evening jacket and white shirt, the effect rather overpowered by an aquamarine satin waistcoat, was staring at her. Unsmiling, unmoving, he was standing near the back wall.

For a moment their gazes tangled and locked, and Vivianna felt a blush warming her cheeks. That he was here was a good thing, wasn't it? And yet she had a strong feeling that, as their eyes had met, he, too, had been thinking of their time together in the coach.

Vivianna took a breath, steadying herself. Mrs. St. Claire, seated on her right, made some innocuous comment and she replied, but she could not later have recalled what she said. Oliver was here. He had accepted her invitation. Why had he come? Had he realized the error of his ways? Well, of course, that must be it. . . .

But she knew that wasn't it at all. Oliver had come here because of her. Aphrodite was correct. He was attracted to her. He had her scent, and he was hunting her like a wolf hunted its prey.

Or its mate.

Vivianna felt the nerves in her stomach jump and her hands tremble before she remembered. Oliver wasn't hunting her; she was hunting him. She wasn't his prey; she was a she-wolf, as fierce and determined as he. The seductress inside her began to stir.

The next speaker's voice droned on, and Vivianna tried to listen. But now that she knew Oliver was there, it was as if she could physically feel him. Her sense of him heightened, and she allowed herself to feel with her body rather than her mind. On impulse, she allowed her Norwich shawl to slip a little, disclosing more white flesh, and wondered whether from where he stood he could see the rise of her breasts above the line of lace upon the neckline of her plum-colored dress, and the way in which her breathing had quickened.

Her mouth curved into a smile, and she lifted a gloved hand and brushed it across her cheek, smoothing a truant curl behind her ear. She was wearing earrings that bobbed when she moved, pearls set in gold, and she touched one, playing with it.

Oh yes, she could not see him but she knew he was there. Her body felt him—the seductress inside felt him, and called out her soft, winsome song.

Oliver knew he was tense. He shifted a little, and observed that he could now see more of Vivianna Greentree—the delicate curve of her cheek, the plump rise of her breasts, the way her chestnut hair tickled her nape in feathery ringlets. It wasn't enough, of course. He should have known that coming here would only be an exercise in frustration for him. And she seemed to know she was safely out of his reach. He could have sworn she was teasing him—the way her fingers were playing with her fleshy earlobe—but it seemed so unlikely that he dismissed it.

She was probably just concentrating on the lecture. The *meeting*. Damn her, she had managed to get him to one of her damned meetings after all! Not that he had heard a word of it. He'd been far too engrossed in Vivianna.

More applause, and then their hostess was announcing that supper would be served and after that another lecture from another worthy gentleman. Oliver tried not to groan aloud. He could leave, he supposed, but that would mean missing out on speaking to Vivianna.

Look at her, he thought crossly. She was already surrounded by gentlemen who knew more about soup kitchens than they had any right to. Were they really interested in her conversation or were they just there to gaze into her hazel eyes? Oliver felt disgust at himself for the thought, but he couldn't help it, just as he couldn't help a great many of his thoughts and actions since he had met Vivianna Greentree.

He moved closer, until he was near enough, if he had wanted to, to reach out and touch her. Her scent filled his nostrils—lavender and woman. The pulse in her neck was beating beneath the skin, and he had the urge to bend his head and suck upon it. Put his mark upon her, just so that everyone in the room knew she was his. She knew he was standing behind her, didn't she? She must know. Then why was she continuing her damned conversation with the bore in the blue jacket? Did she enjoy the company of such men? Oliver, his irritation growing with every second, was on the point of rudely interrupting when she finally turned.

Her hazel eyes lifted to his and she regarded him quizzically, but her lips were curved in a little smile that told him she was pleased to see him. "Lord Montegomery," she said, and lifted her hand to rest it upon his bicep. And left it there, lightly, so that he barely felt it through his clothing. But that butterfly touch was enough to heat every part of him. Oliver forced his eyes from her delicate, gloved fingers and met her bright gaze.

"Are these things always so tedious?" he said grumpily.

Vivianna raised her dark eyebrows. She leaned forward, so close he could see down her cleavage where the shadows promised him a rare treat, and whispered, "Shhh, it is for a good cause."

His body was rigid with lust. He wanted to throw her over his shoulder, carry her into a dark corner, and do what he should have done in the coach. Why had he allowed himself to be upset by memories of Anthony and Vivianna's damned lecturing? He had had his opportunity on the way back from Candlewood, and he should have taken it. She wouldn't have resisted. He could have had her up against the squabs and forgotten her by the time they reached Bloomsbury.

Oliver swallowed. He was fooling himself. He doubted he would ever forget Vivianna; his body, his mind had never been more alive. She had offered him redemption but he did not think she had meant through the enjoyment of her body. Still, a lost soul had to find his salvation where he could.

She was watching him, her eyes slanted and gleaming through her lashes. As he had in the coach, he noted the triumphant expression in them, as if she knew what she was doing to him, and she was enjoying it. Of course she was, she had brought him to this meeting, hadn't she? After he had sworn never to attend such a thing?

Oliver took her arm firmly in his and, as her brow creased with sudden unease, began to thread his way through the crowd heading for the supper table.

Vivianna tried to tug herself free of his grip, but he did not release her. "Lord Montegomery," she said a little desperately, and she wasn't smiling now. "I am a guest here. I cannot just leave. I must say goodbye—"

"Miss Greentree!" a bright-eyed woman twittered. "And Lord Montegomery! How wonderful that you have come to our little meeting. So gratifying to see a new face in our midst."

"Mrs. St. Claire, I am sure that Lord Montegomery would be more than happy to—"

"Miss Greentree has another engagement," Oliver said, barely pausing. "An urgent one. My apologies, Mrs.—eh—St. Claire, but her presence is needed at once at the Shelter for Poor Orphans."

"Oh dear," the woman cried. "I hope it is not bad news?"

"I'm afraid it is. The orphans are revolting," he said, and strode determinedly toward the door.

Behind him, Mrs. St. Claire gasped, but in a moment the door had closed on them all and he was alone with Vivianna in a wide corridor lit by gaslights. The babble of voices receded behind them until the only disturbance was the sound of their steps, the rustle of Vivianna's skirts, and the soft hissing of the gas.

"That was very rude," she said, a tremor in her voice.

She was angry with him, and rightly so. He had behaved abominably, but he couldn't seem to help it. She drove him to it.

Doors were closed on either side of them. On impulse, Oliver opened one and glimpsed a smallish sitting room. It was empty, and he drew Vivianna inside and closed the door.

"What *are* you doing?" she demanded, and finally tugged free of him. She straightened her sleeve with quick, angry jerks, her cheeks flushed, her eyes sparkling. "I think you should apologize, my lord."

"I apologize," Oliver retorted. He stood watching her as she attempted to smooth out every crease in her attire, and gradually the irritation drained out of him. "What are you up to, Vivianna?"

She didn't look at him. "Up to? Nothing at all. Now, if you will excuse me, I must—"

"No, I won't excuse you, and yes, you are up to something. You're driving me to madness."

She was pleased! He saw the flicker in those hazel depths.

"Aha!"

Warily she watched him step closer, until the toes of his shoes brushed her skirts. "What do you mean, aha?"

"You want to drive me mad," he retorted. "I wonder why." Her skirts and petticoats gave way before him, pushed back by his forward movement, and he took another step. He was close enough now that her breasts were brushing his chest. He did not touch her with his hands, not yet, although he had to clench his fingers into fists at his sides to stop himself. But he was not ready yet.

"I want you to see that to demolish Candlewood is a terrible mistake, that is all."

Vivianna heard her own voice waver and swallowed down whatever emotion was trying to break free. He was looming over her in a most intimidating manner, but she wasn't intimidated. All she could feel was the warmth of his body against hers, the hard muscle of his thigh where it rested hard against her skirts, and the low timbre of his voice vibrating through her.

"I think, after what I have been through tonight I deserve some reward," he said in that drawling tone she knew so well.

"Nonsense."

He smiled and loomed closer. "But I do, Vivianna. You forget, a bad man like me isn't used to being surrounded by so much goodness."

"Even rakes can change their habits," she said, and then wished she could bite the words back. Of course rakes couldn't change their habits! She knew that, she had seen it firsthand.

But his smile broadened and he ducked his head and took her mouth in a hot, all-enveloping kiss. Vivianna, surprised, was quickly overtaken by the feel of his lips on hers. She moaned softly. Somehow she had slid her own hands around him, beneath his jacket, her own palms flat against the hard muscles of his back. He felt marvelous, and the seductress inside her wanted more.

Oliver's fingers had fought their way beneath the tight bodice, beneath the soft cotton of her chemise, and found her nipple. A shiver of surprise and pleasure ran through Vivianna as he stroked her. The intimate place between her legs tingled as if it had suddenly come alive.

"I like that," she purred, remembering Aphrodite's instructions. "Do it again."

His eyes glittered. "I have a better idea. . . ." He reached around her, his hands dangerously quick and practiced, and opened several of the fastenings that held the bodice in place.

The plum dress sagged, slipping down her arms, revealing the curves of her breasts and the delicate stuff of her chemise and boned corset. Her bosom was pushed up by the stays, and he brushed away the coverings and bared her to his gaze. Her full breasts looked swollen, and her nipples seemed to point at him.

Shocked at the sight of herself naked before him, Vivianna gasped and put her hands up to hide her flesh, but he caught them and slowly, firmly drew her hands away. For a moment he just looked, his eyes caressing her, exploring the full curves and soft white flesh, the darker tips and hard little nubs of her nipples. And then, when she thought she would die if he did not do something, say something, he lifted his hand and stroked his finger across one nipple and then the other.

"Oh," she gasped, the sensation so intense her knees went weak.

He took no notice and, bending his head, closed his hot, moist mouth over the peak of her breast and began to gently suck upon her.

It was like nothing Vivianna had ever imagined. She heard herself make a sound like a little growl, and reached up to cup his head in her hands, holding him closer. His tongue played with her, and then his teeth grazed across that so-sensitive flesh. His other hand lifted to squeeze and mold her other breast, and as she looked down at him touching her, Vivianna felt as if she had never seen anything more exciting.

A sound beyond the door, out in the corridor. Vivianna jumped back, covering herself, suddenly aware of where they were, how dangerous this was. The danger was part of the excitement, she accepted that, but that did not mean she wanted to be found here by Mrs. St. Claire or Lady Chapman.

She began to tug up her bodice, though the rasp of the cloth against her breasts was almost painful.

After a moment of watching her struggle, Oliver gave an impatient sigh and turned her gently but firmly about, refastening the back of her dress himself. "We seem fated to be interrupted," he said. "I see another long sleepless night ahead."

Vivianna glanced at him over her shoulder. "I did not realize. Do you mean that you suffer, because you do not . . . ?"

Oliver's brows lifted. "I suffer," he agreed.

She smiled.

Oliver ran his hands over her shoulders and down over her bodice, cupping her breasts through the cloth, and his breath was hot against her ear. "That pleases you, you little devil," he whispered. "There is nothing saintly about you after all, is there, Miss Greentree?"

Vivianna shivered from his hands and his warm breath, but her voice was firm. "I am no shrinking violet," she agreed.

He laughed. "Indeed you're not."

He dropped his hands and stepped away, and she was sorry, but also relieved. She had enjoyed the feel of his mouth on her, but she had felt as if she were on the verge of losing control again. The seductress in her had awoken and stirred and Vivianna had set her free, but there had not been enough time for her to test all her powers.

Tell him how you feel. . . .

"I cannot sleep either," she said quietly.

Oliver looked up from straightening his jacket and smoothing his hair, his dark blue gaze suddenly intense.

"I dreamed of you," she went on, forcing all thoughts of self-consciousness from herself, concentrating on him, on pleasing him, and on pleasing herself. "I dreamed you were touching me, your fingers inside me, and then I . . ."

"You climaxed," he said, but there was a rigid tension in him that made her think he was very interested in what she was saying.

"Yes. I wished you were in my bed with me. Your bare skin against mine."

He groaned and shook his head. "Go away, Vivianna, please. Go home. If you don't, I can't be responsible."

Vivianna went to the door, but stopped to glance at him once more. He was watching her with a mixture of longing and irritation, as if he did not like the things he was feeling.

"Go home," he repeated, "and get some sleep." His eyes narrowed. "Believe me, you'll need it."

Vivianna closed the door behind her and found she was quite breathless. Her breasts still ached and her lips felt swollen, but she did not mind that. She did not mind that at all.

Inside the room Oliver rubbed his hand over his jaw and stared at the empty fireplace. There were too many vital matters happening right now to risk them for an affair with Vivianna Greentree.

I dreamed about you.

Her words drifted through his mind and he shook his head again, as if he would dislodge them. Why had her admission shaken him so? And yet the thought of Vivianna dreaming of him, thinking of him, alone in her bed at night, made him desperate to hold her in his arms. Not to kiss or touch her, although he would do that, but rather just to hold her. To hold her close and warm, and enjoy the feeling of no longer being alone.

Lord Lawson was weary. He felt the weariness in his mind, in his eyes, in his very bones. He was so close to his goal, so very close. Sir Robert Peel might well be the next prime minister, but Lawson knew he would follow soon after. He could taste victory.

He clenched his fist in sudden anger. This weariness was Oliver Montegomery's fault!

He had believed he was safe. Candlewood was to be demolished, and with it any chance of discovery. That Anthony had hidden the letters in that monstrosity he was so fond of was no longer in question. They were there, somewhere. The idea that they might be found at any time had almost driven Lawson mad, but when he learned the house was to come down, the relief had been indescribable.

And now there was a secret chamber. . . . Curse the man! To drop that little gem into the conversation like that, as if it had no importance whatsoever. Lawson had no doubt Oliver would find the hidden chamber, he was lucky like that. He would find it, and the letters inside it, and then all would be lost.

Lawson knew he couldn't allow that to happen.

All these years he had worked toward his own success and now one mistake was threatening to pull him down. Disgrace. Scandal. It didn't bear thinking of, and he wouldn't think of it! Surely a man of his talents and intelligence could overcome a drunken fool like Oliver Montegomery?

Then why did he feel as if he were being purposely led down a path he had no desire to follow?

There was something wrong. Lawson felt his weariness begin to lift. Yes, that was it. Something was not as it seemed. Oliver? Could it be Oliver?

His first reaction was to laugh and dismiss his doubts. Oliver had reached the point of no return and Lawson had watched his downward slide with scorn and some pleasure. Anthony had always been so fond of his younger brother, so tolerant of his follies. Anthony had believed that in Oliver there was a great man and in time he would declare himself. But Anthony was a fool, after all. Lawson had offered him a chance to live, had explained how important it was that the letters remain secret, but Anthony had not wanted to listen. He hadn't understood that the good of the nation was more important than such a minor consideration.

What a fool! Lawson had lost count of the number of times he had told a lie or arranged a situation to his own benefit through bribery or worse. Sometimes it was necessary to force a path through the obstacles in order to win the day. Everyone knew that!

Oliver . . . was he really what he seemed? Lawson would find out, and if Oliver had been playing him for a fool . . . Lawson smiled. Well, Oliver would pay the same price as his brother.

Vivianna, returning to Queen's Square after a visit to Aphrodite and an hour of shopping in busy Regent Street, found Aunt Helen all aflutter.

"Lady Marsh is here!" Helen hissed, catching Vivianna's arm as she began to divest herself of her packages—she had bought presents for all her family. "She has been waiting almost half an hour. I think she was on the verge of leaving when you came in."

Vivianna stared at her blankly. "Lady Marsh? Lord Montegomery's aunt?"

"Yes, yes." Helen gave her an agonized look. "She is very formidable, Vivianna. I do not think I could have stayed with her much longer without saying something quite idiotic."

"I see." Vivianna straightened her back and gave a determined smile. "Lead me to her, then, Aunt Helen, *I* am not intimidated."

With obvious relief, Helen did so.

Lady Marsh was ensconced upon the large armchair in the corner of the sitting room, like a queen upon her throne. She sat bolt upright, her gray hair smoothed into submission beneath her muslin bonnet, her gray silk gown subtle in its richness. Lady Marsh—despite marrying a man beneath herself—was every inch an English aristocrat, and she wanted them to know it.

Vivianna made her curtsy. "Lady Marsh, how kind of you to call."

Lady Marsh inclined her head, but her eyes—dark blue, just like Oliver's—fixed upon her. "You were out a very long time, Miss Greentree."

"I am sorry. I was looking at the shops in Regent Street."

"Not alone, I hope?"

"No, I had my maid with me."

"Good. A young lady cannot be too careful when it comes to her reputation."

Vivianna had the urge to tell Lady Marsh who she had been visiting before shopping, but wisely bit her lip.

"Sit down, Miss Greentree, I wish to speak with you." Lady Marsh glanced at Helen. "Alone."

"Oh." Helen backed toward the door, relieved. "Of course, of course. I will leave you to talk or . . . I will leave you." The door closed.

Vivianna lifted her brows at Lady Marsh, thinking her rude, and waited. Lady Marsh gave a thump on the floor with her cane, and Vivianna noticed how twisted her fingers were within the gloves. She had heard that the woman was an invalid, and it seemed the rumors were true. It must have cost her much to come here today, and if that was so, then what she had to say was clearly important to her.

Vivianna's annoyance at Lady Marsh's high-handed behavior, and her indignation on her aunt's behalf, faded a little. "What did you wish to talk to me about, Lady Marsh?" she asked, more gently. "I am here now."

Lady Marsh seemed to read her thoughts in her face, for she gave a sardonic smile, also very much like Oliver's. "I am not at death's door yet, Miss Greentree, although some would have you believe I was. I have come to see you because I like you. There are not many young ladies I like, but I find you are one of them. My nephew likes you, too. He is not an easy man to manage, but you seem to have the knack."

Vivianna smiled—she could not help it. "I do not want to 'manage' him, Lady Marsh. I only want him to change his mind about Candlewood."

"Nevertheless, he seems quite taken with you, Miss Greentree."

Vivianna felt the color in her face. A little earlier she had been discussing with Aphrodite how taken with her Oliver was. . . .

"I told him about the dream," Vivianna had said, trying not to feel self-conscious under Aphrodite's scrutiny. "It pleased him, I could see that."

"Of course it did, *mon chou*. And he came to this meeting? A thing he professed to hate, just to see you?"

"I think he must have. I cannot believe he came for his own edification. Besides, he was very rude to some of the other guests."

Aphrodite had smiled. "He fights it, but he cannot win. You must play along with him, Vivianna, listen to your body, and then, when the moment is right, you will close your hand upon him and force him to your will."

"When will the moment be right?" Vivianna had asked softly.

"You will know. The seductress inside you will know."

"Miss Greentree?"

"I—I am sorry, Lady Marsh. I am sure that your nephew is not at all—"

"I am sure he is, and that you know it, no matter how modestly you may protest."

Vivianna laughed. "You must be right, then, Lady Marsh."

"I am always right," the older woman said. "You may not know it, but Oliver has altered a great deal since his brother died. He needs someone to help him forget that particular episode, although his feelings for his brother, of course, do him proud. But it is time for him to put Anthony's death behind him and move on. He has his life before him, and he is the last of the Montegomery line."

"He needs a wife and an heir," Vivianna replied.

Lady Marsh's eyes narrowed. "Indeed he does. I am

a little surprised, however, that you would say so. And yet . . . I am glad you speak plainly, Miss Greentree. I prefer it. This new generation is far too easily shocked for my liking."

"Then I will be plain, Lady Marsh, for I prefer it, too. My interest in your nephew is his ownership of Candlewood. That is all. And I think you exaggerate *my* importance to *him*."

Lady Marsh thumped her cane again. "Hmm, well we shall see. There was something more I wanted to ask you before I leave. My nephew is accompanying me to the opera tomorrow evening, Her Majesty's in the Haymarket. Italian Opera—it is all the rage these days—the queen is very fond of it. They are performing *L'elisir d'amore—The Elixir of Love*. Sounds appalling to me, but it might be just the thing for Oliver. Will you join us?"

Vivianna's amusement at Lady Marsh's description of Donizetti's opera gave way to genuine surprise. The invitation was so unexpected. "I don't know if I—" she began.

"It would please me very much, and you will be able to speak to my nephew about your shelter. Surely such opportunities should not be missed, Miss Greentree, in the circumstances? How many days is it now, until your orphans must vacate?"

She was right, of course she was. A rebellious tingle of excitement curled through her. Yes, she wanted to see him, to talk with him, and Lady Marsh—who seemed so supportive—would be there, so matters could not get out of hand. It would be a perfect opportunity.

"I accept, ma'am."

Lady Marsh's harsh face relaxed into a smile of approval. "Excellent. Now, if you would call my servant to help me, I will bid you farewell."

The servant—a burly man—was called, and Lady Marsh was helped, painfully, to her feet and assisted to her carriage. When she had gone, Vivianna wondered what it had all meant. Was Lady Marsh looking her over, in preparation to adding Vivianna to her list of possible wives? It seemed ridiculous and frightening—Oliver was the last man she wished to marry!—and yet . . . there *had* been speculation in the old woman's gaze as it rested upon Vivianna.

What, she wondered, would Oliver think of that?

Vivianna smiled, and could not seem to stop. Oh yes, she admitted it with a little shiver, she was looking forward to seeing him again. And she was suddenly very happy that Lady Marsh had given her an excuse to do so.

Chapter 12

Oliver nodded at his aunt's elderly butler as he stepped inside her Eaton Square house. "Is her ladyship ready, Bentling?"

Bentling looked slightly to the left of Oliver's eyes and straightened his stooping shoulders. "Her ladyship has become indisposed, my lord. I am afraid she will not be accompanying you to the opera after all."

Oliver frowned. "Oh?" But still Bentling would not meet his eyes.

"Miss Greentree will be attending, however," Bentling went on, showing signs of strain under Oliver's steely stare, "and her ladyship says that you should call upon her at Queen's Square and collect her forthwith. She wishes you to give Miss Greentree these"—he held out a pair of opera glasses—"with her good wishes."

"Does she, now?"

Bentling swallowed. "Yes, my lord."

Oliver sighed. "Tell my aunt . . . I hope she is better

soon, although I doubt she needs my good wishes for a speedy recovery."

"Yes, my lord."

Oliver knew the signs well enough, and knew he should be angry with his aunt for her obvious machinations. He wasn't, though, he thought, as he went back down the steps to his coach. He and Miss Greentree would be alone together at the opera—not exactly proper, he supposed, but not exactly improper, either. The front of Lady Marsh's box, at least, would be well within view of other patrons, and what was wrong in asking a woman to accompany him to the opera? Other men did it all the time. But Miss Greentree was young and attractive and unmarried; her reputation might suffer. Perhaps that was his aunt's plan, that he be forced to propose to Miss Greentree?

Oliver grinned to himself as he climbed back inside the coach.

It would be a brave man who married an unwilling Vivianna. She would make his life a misery. And a joy. He closed his eyes at the sudden image of her, here in this very coach, in his arms. Perhaps being alone with her was not such a good idea after all—she was a complication and he didn't need any more of those. He would call upon her and explain that his aunt was ill, and suggest another night.

Regret filled him, but he ignored it. A few weeks ago he had never heard of Vivianna Greentree; how could he suddenly be feeling her loss? As if . . . as if she were a part of him, he thought suspiciously.

The house in Queen's Square was lit up and waiting for him. "Miss is just coming now, my lord," the maid who answered the door informed him.

"I am afraid that—"

"Montegomery, how do you do?"

He felt the skin at the back of his neck bristle. Toby Russell, the sort of man he despised and usually avoided. Toby's handsome face was deeply lined, as though his vicious ways had caught up with him at last, and there was a calculating air to his smile.

Oliver bowed politely. "Russell, I have come to collect your niece."

"I know, I know. Lovely girl, isn't she?"

Oliver did not allow the other man to see what he was feeling. "My aunt thinks so. It was her invitation."

"Ah, nice to know she is looked upon favorably in that quarter, eh?"

Oliver wondered whether it would be very rude of him not to answer at all. "My aunt is an invalid and does not get out much," he said neutrally.

"Of course, of course." Toby eyed him cautiously, as if he were a firework that had fizzled out and yet still might go off.

Oliver heard the sound of steps on the stairs. Vivianna's. He knew her step. He knew the rhythm of her movements. He could smell her soap and the scented water she used in her hair. It took all his willpower not to hurry to meet her.

"Here she is!" Toby said unnecessarily.

Vivianna came down the last flight of stairs. She was wearing a cream shot-silk dress that caught the lamplight and gleamed and shimmered as she moved. The full skirts rustled about her and the fitted bodice was lower than any he had yet seen her wear, disclosing the opulent swell of her breasts—he remembered those breasts, naked in his hands. . . . He blinked, took in the dark green lace-trimmed shawl that was arranged to display rather than hide her charms, and the cream lace mittens that reached almost to where her short sleeves ended. Her hair was simply dressed in long, loose ringlets at the sides, the remainder fastened in a heavy knot at her nape.

She gave him her beautiful smile, as if she were truly pleased to see him. And then she saw her uncle. Vivianna's eyes turned wary, and the smile less brilliant. "Lord Montegomery," she said politely. "Your aunt said eight o'clock."

"Eight o'clock, eh? Well, it's near enough to it, isn't it, Niece? Why make a fuss over a few minutes?" Toby asked her testily, thinking he was being amusing.

Vivianna fiddled with her shawl, enduring him until he had finished, and then she glanced to Oliver for her answer.

"The opera starts at eight. My aunt does not mind being late—she finds missing the first act a blessing, I think. But in actual fact I—"

She was watching him inquiringly, her hazel eyes honest and warm, that smile curving her mouth. He had been about to tell her that they were not going after all—that his aunt had tricked them into a situation he did not feel comfortable with—but suddenly he knew he didn't want to say that. Toby Russell was standing listening, so smug and awful, and Oliver wanted to take her away from the man. More than that, though. He wanted her company, he wanted to be with her, even for a short while.

"Are you ready, Miss Greentree?" Oliver said quietly. "The coach is waiting outside."

She glanced away, again fiddling with her shawl, and he knew she was remembering what they had done in that same coach. And all the while Toby's eyes were flicking between them, watching, while he came to his own conclusions. Ignoring him, Oliver held out his hand. Gratefully, without a moment's hesitation, Vivianna rested her fingers upon it.

The maid at the door hurried to open it, and Vivianna thanked her by name and with a proper smile. Then, with a cool nod to her uncle, she allowed Oliver to accompany her outside. He helped her into the coach, arranging her skirts about her so that they would not be crushed, and then climbed in opposite her, instructing the driver to drive on.

"Your uncle watches over you very particularly," Oliver said.

"Yes." Her voice was restrained. "He does."

"You do not like him."

"Is it that obvious?" Vivianna glanced at him and sighed. "I admit he is my least favorite relation. I love Aunt Helen dearly, of course, and feel very sorry for her. I have another uncle, my mother's brother William, and he is always very kind to me. But I cannot like Toby."

"He is a blackguard," Oliver said seriously. "Never trust him, Vivianna. He would do you harm if it was in his own interest."

She was quiet, and he watched her, wondering what she was thinking. At last she said softly, "I have just realized. Lady Marsh is not here. Are we going to collect her now?"

"No, I am afraid not. My aunt is unwell, and she has asked that we go to the opera without her."

Silence again. Now, he thought, she would ask to be returned to her home. But she said nothing and, as the wheels of the coach rumbled on over the cobbles, he began to relax a little. Gas lamps glowed against the night mist, making little haloes along the street, and people strolled in the evening air. Everybody seemed to be out enjoying themselves.

"When I first arrived in London," she said, "I thought it crowded and noisy and smelly. A ghastly place. A sprawl of humanity with no heart or soul. Now I am growing used to it. In fact I quite like it."

"Not like Yorkshire, then."

"Not like Yorkshire, no."

"I did not intentionally deceive you, Vivianna. I meant to tell you that my aunt was unwell, but your uncle—"

"Put your back up."

He laughed at the droll note in her voice. "We understand each other, then, do we?"

She met his gaze and held it. "Yes, I think perhaps we do."

Her Majesty's Theatre had been renamed when Queen Victoria ascended to the throne, and it was a venue where only the queen's favorite Italian operas or French ballets were performed. Most nights the magnificent building was full to capacity. Outside, flower sellers held up their neat and fragrant bunches, while the crowd streamed by. Vivianna admired Nash's elegant colonnade, and inside, the gas chandeliers that lit their way. Lady Marsh, explained Oliver, hired a private box for the entire year, despite the fact that she rarely attended the opera.

"Because she is an invalid?"

"Because she loathes it."

Vivianna smiled, enjoying herself and the feel of his hand lightly brushing her waist as he led her through the door to their box. His touch was enough to set her body tingling. He was very handsome tonight in his black and white evening dress, his trousers tapered to black shoes, his tailored black jacket and his white frilled shirt and white cravat. His silk top hat he carried in one gloved hand. He was probably the most handsome man here, she decided seriously.

The chairs were padded brocade, and when they were seated, Vivianna admired their view of the theater. It was overflowing with patrons, from the colorful occupants of the stalls to the tier upon tier of boxes full of gentlemen in evening dress and ladies beautifully gowned, to the noisy and unseen gallery far above, where there were cheaper seats to be had. Some dandies in the stalls had turned their backs on the curtained stage and were eyeing the new arrivals through their monocles.

Vivianna ignored them when they focused en masse upon her. An officer in a red coat covered in medals and ribbons was speaking in a loud voice to a smallish plump lady with dark ringlets, wearing a wide-skirted white satin gown, a sash about her tiny waist, and a necklace of diamonds about her white throat.

She didn't look to be much older than Vivianna, but when she noticed Vivianna staring, gave her a reproving frown.

"She doesn't like to be watched," Oliver murmured at her side. Then, meeting her blank gaze, "The queen, Vivianna. Her Majesty, Queen Victoria."

"Oh!" Vivianna felt horribly embarrassed, but still she gave the box another glance. "Is her new husband there? Prince Albert?"

"Yes, there he is, in evening dress. Tall with dark hair, very serious—the ladies think him very handsome."

Vivianna saw him. He was much taller than the queen, and Oliver was correct, very handsome and very serious. As she watched, Victoria rested her gloved fingers upon her husband's arm, as if she could not resist touching him, even in public. They were in love, then, just as Vivianna had heard.

"Vivianna."

"I'm sorry. Am I staring again? It is all so exciting. I

do not go to the theater very often. And I have only been to an opera once, although I read as much as I can about such things. I believe this one is by Donizetti."

"*L'elisir d'amore.* Rather sentimental, but some of the melodies are quite bearable. The tenor is Rubini, and Madame Grisi is playing the part of Adina."

Some of the dandies were calling out, and Vivianna saw that a woman with bright red hair had seated herself in one of the boxes. Her gown was very low cut, her bosom almost spilling over, and she was wearing more jewels than the queen.

"Who is that?" she whispered, leaning closer to Oliver.

"Someone you shouldn't have heard of," he retorted.

Vivianna examined the redhead closely. "You mean like Aphrodite?" she said.

He smiled. "Yes, like Aphrodite."

"But *you* know her?"

"That's different."

"Is it?"

His eyes were dark, intense, and very close to hers. She felt his breath upon her skin, and despite her determination not to, her lashes fluttered down, hiding her feelings from him. She could feel the pulse in her neck, hear the rush of blood in her ears. For a moment the noise of the theater was washed away beneath the tide of her desire.

"I want you," he said, his voice a whisper in her ear. "And I think you want me, too. Don't you?"

Vivianna drew back a little and looked again into his eyes.

"Don't you?" he insisted, and there was something naked and vulnerable in his face.

She should lie, she supposed. Tease him. Play at indifference. But she could not. This was too important for teasing or lying. The passion and desire between them lay heavy, so that she was finding it difficult to breathe.

"Yes," she said. "I do."

The opera had started. Vivianna did not speak again, and neither did Oliver. It was as if, now the truth had been stated between them, they had to consider their next words very carefully. Perhaps, she thought, he wanted to draw back. Perhaps he had not expected her to say what she did.

Doubts gripped her, making her feel faintly queasy.

What would Aphrodite think, when she learned what Vivianna had done? Would she approve or shake her head with displeasure?

Rubini's voice soared, along with that of the beautiful Madame Grisi. The audience was spellbound. Someone called, "Brava!" Someone else cried, "Hush!"

"Do you speak Italian?" Oliver asked her softly. His hand reached over and covered hers, where they were clenched together in her lap.

She jumped. "I . . . no, I don't. Mama could not find an Italian instructor who would make the journey across the moors."

"Ah." He had taken off his gloves, and his fingers were strong and warm, and they held hers firmly, possessively.

"I understand the story despite the Italian, I think. The woman . . ."

"Adina."

"Yes, she will not marry the man . . ."

"Nemorino."

"He has bought a love elixir, but it does not work,

and now Adina is going to marry someone else . . . the soldier."

Oliver's breath warmed her cheek. "Very good."

"Will the ending be a happy one? Or is someone going to die?"

His eyes clouded, as if he were thinking of his own circumstances, his brother and the woman he had been meant to marry. "You will have to wait and see, Vivianna," he said, but his voice had lost its lightness.

"Tell me about Celia Maclean."

She had asked the question on impulse, and she could see that she had surprised him. He drew back a little and removed his hand. Vivianna supposed she was setting him a test. A chance to tell her the truth about himself, to be frank with her, to answer some of the questions that puzzled her about him. There was always the likelihood that he would refuse, and she must not be disappointed if he did not answer . . .

"Celia and Anthony were not officially engaged," he said, his voice low and level, and she felt a frisson of relief. "But it was understood they would marry. Her father wanted it, and Anthony was in love with her. Celia . . . she was reserved, but she did not protest the match, not aloud, anyway. She came to my house in the evening—late. I was . . . I had been to a dinner, and I had drunk far more than normal. I was surprised to see her."

"But you let her in."

"Of course. She was . . . upset, and she was Anthony's fiancée, nearly. She said she needed to talk to me urgently."

"And then?" She glanced at him now. He was staring unseeing at the stage, handsome and somber.

Act One was over. All around them the applause

thundered out. Patrons began to move about. The dandies in the stalls had their monocles up again.

"And then?" Vivianna repeated.

"I can only think she knew Anthony was coming to see me; he must have told her so. She had timed her own visit so well."

"She compromised herself," Vivianna said, surprised. She had not expected this. The bad man, the rake, had not been as much at fault as rumor would have everyone believe. Vivianna didn't know what to think.

"Yes." He looked at her now, his dark eyes full of so much pain and regret, she felt an ache of empathy. "She didn't want to marry Anthony. I didn't realize at the time, but I have heard since that her father was forcing her to make the match. She was in love with someone else, someone totally unsuitable. The only way out was to ruin herself and drive Anthony away."

Vivianna nodded. "Did you kiss her?" she demanded, determined to hear the worst.

Oliver's eyebrows rose. "She kissed me first."

"But you did kiss her back?"

He shrugged his shoulders. "Of course."

"Did you touch her?"

"Vivianna," he groaned, and bowed his head. Clearly he was ashamed and embarrassed, but she would not let him avoid the truth just because he did not like it.

"I want to know, Oliver. You said the other day that you wanted to avenge your brother. I want to know everything that happened that night. Tell me."

Upon the stage the curtain had risen once more. The orchestra in the pit struck up, and Act Two opened inside a *taverna*, where a wedding celebration was taking place.

"Yes," Oliver said softly, "I kissed her, and yes, I touched her. I was drunk and confused, but I don't claim that as an excuse. I should have pushed her away—she was Anthony's."

"And then he found you both."

"Yes." He looked at her through his lashes, and his mouth curled in a smile that held no humor. "She was wrapped around me like ivy, her dress half off, her hair down. She'd pulled off my cravat and my shirt was hanging out of my trousers. Yes, Vivianna, you wanted to know!"

She had looked away, but she forced herself to turn back. "You didn't consummate your . . . eh . . ."

His eyebrows lifted again. "Are you an expert on copulation, too, Miss Greentree?" he asked her with an edge of anger.

"No, of course not. There . . . there was a booklet I read once, and it showed illustrations of men and women."

His lips quirked. "Oh?"

"It was an instruction booklet, on how to prevent children. There was a Latin term . . ."

Oliver looked as if he wasn't sure he was having this conversation. "Coitus interruptus."

"Yes!" She smiled, relieved he knew what she was talking about.

A muscle twitched in his cheek. Oliver swallowed and shifted in his seat. "Vivianna, as much as I am enjoying talking with you about connection, I think we have strayed from the point."

"Oh, of course." She flushed. "W-what happened then, when Anthony came into the room?"

"He just stood there. Celia started to scream, saying she didn't love him. The inference being, I suppose, that she loved me. I sat down and started to laugh. I was drunk and it was all so absurd—like this opera. Anthony turned around and left. The next time I saw him . . ."

"He was dead."

"Yes. I tried to persuade her to marry me, you know. Do the right thing. She wouldn't. Didn't want me. It was all a game to get out from under her father's thumb. I can't blame her, I suppose. I *don't* blame her; I blame myself."

Vivianna felt her heart swell with compassion for him, and relief that after all he had not been so very bad. "It's not so terrible," she said gently. "You were foolish, but the scene was not engineered by you. Probably, in time, your brother would have forgiven you, and you would have been friends again. You should not think he hates you from beyond the grave—I do not believe the dead would hate the living for one simple mistake. Surely they are past such petty concerns."

Anthony's death had destroyed all chance of a reconciliation between the brothers. It was no wonder Oliver spent his days and nights trying to forget. And yet what was it he had said in the coach? *I hope to avenge my brother, Vivianna, not placate his restless spirit.* Avenge him in what way? By hurting Celia? Vivianna did not believe it. There must be something else. . . .

She turned to ask him further questions, but he was smiling at her, his gaze sliding over her face like a caress, and the words flew from her head.

"You are a very unusual woman, Miss Vivianna Greentree."

"Is that a compliment?" she asked frankly.

"Oh yes." He nodded slowly. "You've forced me to reveal something to you that I had not intended to, and

I actually feel a sense of relief. Are you my confessor now, Vivianna? I warn you, you would not like to listen to all my sins."

"Are they very numerous?"

"Very."

Vivianna sensed the return of desire between them. The heavy liquid weight of her limbs, the lazy thud of her heart, the tingling tightness of her skin.

His lips brushed her cheek, then the corner of her mouth. She closed her eyes. The opera continued, but Vivianna neither saw nor heard the agonies of Adina and Nemorino. Her own feelings filled her to bursting, and at last, with a soft groan of surrender, she lifted her face to his.

His mouth was hot, barely controlled.

A mistake, she told herself. *This is a mistake. Everyone will see . . .*

Evidently he knew it, too. In the time it took Rubini to draw breath for his next note, Oliver had propelled her to her feet and back, into the shadows to a small anteroom, offering privacy and hiding them from the eyes of the audience. Oliver had earlier explained the anteroom had been built at Lady Marsh's request, because she often had to recline when the pain was too great, and she did not wish people to see her.

Tonight it hid Oliver and Vivianna, and she was in his arms.

"I've thought of this for days." He kissed her face, and then his mouth was against her throat as she arched it for his pleasure. She could feel his chest to hers, the frill on his shirt tickling her skin, and only the width of her skirts defeated her ability to feel his legs and his hips.

Protect your heart.

That was all very well, but what about this burning,

aching need? How did she protect herself from that and at the same time use it to her advantage?

His hands stroked over her ribs, and upward, to cup her breasts through her stays and chemise and the silk of her bodice. The feel of his palms on them, even through so many layers of cloth, reminded her of his fingers against her bare flesh, and Vivianna moaned aloud.

He covered her mouth with his, and he reached back, his fingers working on the hooks that held the back of her bodice together. A tug, the lined silk bodice loosened, and in a moment he had drawn it down. He lifted aside the soft cup of her stays and the thin chemise, and bared her breast. Her nipple was already puckered against the dark aureole, and Vivianna gasped and touched herself in wonder.

"It is as if I am ready for you," she murmured. "Wanting you to kiss me there."

Oliver groaned at her words, and then he stroked her, covering both her hand and her breast with his own hand.

Vivianna gasped at the warmth of his palm, and then his mouth was on hers. He was rolling the stiff peak of her breast between his fingers, tugging gently at the nipple in a manner that made her want to scream at him. Not to stop, though, never that. But the sensation jolted her right down to her toes, though mainly it was in the place between her legs. She ached for him, and pressed her thighs hard together to try and ease it.

"Beautiful," he whispered against her lips. He stroked her again, and then he stooped and took her nipple in his mouth, sucking gently upon it. Beyond them, out in the theater, applause erupted, and laughter as something upon the stage caught the audience's attention.

Vivianna was oblivious to everything but Oliver.

"You make me feel . . ." she began, her voice strange and husky. "I feel as if I have drunk too much champagne."

He laughed softly and, holding her face in his hands with tender care, kissed her mouth again, opening her lips, using his tongue. "You're drunk on desire," he murmured. Then, holding her still and looking down into her eyes, "I want to kiss you."

"You have," she breathed, and reached up to touch his lips with her own.

He smiled against her mouth. "Not there. I want to kiss you between your legs."

"Oh." Aphrodite had not mentioned that sort of kissing, but Vivianna knew by the tremble in her knees that already she was longing and eager for him to do it. She told him so, meeting his gaze. "I would like that. Will you let me kiss you, too?"

His eyes blurred, as though the vision she had created in his head had temporarily scattered his thoughts. "You can kiss me another time," he said huskily, "and I would like it very much."

And then he knelt down at her feet and began to pull up her bulky skirts and petticoats. Vivianna clasped the many folds in her hands, holding them for him, until he had exposed her stockinged legs. Cool air brushed her most sensitive places. Oliver swallowed and looked up at her, his eyes black with desire.

"You aren't wearing any drawers," he said as if he couldn't believe it, although the evidence was there before him.

Vivianna smiled. "I know."

Slowly, with extreme concentration, he reached out and stroked her thighs above the ribboned tops of her stockings. His palms curved over her hips, then down, molding to the rounded curves of her bottom. His warm breath stirred the soft curls at the apex of her legs.

Vivianna felt her body tense in anticipation. She leaned her head back against the wall and wondered if she would be able to stay upright much longer.

His fingers eased between her thighs, sliding down through the curls that hid her outer lips, searching the delicate folds, to the slickness within. He made a sound of satisfaction in his throat and then . . . good Lord, and then he bent forward and . . .

A bolt of sheer pleasure rendered Vivianna momentarily speechless, and then she gave a deep moan. She lifted her wrist to her mouth and bit upon it, muffling her cries. His tongue circled her swollen nub, sending more quakes through her trembling body, and then he proceeded to suck upon it, gently but firmly. Vivianna arched her back, and at the same time her knees gave way a little more.

He held her up, his fingers pressing into her bottom and opening her thighs at the same time, while his mouth and teeth and tongue did their wonderful work. Vivianna gasped and moved against him. His fingers were inside her, she could feel the pressure, thrusting as his tongue teased her toward the precipice. She bit into her glove, but what she really wanted to do was scream. It was almost too much to bear.

She felt herself erupt, and her legs gave way.

He caught her, holding her up, and the next thing she knew she was in his arms, his skirts rumpled up between them, as she sobbed and gasped out her pleasure in the warm crease between his shoulder and neck. His heart was thudding as loudly as hers, and his chest was rising and falling as he tried to catch his breath.

Vivianna took several deep breaths of her own, trying to calm herself, but it was as if her feelings were all confused and jumbled up inside her. Surely what he had just done was not typical of a rake? She had always believed rakes cared only for themselves, for their own selfish pleasures. What he had just done to her was for her pleasure alone, wasn't it?

She murmured something of the sort into his cravat.

Oliver's breath warmed her ear. "You're beautiful, Vivianna. Pink and sleek and beautiful. It was for my pleasure, too, believe me. Next time I am inside you it will not be with my tongue."

Protect your heart!

Her head was spinning with what he had said, but worse than that, her heart was melting. He had given her such joy, and denied himself release, and now he spoke of the next time. Vivianna knew he would not hurt her, not physically anyway. He would not hurt any woman. There was such goodness in him. Surely he would not deny her her request if she asked him now . . . ?

Yes, ask him to save the shelter. This is your chance. You have him in your control, in your power. Do it now. Now!

He was kissing her again, his mouth feeding on hers, his hands hot against her breasts. He pushed against her, against the place he had just been kissing, and with each movement a new jolt of hot pleasure went through her. And then he turned so that his body was hard against hers and she felt him, the hard urgent length of him, against her belly.

"Vivianna," he groaned, "come with me now. We can go somewhere private. We can make love in safety."

A warning sounded in her head. *And then what?* it

demanded. *Will he call you a hackney and send you home? Why not, once he has what he wants from you?*

And yet he had been so unselfish. He had lavished all his care and attention upon her, given her pleasure such as she had never before experienced. Surely he would not abandon her?

Vivianna tried to clear her head.

The shelter. *Save the shelter.* That was what this was all about, wasn't it? Aphrodite had said she would know when the moment was right. Was this it now? Had the right moment come? He wanted her, that much was clear. If he really wanted her, if she was really important to him, he would say yes. Simple. *Just ask him. . . .*

Again his mouth was on her breast, and he ran his tongue over her nipple, making her flesh jump and squirm. His fingers brushed her inner thigh, stirring the desire he had only just sated, making her think of being in his bed for an entire night.

The image made her dizzy.

Ask him now, before it is too late. . . .

"Oliver," she managed. "How much do you want me?"

His hand cupped the hot moist core of her, and his mouth stilled against her skin. "More than life," he said.

"More than Candlewood?"

It was said. The words hung between them, and she knew. As soon as they were said, she knew. This wasn't the right moment, this wasn't it at all.

Vivianna had just made a most dreadful mistake.

Chapter 13

He looked up at her, his dark eyes blurred. He was stunned. His dark hair tangled and untidy, his necktie askew, his face flushed with passion. One hand was still upon her breast, the other cupping her between her legs. He blinked, slowly, regaining his composure.

"The shelter. Of course." He shook his head. "Of course."

And then he stepped back from her and left her cold.

The applause in the theater was growing, and she realized that Act Two must be over. With shaking hands she began to straighten her clothing. The hooks of her bodice were a problem, but she could use her shawl to cover herself. She may look somewhat less well turned out than she had before, but in the crush beyond the door, no one would notice.

Oliver stood a moment and watched her make her repairs, his hands loose by his sides, and then he laughed without humor, and began to jerk his coat back into shape and smooth his cravat.

"I thought . . ." He shook his head. "My mistake, Miss Greentree. I have long suspected where your real passions lay, now my suspicions have been confirmed."

Vivianna licked lips that were suddenly very dry, but she had gone this far. It was too late to back out now. "You say you want me, and in return you will not reconsider extending the lease on Candlewood? You cannot want me very much."

He smiled, a polite mask through which Oliver's eyes glittered. "I am surprised you have stayed a virgin so long, Vivianna. Or perhaps you are not? Perhaps some Yorkshire worthy has got there before me?"

She slapped him.

The sound of the blow was hidden in the applause, but Vivianna saw his head swing to one side with the force of it, and the red mark bloom upon his cheek.

She had never struck another person in her life, and now she felt sick. Wretchedly sick with anger and hurt. *Protect your heart.* It was too late, too late. . . .

Vivianna made her voice flat—if he could play a part, then so could she. "You're just like Toby, aren't you? A rake who cares nothing for anybody but himself."

He looked at her, and then he smiled. That lazy, reckless smile that struck her to the soul. "And you are just like Aphrodite, aren't you? Selling yourself for gain."

"The shelter isn't—"

"It may as well be an emerald or a ruby."

"Believe what you like," she hissed.

"Oh, I will," he said grimly. "Believe me, I will."

She marched toward the door and wrenched it open. Vivianna exited the box into the crowd.

The audience was spilling out from their boxes to chat and sip champagne. Supper was being served. Although the opera was finished, there was a ballet to be performed for those in the crowd who wanted to maked the most of this "occasion."

But Vivianna knew that, for her, the evening was over.

She felt as if her life were over, too, but it could not be that bad. No, she told herself bleakly, she would rally. A few weeks ago she had not even met Oliver Montegomery. He could not possibly mean so much to her in so short a time.

Oliver followed her down the staircase, not touching her, but never too far from her. Once she would have thought he was hovering protectively, but now she knew he hated her.

Perhaps some Yorkshire worthy has got there before me . . .

She had wounded him. Who would have thought her words would hurt him so much? And yet Vivianna understood now. *You are just like Aphrodite.* He had put her on a pedestal, and she had fallen off it with a bang.

Well, that was his mistake, surely, not hers? She could not help it if he had thought her an angel and she was mere flesh and blood!

Or was it not so simple?

Oliver was a mystery to her, all mazes and complications. He had secrets, too, and he had made mistakes. He felt responsible for the death of his own brother, and he refused to give in when it came to Candlewood. But those things did not stop her from liking him, being attracted to him.

Sometimes she thought she was attracted to him despite herself.

And now that was all over.

"Oliver!"

The loud deep voice startled Vivianna, but it shocked Oliver. For a moment his face was blank, and then in another moment he seemed to consciously relax, his eyelids lowering, his mouth curling in that lazy smile, his body turning fluid. He was like an actor taking on a role, she thought in amazement.

He turned and faced the man behind him. "Lord Lawson."

Lord Lawson was a gentleman in his fifties, tall and lean, his hair more gray than brown, and with an energy about him that spoke of the ability to get things done. But his eyes were as cold a blue as Vivianna had ever seen.

"The worse for drink again I see," Lawson said with a smile, but the note in his voice was not amused.

"Alas, yes."

"You are leaving early?" he asked Oliver. His icy gaze slid to Vivianna and back again. He was still smiling, but it was a meaningless gesture—his eyes weren't.

"Yes, a prior engagement," Oliver said, blinking sleepily, in a manner she had seen before, as if he had drunk too much brandy. And yet she knew he had not drunk any at all.

"I see." Lawson glanced at Vivianna again, clearly waiting to be introduced. When Oliver didn't oblige, Vivianna assumed it was because he was still angry with her, and she stepped forward and held out her own hand.

"Lord Lawson, how do you do?" she said briskly, ignoring the surprised lift of his brows at her forwardness. "I am Miss Greentree, patron of the Shelter for Poor Orphans."

"Ah." Lawson took her hand firmly. "I have heard of you, Miss Greentree. But I am a little surprised you would accompany Oliver here to the opera, not when he is being so stubborn about Candlewood."

Oliver laughed idiotically. "She's a glutton for punishment," he said. "Now, Lawson, you'll have to let us by. Things to do, you know."

Lord Lawson bowed, but his gaze remained on Vivianna. "Goodbye, Miss Greentree. If I can ever be of any assistance . . ."

"Thank you," Vivianna managed, but Oliver's hand on her arm was like iron, and he was pulling her steadily away. "Will you stop it!" she hissed. "What is the matter with you? Why did you pretend like that?"

"None of your business, Vivianna."

"Oh yes, I forgot, I mustn't ask questions. You prefer me with my mouth closed."

"Unless I want to put my tongue in it," he answered in that droll, hateful way.

Vivianna said nothing. He was beyond reaching with logic, and besides, she was still reeling from what had happened between them during the opera.

By the time they reached the street, the coach was waiting and he followed her to the door. His hand was still strong on her arm, helping her in, but when she had been seated, she saw that Oliver had stayed outside. He was looking in at her, his face a shadow against the gaslights on the street, his expression unseen. But Vivianna heard the coldness in his voice.

"I will leave you here."

"Leave me?" There was an anxious note in her voice, but she swallowed it back, and with it the sense of panic. There would be no journey home with him, no chance to right the wrong, no time to apologize.

"My coachman will take you home, Miss Greentree. I prefer to walk."

"Walk to Aphrodite's?" she said bitterly, and then wished she hadn't.

He did smile now; she saw the gleam of his eyes. "No, I think not. I have had enough of love for profit for one night."

Her heart lurched a little, but she held it in check. She told herself it did not matter to her. "Then I will say goodnight, Lord Montegomery. Thank Lady Marsh for the chance to see an Italian opera, and I hope she is well again soon."

He stepped back and bowed. His voice had a grave finality. "Goodbye, Vivianna."

"Oh, and Oliver . . ." She managed a smile, though her face hurt with the effort. "I think I will be taking Lord Lawson up on his offer to help."

Just as she thought, he did not like that. Something in his eyes flickered, but it was gone as quickly. "Drive on!" The coach jolted forward, and her last view of Oliver was of him turning away and walking into the crowd outside the theater—the flower sellers and link boys, the street women, the hungry and the homeless.

This was not as she had envisaged the evening ending. No wonder she felt bereft. *Protect your heart.* Easier said than done. Would she ever see him again?

Of course she would! There was still the matter of Candlewood, and she must continue to try and save it for the children, and Lord Lawson had offered her his services. But she admitted to herself that inexperience had caused her to make a dreadful mistake. She had thought it was the right moment to speak of Candlewood, but it wasn't. Maybe it had all been a mistake; maybe she had confused her passion to save the shelter with her passion for Oliver.

Vivianna groaned and put her face in her hands.

When she reached Bloomsbury, Helen was abed and

Toby was out. She was glad to climb into her bed and be left alone.

For a time she lay in the candlelight and listened to the stillness. Queen's Square was not one of the busy areas of London. It was old and out of fashion, but what it lacked in *savoir-faire* it made up for in quiet. The people who lived here were those, like Helen and Toby, struggling with their finances, or those who were on the fringes of polite society, or seeking to make their ways into it.

Queen's Square was not like Mayfair, or the Boulevard de la Madeleine.

That was when she remembered the red leather-bound book that Aphrodite had given to her. Her life story, or the beginnings of it.

She had not had a chance to look at it before—she wanted to be certain she would not be interrupted. Now she rose again from her bed and searched in her trunk, finding the book tucked away among her plain woolen Yorkshire gowns.

For a moment Vivianna felt strangely wary of opening it. What if it was dreadful? Maybe she would be better off not knowing? And yet curiosity won her over, and Vivianna finally opened the book and, moving the candle nearer, settled herself to reading at least a part of it.

> *It is 1806 and I look out of my window and down into the narrow street, piled high with the filth of generations of families, of men and women and children, trapped here, just as I am. And I wish I could escape this life of mine.*
>
> *My mother works for a milliner on Dudley Street, and brings home barely*

enough to pay for the ale my father drinks. He works in the stables on George Street, but sometimes he doesn't come home. There are other children, four brothers and three sisters, and we sleep and live in this small place. Outside the air is full of smoke and dust and dirt, and the smells of so many people packed into one small area of London.

This is the Dials. Seven Dials. And this is what I have to look forward to. Unless I leave in a wooden box, says Jemmy. He makes me laugh. He works in the stables with Da, and he loves it. His dream is to have horses of his own, maybe drive a coach or a cab, or work for some gentleman as a groom.

Jemmy tells me to stick with him and everything will be all right. He says we have love for each other, and that love makes all the difference. But does it? I think even love like that between me and Jemmy would wear out in this place. It might even turn to hate, eventually. I think I'd feel trapped, like a fly in a jam jar, buzzing and buzzing against the sides and never being free.

I don't want to hate Jemmy.

Vivianna found herself intrigued. The young girl, never named but obviously Aphrodite, observed the lives of those about her with quiet despair. She didn't want to be one of them. Soon she had turned her eyes, instead, toward the ladies and gents she saw on her way to one of the slop-shops, or sewing rooms, on Monmouth Street, where she now worked. The slop-shops made clothing for some of the top modistes, who then sold them to the wealthy for far more than the girls could imagine.

Elena was there, young and full of hope. But whereas Elena gazed upon the clothing worn by the rich, and dreamed of one day having her own shop, or of being a modiste with a list of aristocratic clientele, Aphrodite looked at the ladies and gentlemen themselves.

And longed to be one of them.

Jemmy wants us to marry soon. He has saved a little from his work, and as he has no family to support—he was left when he was five and has lived by his own wits ever since—he puts it aside. He hides it in a space in the wall, behind the bed, at his lodgings. He says we can use it to rent a room of our own, and to make a start.

He says we can even leave the Dials and go into the country.

I don't know, though. I see lots of country people here in London, looking for work, looking to better themselves. More of them come every day.

1809—A gentleman spoke to me today. I often see him, outside the slop-shops. They say he preys upon girls, offering them food and a warm bed, and then he sells them into disorderly houses. I would not go with him, but I like to talk with him, just to listen to his voice. Elena pulled me away and swore at him. I told her I didn't mean any harm, that I just wished I could talk like him, all la-di-dah.

I don't think she believed me, though.

Soon Aphrodite was carrying clothing from the slop-shop to the different modistes. She was pretty and personable, and generally liked. She would stay and chat, and make even the most sour-faced person smile. There were always plenty of ladies and gentlemen about such places. One gentleman, whom she called Henry, was particularly attentive. He had come to pay for some clothes for his mistress.

But even as he spoke of her, his eyes were all for Aphrodite.

Henry says he is rich, and he could teach me to be a lady. I would have to learn to speak, to walk, to dress, even to think properly. Everything! But he says I am a quick study and I can do it.

I amuse him; I make him laugh. He says that is what men like best, a woman to make them laugh. I think he is bored with his life and looking for diversion. That is what I am to him, his current diversion. But it will not last. His eye will stray and he will see something else.

If I am going to make my decision it must be soon.

He has a house in Mayfair.

Vivianna could read the temptation between the lines. Aphrodite wanted to go with Henry, but what would become of her, and what would become of Jemmy? Quickly she turned the page.

> *I have said yes. I have told him I will meet him tomorrow and I will go with him. He tells me he has friends, and I will never want for anything. Especially when I have learned to be a lady.*
>
> *I have not told Elena, or my family, or Jemmy. I don't know what I will say to them all, but especially to Jemmy. He will hate me, and yet I know I cannot do as he wants me to, I cannot be what he wants me to be.*
>
> *This is best, for us all.*

And then, at the bottom of the page:

> *Jemmy has joined the army and gone to fight Napoleon.*
>
> *I do not suppose I will ever see him again.*

Tears flooded Vivianna's eyes.

Was this the love Aphrodite had spoken of, the man she had loved and left behind and now regretted beyond words? Strange, that a woman who had done so much, seen so much, lived such a rich and full life, should regret something that happened when she was a young girl, at the beginning of it all.

Beyond her room, Vivianna heard Helen's voice, and then Toby's deeper tones. He was home, then. After a moment Helen began to cry. Vivianna wanted to keep on reading Aphrodite's diary, but she knew she could not. Helen would need her company and support when morning came. Fascinating as the beautiful courtesan's life was, it had nothing to do with her.

She closed the diary and hid it away again, promising herself she would read more as soon as she was able.

After he had left Vivianna, Oliver wandered for a long while, undecided upon his destination. His body ached for hers, but he was glad it had come to nothing—*could* come to nothing. He had known all along that even if he had her, it would not be the end of his reluctant obsession with her. More likely it would be the beginning of something more.

She was not the woman he had wanted her to be.

Now he knew the truth.

It was Candlewood she thought of when she was kissing him and touching him. It was Candlewood making her gasp and cry out when he did the same to her. She had believed she could barter her body for his compliance.

Oliver had met too many women like that in the past year. He was jaded with them and their view of the world. He had thought Vivianna was different; he had wanted her so much to be *different*.

But beyond his disappointment, now there was something more to keep him awake at nights.

Lawson and Vivianna.

He had no doubt Vivianna would contact Lawson and take up his offer of help. She had said as much. And Lawson, his cold eyes smug and confident, knew he had found a lever to use on Oliver.

"Bastard," Oliver muttered. "Murdering bastard."

Lawson, through Vivianna, would try to stop Candlewood's demolition—he would use her crusading spirit to buy himself time.

He looked up at the dark, cloud-strewn sky. Lawson was a dangerous man. A killer with powerful friends. On their way home from Candlewood, Oliver had let slip to Vivianna that he wanted to avenge his brother. She hadn't forgotten it. She would repeat it to Lawson. Naturally she would, because Lawson would assure her that he and Anthony were the best of friends. She would tell him everything.

The game would be up—Lawson would know Oliver was on to him. A year of slowly reeling in Anthony's killer would have been wasted. But, more than the destruction of all his hopes and plans, Vivianna would be in Lawson's power. She would be in danger.

Oliver's blood turned to ice.

He took a deep breath and looked around. The white columns of White's were right in front of him and he didn't even remember making the journey. Lawson was probably there now—the opera had long since finished. There was a chance Oliver could still salvage his plan. He could throw Lawson off the scent, make him believe Vivianna was of no importance. He had to try. With a tired shrug of acceptance, Oliver climbed the steps and made his way inside. The gaming rooms were as full as ever, and there were quite a few members deep in conversation, or partaking of a late supper in the dining room.

Oliver refused a number of requests by his acquaintances to join them. Instead he sat with a glass and a bottle of brandy before him, and pretended to be busy with his usual pastime of getting drunk.

"Oliver!"

He didn't jump, although his entire body went rigid and his heart began to pound. As if he had suddenly come face-to-face with tremendous danger. Slowly, taking his time, Oliver rose unsteadily to his feet.

"Lord Lawson."

Lawson returned his bow briefly.

Behind him, Toby Russell's handsome, dissolute face appeared, his eyes as watchful as ever. "Lord Montegomery!" he said with false joviality. "This is a surprise, eh? I thought you were at the opera with my niece. Don't say it's finished already? Those things usually go on for hours, don't they?"

Lawson gave Toby a curious glance. "With your *niece,* Russell? Is the forthright Miss Greentree your niece?"

"She's come down from Yorkshire. She's my wife's sister's girl."

"And you asked her to the opera, Oliver?" Lord Lawson was smiling at him, but there was calculation behind it. "Alone?"

Oliver affected disinterest. "Lady Marsh asked Miss Greentree to the opera and then fell ill. I took the young lady in her place."

Toby raised his eyebrows, but before he could question Oliver's statement of events, Lawson said, "I thought you were hanging out for a wife, Oliver. Perhaps your aunt sees Miss Greentree as filling that role?"

"Not me, my lord. I have no intention of being leg-shackled yet. Look at Russell here, he's a warning to us all."

Lord Lawson laughed loudly and Toby smiled in a manner he probably believed to be good-humored, though looked anything but.

"She is a pretty thing, Oliver, this niece of Russell's."

"I suppose she's attractive in a countrified way," he said offhandedly.

"So you didn't enjoy the opera?"

Oliver yawned. "No, my lord, I didn't."

"Strange, that wasn't what I thought."

Oliver felt his blood freeze as he looked into Lawson's famous ice-blue eyes. There was amusement in them, and triumph, but worst of all, there was knowledge. Lawson had seen them, or someone else had done the spying and then reported to him. Oliver knew he should have thought of that—he should have planned ahead. And yet it had been innocent enough, until he kissed her.

Then the situation had spun rapidly out of control.

How could he have been so blind and so stupid? He must defuse the matter, brush it off as one of his escapades. He wasn't supposed to care what happened to someone like Vivianna, and Lawson wouldn't expect him to.

But he did. Despite what he had said to her tonight, despite what she had said to him, she mattered to him. He realized it now as he sensed the danger he had brought down upon her, and he also realized just how much.

"Ah." Oliver wagged his finger at the other two men. He made himself smirk and swagger a little, playing at being the drunken fool. "Then you know, Lawson, that Miss Greentree isn't very happy with me."

Lawson smirked back while Toby looked from one to the other in frustrated silence. "And why is that, Oliver? Do enlighten us, and I will tell you whether your story tallies with my own. What did you and Miss Greentree talk about at the opera?"

"Damned if I know. I wasn't particularly interested in her conversation," he said.

Lawson laughed, but his eyes were bright with contempt. "Do you often copulate with girls in public, Oliver? Very bad form. Especially when Her Majesty is present."

Toby's eyes popped. "You did what?"

"I didn't manage it," Oliver went on thoughtfully, as if he were discussing a horse race and not a woman's honor. "I tried, but she wasn't having any. I do believe I'll have to let that one go. I don't think Miss Greentree will come out with me alone ever again. Or that her uncle here would allow it, eh, Russell?"

Toby looked annoyed, but Oliver thought it was because he felt an idiot for not seeing the truth before now, rather than that any harm might have been done to Vivianna.

Lawson gave Oliver a wink. "I don't know, Oliver, you used to have quite a reputation where the ladies were concerned. Strange, but my information is you were more interested in gazing into her eyes than watching the opera. But you're not the man you were, Oliver, are you? Maybe these days you need someone else to hold her down for you, open her legs while you find the right—"

"I don't . . . don't know what you're talking about."

His voice was tight and hard, his hands clenched at his sides. If Lawson had wanted to flush the truth out of him, then he had almost succeeded. Oliver swallowed his fury and looked away from those ice-blue eyes and hoped he had not given himself away.

"Well then," Lawson said softly, sounding pleased with himself, "you won't mind if I take an interest in Miss Greentree, will you, Oliver? Between us we might be able to save Candlewood for those poor little children."

Oliver stiffened.

Those cold eyes stared into his, and Oliver couldn't think of a thing to reply. Lawson smiled, as if he had won some bet with himself. "Good, good. I thought not."

Oliver felt his stomach drop away. Anger and dismay made his hands shake, and he had to slip them into his pockets. It could be that Lawson was just amusing himself, that perhaps he believed that Oliver was in love with Vivianna and he simply wanted to cause him pain. Revenge for the inconvenience Oliver had been causing him for over a year now. But Oliver did not think so. Lawson had another agenda. He was suspicious. He was beginning to doubt. And he saw Vivianna as a way of forcing Oliver out into the open.

"I'll be keeping an eye on your niece, Toby. Can't have the girl corrupted by a rake like Oliver, can we?"

Toby sniggered.

Oliver promised himself that one day soon he would bloody Toby's nose, but not before he had saved Vivianna from Lawson's clutches.

If, that is, she would let him.

Chapter 14

"I made a mistake."

Aphrodite was watching her in her usual aloof manner. "You are a novice, *mon chou,* you will make mistakes."

"No, I . . . I thought the moment had come to tell Oliver what I wanted from him. He seemed so approachable, so tender, and I believed he would listen to me and grant me my wish."

"So you asked him to give you Candlewood?" Aphrodite prompted.

Vivianna nodded, swallowing tears. "He said I was selling my body for Candlewood, and that he had had enough 'love for profit.' "

Aphrodite was silent, and Vivianna wondered if the courtesan was insulted. After all, love for profit was what she herself sold.

"I don't want him to despise me," she went on quietly, her head bowed, and a tear dropped onto the cloth of her skirt. "I realized then that I don't want him to think I am only pretending to enjoy his company for the sake of Candlewood. I know he is a rake, but he . . . that is, I know that I can . . . I can . . ."

"Save him?" Aphrodite said woodenly.

Vivianna looked up in surprise and realized that there was a deep compassion in the courtesan's dark eyes. Aphrodite pulled a lacy scrap of handkerchief from her sleeve and passed it over, watching as Vivianna tidied her tears.

"It is your nature," the older woman said at last. "You cannot help but believe the best of people and want to help them. I should have foreseen it. You see a man like Oliver, a rake whose life revolves around his own pleasure, and you immediately begin to believe he is redeemable."

It sounded so very like what Vivianna had been thinking that she was shamed into silence.

"Perhaps, despite what you think, he wanted you to admit to it, *mon chou,* so that he could bargain with you. He wanted you to say to him, 'Yes, I am willing to sell my body for Candlewood,' and then he would not have to pretend to care to get what he wanted. Some men think they have to play a game, a part."

Play a part? Vivianna remembered when they had run into Lord Lawson at the opera, and Oliver had pretended to be a drunken fool. But surely that wasn't the sort of part Aphrodite was speaking of, it was only one more mystery that Vivianna had yet to solve.

"You think I should bargain with him, then, honestly and openly?" Vivianna asked, her fist closing over the sodden lace. "You think he never cared for me, only for what he could get from me?"

Aphrodite made a face. "I am tempted to say that it is so. For the past year, Oliver has certainly given all who know him the impression that he is on his way to hell. And yet, *mon chou,* I have sometimes wondered if Oliver is being completely honest with us." Her eyes narrowed. "You are very strongly attracted to him, *oui*? Your body longs for his?"

"Yes," she whispered. "I *ache* for him."

Aphrodite reached out and clasped her hand. "Then you must do something about it. You should take him, Vivianna. Not with your heart, but simply with your body. Enjoy what he has to give you and then walk away from him and forget him. A single night, *oui*? One night of passion and then, *psht!* Over. It is the best thing."

"I don't know if I can do that," Vivianna said, gazing into those black eyes. "I don't know if I would be able to walk away."

Aphrodite's fingers pressed hard. "Of course you can. Take what you want. You say he is a man who makes you ache; satisfy that ache. Satisfy your curiosity. You will always regret it otherwise."

Vivianna nodded, but she wondered if it was that simple. Somehow Oliver had already entangled himself in the threads of her life. And yet the thought of enjoying him for what he could give her—pleasure and expertise—made her quiver deep inside. A night of unbridled passion and then goodbye. Perhaps it would be worth the pain, to have such memories?

"I want to touch him, too," she said quietly. "I want to touch that part of him that makes him a man."

Aphrodite smiled. "Why not? He will not expect you to be trained like a courtesan, so do not be afraid of being bold. Your innocent fingers on him will make him very excited, *mon chou.* Stroke his shaft, hold him, kiss him. If you like, you can take him into your mouth. Gently, though. That part of a man may appear powerful and strong, but it is his most vulnerable part."

Vivianna felt a little dizzy at the thought of doing such things to Oliver. But Aphrodite was right. If she did not satisfy her curiosity, if she did not have her night of passion, she would always regret it.

Aphrodite, watching the thoughts flit over Vivianna's face, wondered if she was doing the right thing. There were those who would be appalled at such advice as she had just given, but Aphrodite had seen much of life. Vivianna needed Oliver Montegomery, and if she wasn't very much mistaken, Oliver needed Vivianna.

She was no matchmaker, but she had sensed a connection between the two of them from the first. Maybe, with luck, this might do the trick. If not . . . She shrugged her shoulders, Vivianna would have a night to remember and no harm done. She might think her heart broken for a little while but Aphrodite knew that hearts did not really break, and they were remarkably good at mending.

She knew now that Vivianna was made of sterner stuff. She would endure, just as Aphrodite had endured.

Such is life. . . .

Oliver,

It has occurred to me that, being financially stretched as you are, you might be amenable to an offer from me for Candlewood. I am concerned that the Montegomery name is suffering over this business with the Shelter for Poor Orphans and, being an old and dear friend of your brother, I am anxious to help in any way I can. Would you meet me for discussions as to an acceptable figure?

Yours Most Sincerely,
Lawson

Lawson,

Much as I appreciate your concern and your offer, I am quite content with matters as they are. No need for you to bother further.

Oliver Montegomery

The following day Vivianna went to Candlewood. The Beatty sisters questioned her thoroughly on her progress with Oliver, and it broke her heart to have to tell them that she feared they had lost the battle.

"He is set in his determination to have Candlewood demolished. I wish I could give you hope, but I think . . ." She could hardly bear to meet their stricken eyes. "I think it best if you go ahead and accept Lord Montegomery's offer of the other property."

"Oh no!" Miss Susan cried.

"The Bethnal Green house will have to do, until something better comes along." Miss Greta, more practical, drew a sustaining breath. "I admit I have looked over it."

"Greta!"

Greta took her sister's hands and squeezed them gently. "I know, I should not have gone without you, but I thought, if worse came to worst, we would at least know what to expect."

Vivianna was in agreement. "In hindsight, you were wise. What is it like?"

"I have to say that I do not think, by our standards, that it is the proper place to lodge children. The building is damp and some of the floors are rotten. The roof leaks."

"Poor little souls." A tear streaked down Miss Susan's cheek.

Vivianna, herself close to tears, glanced up at that moment and saw one of the "poor little souls" outside the window, aiming a slingshot at a bird in a tree. It was Eddie, and he released his shot, sending the bird into angry flight. Her sadness lightened, and she actually found herself smiling. These children were resilient, they had had to be. Maybe the Bethnal Green house was far from ideal, but for the time it would have to do, at least until they were able to find somewhere more suitable to carry on their dream.

Back in Queen's Square, she had barely stepped from the coach when the man who had been monopolizing her thoughts stepped in front of her, blocking her path to the front door.

Vivianna started and said, "What are you doing here?" before she could think to affect indifference. Besides, she wasn't indifferent, she was angry. Her body began to tingle and melt, as if it were greeting him in its own passionate language, and that infuriated her even more.

"I want to speak with you, Vivianna. I left my card, but you were out."

"Speak with me?" Her eyes narrowed. "I have been at Candlewood. Have you been lurking out here waiting for me to return?"

"Lurking?" He gave an angry laugh.

"What is so urgent that it could not have waited until tomorrow?"

There was something strange about him, something edgy and anxious.

"I want to speak with you about Lawson," he said bluntly, not bothering to answer her question.

"Lord Lawson?" Vivianna raised her eyebrows. She had forgotten all about Lord Lawson.

He glared at her. "He's already written to me asking to purchase Candlewood on behalf of the shelter. I have refused. Was that your doing?"

Vivianna could not hide her shock. "No, it wasn't my doing. I had no idea. . . . But I must say it was very kind and generous of him. Why did you refuse? Isn't money the same, whoever it comes from? Surely it would not matter to you who paid it as long as you could spend it on . . . what was the term, now? 'Whores, brandy, and gaming.' Wasn't that what you told me the first time I met you?"

Oliver frowned, clearly not liking to be reminded. "I lied," he said bluntly. "I don't want Lawson's money."

"Well, I am disappointed. Lord Lawson promises to be very useful to us, and I mean to beg his continued support. I am very sorry for your brother and any guilt you might feel, if that is the real reason you want Candlewood turned to dust—and I have to say I am beginning to doubt that is the real reason, Oliver. But that is beside the point. I cannot allow you to ruin the lives of the children for—"

"Damnation, Vivianna, will you be quiet? Do you never listen? I have come to warn you that Lawson isn't to be trusted. You think he wants to help you? He doesn't want to help *you*; he wants to hurt *me*. He is using you because he thinks he can get at me."

Vivianna stared at him. It made no sense to her, and

yet he looked sincere. But then, Oliver was very good at looking anything he wanted to. "You are very arrogant," she said at last. "The world doesn't revolve around you, Oliver—"

She broke off as he stepped closer, and now he was almost touching her. The warmth of his body, the scent of sandalwood from his clothing, in fact everything about him weakened her. In another moment she would put her arms around him and kiss him. It didn't matter what he might or might not have done; it did not matter whether or not he was an unreformable rake.

That was what made Oliver so dangerous to her.

"Are you wearing drawers?"

She blinked, wondering if she had heard him right. "Oliver!"

He shook his head, and rubbed his eyes as though he, too, were having difficulty concentrating. "I'm sorry."

Vivianna knew she needed time alone, to think. To plan her next move. To gather her scattered thoughts.

"Will you let me talk to you?" Oliver added quietly, urging her to say yes. "Vivianna, will you please ask me inside your aunt's house so that I can speak to you in private?"

She stepped backward. "I don't think so. You are clearly not in your right mind."

He rolled his eyes to the heavens. "If I am insane then you are the cause."

"I must go, my lord, excuse me."

Oliver glared at her a moment more, and then turned his back and walked away. Vivianna watched him disappear around the corner. Why was Oliver so determined to keep her from Lord Lawson? It was most bizarre, and yet she sensed from Oliver's demeanor that something very serious was happening. Perhaps she should have spoken to him further.

But Vivianna was still trying to decide whether or not to take Aphrodite's advice, to give herself one night with the rake and then walk away. Being in his company confused her. Such decisions must be made out of his influence.

Vivianna sighed. "I wish Mama were here."

And yet, she thought at the same time, better that she was not. Vivianna had too many secrets to keep from her, and it was never easy keeping secrets from Lady Greentree.

Chapter 15

Sounds outside. Guests arriving. Servants calling, doors banging, and familiar voices speaking in excited tones. *Beloved* voices.

"Mama!"

Half awake, Vivianna was out of her bed and barefoot on the stairs, just as Lady Greentree and Marietta entered the house and looked up. Lady Greentree, her face pale and wan from the long journey, smiled with sheer relief.

"My dearest girl!"

Vivianna was down the final stairs in an instant and into her mother's arms. She had not realized, when she came to London, just how much she would miss Lady Greentree. That calm, practical woman who was always there to advise her, to discuss her problems with, or to simply offer loving support.

She needed all three of those comforts now.

"Vivianna, it's me! I am here!" Marietta, her blond curls bouncing, claimed a hug from her sister, although she could hardly keep still at the same time.

"We have left Francesca home," she announced triumphantly, "because she is too young to come."

"She did not want to," Lady Greentree admitted, wiping her eyes. "Not without her dog."

"And we could not have that smelly lurcher in the coach with us," Marietta said, wrinkling her nose.

"Amy!" Now it was Helen's turn to come running and throw her arms around her sister. They hugged and wept, while all about them an alarming amount of luggage continued to be brought in. When eventually order was restored and the newcomers had taken off their cloaks and bonnets, they all partook of breakfast in the breakfast room.

Vivianna had, by this time, washed and dressed and was feeling much more herself. On her way down the stairs for the second time, she had met Mr. Jardine, Lady Greentree's trusted secretary and steward, coming up. A man of medium height with gray hair and twinkling blue eyes, he gave Vivianna a warm smile of welcome.

"I am glad to see you safe and well, Miss Vivianna."

"And I, you, Mr. Jardine. We had no warning that you would all be coming to London."

"It was rather sudden. Lady Greentree decided it was time she paid her sister a visit, and we set out the next day."

"To pay Aunt Helen a visit or to check up on me?" Vivianna said drolly. "Well, I do not mind. I am so very glad to see you all."

Above them, at the top of the stairs, Lil gave a little cry of excitement and burst out, "Mr. Jardine, sir! I didn't know you was coming to London. Oh, I am that pleased to see you!"

Vivianna laughed at the maid's enthusiasm, and Lil blushed a fiery red. Mr. Jardine took the remaining stairs, and captured one of Lil's hands, as if she were a lady, and gave it a little pat. "Dear Lil, it is I who am pleased to see you, as always. Tell me, have you seen all the sights of London yet? Or are there still some I can show you?"

"I've seen the Tower and the zoo, sir," Lil said shyly.

"Well, that's a start."

Mr. Jardine was somewhere over forty, and still handsome, his skin browned from a life lived mostly in the West Indies. He had been an adventurer when he was young, and had made and lost a fortune, so it was said, although he spoke little of the matter himself. Now he was gazing down at Lil, a little smile on his lips—and Vivianna knew that he was very fond of her, but as a father might be fond of his daughter. He had been there when Vivianna brought Lil to Greentree Manor, and he felt a paternal responsibility toward her.

"Jacob is here, Lil. He drove the coach."

"Oh." Lil looked uncertain, and then she pursed her lips. "I hope he didn't come to see me. You know I will not marry him, Mr. Jardine. I am looking higher than a coachman."

Lil was twenty-five, a girl who had once lived on the streets and made her living from selling her body to men. She had regained her self-respect, and was fiercely loyal to the Greentree family, particularly Vivianna. Mr. Jardine had made it his task to look out for the girl, as he did all the Greentree servants, and he thought Jacob would make her a good husband. But Lil did not see it that way.

Mr. Jardine released her hand. "Well, I'd better get on, then, Lil, and leave you to your work. Miss Vivianna," he said with a small bow. And he strode off toward his room on business of his own. Lil gazed after him, and the look in her eyes was certainly not daughterly.

"Perhaps I should marry Jacob," Lil said miserably. "No other man'll have me. Not the man I want, anyway."

Mr. Jardine and Lil? Vivianna thought. Surely not. Not on Mr. Jardine's part anyway, even if Lil did nurture hopes. The chasm between them was great indeed, too great to breach.

"Lil, you will find someone," she said gently. "Just wait and see. If not Jacob, then another young man will come along, a handsome stranger who will sweep you off your feet!"

"You sound as if you've already been swept off yours, miss," Lil replied tartly.

Vivianna frowned. "Not at all, Lil. Quite the opposite, in fact." And she made her way down to the dining room for breakfast with her family.

"Helen has told me that things are not going very well with Lord Montegomery and the Shelter for Poor Orphans," Lady Greentree said, sipping her coffee.

Vivianna glanced sideways at Helen, but her aunt was busily spreading toast with marmalade.

"Unfortunately, he does not seem to be as easily persuadable as I had hoped, Mama. The Beatty sisters and I have decided we will have to take advantage of his offer of the lodging house in Bethnal Green—until something better comes along."

"Is he unpleasant? This Montegomery?"

"N-no, not unpleasant, not really. Just . . . stubborn." And for some reason she smiled; she couldn't help it.

Lady Greentree's eyes narrowed. "Oh? Then he's just like you, my dear."

Marietta giggled and, jumping up from her chair,

took a turn about the room. "Can we go to the shops, Mama? I want to buy a new bonnet and a gown and new shoes and—"

"For heaven's sake, Marietta, sit down! I am exhausted and I am not going anywhere for at least a day. You will have time enough to go looking at the shops tomorrow. I am sure Vivianna will be happy to accompany you."

Then Lady Greentree turned to her sister, taking advantage of a private chat while Toby was not there. Marietta came and sat closer to Vivianna, her bright blue eyes shining with mischief.

"I know you haven't told us everything," she whispered, so that the others could not hear her. "You have fallen violently in love with Lord Montegomery, haven't you? Mama heard from one of her London friends that he is very handsome and a terrible rake. She was so worried you might fall under his spell that she came to keep guard on you. Like one of the beefeaters at the Tower of London. *I* would like to fall under the spell of a rake. Have you? What is it like?"

"Marietta, will you be quiet!" Vivianna gasped. "You are talking nonsense. I have not fallen under anyone's spell, and he is not a . . . well, maybe he is, but I came here to try to persuade him not to demolish the shelter. It is just that it is taking longer than I had hoped."

"But he *is* handsome? I know he is. Your mouth is all primed up, like it always is when you're telling fibs."

Vivianna didn't know whether to laugh or cry. "Yes, Marietta, he is good-looking, but it is of no consequence. I don't notice that when I am with him. I am too busy thinking of more important things."

Marietta frowned, looked doubtful, and then

sighed. "Well, I think that is very dull of you, Vivianna. If I met a rake I would make the most of it, and I wouldn't be talking about any old shelters!"

Later, Lady Greentree had some time alone with Vivianna. "I *was* worried," she admitted, her pale eyes, so like Helen's, searching her elder daughter's. "And besides, Marietta was driving me to madness with her pestering. I thought we should come to London for a little while, just to see all was well with you, and to give her a chance to work it out of her system."

"There was no need to worry," Vivianna assured her, while knowing in her heart there were plenty of reasons. If her mother knew half of what she had done, she would be appalled and insist she return to Yorkshire with them immediately.

That was why she had decided not to tell her.

"Maybe not, but I must admit I feel better having seen so for myself. Oh, I forgot, Francesca has sent you her latest watercolor." She fetched out a small bleak picture of the moor, with a single stunted tree as its centerpiece, flattened against the gales.

Vivianna looked at it in dismay. "I think she is getting worse," she said.

Lady Greentree smiled. "I am sure she is. But I think she has a real talent all the same. Remember, she is but fifteen; in a few years' time, she will be just like any other girl, painting pretty cottages and . . . and kittens."

Vivianna laughed. "I think you are being optimistic, Mama, but I hope you are right. I do not think I could bear to have any more of her watercolors—they bring down my spirits."

Lady Greentree sighed. "They do, rather, don't they?"

"We are all of us different, aren't we?" Vivianna

went on thoughtfully. "Marietta is vivacious and lively and full of mischief, whereas Francesca is solitary and dramatic and intense, and I . . . well, I am headstrong and difficult and . . ."

Lady Greentree took her hand and held it tightly. "You are passionate and caring and determined, my dear, and it does you credit. Believe me, I would not change any of you."

For a moment Vivianna was tempted to tell her mother everything, but she stilled her tongue. What was the use of upsetting her? Comforting as it would be to unburden herself of her secrets, it would only lead to more trouble. Vivianna told herself that she had created this situation, and she must extricate herself from it.

After Oliver had left Vivianna he had gone to one of his clubs, and then another. He had thought of calling upon her again in Queen's Square despite the late hour, but she would refuse to see him.

So he had gone on to play cards at White's, and then to watch some fistfighting at the Bucket of Blood. Both occupations bored him, though, and he was home again long before midnight. He ignored Hodge's long-suffering look and sat morosely in the library, trying to get drunk. And that was where he went to sleep.

And dreamed.

Strangely, in the dream he was running through Candlewood. His feet were slapping against the wooden floors on the upper story, bare feet, as though he had just risen from his bed and forgotten to put on his slippers. There was someone behind him. Someone following him, relentless in pursuit.

He knew then that he was running for his life.

There was something in his hand. Some papers. Letters? Thick paper and black ink, clutched in his fingers. Instinctively he knew it was the letters that whoever was behind him was seeking.

Down the uncarpeted servants' stairs, dark and narrow. In front of him was the door to the unfinished wing of the house, and he wrenched it open and went through.

He ran on.

There was a huge mural on the ceiling with gods in battle armor and nymphs in not very much at all. He heard the sounds of pursuit, and knew in his heart that soon he was going to die. But, he told himself desperately, if he hid the letters, if he left a clue, then his brother would find them and avenge his death.

His brother, whom only hours before he had felt betrayed him. But now, in his moment of great peril, his feelings were redefined, made simple. He knew his brother loved him. Just as he loved his brother.

He turned again. There was a huge mirror on the wall, tarnished and cracked, but he could see into it. He could see himself.

Anthony. It was Anthony who stared back at him. Anthony, in the last moments of his life.

The dream began to fade.

Oliver struggled to retain it, to keep himself within it, but he was spinning away, the room revolving, his brother's face growing pale and distant below him.

"No!"

Oliver sat up in the library, his heart pounding, his breath heaving, the sweat dripping from him. He was alone, he thought, glancing to the dying fire and the smoking candles. All alone. He should be reassured by the fact, but he wasn't.

He wanted someone to turn to and hold. He wanted a warm body beside him in bed at night. He wanted someone to smile when he smiled, and show concern when he was sad.

He wanted Vivianna.

He might not trust her, but he could not seem to stifle the feelings he had for her. Whatever she felt for him, he wanted her, and yet for her own sake he must stay away from her.

I'll tell her the truth first. I must. I have to warn her about Lawson. And after that I won't see her again, ever . . .

Vivianna was late retiring, but despite her confused thoughts, or perhaps because of them, she sought out the diary given to her by Aphrodite, and settled down to read.

Aphrodite was older now, and Jemmy had gone off to be a soldier and fight the French. She found it strange and difficult at first, learning to be all that she had admired. Because there were so many French émigrés about, it had been decided that she should play at being one.

> *The gentlemen like French ladies in distress.*
>
> *In time, I moved on to other lovers. There were always gentlemen willing to share my life, for the sake of a moment of kindness or passion. And it was interesting and exciting, and I had many beautiful things. Once I returned to Seven Dials to visit my mother, but the rotting houses seemed worse than ever, and I could tell she did not want to see me. I never returned, but out of that visit something good came.*
>
> *I saw Elena again, my friend from the days in the slop-shop.*

She was pleased and happy to see me, and asked to hear my stories. I wanted to help her, and though at first she was uncertain whether to trust me, in time we grew close again. I bought her a place in which to sell her clothing, and she began to make my dresses. When I wore them to the theater or the opera, others would admire them, and I would give them her name.

In such a way are fortunes and reputations made and lost.

At first I did not miss Jemmy. I cannot pretend that I wanted that life back, when the new one was so full of color and excitement. Only sometimes, in the dark of the night, I would dream of Jemmy and his smiling face, and wake suddenly, wondering where he was. Dead, I thought. And if his voice called out to me from the throat of some man in the street, or I caught a glimpse of him in the face of a groom, then I would think, "Ah, it is the ghost of Jemmy."

Because despite my many friends and lovers, and my jewelry and pretty things, I am alone. I am always alone.

Vivianna closed the diary. There was no more to read—Aphrodite had not written any more—and her tale's moral was one Vivianna already knew. It was not jewels or pretty things that made one happy; it was the people with whom one shared one's life.

Oliver would make her happy.

His voice was the one that called to her in the darkness, just as Jemmy's had called to Aphrodite. It was his ghost she saw, his smile that made her smile. She lay in her bed and felt her body tingle and ache for his, and knew that there would never come a time when she did not miss him. Even when she was an old lady, she would be thinking of him, dreaming of him, and wanting him beside her.

So what on earth was she going to do about it?

But in her secret heart Vivianna already knew.

Vivianna was just setting out with her sister for the promised assault upon the London shops when Oliver called to see her. Unfortunately, they were standing in the hall awaiting the coach, or Vivianna might have managed to put him off or receive him alone. As it was, Marietta's eyes lit up like blue beacons when the maid showed him in. Fortunately, he seemed to have regained his senses.

Vivianna kept her voice cool and polite as she introduced him, despite the fact that the sight of him made her tremble. Marietta shot her a look that said: *Now I know you were fibbing!*

"I am pleased to meet you, Miss Marietta," Oliver said, taking Marietta's hand and bowing over it. His smile held its usual charm, his attire and person was immaculately turned out—apart from a savage red waistcoat—but Vivianna thought he looked fraught. Perhaps she looked the same.

He had attuned her body to his touch, and now she found she could not do without him.

"Vivianna and I are about to go shopping," Marietta was bubbling on, as he bent his head attentively toward her. "Perhaps you could escort us, Lord Montegomery?"

"It would be my pleasure, Miss Marietta, but I fear I have a prior engagement."

"Oh no. Can you not cancel it?"

"Marietta!" Vivianna admonished, her face fiery. "Remember your manners. Lord Montegomery is not interested in ladies' clothing!"

Oliver glanced at her, and something in the depths of his blue eyes made her breath catch in her breast. It was as if the heat of their passion was replaying in her head. His mouth on hers, his hands and his body. *She could not look away. . . .*

"Mama! It is Lord Montegomery." Marietta's voice broke the spell between them, and Vivianna turned shakily toward her mother, feeling as if she might fall over.

"Mama, this is Lord Montegomery," Vivianna said dutifully. "My lord, this is Lady Greentree, my mother." She did not look at him again, not directly. She did not dare.

Oliver smiled his charming smile and bowed over her mother's hand. Vivianna saw the uncertain look on her mother's face, the quick glance to her, the fear that her daughter had become entangled with this elegant rake. Vivianna understood her mother's concern. Toby was rake enough for any family—they did not need another.

"You have business in London, Lady Greentree?" Oliver asked her, polite, interested, the perfect gentleman. Only Vivianna felt his lapse of attention, saw the tension in his shoulders and his jaw, sensed the urgency in him to be alone with her. She did not know whether to be sorry or glad.

"I have come to support my daughter, Lord Montegomery."

"Of course."

"I believe you will not give in to her pleas regarding the orphans' shelter?"

"I'm afraid that is impossible."

They sized each other up, and then Lady Greentree sighed. "I see."

"I . . . that is, the Beatty sisters ask that you make all ready for them at Bethnal Green," Vivianna said stiffly. "We will have to avail ourselves of your generosity until we find somewhere else more suitable."

Oliver raised his eyebrows. "I think you will find the house at Bethnal Green more than suitable, Miss Greentree."

Vivianna's eyes narrowed at him, and she forgot her longing for him in a spurt of righteous anger. "Miss Greta has been to visit and she does not believe that to be the case. Children should not be made to live in such squalid surroundings."

Oliver looked blank. "When did she visit the house in Bethnal Green?"

"I do not know. Some weeks ago, I think."

"Ah." He gave her a little smile.

"What do you mean, ah?" Vivianna demanded.

Lady Greentree hissed her name in displeasure, and Marietta giggled with excitement. But Vivianna ignored them, and Oliver took her lead.

"I mean she has not visited since I made the repairs. I think you will find the lodging house is now more than suitable for your children, Miss Greentree."

"More than—"

"No, no, don't thank me."

Vivianna's eyes shot fire. "Thank you!"

"You must forgive my daughter, Lord Montegomery," Lady Greentree said quietly. "When it comes to her children she can be formidable, and sometimes she forgets her manners."

"That's because she was an abandoned child herself," Marietta announced. "Francesca and I were, too, but we were too young to remember it. Vivianna looked after us. She's been looking after abandoned children ever since."

"Please, Marietta, Lord Montegomery isn't interested in ancient history."

Oliver was looking at her. She could feel his eyes on her profile. "I wonder," he said, "if I might have a word with you alone, Miss Greentree?"

"Oh." Vivianna looked at her mother. "We were just going out."

Lady Greentree raised her brows. "Perhaps a very brief word, my lord. As my daughter says, we were just about to go out."

"Of course, I will be as brief as possible."

Stiff-backed, Vivianna led the way into a small parlor that was rarely used. Vivianna had chosen it, not for its lack of comfort, but for its distance from her mother's listening ears. However, she did not shut the door.

"Vivianna," he said gently, "why didn't you tell me about your childhood?"

"It wasn't important. Besides, would it have made you change your mind?"

He gave an elegant shrug.

"Then I was wise not to discuss my past with you."

He touched her shoulder, then tried to draw her closer, but she remained rigid and unbending.

"I want to ask you something," Vivianna said, and heard her own voice like a stranger's. Was she really going to do this? Was she really going to suggest Oliver use his expertise upon her? No, she wasn't, Vivianna reminded herself. She was going to take what Oliver offered and enjoy herself, totally, for one night. And then . . . she would say goodbye to him, and mean it.

"You can ask me anything you wish."

So reasonable! "I find I—I cannot sleep," she said evenly, although her heart was thudding. She turned her face away. "No doubt you have performed some spell upon me that makes it so. I want to sleep peacefully again. I need you to . . ."

His eyes flared, and he bent his head, his breath warm on her lips. "Meet me."

"Yes, I will meet you," she said a little desperately. His mouth brushed hers, the kiss so light, so teasing, it was barely there. "But it will be difficult. Mama will be watching."

As if to give credence to her concerns, Lady Greentree called out, "Vivianna! We are waiting."

Oliver brushed her lips again, maneuvering himself so that he could see into her eyes. "I need to speak to you," he said. "It's important."

She laughed a little wildly. "I need more than words, Oliver. It is my belief that a woman should live her life as she sees fit, and not be forced into marrying a man simply because she wishes to have him in her bed. Men are not governed by such things, so why should women be? I have never had a man in my bed and now I find I am very curious as to what happens in such situations. I am . . . attracted to you. I would like it to be you who . . ."

Oliver blinked. "If you're saying what I think you're saying, then I accept."

Vivianna eyed him uncertainly, but he seemed sincere. She stated her terms. "For a single night. Just one night with an experienced rake, Oliver, that is all I require. I will not be your kept woman or your soiled dove. Nothing of that nature. It will be a night of passion, both of us free and untrammeled by the rules of society, and then we will separate with only our memories."

"I have told you I accept." He looked almost relieved, and the idea that he would not argue or resist, or plead for longer, hurt her. But Vivianna said nothing—she had made the rules, after all. It would be ungracious of her to now argue against them. . . .

"I don't want you to agree to something you later regret," she burst out, and couldn't seem to help it.

"Vivianna," he groaned. "How can I regret it? I've wanted you ever since I met you. I'm hardly likely to refuse."

"Oh."

Deliberately he bent his head and took her mouth with his. It was the kiss of a desperate man, but it made clear its message. When he had finished, Vivianna was breathless and weak.

"Oh yes," he said grimly, "I want you."

"Wherever, whenever?"

"Vivianna!" Lady Greentree's voice was anxious. In a moment she would come and fetch her.

He smiled. "Yes."

"Then I will meet you tonight."

"What about Lady—"

"I will manage."

"Then meet me tonight, outside, around the corner. At ten o'clock."

"Vivianna?" Footsteps.

"Coming, Mama!" Vivianna hurried out into the hall, her skirts rustling about her. Oliver followed more slowly.

"We must go," Lady Greentree said impatiently, her gaze all over them.

Oliver took Vivianna's hand, his fingers closing so firmly on hers it was almost painful. "Goodbye, Miss Greentree," he said. And then he had released her, turned politely to her mother and sister, and the door had closed behind him. There was a little silence, before Marietta broke it.

"Oh, I do like him! You are lucky, Vivianna!"

"Don't be ridiculous." Vivianna could feel her face turn fiery red.

Lady Greentree was pulling on her gloves. "He is very good-looking, my dear, but . . . I cannot help but wonder what his aim is, in making himself so agreeable to you. Why come here as if he is our friend, when he is refusing to do as you ask? And why do you receive him as one?"

"He is being polite, that is all," Vivianna said quietly. "He was born a gentleman, Mama."

"But is he one now?"

Lady Greentree was thinking of Toby Russell, who also went by the title of "gentleman." And she could not blame her for that—had she not also been afraid Oliver and Toby were very much alike? Only it no longer mattered. The fact that Oliver was a rake would make her night with him even more memorable.

She would give herself to him, she would set the seductress in herself completely free, and she would not allow a single doubt or fear to spoil it. And tomorrow, well, she would walk away from him forever.

Vivianna allowed the realization to trickle through her, soothing her fears, accepting the inevitable.

"You should have no concerns for me in regard to Lord Montegomery, Mama," she said firmly. "I do not expect to see much more of him."

Lady Greentree stared at her hard a moment more and then looked away. The line of her mouth was sad, as though she feared the worst. "Very well, my dear."

Guilt assailed Vivianna. She was deceiving those she loved.

"Come on, you two!" cried Marietta. "Let's go shopping!"

Chapter 16

Marietta was determined to see every fashionable shop in Regent Street—from drapers and dressmakers to shoemakers and bonnet warehouses—and it was afternoon when they finally headed for home. Loaded down with parcels and packages and boxes, and with Marietta suffering from a headache—she was prone to them when overexcited—they reached Queen's Square.

"I think I shall put Marietta to bed," Lady Greentree said, removing her bonnet and tossing it onto a chair in the hall. "And then I will lie down, too, until supper."

"You should not let her run you ragged, Mama."

Lady Greentree smiled, her gray eyes lighting. "I know, but she is such a dear girl. Not an ounce of spite in her. If she was vain and full of self-importance, than maybe I would be firmer, but she isn't. Most of the presents she has bought are for all of us and her friends at home. You know it is so, Vivianna."

Vivianna sighed. Marietta was a dear girl, it was

true, and no doubt as she grew older her temperament would grow calmer and more considered. It was just that Vivianna herself had never been like Marietta. She had always felt far older than her years, with the responsibilities of her family, and the world, heavy upon her. It was only lately, since she had met Oliver, that she had felt young. And happy. As if, for the first time in her twenty years, she knew what it was to be a young woman. To look at the world with young eyes.

To be a woman in love with a man.

"You go up and rest, Mama," she said now, gently. "I will fetch you some tea from the kitchen. Aunt Helen hasn't enough servants to run after us all, I am afraid, so I help when I can."

"You are a sweet girl," Lady Greentree said, and kissed her cheek. "I do not know what I would do without you all. I am very fortunate, my dear."

"As are we."

"I . . . do not take this amiss, Vivianna, but you have not been much out in the world. Oh, I know you have done a great deal to help those less fortunate, and that you have seen the seamier side of life. But you have remained innocent in matters concerning young gentlemen. I would not want to see you hurt by someone who is undeserving of you."

Vivianna managed a smile. "I promise you, Mama, that I would not let anyone undeserving hurt me."

Lady Greentree nodded. "Good," she said.

Vivianna watched her make her weary way upstairs. Guilt seemed now to be her constant companion, but she knew it would not prevent her from finding her way out tonight. She felt a little nervous, of course she did, but she also felt alive. Intoxicated.

This was to be her one night, her only night.

And Oliver would be awaiting her.

* * *

The coach *was* waiting. No insignia, nothing to show who it belonged to. As she approached, the door opened, and Oliver reached out and drew her in. The driver's whip cracked and the horses' hooves clattered away over the stones.

Vivianna leaned back in the corner. It was dark, but she could see the shape of his face, the shine of his eyes. Her voice was breathless when she asked, "Where are we going?"

"I have arranged for somewhere special."

"Oh."

"Don't worry, Vivianna. You will enjoy it. We will both enjoy it."

Vivianna didn't answer. Now that the time had come, she found she was very nervous indeed.

The gloom of the coach was claustrophobic, and as she huddled smaller into her corner, Vivianna knew she could not stay like this. By the time they reached their destination, she would be too anxious and frightened to come out. This was meant to be a night of celebration, of intense enjoyment.

She should begin as she meant to go on.

Vivianna closed her eyes and took a deep breath. *Let the seductress free,* she thought. *Pretend I am a courtesan like Aphrodite. What would she do in such a situation as this? She would not cower in the corner and hope for the best. She would take charge.*

Vivianna shut her mind to doubts and let herself *feel* instead. And what she felt was Oliver's presence, and what she wanted to do was touch him. Instinctively she reached out and rested her hands gently just above his knees, and before he could do more than catch his breath, she was sliding her fingers along his thighs, feeling the hard muscles shift and contract.

It felt good; *he* felt good.

So hard and strong, so different from her own body. Before she realized it, Vivianna found herself dropping to the floor of the coach, using his knees as support. "Vivianna," he groaned. His body was frozen, rigid, but she could hear him breathing. Heavily.

"I just want to touch," she whispered. She leaned forward and rubbed her face against his inner thigh. He was so warm and hard and the sensation of having him in her power was intoxicating. Vivianna smiled. In the dim light from the coach lamp, she could see before her clear evidence of his desire for her: the outline of his swollen member beneath the cloth of his trousers.

Vivianna did not allow herself to think. She stretched out her hand and stroked her fingers over him. Lightly. Curiously.

He made a sound in his throat, as if he weren't sure whether to urge her on or tell her to halt. He hardly seemed to be breathing at all now. She brushed her fingertips over him again, more firmly this time, exploring the shape of him, her eyes closed, the better to imagine those dimensions. He quivered beneath her, and then his hand rested lightly upon her hair.

She wondered if it was really possible to seduce a rake. A dichotomy, surely? And yet Oliver Montegomery seemed more than happy to allow her to continue. She found the buttons that closed the flap of his trousers and began to slide them from their fastenings, one at a time.

"What is his name?" she whispered. "What do you call this part of your body?"

His laugh was husky and strained. "The Duke."

"Why the Duke?"

"Because he is arrogant and demanding."

"Oh."

Vivianna was breathing quickly, and she realized with surprise that she had become intoxicated and aroused by what she was doing. The feel of him, the scent of him, the knowledge that he was excited had all served to urge her on to be bolder than she had ever been before.

Vivianna eased her fingers within and discovered that, like herself, Oliver wore no undergarments. The thick, hard length of him filled her hand. So warm, so alive, so big. It was nothing like the illustrations she had seen in that wretched pamphlet. For a moment she simply held him, caressing him, enjoying the velvet strength of him. And then she bent forward and pressed her mouth to him.

"Vivianna," he groaned, a mixture of wonder and pleasure.

"I want to," she murmured.

She felt voluptuous, powerful, all woman. Vivianna licked him with her tongue, tasting him, enjoying the smooth velvet skin that ran from root to tip. He arched his body slightly toward her, and she took him in her mouth.

It was too much for him, evidently. He caught her up, his hands gripping her beneath her arms, and bore her backward, onto the seat behind her. His weight came down upon her, and her breath whooshed out. "Damn, I'm sorry. . . ." At once he eased up, supporting himself, but he was still heavy as he lay over her.

"I'm all right." The unfamiliar position wasn't uncomfortable. She was his prisoner, and yet she knew she was perfectly free to tell him to get off her. She just didn't want to.

Oliver was looking down at her, examining her in the dim light of the coach lamp. He ran his fingers across her temple, down the side of her face, and traced the shape of her lips. She opened them and took his thumb between her teeth.

He smiled. And then he was kissing her with a desperation that told her more than words could just how much he wanted her.

"Hmm," Vivianna sighed. His mouth was hot and open against hers, and then he was branding her throat and shoulders and the swell of her breasts above the line of her bodice.

"No stays," he murmured, his hands cupping her, his thumbs rubbing the hard buds of her nipples. "What other surprises do you have for me, Miss Greentree?"

Vivianna smiled and then gasped as his mouth closed over her breast through the cloth of her dress. His teeth teased her, gently, and she gripped his shoulders, her head arched back. When he took his mouth away, the cloth felt damp, cool, against her aching flesh. His hand had found its way beneath her skirts, and he had bundled them up, so that she felt the cloth of his trousers against her bare thigh.

"You really must wear your undergarments," he drawled, and she felt the heat of his palm sliding over her belly. Vivianna shivered, unable to help herself, as he neared his goal.

"There," she told him breathlessly. "Please, touch me there. . . ."

Obediently his fingers slid between her bare thighs, a feather-light touch, teasing aside the folds to find the place where she wanted him most. But he was gone again in a moment, caressing her hip, her knee, kneading the cheek of her bottom.

"Oliver," she whispered urgently. "You didn't touch me."

"I did. I will. Be patient, Vivianna."

His finger continued to tease, returning to stroke her for a moment, and then, just when she felt the quivering inside her, the climb to completion, he moved away, finding some other, less sensitive spot. She shifted restlessly, aching, then sighing with relief when his fingers returned again. Once he used his cock to touch her, sliding it through her soft curls, circling the entrance to her body, promising her so much. As the coach rattled toward its unknown destination, Vivianna lay gasping and twisting beneath him, calling his name plaintively, not sure whether to kiss him or to bite him.

"Oliver," she groaned, "you must . . . you must do it now. I can't wait."

Oliver settled himself between her thighs and looked down into her flushed, beautiful face. Vivianna Greentree. His nemesis, his curse. And very probably the love of his life.

He pushed his cock into her, as gently as he could, wanting to be tender—the practiced and perfect lover—and yet the beast inside him needing to have her all, right now, to make her his. She surged against him, too aroused to care if he was hurting her. He held back, easing himself in farther, groaning at the exquisitely tight, hot fit of her, until he felt the membrane that he must break. Oliver bent and kissed her mouth, and felt her immediate and eager response.

Vivianna Greentree was more than ready.

Oliver plunged himself inside her fully, and experienced the mixed torment of knowing he had hurt her and the aching joy of knowing he was the first. She went still, and cried out against his lips. He held her, kissing her, soothing her, but in a surprisingly short time she was kissing him back, her hands running through his hair, rubbing against his back, pulling his shirt from his trousers, and sliding up over his skin. And then she lifted her hips, opening her thighs, and pushed up against him with a sound in her throat like a purr.

Oliver shuddered as her sheath clenched around him. He had held back long enough; he could hold back no more. With a deep breath he withdrew from her and drove deep. And then again. The movement was smooth and steady and required all of his control and his skill. She was so hot, so tight, he wanted to plunder her like some ravening barbarian, but again he kept the beast in check. She was a virgin, she was a gentlewoman, and she deserved the best of him.

This was her one and only night with him, after all.

And his with her.

Vivianna was beyond thought now. She was pushing up against him, seating him deeper and deeper. He felt her stretch, then he felt the muscles inside her begin to contract, tightening around him. The pleasure roared through him, begging for release, but he held on, driving into her again and again.

And then she cried out, a sharp wail of ecstasy. Vivianna went to pieces, arching against him, her arms clutching him to her. Oliver stopped and held her as her climax rippled into calm, and then he began to thrust again. His heart was pounding so loudly he could not hear above it, his body was screaming to let go, and so he did. With a deep, low moan, Oliver gave himself to her.

For a time after that there was silence.

Stillness. Repletion.

And wonder.

Tenderly he lifted her into his arms, and knew he had never felt like this before for any woman. He cradled her against his chest as he sat propped up at one end of the seat, his legs spread out along it, her own legs between them, her voluminous skirts covering them both. Vivianna was limp. She was momentarily beyond even speech, thought Oliver with a smile.

"You smell wonderful," he said, and nuzzled her hair. And she did. Like no woman he had ever known before. She was unique. He knew he would recognize her blindfolded.

Vivianna chuckled and burrowed closer into his arms. He was content, he thought, just to hold her, but then her full breast brushed against him and he found himself cupping it, rolling the nipple in his fingers.

She stroked the back of his hand and made a sound in her throat. "Where are we going?"

"A place I know. We're nearly there."

He found her other breast, and now he was hard again, but this time he would have to wait. Oliver supposed that a gentleman would have waited for the first time, too, but she had been so hot, so ready, it had made more sense to make use of that eagerness. The losing of a woman's virginity could be a painful business, so he had heard, and the less time she had to think about it, the better.

Besides—he smiled to himself—he was no gentleman, not tonight. Tonight, Oliver was the ultimate rake.

Vivianna had not known what to expect when they arrived at their destination, but the Anchor Inn, a remote and extremely selective establishment overlooking the Thames, was as discreet as it was sophisticated. She had no time to feel conscious of her dishevelment or embarrassed by her situation. A bowing gentleman and two maids took them immediately upstairs to their room, where food and drink was laid out, warm water and towels were quickly brought, and the door was then closed firmly behind them.

They were alone.

That was when the shyness and unease that Vivianna had felt when she first entered the coach returned to her. It was strange, she thought with a little shiver, but suddenly it was as if the hot, earthy love they had made was a dream. In the dim light, driving through the night, it had seemed safe, somehow. Now, here alone with Oliver, in the bright light of lamps and with a bed the size of India, Vivianna was very uncertain. She was even wondering whether she had made a rather dreadful mistake.

The fire in the grate was burning merrily. She went and held her hands to it, avoiding looking at him. The warmth helped a little, but the chill seemed to be inside her.

She did not hear him come up behind her, but when his hands rested upon her shoulders she jumped. *Oh please,* she thought, squeezing her eyes tight shut. *Don't pounce on me now. I don't think I could play at being the courtesan again so soon. Whatever strength I found has vanished. Where are you, seductress? Where have you gone now I need you?*

"You should take off your cloak," he said matter-of-factly. He didn't sound as if he was going to rip off her clothes and fling her onto the bed. Vivianna allowed him to unfasten the cloak and slide it from her shoulders. "That's better," he said softly, and stirred a memory of those same words, spoken by her once, when they were also alone together.

"What is this place?"

"The Anchor. It's famous for assignations between people who don't want it known they are lovers. These walls keep their secrets, and more importantly, so does the owner and his staff. Gloves."

For a moment she didn't understand him, and then she realized what he wanted and automatically held out her hands. He tugged off the gloves she had pulled back on before they exited the coach.

"I did not realize such places existed," she said, avoiding his eyes.

He smiled, his handsome mouth curling upward, his eyes narrowing in that sleepy way that made her heart thud faster. "They've always existed," he said. "Hairpins."

Vivianna reached up and touched her braids. "Oh. I . . ."

"Never mind, I'll do it." He reached up and slipped out the pins, and her braids fell down her back. "Prince Albert wants to close places like the Anchor down," he went on, as quickly he raked his fingers through her plaits, freeing the twists of hair, shaking it out into a thick chestnut curtain about her shoulders. "That's better," he whispered, and his eyes gleamed.

"Close them down?" Vivianna repeated nervously, glancing at him sideways. "Even Aphrodite's Club?"

"Especially Aphrodite's Club. Now your dress. . . ." He was already unfastening the back, loosening the bodice. "He does not believe in immorality, and being a happily married man himself he does not think it necessary."

"Can he do that? Close down Aphrodite's? I do not like to think that Madame might be driven away from London."

The dress slipped over her shoulders to her waist. She wasn't wearing stays, but her chemise covered her adequately. "I think he would find that a great many of the court and the government are members of

Aphrodite's," Oliver said wryly. "Petticoats." She felt his fingers on the ties, and the dress and petticoats fell to the floor at her feet.

She was almost naked, Vivianna realized with surprise. He had stripped her after all, and she had been too involved in his conversation to really notice. But now the fire was warm against her bare arms and through the thin silk of her chemise. Only his hands were warmer. He knelt at her feet and, already having removed her slippers, had wrapped his fingers about her ankle. He looked up at her, his eyes very dark.

"Stockings," he said quietly. Vivianna bit her lip as he ran his fingers up over the curve of her calf to her knee, and found the ribbon that kept her stocking from falling down. The bow undone, he drew the stocking down over her bare skin slowly, caressing her with his movements. She lifted her foot for him, her hand upon his shoulder for balance. He smiled, and then proceeded to remove the other stocking.

Vivianna found her breathing had quickened. Her skin was tingling with awareness, flushed from the fire's heat. There was an ache in her breasts, and the place between her legs throbbed a little, so that she wanted to squeeze her thighs together.

"Now," Oliver said, rising once more to his feet, "that leaves your chemise."

"Oliver," she gasped, "I don't know if—"

"I want to see you naked," he said implacably, and ran his hands down over her bare arms, smoothing her creamy flesh.

"I find I am suddenly shy," she said stiffly. "Silly, I know, after what we have just done."

He didn't laugh, although he bit his lip. Vivianna gave him a narrowed look, and he appeared contrite. "I'm sorry. You're so beautiful, so exactly perfect, I didn't think you could be shy." His hands reached to encircle her waist, then cupped the rounded cheeks of her bottom. "All perfect," he murmured, and pressed his body against hers. Vivianna could feel him jutting against her belly, hard and erect, and she knew he wanted her, and the thought of it brought a hot flood of sensation to her own body, chasing away the doubts.

His hands were cupping her breasts now, squeezing gently, molding the flesh to his palms. "Gorgeous," he whispered, and kissed the curve of her shoulder where it joined her neck. Vivianna tilted her head and shivered, and then groaned as he tugged at her nipples. One of his hands stroked downward, over the swell of her belly and down, down to the soft curls between her thighs.

"Oh yes," he growled softly, and stroked her there boldly through the silken cloth of the chemise. "Perfect."

Vivianna groaned, arching her back, opening her legs for him.

Her head was spinning, and it was a moment before she realized it was, because he had lifted her up in his arms and was carrying her toward the bed. An opulent piece of furniture, the bed was a four-poster with draperies in the deepest cherry red and a thick, soft quilt of the same color. A mountain of pillows and bolsters were piled at the head. Oliver swung her over the mattress and lay her down, and before she could even move a muscle, he had captured the hem of her chemise and stripped her of her final piece of clothing.

She lay naked, sprawled before him.

But instead of joining her, he stood over her, his gaze moving, caressing her, heating her flesh. The way he stared should have intimidated her, but it didn't. There was so much admiration and desire in his dark eyes, she felt beautiful and seductive. He had made her the woman she wanted to be, and now as he looked upon her, Vivianna stretched voluptuously, thrusting up her breasts, arching her back.

"Oh yes," he drawled, "I like it when you do that. I like it very much." There was no disguising the hot need in his face as he began to undress. He pulled off his jacket and then his white shirt, tossing them both on the floor. Then he unbuttoned his trousers and stripped them down over his strong legs, until he stood as naked as she.

Vivianna ogled him. She couldn't help it. She had never seen a naked man before. The sight of him caught in her chest, made her senses swim. He was tall and broad-shouldered, and his chest was hard-muscled and dark-haired. His belly was flatter than hers and his hips leaner, and his thighs strong and firm, and between them rose the part of him she had stroked and petted in the darkness of the coach.

Vivianna shivered, and suddenly the air in the room seemed heavier, hotter. Oliver came and stood at the edge of the bed and clasped her knees, opening her legs wide and drawing her toward him. She thought of struggling, but he was gazing upon her most intimate places with such a fierce, hungry look that she was shaken. He stooped and covered her with his mouth.

"Oliver!" she wailed. The pleasure was intense, and suddenly she knew that she wasn't going to be able to stop the rippling, pounding climax that was about to take over her.

When she came back to herself, he had pulled her over to the side of the bed so that her legs dangled down. It was a very high bed, exactly the right height so that when he lifted her hips and moved between her thighs, he was able to slide his cock into her.

Vivianna gasped. She wanted to look away, but there was something completely and utterly fascinating about the sight of his body entering hers, sliding so slickly into her and out again. The muscles in his arms tightened, his thighs were hard and tense as he held her before him. A living, breathing, and oh so willing sacrifice. Oliver's hands gripped her more firmly and he quickened his pace, thrusting still deeper. He was watching, too, his narrow, sensuous gaze fixed upon the joining of their bodies, and Vivianna could tell it excited him as much as her.

She realized that her passion was building again, when only a moment ago she had thought herself limp with completion. "I didn't think a man could make love more than once a night," she gasped.

"This man can," he growled.

And suddenly she knew she wanted to touch him, to press against him, to be in his arms. Vivianna pushed up with her hands on the mattress, struggling to sit, and immediately he stopped and drew her to him. He lifted her from the bed as if she weighed a feather, and she clung to his neck, her legs wrapped tight above his hips. Then he turned and sat upon the bed and eased across it, supporting her. Vivianna found herself seated in his lap facing him, her thighs resting upon his, her body still joined with his.

His skin was rough against hers, especially the dark hair of his chest. She bent her head and licked at him, tasting his salty sweat. And then the powerful muscles of his legs and arms cradled her, and he bent his head and claimed her mouth in a hot, erotic kiss.

Her breasts ached, and she pressed them against

him, enjoying the friction. She tangled her fingers in his dark hair, her mouth feeding from his, and let the moment slide. Slowly, in no hurry now, Vivianna moved against him, feeling the heavy length of him inside her, her sheath holding him tightly. He clasped her hips and thrust back, deeper, urging her to mimic his movements, and soon they were lost in the pleasure of their bodies and the only sounds in the room apart from the crackle of flames were gasps and groans and soft cries of completion.

Later, he fed her with pieces of food and dribbled champagne over her and licked it off her again. Vivianna laughed and lay atop his body, smiling down into his half-closed and decidedly wicked eyes. He taught her to ride him from on top and held her tight when she thought she was going to fly into the night sky with the wonder of it. And he bathed her body with warm scented water and patted her dry with a towel, and spooned her against him when she slept.

Vivianna had never felt so pampered, so replete, so wonderfully alive. She did not think of tomorrow. She did not want to. This was a moment out of time, a dream that could have no place in the real world. To think that anything more was possible was to let in pain and hurt, and Vivianna was too clever for that.

She had her rake and he had been more than she had hoped for, but soon they must part forever.

"Vivianna?"

Oliver was shaking her gently. "Vivianna, we must go." He was helping her up, pulling her clothing on, lifting her arms as if she were as helpless as a rag doll. Her body was stiff and sore, and once or twice she caught her breath in pain. "Poor sweetheart," he murmured, and kissed her temple, but she felt that he was mocking her, just a little.

He was a rake, after all, and Vivianna knew that you couldn't trust rakes.

When they reached the coach and climbed inside, she moved to her own corner, but he wasn't done with her yet. He sat beside her and pulled her into his arms.

She gave a feeble protest, but he laughed.

"I won't touch you if you don't want me to, Vivianna. I want to tell you something."

"I'm sore, Oliver. I don't say it wasn't worth it, but I don't think . . . What do you want to tell me?" She glanced up at his profile in the darkness.

"I want to tell you something very important. Are you listening?"

Suddenly he sounded so serious. She felt uneasy. "I'm listening," she said warily.

"Good. I want you to stay away from Lord Lawson. He is an extremely dangerous man. Do you understand? I am going to tell you something now that you must not repeat to anyone, especially not Lord Lawson."

"What is it?"

"Lawson killed my brother."

Weariness and shock combined to make it difficult for her to take in what he had said, but she did her best. "You mean it was an accident?"

"No, I mean he murdered him. Anthony had something Lawson wanted, something that would cause the ruin of his political career, and he killed him for it."

He was serious.

"Is that what you meant when you said you were going to avenge your brother? You meant Lord Lawson?"

"Yes. I'm going to bring him down, Vivianna. I'm

going to see him in a court of law, and then I want him hanged by the neck."

His voice was cold and deadly, and Vivianna suddenly had no doubt he meant what he said. This was an Oliver she had not seen before and it shocked her. Where was the rake with the lazy smile and mocking stare? Confused, she forced herself to listen as he went on.

"The night Anthony died he was coming to see me, to ask my advice. Some letters had come into his possession, letters concerning his friend Lord Lawson. Anthony did not feel comfortable about them, and he had thus far refused to return them to Lawson. But Celia was there, and Anthony walked out and made his way to Candlewood and the letters were forgotten. But not by Lawson. He followed Anthony there. I don't know exactly what happened. I suspect he demanded that Anthony return the letters and Anthony again refused. Perhaps he had decided to make them public. Lawson shot him, trying to make it seem like suicide, and then he looked for the letters. Only he couldn't find them. And over the following weeks and months he continued to search and still he could not find them."

Vivianna found her voice. "Where are they?"

"At Candlewood. My grandfather had a secret chamber built and Anthony knew of it. I suspect they are in there."

"And you don't—"

"No, I don't know where it is. I plan to take Candlewood apart stone by stone until I find it."

"What if you don't?"

Oliver looked down at her, and he was a stranger. All the warmth had gone from him. Suddenly she understood the sense of aloneness she had felt the first time she met him.

"I will. That is why Candlewood must be demolished, stone by stone, brick by brick."

Candlewood would not be saved. It could never be saved. She had been working toward something that was an impossibility in Oliver's eyes. Her heart plummeted with the realization, and suddenly she felt like a fool.

"When we met Lord Lawson at the opera . . ."

"I didn't want him to know who you were."

"You pretended to be drunk." She sat up straighter, cold now, the pleasures of the night forgotten. "You have been pretending all along, haven't you!"

To her horror, Oliver didn't deny it. "I didn't need the complications you brought with you. I wanted to frighten you away, Vivianna, by playing the bad man, but you wouldn't be frightened. I don't say I didn't enjoy it. But now it isn't safe any longer to continue with our little game. Lawson has his gaze fixed on you. He thinks he can use you to stop me from tearing down Candlewood and finding the letters. He pretends he's concerned for the orphans, but he isn't. Don't ever believe that. Lawson does nothing that does not benefit himself."

Vivianna was turning the information over in her mind. Well-worn memories, beloved scenes, returned to her, one after the other, but now they looked so different. They had taken on a new aspect, as if she had been looking at them from the wrong angle. When Oliver had followed her to Lady Chapman's meeting he had been playing a part. When he had taken her to the opera, he had been playacting. When he had made fierce love to her just now, it had been make-believe. He had said it was a game to him, and so it was.

Oliver was no more a lost soul than she! He had been pretending all along, and probably laughing at her behind her back.

"You're not a rake," she said tightly, and the pain in her chest made it hard to breathe.

"You're not happy with your one night in the arms of the lecherous scoundrel Oliver Montegomery?" he mocked. "I thought it was rather fine."

"Stop it," she whispered. Anger made her tremble, the heat rising up her throat and into her face. Tears blossomed in her eyes, but she blinked them back furiously. He would not make her cry, he would not.

"Well, I gave you what you wanted," he said in that cold, stranger's voice. "A night in the arms of an experienced rake. After this past year I feel I have the necessary qualifications."

He seemed to be waiting for something, but Vivianna did not know what it was. Her pride forced her voice to mimic his indifference.

"Yes, you were the perfect rake. I have no complaints. But now it is over, Oliver. You will understand if I say that I never want to see you again."

He gave a humorless laugh. "I understand, and I'm sure you will not take offense if I add that the feeling is mutual."

She nodded stiffly, then pulled away from him, moving back into her corner.

Her body ached, her head ached, but most of all her heart ached.

He had lied to her, fooled her, used her. She felt humiliated as she had never been before. Her night of wondrous passion had turned into a night of heartbreak, and the memory of it would never leave her. It had never been real, none of it, just as Oliver had never been real.

Vivianna knew to her despair that she had fallen in love with a man who did not even exist.

Dawn was breaking across London, and the street sweepers had long been up. The horses were weary, and so was Oliver. For the final part of the journey he had sat staring at nothing, aware of Vivianna's outraged silence nearby. He had fully intended her to be hurt. He had had to wound her so severely that she would not wish to see him again.

Knowing Vivianna as he did, Oliver had understood that if she believed him to be in need of her help she would never leave him. She would put herself at risk for his sake. He did not want that. If she was ever to be safe, then Lawson must believe that she was estranged from him. And Lawson was no fool—he would see through one of Vivianna's lies. It had to be the truth.

Well, now fiction had become fact. Vivianna hated him, and her hatred made her safe. She would never know how his heart ached, awash with regret and memories of the night he had just spent with her. A night he intended never to forget.

She must believe him a monster, but the fact was Oliver was suffering just as much as Vivianna. More, because he had to hide it. For her sake, he had to pretend. And he was so, so tired of being something he was not.

The coach drew to a halt. In a moment she was out of the door and jumping down to the street. She glanced back, her face white and pinched, her eyes dark hollows.

"I never want to see you again," she said bitterly. "Understand that, Oliver."

"Of course," he drawled, and lifted his eyebrows as if there had never been a question of it being otherwise.

She cast him one, last, fulminating look and then she was gone. Her slippers hardly made a sound as she reached the corner and turned. And then there was nothing, only silence and an empty street.

She couldn't know it, of course, he thought idly, but Vivianna had changed him. She had brought a sense of purpose back into his life. A sense of looking toward a future that held more than just the destruction of Lawson and the avenging of his brother.

He bit back a groan of despair. There was nothing he could do. "Drive on!" he called out, and the coach lurched forward.

Lil had left the back door unlatched, and Vivianna slipped in. There may be servants about, but she could pretend to be up early rather than in late. In this household, they were used to Toby coming in at all hours; probably no one would notice. In her room, Vivianna fell exhausted onto the soft mattress. She wondered how it was possible to feel so low, so humiliated, so utterly destroyed. She had given herself to Oliver, enjoyed the most wonderful night of her life, and in return he had shown her that it had all been a lie. A grand plan to avenge his dead brother.

How honorable of him! How brave! And how utterly, utterly selfish! Didn't he think she would mind? Or did he simply want her to fade away and let him get on with his wretched plot?

Vivianna felt as if she were dying, all the warmth and passion he had brought to the fore curling up and turning brittle. The ache from his lovemaking mocked her, taunted her, and broke her heart.

She had once feared that Oliver was as bad as Toby,

but now she realized he was worse. Oh, far, far worse. . . .

Another tear slid down her cheek but she turned into the pillow and rubbed it off. If she cried any more she would not be able to stop, and her mother must not see that she had been weeping. Nor her sister. She had never felt so *alone*. . . .

Vivianna lifted her head. There *was* a place she could go to. A person she could talk to. Someone who would not be shocked or appalled by the depths to which she had sunk.

Someone who would understand.

Chapter 17

Dobson answered the door in his red jacket, and his gray eyes widened in surprise at the sight of her.

"Miss Vivianna? Whatever is't? You look like you've seen a ghost."

"Dobson, is Miss Aphrodite here? I need to speak with her." And then, as if her lack of manners had just occurred to her, "Please."

He eyed her curiously, but whatever he saw caused him to stifle any questions. "You wait here a moment, and I'll see what I can do. We ain't long been closed, you know."

Vivianna realized then that Aphrodite, too, had been up all night.

"Thank you, Dobson," she whispered.

He touched her arm, his big fingers gentle, and then went to a door across the hall and gave a smart knock. "Miss Vivianna to see you, ma'am. I don't think she can wait."

There were steps behind the door, and then a girl

with a pretty, sulky face opened it. She winked at Dobson, pouted at Vivianna, and tripped away up the stairs. Aphrodite's familiar voice came from inside the room.

"Send Miss Greentree in to me, please, Dobson."

But Vivianna felt as if her feet had taken root. Seeing the other girl had reminded her what this place really was. A high-class brothel, where men came to satisfy their lusts. If, she thought miserably, they could not find a gullible virgin to do it for them.

And yet despite all that, despite her doubts, she knew this was where she had to be. She knew that Aphrodite would understand completely.

And that was what she needed right now.

Understanding.

"You go in, miss," Dobson said quietly, and his hand was on her arm again, leading her gently toward the door. "You go and tell Aphrodite what's the matter. She'll be able to help you."

Vivianna glanced at him.

Dobson nodded, as if to affirm it, and she took a deep breath before she brushed by him into the room.

It was a smallish and rather insignificant office. But Vivianna was not deceived. There may not be the opulence and the beauty here that was present in the other rooms of the house, but this was the business heart of Aphrodite's empire. It was from here that she controlled everything.

Aphrodite had been seated at the desk, but now, seeing Vivianna, she rose with a rustle of black skirts. Diamonds shimmered upon her fingers and about her throat. An ebony pendant rested upon the swell of her breasts. Her face seemed to blur and shimmer a little, as if it, too, were a precious stone, and too bright for

Vivianna's eyes. Her dark gaze narrowed and grew sharp.

"Whatever is the matter, *mon chou*?" she cried. Then, "You have read the diary? Is that it?"

Vivianna hardly heard her. "Miss Aphrodite," she said, "I need to speak with you. I really do need to speak to you now. I have come from Queen's Square, and I know I have not made a prior appointment. I know that. But I have to speak to you."

Aphrodite had reached her side. Her perfume was strong and sweet, and yet somehow comforting. She looked into Vivianna's face, her sharp eyes searching.

"What is it, Vivianna? Tell me, I am listening. I do not care for appointments and such. Tell me what has happened to you."

Vivianna drew a breath, and the pain in her heart made her gasp. "Oliver," she said. "He . . . Oh!"

The tears came then. Frustrated, Vivianna tried to stem them, to finish her sorry tale, but it seemed that nothing would keep them dammed. She put her face in her hands, but that just made it worse, because she began to sob from deep inside, and the sobs threatened to tear her apart.

Warm arms enveloped her and her face was pressed to a surprisingly fragile shoulder. She felt a kiss to her temple and a hand patted her back, as if she were a little girl again. And all the while Oliver's perfidy was creating havoc inside her.

"Oh, dear girl," whispered Aphrodite. "Poor child. What is it? What has this *cochin* done to you? Tell me now or I will think the worst."

"It is . . . it *is* the worst!"

"That you have lost your heart?"

"No," sobbed Vivianna, "no, I have lost my virginity."

Aphrodite stroked her hair and gave a little laugh. "Ah. Well, I do not think that is the worst, *mon chou.* I thought that was what you wanted."

"I did!" Vivianna gasped. "It was w-wonderful. He—he was w-wonderful. And then he told me that it had all been a game. He wasn't really a rake at all, but he is involved in some deep plot and he was simply trying to frighten me away."

"He didn't seem to be trying terribly hard, *mon chou. . . .*"

"But don't you see? He lied to me! All this time, he lied! And then when I asked him for my one night with a r-rake, he agreed, and all the time he was lying and probably laughing at me behind my back!"

Her voice ended on a wail of rage and pain, but although Aphrodite's arms tightened about her, her thoughts seemed to be elsewhere.

"I see."

"Of course I said I would never see him again. I said I hated him. But it was as if . . . as if he didn't even *care.*"

Aphrodite squeezed her tighter still. "Do not pay him any heed for now. We must do what is good for you, not for Oliver."

She sounded so sure, so confident. Vivianna felt her sobs subsiding. She took a shaken breath, and then another. Aphrodite led her to a chair and placed her upon it.

"Sit a moment," she said with gentle firmness. "Take a breath. Regain your calm, Vivianna."

"How can I?" she gasped. "I fell in love with a rake and now I learn he never existed. Oliver has taken my heart and now it is broken."

Aphrodite sighed. "I warned you, *mon chou.* 'Protect your heart.' Remember for the next time—people do not take hearts, they give them. Oliver did not take your heart, you gave it to him. There is a difference."

Vivianna opened her mouth, then closed it again. She was right. Of course she was right. And yet the pain was no better for it.

Aphrodite perched herself on the arm of the chair and slid her arm around Vivianna's shoulders.

"You probably think me callous," she said with humor. "But I assure you that is not the case, Vivianna. I do not think you are damaged in any way that truly matters. You are young and the world is big. You will find another man who loves you as you will love him. Oliver Montegomery is not the only *poisson* in the sea."

Vivianna nodded and tried to believe it.

"You are willful and passionate, and find it hard to curb those passions. I understand. I was so when I was a girl. But if you have read my diary you will know that. I thought I knew what I wanted, and so I took it. With maturity comes a calmer view of the world."

"You have come a long way," Vivianna said. "I know that. From Seven Dials to the Boulevard de la Madeleine."

"Oh yes, I have come a long way. But I have suffered, also. I have suffered much sorrow." She hesitated, and then said quietly, "I lost my children."

Vivianna looked up at her, wiping the tears from her face with her fingers. She could not remember crying so since she was a little girl and she had tried to keep her sisters from harm.

"You lost your children?" she whispered.

Aphrodite nodded, and her eyes were awash with sorrow.

"I was abandoned," Vivianna said, as more tears dribbled down her cheeks.

"No!" Aphrodite's voice was harsh, and suddenly she gripped Vivianna tightly, almost painfully, against the black silk of her gown. "You were never abandoned! You were stolen. Taken from your mother by a cruel and wicked man."

What is she saying?

Vivianna's head had begun to ache from crying. Surely she hadn't heard properly, or maybe she hadn't understood. What cruel and wicked man?

"Your mother was not at home, but she thought her daughters were in good hands. There were loyal servants to care for them, and she did not believe they could be in any danger. She was wrong. The wicked man came for them and brought with him a harridan called Mrs. Slater. She took the three girls away in a coach, and their mother never saw them again."

"Aphrodite?" Somehow Vivianna managed to get the word out.

"She tried to find them, of course she did! She searched and searched, but he had hidden them well, that man. For reasons of his own, you see, and I will not tell you those now, not here, not now. It is still too dangerous to know. But she did try to find you all, for her heart was breaking with the sorrow of her loss. He pretended to look, too, but I see now that was not the truth, although at the time I trusted him. In the end he said you were lost forever and that I should get used to it."

Aphrodite's face was against Vivianna's hair—she felt her warm breath. Her arms clung, as if she did not want Vivianna to look into her face. As if she could only speak these words if she could not see her response. Not that Vivianna could have moved. She was frozen to the spot.

"I collapsed. I was ill for a long time, nearly a year,

and even then I did not recover completely. I have never recovered. I have never worn anything but black since you were taken. I have been in perpetual mourning for my daughters. And then you came to me, and said your name, and that you had two sisters, and I realized . . . I could not believe at first. I thought it was a cruel coincidence. And yet, your face, your eyes. I knew you, I know you. You are my daughter. You are my Vivianna."

Vivianna, her cheek pressed to the black silk, wondered if she had lost her mind. For suddenly it was as if she really did remember. The past was swimming up to her out of the darkness. The other woman's warmth beneath her cheek, the sweet scent of her, the timbre of her voice. All familiar. Her mother, so long lost, come back to her. Could it be? Was it possible?

But Viviana's silence had been too long, and Aphrodite believed it had another meaning.

"I'm sorry." Her voice was harsh with pain and emotion. "I did not mean to tell you. I promised myself I would never tell you. You seemed so . . . so happy with your life, as if you preferred not to know after all these years. You had accepted yourself as yourself, you said. I am not ashamed of what I am and what I have done—I see no shame in it—but I can understand why you would not want such a mother as me."

Vivianna lifted her head and looked up at Aphrodite. And now she could see the resemblance, particularly to Francesca. The dark eyes and dark hair, the pale skin, the beauty and passion in her face. This was indeed her mother, found at last, and she no longer had any doubts.

What did it matter who she was or what she was or had been? It only mattered that she had been found.

Strange, that Aphrodite was the person she had run to when she was in desperate need.

Perhaps, deep in her soul, she had always known the truth.

Vivianna gave a trembling smile. "Mama?" she whispered.

Aphrodite gave a low cry and tears ran down her cheeks. She wept unrestrainedly, and now it was Vivianna who tried to comfort her, patting her back and shoulders, murmuring words that meant nothing, kissing her cheeks.

At last they were quiet, Vivianna's head upon her mother's shoulder, and Aphrodite's arm about her waist. Vivianna felt exhausted and yet oddly content. Oliver was still there, a constant ache in her heart, but he had been set aside for now. She had other things to think of.

"Who is my father?" Vivianna asked in a soft voice, as though she were indeed a child again. "I cannot remember him. I do not even remember speaking of him, or knowing anything about him. It's as if he was a secret."

"He *was* a secret," Aphrodite said. "All of my three daughters had different fathers—shocking, is it not?" with a smile. "Having children is not the cleverest thing a courtesan can do, Vivianna, but if there is a man willing to care for her and the child, to make her life comfortable while she carries the child and bears it, and to help bring it up, then why shouldn't a courtesan become a mother? Besides, I was lonely. I wanted a family of my own. For your father, I chose a man who was also alone, and who had no wish to marry. He had no children, and he agreed that to have one as an heir would be prudent. Although, when he learned you were a girl, he was not quite so keen. Your sisters were conceived in similar circumstances, and with similar results. They are children to men who were otherwise childless at the time—insurance against the future. But for myself, well, I was content with my daughters."

"I see," Vivianna said, and she did. "Can you tell me now who my father is?"

Aphrodite gazed down into her face a moment and then she sighed. "Perhaps. I will have to ask him first. Yes, he still lives, Vivianna, but I have not seen him for a great many years. Not since I had the awful task of telling him you had been stolen. But I promise I will speak to him, and tell him you have been found, and if he is agreeable, I will give you his name. As for your sisters, I think it is best to wait until they are older before I speak to them. I fear for you all. I would rather suffer myself than have more harm come to you. I could not bear to lose any of you again, but especially not you, Vivianna. I know you now. I see you, living and breathing and standing before me. Your sisters . . . they are still memories, still little girls."

"Why should you be afraid?" Vivianna asked, with something of her usual spirit. "You can name this man. He can be punished for what he did."

Aphrodite shook her head. "This man will be watching; he always watches. If he thinks the truth might come out about what he has done, I know he will not scruple to act again. Or he will deny it, and why should anyone believe me over so important a gentleman? Let me deal with this, please. I understand your longing to know all, but believe me, it is safer if you do not. Not just yet."

"I do not mean to press you. . . ."

"I know. You are impatient. I will speak with your father, and then I will contact you. You must understand, *mon chou,* there were promises made before you were born. I swore I would do only as he wished in that regard. I cannot break them now."

Vivianna understood, of course she did, but that did not help her to feel any more patient. She had found her mother, looked upon her, and now she wanted to know her father, too.

"I can hardly believe it," she murmured. "Where was it we lived? I tried so hard to remember it, and to name the village nearby, but I could not remember! I could not remember enough to enable them to find us our home. I failed my sisters. I could not bring them home again."

Aphrodite gave her a fierce hug. "You did not fail! You were magnificent. You saved them, Vivianna. And it is my fault, and your fathers', that you did not know enough to find your way home. I kept you all secluded and, I thought, safe. You and your sisters lived a sheltered life in the country. You were my treasures and I thought you would never be stolen. How wrong I was!"

"This man . . . are you certain he cannot be punished?"

"I cannot prove he did it. Nothing is so simple. I must tread very carefully, my daughter, for all our sakes. There is danger. Do you understand? I must have your promise you will not act alone or tell your sisters before I am ready to do so. Will you promise me?"

Vivianna nodded reluctantly. "Yes, I promise."

"Then trust me in this. I swear I would die rather than allow you all to be harmed again. I will send word when I have news."

Again Vivianna nodded. It was, she realized, time to go. She did not want to go, but she knew she must. This was not her home, and although Aphrodite was her mother, she had not been in that position for many years. Lady Greentree—Mama—would be wondering where she was. Lady Greentree had been her mother since she was a child, and Vivianna realized, with a sense of regret, that Aphrodite must remain in the shadows.

Aphrodite must have known that herself, for she gave a sad little smile. "You go home now," she said. "I know you must. I do not hate Lady Greentree. She has cared for you and loved you, and I am grateful. I lost you long ago, and now you are back, but it cannot be as it was. I know that. I know that." She sighed and shook her head. "Go, *mon chou,* and I will send word when it is time to meet your father. But please, you may come back to me. Whenever you wish."

"Thank you. I will. I think I will need time to believe this is not a dream."

"Of course. Goodbye, Vivianna. Goodbye, my daughter."

She fell into her arms again, and then she was beyond the door. Outside, the birds were singing. She could hear them above the noise and chaos of London. She had found her mother. After so many years they were reunited.

She could hardly believe it.

And the birds were singing.

"I have lost her. I have found her, only to have lost her. Oh, Jemmy, Jemmy, I never thought . . . I never realized it would hurt so much, when I am so happy."

"My love, my poor love."

Aphrodite took a deep breath, though it cost her dearly. "I cannot grieve for her anymore. I cannot. She is safe and happy, she is a wonderful person. I should be proud and pleased, and I am, Jemmy. I am!"

"She is an awful lot like you, my love."

Aphrodite's eyes brightened a little, and she wiped her cheeks with her fingers, rather like Vivianna had done earlier. "Is she?"

"You know she is." He handed her a handkerchief. "What will you do about the father?"

Aphrodite attempted to marshal her thoughts. "I will go and see him, as I promised. Fraser was never a problem, but he is not a young girl's idea of a father. She will be disappointed, Jemmy."

"That isn't your fault."

"No, that isn't my fault."

"And the others?"

Aphrodite shrugged, her eyes mournful. "There will be time to decide what to do. There must be. I cannot risk such a thing happening again, or worse."

"I will kill him for you. You know I would do anything—"

"But I cannot be sure. I was never entirely sure. I feel he was responsible, but there was never any proof. How can I accuse a man of such a crime when I have no proof? It is his word against mine, Jemmy."

"Let me kill him for you."

"Hush, Jemmy, hush." She leaned against him, feeling the strength in his arms, the familiarity of the man she had loved all her life. The man she had lost, only to find again years later.

He kissed her and stepped back. Jemmy unbuttoned his red jacket. "You need to rest, my love," he said. "Let me take you upstairs."

She smiled. "Yes, I would like that, Jemmy. I still have you, don't I? Though after all I have done, I do not think I deserve you."

"You did what you had to, as I did what I had to. The past is over, and we are together now."

Jemmy Dobson bent his head to kiss the only woman he had ever loved.

Vivianna was in a daze when she returned to the house. She did not know what to say to her family, so she said nothing, removing herself to her room and pretending she had a headache. Another lie, but she could not think of that now. The humiliation, the sense of betrayal, and her broken heart were all still there, but they were juxtaposed with this new joy.

She had found her mother. She was Aphrodite's daughter. Her past was suddenly a little less mysterious, although not entirely. There were still secrets, and it seemed that Aphrodite meant to hold them close to her and not reveal too much. Maybe it was, as she said, for Vivianna's sake and the sake of her sisters, but Vivianna wished with all her passionate nature she could solve the problem now.

By the time she came down to supper, Vivianna felt a little better, though she was still pale enough to cause comment. Marietta was full of the wonders of London—she had spent the afternoon with Mr. Jardine and Lil, wandering about Madame Tussaud's at the Baker Street Bazaar. Lady Greentree had been closeted with her sister, no doubt offering sympathy and advice concerning her husband. Lady Greentree had loved her own husband and sincerely mourned him still—he had died in India with her brother, Thomas Tremaine. They were best friends, had served in the same regiment and had both succumbed to fever within days of each other. In fact, it was through Thomas that Amy Greentree had first met her husband all those years ago.

Speaking of him now, Lady Greentree sighed, "Even after all this time I miss him so."

"It was a love match," Helen said. "You were fortunate that it worked out for you, Sister. Sometimes, in the first flush of love, one is blinded."

There was an uncomfortable silence, as they all thought of the horrid Toby—and Vivianna of Oliver. Mr. Jardine cleared his throat. "I never had the pleasure of meeting your husband, Lady Greentree. I wish I had. He sounds an admirable sort of man."

Lady Greentree gave him a grateful smile. "He was, Mr. Jardine. I am sure you and Edward would have got on very well together."

Although, thought Vivianna, if Edward had not died, then Mr. Jardine would not have found himself a home at Greentree Manor. It occurred to her now, watching them together, that her mother and Mr. Jardine were extremely well matched. Perhaps because of her own new and tender position as a brokenhearted lover, she saw them from a different perspective. It was odd, that they had never considered marriage: Mr. Jardine was a gentleman, even if he had lost his fortune, and a personable man in looks and manners; Lady Greentree was calm and lovely, and universally admired. And yet, still mourning for her husband as she was, perhaps Lady Greentree did not notice other men. At least, she did not notice them as prospective bridegrooms!

"Edward would have been a wonderful father to you all," Lady Greentree said now, looking about at her two daughters. "He longed for children."

"I wonder who my real father is."

It was Marietta, as usual saying exactly what was in her mind, without thought for the consequences. Vivianna, who now knew of the past, bit her lip. A crease marred Lady Greentree's usually serene countenance.

"Dear child, I, too, wish I knew! After you were all

found, we tried to discover the secrets of your past, but without success. William searched high and low, and even placed advertisements in some of the more widely read newspapers and circulars, but there was no response. Not one person came forward. Not one clue did we receive. We tried our very best, indeed we did, but to no avail!"

"I am sure Marietta did not mean to criticize you, Mama," Vivianna said quietly, with a glance at her sister. "We know how hard you tried to find out the truth about us."

Marietta gave her sister a cross look. "Of course I was not criticizing Mama! I was merely wondering out loud."

"Perhaps it would be better for you not to know," Vivianna retorted. "Not everyone is ready to hear the truth, and sometimes knowing it can be more dangerous than ignorance."

She should not have spoken; she knew it as soon as the words spilled from her lips. But she had had a difficult day and her head was not as clear as it should have been. Marietta tossed her fair curls and sulked, while Mr. Jardine gave her a little smile. Helen sipped from her glass. It was Lady Greentree who seemed most struck with Vivianna's words. She was watching her eldest daughter with a clear, pale look that Vivianna knew well.

Amy Greentree sensed that something was amiss.

And Vivianna knew that Amy Greentree would not rest until she had winkled the truth out of her.

Lady Greentree's visit to her bedchamber was no surprise to Vivianna. She smiled at her mother in the mirror as Lil busied herself brushing out her hair.

"I wanted to speak with you," Lady Greentree said,

and sat down on the chair by the window. Outside, the street was quiet, only the occasional rattle of a coach or the clip of a horse's hooves.

Vivianna caught Lil's eye, and the maid gave a little bob and left them alone. Vivianna began to tidy her dressing table, moving the few pots and jars about. She had never been much for lotions and potions—for devices women used to hide behind. Perhaps that was why Oliver had found it so easy to hurt her—she was honest and true, while he was devious.

"Vivianna?"

"Yes, Mama." The word came naturally and Vivianna knew it always would. Lady Greentree was her mother and nothing could change that. Aphrodite was . . . well, she was Aphrodite. It was too late now for Aphrodite to assume that place in Vivianna's life, but she could be a friend. A special friend.

"Something has happened," Lady Greentree said, watching her daughter from the shadows. "You are sad, my dear. Is it Lord Montegomery? Has he done something to—"

Perhaps it was to prevent her mother probing any further with her questions about Oliver, perhaps it was just that she *wanted* to tell her. Needed to tell her. Or perhaps it was the right thing to do. She had promised Aphrodite that she would not tell her sisters, but she had said nothing of Lady Greentree. Vivianna ached from holding this secret in, and if anyone had a right to know, then it was this woman who had shaped her life.

"I have found my mother," she said evenly, and thought how strange it sounded.

Lady Greentree started forward, her lips open, her face chalky white. "You have found your . . . mother?" she whispered. "How . . . ?"

"It was purely accidental. I was following Oliver and I . . . I met a woman. She asked to know a little of my past and I . . . we realized that I was her daughter. Lost all these years. Mama, she looked for us, she searched, but we had been taken from her. After we met again, she did not even want to tell me the truth. She knew I was happy with my life as it is now, and she thought she would spoil it. In the end it slipped out."

Lady Greentree was listening, but Vivianna could see she was growing more and more concerned. Worried for her own relationship with Vivianna? Perhaps. But Vivianna thought it more likely she was worried that Vivianna would be hurt.

"Are you certain she is your mother?" she asked. "There are unscrupulous people in this world, and—"

"Oh yes, I am certain. I know you are thinking that she may have duped me, but Mama, she has Francesca's looks, and . . . there is me in her face, too, and Marietta, sometimes. She is our mother. I know it, in my mind and my heart." Vivianna smiled wanly. "Mama, you will not like this, but her name is Aphrodite and she is a . . . was a courtesan."

Lady Greentree blinked. "Good Lord," she said faintly.

Vivianna pulled a face. "Wait, there is more. The three of us are the children of her lovers, three different lovers. She will not tell me their names. She means to protect them, and us, I think. When we were taken from her she thinks it was by someone connected to her, and she fears that person will harm us again. I must wait. I must be patient while she contacts my father."

Lady Greentree searched for words. "Will I be able to meet her, this Aphrodite?"

"Do you wish to?" Vivianna asked, hardly daring to hope.

Lady Greentree smiled, and now there was genuine amusement in her eyes. "Am I so straitlaced, my dear? I admit it is not the ideal situation, but if it is what you wish, then I am more than happy to meet with Aphrodite."

Vivianna went to her mother and knelt by her, resting her head upon her lap. Lady Greentree stroked her hair, much as Aphrodite had done earlier, each touch of her fingers filled with love.

"You are my daughter, Vivianna. You know that, don't you? I do not think of you in any other way. Greentree Manor is your home. I would hate to think that you might feel you had to live with Aphrodite, and yet I would also hate to think you felt obliged to stay with me because you owed me some debt or other."

Vivianna shook her head. "You are my mama," she said, "and nothing will change that. Aphrodite was lost to me many years ago, and although I am glad to have been reunited with her, I do not think either of us wants to suddenly set up house together. She has her own life and I have mine. But I would like you to meet her, Mama, and I would like to know the name of my father. I have never felt entirely whole, you see. And I think, if I can know these things, then I may."

"Of course I understand that, Vivianna. And of course I will meet her."

Vivianna smiled through her tears. "Thank you," she whispered, and they both knew it was not just the willingness to meet Aphrodite she was thanking her for. "I . . . I would suggest tomorrow, but I promised I would help Greta and Susan. There is much to be done if we are to move the children to Bethnal Green."

"My love, I am quite happy to wait until you are

ready. This must have come as rather a shock to you—I know it has to me. Perhaps you need time to adjust."

Vivianna did not know what she needed. She had found her mother, but it had not made her life complete. For a moment a memory of Oliver flitted into her mind, his lazy smile and the gleam in his dark blue eyes as he looked at her. Her heart squeezed and the pain was enough to make her stop remembering.

Chapter 18

The following morning, Vivianna met the Beatty sisters at the former lodging house at Bethnal Green; it was not at all as Miss Greta remembered it. The three women gazed about in surprise at the newly painted walls and the repairs that had turned a sagging, soggy dwelling into a place pleasantly smelling of sawdust. There was even a small garden at the back, the soil already tilled and waiting.

Oliver had warned her he had made repairs, but she had not appreciated how much he had done. She could hardly believe it. All this, for the children? *Or was it for you?* teased a mocking little voice in her head.

"Of course not!" she muttered, and then bit her lip. Luckily the two sisters were as flabbergasted as she and did not hear her talking to herself.

"Well!" Miss Susan's eyes were brighter than they had been for weeks. "I still don't want to leave Candlewood, but I think we can have no qualms about moving the children here."

Miss Greta had a little smile on her mouth. "Lord

Montegomery has certainly taken some time and trouble to please us." Her glance to Vivianna was quizzical, "Or to please someone."

Vivianna sniffed. "We must have pricked his conscience enough for him to feel obliged to make the place habitable."

"I think we can safely begin to move our belongings from Candlewood," Miss Greta said, practically.

"Yes." Miss Susan smiled. "Oh, the children will be pleased."

When Vivianna returned to Queen's Square, she found that Aphrodite had sent Dobson with a message that her father had been told and wanted to meet her. It was as if a new phase in her life was opening, and Vivianna welcomed it.

And once more determined to put Oliver behind her.

Angus Fraser lived in Grosvenor Square. The house was certainly imposing; it spoke of opulence and wealth and grandeur. But Fraser was no aristocrat, he was a self-made man. Aphrodite had told Vivianna that by living in such a house Fraser was showing off to the nobility who had mocked and snubbed him all his life. "He is rubbing their noses in it," Aphrodite had explained with a wry smile, "and that is very Fraser."

Inside the house it was more like a museum. Cold and empty and full of beautiful things. A little dusty, too. Vivianna only saw two servants on her way up the sweeping grand staircase to her father's bedchamber.

"Is he all alone in the house?" she asked Aphrodite.

"It is how he wants it to be," Aphrodite said with one of her shrugs.

Vivianna wished she could accept such things as

matter-of-factly as her mother, but the echoing house saddened and disturbed her. And the thought that in just a moment she would be face-to-face with her father frightened and yet elated her at the same time.

Despite everything, her treacherous heart longed for Oliver's arms about her. Instead, she slipped her fingers into Aphrodite's, and was grateful for her comforting squeeze.

"I know I promised not to tell my sisters about you," she said quietly, "but I have told my mother . . . Lady Greentree. I am sorry, but she knew something was wrong, and I have lied to her enough lately. Did I do the wrong thing?"

Aphrodite turned toward her with a suddenly still and pale face. She then looked away and chewed on her lip. "I . . . maybe not. Maybe it is for the best that you did so, Vivianna. Yes, I think you did the right thing. Anyway"—with a forced smile—"it is done now."

They reached an arched doorway with double doors; the way into Fraser's bedchamber. Aphrodite halted.

"I have told you that Fraser is dying," she said. "He has no legitimate heirs. You are his only child, Vivianna. I do not know what he plans to say to you; Fraser does not show his feelings to me. He has asked to speak to you alone."

"But—"

"Do not be afraid. His bark is worse than his bite. You will see."

Vivianna moved to open one of the doors. Aphrodite had told her a little about her father in the coach on the way here. Fraser was very rich, but he was not a gentleman. Most of his wealth came from breweries in London and elsewhere about the country. He could be blunt and rude.

Growing up, Vivianna had imagined her father to be a kind and generous man. The sort of father a young girl would adore and an older girl would look up to. Somehow, despite what Aphrodite had told her, she could not rid herself of that image.

Fraser was dying, and she was the only part of him left.

Surely that would make a difference to him? Surely he would love her and she would love him, simply because of that?

The room was lit by a lamp, but it was still dark. The curtains were drawn and the colors were muted. An enormous tabby cat sat upon a chair and watched her with calm yellow eyes. Vivianna edged closer to the figure beneath the bedcovers in the ornate four-poster bed.

Fraser had been a big man. His length still made an impression, but now he was so thin his body barely lifted the bedding. His face, upon the pillows, was gaunt, and his hair red as fire. His eyes, hazel like Vivianna's, were open and watching her approach.

"Mr. Fraser?"

He crooked a finger impatiently. "Come here, lass! Ah, that's better. I can see ye now. Plain, aren't ye? Pity. Not that it matters. Not for what I have in mind."

Vivianna crept closer, knowing she was a coward but unable to help herself. *Plain.* The dismissive manner in which he had said it hurt. Oliver had called her beautiful, but then she could no longer believe anything Oliver said to her. Perhaps it was better to believe herself plain than to be lied to.

"What is your name, lass?"

Vivianna met those hazel eyes, so like her own. "Vivianna."

Fraser's lip curled. "That's no' a name for my

daughter. I'll call ye Annie. I suppose she told ye I was a rich man."

He sounded gruff, but at the same time rather proud of the fact that he was rich.

"If you mean Aphrodite, then yes, she did."

"And is that why ye're here? To get yer hands on it?"

Vivianna glared, forgetting to be nervous. "No, it is not! I have money of my own, Mr. Fraser. I am content as I am."

"Oh, are ye!" He beckoned her again. "Come closer, lass. I canna see ye. That's better. Now sit yoursel' down. I have a proposal to put to ye."

She sat down on a stool beside the bed. Aphrodite had warned her that Fraser was blunt and rude. *He's dying, I am his daughter.* She must remember those two things. Perhaps they may yet find common ground. . . .

"I want to name ye as my heir. I want ye to have it all."

"I had not intended to—"

"Yes, yes, but if ye don't have it, it'll go into the government coffers, and I dinna want that."

Vivianna did not want his money, but Fraser did not seem able to accept that. Maybe because it was the only thing he had left to leave, he did not want to believe she was not as attached to his fortune as he was.

"I know there will be a scandal," he said now with relish, and his ravaged face twisted into a chuckle. "It'll give them something to talk about, won't it? Fraser's last *faux pas*. They'll be whispering about Old Fraser's bastard daughter for years to come. They mocked me in life; I was ne'er good enough for them. I'd like to give them a wee shock before I go, aye.

"I made my money from the breweries," he went on, his eyes on her. He blinked slowly, and moved his head as if his neck hurt.

Vivianna rose and leaned over him, adjusting the pillows. He did not thank her, but the creases in his face smoothed out, and he sighed.

"And there are the lodging houses. People will live in anything, aye they will, ye look surprised, lass! A house with only four small rooms in it will fit at least twenty people, each paying rent. Thirty, at a pinch. Such folk are used to dirt and the like, and they dinna complain too much 'cause they know they're lucky to have a roof over their heads at all."

Vivianna said nothing. She had seen the places he spoke of. Those who made money from such suffering without seeking in some way to alleviate it were beyond her understanding. There were good landlords and masters, of course there were, but Fraser was not among them.

Her own father was not among them.

"I cannot take your money," she said coldly.

"What, what?" He peered at her. "Canna take it? Oh yes, ye can, girlie! My fortune will buy ye more bonny gowns and baubles than ye'll know what to do with. Ye're my heir. This is why I bought that woman out there to breed with. For this very day. Now I have ye, and I want my money's worth."

Vivianna managed not to press one of the pillows over his face and hold it there, although she was sorely tempted. She knew she could refuse to take his money, of course she could, but now her mind was beginning to work in other ways.

Why not take it? Take his money.

Not for herself, never that, but for the good she could do with it. She would be able to set up homes for the poor all over the country. The Fraser Memorial Homes. That had a nice ring to it. Homes built specifically for those who could not afford decent accommodation. And then there would be hospitals and schools.

Vivianna smiled. Why not?

"Ah, like the sound of that, do ye?" Fraser had been watching her, and evidently thought the mention of baubles had won her over. Well, let him! Vivianna would be his heir, if that was what he wanted, and then she would spend his money making recompense for the harm he had done.

Outside in the gallery, Aphrodite anxiously searched her face. "What did he say?"

"I am to be his heir. That is why he paid for you to have me all those years ago."

Aphrodite closed her eyes. "*Mon dieu.*" After a moment she pulled herself together enough to remind them both, "He is dying—"

"I know." Vivianna said it bleakly. "I'm sorry, Aphrodite, but I do not like him. I wish I could. He's my father! But I do not. I have said I will be his heir, but when he is dead I will use his money for good works."

A slow smile spread over Aphrodite's face. "Did you tell him this?"

"Not yet."

"Then don't, Vivianna. Let him enjoy his last weeks, it cannot hurt."

Vivianna looked at her in surprise. "You are fond of him, aren't you?"

Aphrodite's smile turned sad. "I had a child with him. It makes a difference."

Oliver was still asleep late the next morning when Hodge woke him. "Lady Marsh is awaiting you in the sitting room, my lord."

Oliver opened one blurry eye. "You let her in?"

"I could not prevent her, my lord."

"What does she want?"

"She wants to see you, my lord."

Oliver groaned and sat up. "I will be half an hour, Hodge. I can't be any faster. I haven't long retired."

"I know, my lord. I will see her ladyship has some refreshment while she waits."

Oliver rested his head carefully into his hands, wincing as Hodge closed the door. He had drunk far too much and slept far too little. Last night at White's replayed in his mind. Lawson, his breath hot against Oliver's ear, murmuring, "Where is this secret chamber, Oliver? Your grandfather's secret chamber?"

Oliver had swayed dangerously, almost losing his balance. "Just a story," he'd muttered drunkenly. "Nothing to it. Why? Why do you want to know?"

Lawson had smiled, but his eyes were lethal. "You need to tell me soon, Oliver," he had said, not drunk at all. He had only been pretending. "You need to consider your future very carefully, or the fact that you may not have a future. . . ."

"Like Anthony, you mean?" he had asked levelly.

And suddenly the game was over. They had stood facing each other, wearing their true skins.

Lawson had observed him as if he were an interesting specimen of insect. "Yes," he had said softly. "Just like Anthony."

"You're finished," Oliver retorted, and the rage in him threatened to boil over. "I'll see to it."

Lawson smiled. "Your brother said that, too. And look what happened to him." And then he'd simply turned and walked away.

In his bedroom, with the sunlight creeping through the curtained windows, Oliver contemplated the danger he was in. He wasn't afraid. He was only the more determined to find the letters and see Lawson punished. But he was vastly relieved Vivianna was out of it—whatever happened to him now, she would be safe.

It was the only thing that kept him from going to her house and begging her forgiveness.

A pain stabbed at his chest at the thought of her, but he ignored it. Surely all he had to do was remember how she used to lecture him and argue with him to be glad he never had to spend time with her again? But somehow it just didn't seem to be working. . . .

Exactly thirty minutes later, immaculately dressed, Oliver made his way to the sitting room. Lady Marsh set her cup down with a clatter and gave him a stern look.

"Oliver, have you heard? I have never been more shocked."

"Shocked?"

"You mean you haven't heard?"

Oliver knew his head was fuzzy, but surely his aunt couldn't mean the Anchor Inn? No, she couldn't. If she'd heard of that she would be tearing strips off him.

"Oliver! Are you asleep?"

"No, Aunt, I'm not asleep. You put a stop to that." He settled himself on the chair opposite and she proceeded to pour him some tea.

"Miss Greentree is not the daughter of Lady Greentree after all," she began with relish. "Angus Fraser, the brewery millionaire, has named her as his heir! She is his daughter by some drab or other, and she became lost when she was a child. Baby farmers or some such thing. Now they are reunited, Fraser is on his deathbed, and she is his heir."

Oliver tried to take it in. "I thought you always rather liked Fraser," he heard himself say.

"I did. He says what he thinks, and that is rare enough in our world. But that's not the point! The point is, I rather thought *you* liked *Miss Greentree.*"

"I did." He blinked at her, rubbed a hand across his freshly shaven face. "I do."

"And you did not know?"

"I knew she was abandoned as a child, but I did not know her parentage."

Vivianna, the daughter of Fraser, the brewery millionaire? It hardly seemed credible, except his aunt was a sharp old bird. If she believed it, then it must be true.

"Oliver! Are you listening? I just said that you cannot possibly marry her now. Your wife must have an unsullied reputation, the mother of your heir must be beyond reproach. No, I am afraid you must choose one of the girls on my list. You must find a girl who is more acceptable."

Oliver stood up. The tea table rocked dangerously. "I'll be damned if I will!"

"Oliver, really—"

"I will marry whom I like. Who am I to quibble about Vivianna's reputation anyway? She's worth a hundred of me. A million!"

"Oliver, calm yourself—"

"No, I won't." But he did. He drew a long, slow breath and sat down again. "I'm sorry," he said formally, "but I won't have Vivianna slandered."

Lady Marsh fixed him with a stare. She looked as if she were trying not to smile. After a moment she said, "Well, Fraser *is* very rich."

"I don't want her money."

"I'm sure you don't," she retorted, raising her brows, and making Oliver wonder whether she had heard of the Anchor Inn after all. "Well, are you going to ask her to marry you or not?"

Oliver blinked. "Of course not!"

"Why not? Ask her."

"She won't see me."

Lady Marsh shook her head at him. "Why not?"

"I told her about Lawson. Now she hates me for pretending to be a rake."

Lady Marsh's eyes widened. "Good gad, is she so partial to rakes? Well"—with a heavy sigh—"pretend to be one for her. I like that girl, Oliver, and I want her as your wife. Be the best rake in London and win her over!" Lady Marsh rose to her feet with difficulty, using her cane. "I intend to see a new Montegomery born before I die, Oliver," she said testily. "Get busy."

Lady Greentree and Aphrodite stood awkwardly, facing each other across Helen's sitting room. Lady Greentree had asked that she see the other woman alone, without Vivianna present, and now she didn't know what to say.

Earlier, she had explained to Vivianna, "It will be difficult enough for your mother and I, my dear, without you being there biting your nails. I have sent Marietta off with Mr. Jardine and Lil—I think it best if she is kept out of this as much as possible. Let me speak to Aphrodite alone, and then if you wish you can join us."

Vivianna had agreed, although Amy Greentree could see she was not happy. Amy knew that Vivianna could see very well how her being named as the heir to Mr. Fraser's fortune, and now the truth about her birth, was making everything very difficult for the family. There was talk and gossip everywhere they went.

Several of Helen's acquaintances had cut her in the street, and as for William . . . ! Amy sighed. William, when he had finally come to call upon them, had been furious. She had not seen him so furious since Helen eloped with Tony. He had told Amy that she had no right to keep such news from him, and that if he had known he would have nipped it in the bud, although how he could have done so she did not know. "Bringing disrepute to our family," he had blustered, his face puce, his pale blue eyes, so like Amy's, bulging. "What would Thomas have said? It is not to be borne!"

"I am afraid it will have to be," Amy had replied calmly, refusing to join her brother in hysteria, and wishing their elder sibling were here now. "Angus Fraser has stipulated that to be named as his heir Vivianna must proclaim herself his illegitimate daughter. Vivianna has decided that this is what she wants. And she means to use the money for her good works; the dear girl says that any amount of scandal and humiliation will be worth it in the end."

Though privately Amy had wondered if Vivianna realized just how unpleasant matters might become for her.

"Good works!" William had shouted. "She wants to waste her money on those blasted orphans!"

That was probably the part that had upset her brother most of all, Amy thought now. That all that money was to be squandered on homeless children and the poor, instead of going to the further aggrandizement of the Tremaine family. But William was William, and in time he would come around.

It was Vivianna who concerned her right now.

The dear girl had recently had several offers of donations to charitable institutions returned, simply because of the scandal. It was very unfair, and Amy was still fuming over it. And now she had the task of facing Aphrodite, the courtesan, and making some sort of bridge between them.

"You are not as I imagined," Aphrodite spoke at last. She was beautiful, in a ravaged sort of way, and Vivianna was right, she did resemble Francesca.

Amy gestured to a chair. "Please, be seated, Aphrodite. May I call you that?"

"Please do, Lady Greentree."

"Then you must call me Amy." She raised a curious eyebrow as she sat down opposite. "Why am I not as you imagined?"

"I thought you would be . . . I don't know. You are so tranquil, so restful. I think your household must be very peaceful."

"I am not like Vivianna, you mean?" she asked wryly. "My daughters are all very much their own persons, Aphrodite, and I love them for that. I have cared for them and loved them since the day I found them and I hope I can continue to do that."

Aphrodite blinked. "Of course," she said. "I would not want to take any of them from you. I know they will never be my daughters now. It is too late. If I may . . . if I can look upon them, as if from a distance, like a doting godmother . . . I think I will be happy with that."

"You are very courageous," Amy said gently.

Aphrodite shrugged as if she were indifferent. "They are happy, that is all that matters."

Amy let it pass, although she knew Aphrodite could not be as unconcerned as she pretended. It was the other woman's way of dealing with her pain.

"I wanted to see you alone to ask if you will tell me the story of their disappearance. Vivianna says there is some mystery . . . ?"

Aphrodite gazed at her a moment, as if turning the matter over in her mind, and then shook her head. "No, I cannot. I am not being mysterious, Amy, it is just something I cannot speak of. Not yet. I have given Vivianna her father, although I do not think she is very happy with him," she added with a grimace, "but as for the others, they must wait until they are older and I am certain it is safe. They were taken away once, I am sure you would not wish such a thing to happen again."

Amy leaned forward. "I promise you," she said, "I swear to you, if you tell me, it will go no further. And perhaps I can help."

Aphrodite smiled coolly, suddenly aloof. "You are very kind. I thank you, but no. This is my problem, and I will solve it without involving you or the girls."

Resigned, Amy said, "Very well. I have sent Marietta out, as you requested, but will I call for Vivianna now? She is probably working herself into a state waiting for my summons."

The tension seemed to go from Aphrodite. "Yes, please. I fear Vivianna does not realize how cruel society can be," she added when the bell had been rung. "I wish I could shelter her in some way, but I would probably just make it worse."

"I think she does know." Amy grimaced. "People have been perfectly horrid, and not just to her. At least the family is standing by her, apart from my brother William, but I had expected nothing else from him. He is a great stickler for the proprieties."

Aphrodite smiled politely. "It will be an ordeal for Vivianna, but still she insists she does not mind."

"She has never cared much for those rules society values. Vivianna is very much her own person."

"Yes," said Aphrodite, and the words went unspoken between them that mother and daughter were very much alike.

Chapter 19

Eddie and Ellen stood at the edge of the staircase, looking down into the shadows. The old stone lion with its chipped ears and broken paw had been pushed hard to one side. Eddie had discovered the trick. The lion was fixed to a large rectangular slab on the floor, but if one of the carvings on the slab was pushed down, the fastening opened with a loud click. Then it was a matter of heaving, hard, to move the lion and slab aside. Beneath it was an opening and a staircase, going down.

A secret chamber.

Ellen was impressed, but she edged closer to Eddie and the lantern he clutched in his hand. The candle flame inside flickered wildly, and they both held their breath until it began to burn more steadily.

"I don't like the dark, see," Eddie explained. "Once my da's lady friend locked me up for a long time—days! I was in a small, dark cupboard. I felt like I couldn't breav. After that I ran away, and since then I can't never go into small dark places."

"It's all right," Ellen whispered, and cuddled her doll to her thin chest. "I'm here, Eddie. I'll keep you safe."

Eddie nodded seriously, as if pale, skinny little Ellen could protect him, and took a step down, and then another. "Come on, then," he said in a voice that sounded too shaky to be brave, "let's get on wif it."

They disappeared down into the darkness, the candlelight wavering as they went, and the lion looked on in silence.

"Miss Greentree?"

Startled, Vivianna looked up from packing books in one of the crates that the wagon would take from Candlewood to Bethnal Green. As far as she had known she was here alone, apart from her coachman waiting outside with the horses. The Beatty sisters had gone to Bethnal Green with the children to begin the process of settling in.

The man standing in the shadow outside the doorway was tall, and for a moment she thought, with a treacherous lift of her heart, that it was Oliver. But then he stepped forward and she realized it was actually Lord Lawson.

Lawson killed my brother.

"Lord Lawson," she said, and dusted off her skirts, seeking time to recover. Instinctively she knew it would be a mistake for him to realize she knew about him and Oliver's brother.

"I hope you do not mind me walking in upon you like this, but I could not find a servant." Lawson was moving toward her now, and Vivianna forced herself to stand still and not to turn and run.

"We are rather short of servants at Candlewood," she replied with an attempt at a wry smile.

He smiled back, but his eyes were cold. They were blue, but not dark and sensuous like Oliver's; Lawson's eyes were like ice, and with just as much humanity.

"Miss Greentree, it is Candlewood I wanted to discuss with you. I know it is something we both hold dear." His gaze went past her to the open trunk. "Are you leaving?"

Vivianna looked at the trunk, too; anything to escape those cold eyes. "Yes, of course," she said. "We have to leave. Lord Montegomery has offered us lodgings in Bethnal Green and we are moving there as soon as possible. Candlewood will soon be empty."

"Will it indeed? Well, I will be sorry to hear it. As you know, I was a dear friend of Oliver's brother, Anthony, and I know he was very fond of this house."

But that didn't stop you from shooting him in cold blood.

He looked at her sharply, and for a moment Vivianna thought she must have said the words aloud, but the next moment he was smiling and asking her in a charmingly tentative manner whether it would be acceptable for him to take a walk over the house.

"I may not get the chance again," he said with a sigh, "and then I will have nothing but memories."

"But of course!" Vivianna could play games, too. "I will come with you, my lord. I think I deserve a rest from packing. It will be interesting to hear about Candlewood from someone who knows it well."

He wasn't happy with her—she could see it in his eyes—but what could he do? He bowed politely, and Vivianna led the way out.

"Miss Greta and Miss Susan are at Bethnal Green," she explained as they meandered up and down corridors. "There is much to be done there." Vivianna glanced at him sideways. "I believe you made an offer for Candlewood, my lord, and was turned down."

She felt his start of surprise but did not acknowledge it. They were moving toward the unfinished wing, where it was forbidden for the children to go. Vivianna wondered whether they should turn back—she felt rather as if she were taking a stroll with a dangerous animal—but Lawson's next words drove all such thoughts from her mind.

"I made the offer for the sake of the orphans, Miss Greentree. I could not bear to think of them losing the home they had grown to love."

Anger curled inside her at the sheer hypocritical nature of his statement. Oliver may have tricked her and humiliated her, but he had never used the children in his plot. He might have refused to bow to her wishes as regards to Candlewood, but he had always been honest and steadfast about his refusal. This man was *wicked*.

"I am sure it is all for the best," Vivianna replied blithely.

She felt his eyes upon her, studying her. "I must say I am surprised to hear you say that," he said at last. "I did not think you would be so forgiving. From what I have heard, you have fought like a tigress for Candlewood, and yet now you seem quite calm in defeat. Perhaps Oliver has won you around to his point of view?"

The door to the unfinished wing was unbolted. With a puzzled frown, Vivianna passed through into the long, colonnaded room with the faded mural upon the ceiling. "I do not think he has won me to his point of view, my lord, but sometimes to continue to fight is pointless."

It was as if he had not heard her, or perhaps he was

just playing his own devious game. "Oliver is a very personable young man, of course. I have often noted how attractive he is to the gentler sex."

"I find Lord Montegomery singularly unattractive," she snapped, but knew even as she said it that her protests seemed forced. He knew something, and now he was smiling at her in a manner that made her queasy.

"I'm afraid Oliver can be rather devious, Miss Greentree, if he wants his . . . way with a pretty girl. You shouldn't believe a word he says. And as for marriage"—he smirked—"I doubt he would look in your direction for a wife. His aunt, Lady Marsh, would expect him to marry the daughter of an earl, at least."

If he thought to turn her against Oliver, he was wasting his time. She told herself that she already loathed Oliver Montegomery, but that did not mean she would take sides with his brother's murderer.

Vivianna had walked another step or two before she realized that Lawson had stopped dead in his tracks. "Lord Lawson? What is it?" She followed the direction of his fixed stare, wondering what it was he suddenly found so amazing.

For a moment she could see nothing. The long gallery was as she remembered it from the few times she had been here. Dusty, bare, apart from one or two sculptures and stone figures fixed into the floor. And then she realized that the statue of the lion was out of alignment with the rest; it was pushed to one side. But how was that possible? It was made of stone and very heavy. Who would have had the strength to move such a thing, and why? And then Vivianna saw that where the lion had once stood was . . . nothingness.

Lawson was striding forward. His face was ablaze

with triumph. "The secret chamber!" he hissed.

Vivianna ran after him, her skirts making a trail through the dust. Fear and shock had caused her to feel a little light-headed, but oddly calm. The lion, she could see, was attached to a slab that had been rolled to one side like a horizontal door. And in the space was a stone staircase, running down into the darkness. The secret chamber must be underground.

"Is someone down there?" Lawson demanded, glancing at her briefly before his ice-blue eyes returned to the shadows.

"I—I don't know. I didn't know such a thing existed. How did *you* know, Lord Lawson?"

Her question seemed to bring him back to his senses. Vivianna could almost see the mask slipping over his face once more. "I had heard of it. I did not know it really existed until now. Has Oliver been here? Maybe it was he who discovered its whereabouts?"

Vivianna knew as if he had told her that if Oliver was down there, then Lawson would kill him. And her, too. He would kill anyone who stood in the way of his secret and his ambition. Why shouldn't he? He had done it before.

"Oliver isn't here," she said a little breathlessly.

"Someone has been."

Vivianna's gaze had been wandering over the dusty floor, around the edges of the "door," and now she realized what she was looking at. Footprints. Small, children's footprints. Before she could think about it, she stepped over the telltale signs and allowed her long skirts to brush across the ground. The work of a moment and the footprints were gone.

Lawson was watching her agitated movements suspiciously and she realized she hadn't answered his question.

"I honestly do not know who has been here, my lord! As I have explained, I did not know such a place existed. Surely this chamber cannot still be in use? Do you think there is anything hidden down there?"

He wanted to go within and search. Vivianna could see it in his face, and the way his gaze kept returning to the steps. But her presence was preventing him. He would not want her to see the letters. . . .

"I had better ascertain whether anyone is there," he said, frowning thoughtfully. "Stay here, Miss Greentree. I would not want you to slip and break your neck."

Vivianna's shiver was genuine. And yet she could not allow him to go alone. If the letters were still down there, he could destroy them in an instant and then Oliver's chance to expose the man who had murdered his brother would be lost.

"Lord Lawson, I really don't think you should go down. It might be dangerous. I should find someone to come and—"

"Nonsense." He was already on the first step. She went to follow him, though her knees were like jelly.

"Miss?"

Eddie's voice brought her up short. She turned and spotted him, standing by the lion, his hand resting upon its lifted paw. Had he been hiding there all along? His freckles stood out on his pale face, his hair was dusty, and the remains of cobwebs trailed across his jacket. Eddie had been inside the secret chamber.

She tried to speak, but the sensation of Lawson, watching, listening, froze her tongue.

"Miss?" Ellen stepped out from behind Eddie, her voice like a soft echo. Her fair hair was festooned with webs and fine dust. "Can we talk with you, Miss Greentree?"

"Talk with me?" She, too, was an echo, it seemed.

"I thought you said you were alone here, Miss Greentree."

Lawson, she realized, had his gaze fixed upon the children. And suddenly Vivianna knew she must protect them at any cost. "Oh yes, I forgot. Eddie and Ellen stayed behind to help. You naughty children, where did you run off to? Well, never mind," she added hastily, in case they answered her. She forced a rather ghastly smile. "We were going to discuss the . . . the . . . children's shoes, weren't we? The box of shoes."

She glanced back at Lawson apologetically. "Do you mind, my lord? We have so little time to organize. Should I send someone to help you?"

Lawson hesitated, and then shook his head. "No, there is no need, Miss Greentree. You run along. But first . . ."

Vivianna had already turned away, a firm hand on the back of each child. She looked back at him over her shoulder. "Lord Lawson?"

He smiled and said softly, "Give me the lantern, lad. It's dark down here. But I think you know that, don't you?"

Eddie looked to Vivianna for instructions. He did indeed have a small lantern in his hand—a simple glass casing with a lighted candle inside. She took it from him and walked over to the entrance to the secret chamber. Her fingers were shaking as she held it out.

Lawson was watching her. She amused him. They both knew, if he wanted to, he could take the lantern and her hand, too.

"My coachman is outside," she said. "Will I send him in to help you, my lord?"

He met her innocent stare for what seemed a long

time, and then gave an impatient shake of his head. He took the lantern. "That won't be necessary, Miss Greentree. I think I can manage."

Vivianna did not wait. She more or less propelled the children from the long, echoing room.

"Miss!" Eddie protested. "You're hurting!"

"Were you down there?" Vivianna demanded softly. "Were you in that room?"

Eddie and Ellen exchanged a look.

"Tell me the truth," Vivianna said fiercely. "It is very important."

"We was down there," Ellen whispered, "and it was dark and cold. Eddie was frightened of the dark, but I held his hand, and we had the candle. It was our last chance to explore, you see, miss, before we left Candlewood forever."

Vivianna's heart contracted at the thought of them doing something so dangerous. But she swallowed down the urge to scold. No time for that now. Lawson might already be after them.

"Did you find anything? Remember, this is very, very important."

Another exchanged glance, and then Ellen lifted a finger to her lips. "Shh, miss," she whispered, "it's a secret. Can you keep a secret?"

Vivianna made her expression sober. "Yes, I can," she breathed. "Tell me what you have found, children."

They had reached the door into the occupied part of the house. Vivianna thought of bolting it, but knew that would not keep a resourceful man like Lawson out. Besides, there were gaps in the walls in the abandoned part of the house, gaps big enough for anyone to climb through.

Eddie was fumbling underneath his buttoned-up jacket, and now he began to withdraw something bulky from its hiding place. Vivianna did not have to pretend to be astonished. It was a bundle of letters tied with black ribbon. They were a little musty and dusty, and it appeared that a mouse had nibbled on one corner, but otherwise they looked to be in excellent condition.

"Eddie," she whispered, "what is that you have found?"

He grinned, looking pleased with himself. "They was in the secret room under the stone lion," he said.

"Shh!" Ellen glanced about them.

"I found the room when I was playing," Eddie said, lowering his voice. "I used to ride the lion like a horse, and one day I touched part of the pattern on the stone base and the floor opened up. No one else knows 'cept us, miss."

Suddenly Vivianna felt dizzy with the knowledge that Eddie now held the evidence Oliver had been searching for during the past year.

"Eddie," she said gently, "Ellen, I know someone who will be very pleased to have those letters. He may even give you a reward. What do you think of that?"

"Cor!" Eddie's eyes popped and Ellen clapped her hands softly. "Who is he, then? Prince Albert, I bet?"

Vivianna couldn't help but smile. "No, not quite. Lord Montegomery."

"Oh," they gasped in unison, and then they grinned like the urchins they were. "Do you think he'll really give us a reward?"

Vivianna nodded solemnly. "I think he will, Eddie."

"I wonder if it'll be enough to buy a new slingshot. . . ."

"I'm sure he'll buy you several. Now listen to me, this is very important. You need to hide. Lord Lawson isn't a very nice man and we can't let him find you. He wants those letters, you see, and I don't think he would care if he hurt you."

Eddie's eyes widened, but Ellen shook her head and said calmly, "Why would we hide, miss? We can lock the gentleman up in the dark, just like Eddie was locked up."

Good God, of course! Vivianna's gaze swung back down the long gallery and found the black space in the floor. Lord Lawson was still down there. But for how long?

She began to run. The children clattered after her. By the time Vivianna reached the entrance to the chamber, she was breathless. She gulped in air, peering down to where the steps vanished into nothingness.

"Lord Lawson?"

A scuffling noise. "What is it?" He sounded some way away, his voice hollow.

"Have you found anything?"

Movement, getting closer. "No. I'm coming back up."

Vivianna's heart jolted. She spun around to face the children. "The lion," she whispered fiercely. "Push it back across!"

Definite footsteps now; the scrape of a shoe on stone. The children began to tug and pull the lion. It barely moved. Vivianna pushed against its cold flank, and felt the slab begin to roll back into position. But slowly, so slowly.

"Where are those children?" Lawson's voice echoed beneath their feet.

He knew!

He was getting closer, and now they could hear him on the stairs. The lion upon its slab was halfway across. And then Lawson seemed to realize what was happening. He shouted out. He began to run . . . and stumbled.

The lion gained momentum. It trundled across the diminishing gap. Just as Lawson's face appeared, white and streaked with dust, his eyes blazing with fury, the door closed with a soft whoosh.

"That was close," Eddie muttered, his freckles even more prominent.

Vivianna leaned against the statue. Her heart was jumping in her chest. "Can he open it from inside?" she asked.

"I don't know, miss," Ellen whispered, and looked frightened.

"It's dark down there anyway," Eddie said grimly. "He won't be able to see much once the candle goes out."

That was true. Vivianna waited a moment more, but apart from some angry shouting and thumping at the slab beneath them, there was no sign of Lawson escaping. She held out her hands and tried not to shake. "Come on, children. There are things to be done."

Oliver spurred his horse down the long driveway. Ahead of him Candlewood awaited in the afternoon sun. He had come as soon as he could and Sergeant Ackroyd was not far behind. Vivianna's message, via her coach driver, had been blunt and to the point.

I have the letters and Lawson. Come at once.

He still found it difficult to believe. Vivianna had accomplished in one afternoon what Oliver had been trying to accomplish for a year. He should be thrilled, but he wasn't. He felt sick with anxiety and all he could think was: How dare she endanger herself in this way!

The whole point of driving her away after their night at the Anchor had been to keep her from danger. Why the hell couldn't she ever do what she was supposed to? *Damn the woman. . . .*

The door to the house was flung open as he dismounted and two small faces peered out at him. Then they began to shout. Almost immediately Vivianna appeared behind them.

He noticed she was wearing one of her woolen dresses, and her hair was pulled back tightly at her nape. She looked as severe and plain as she had the first time he met her. A reformer. A woman who attended meetings and lectured him. A do-gooder who would never be satisfied until he gave her Candlewood in perpetuity.

And he realized he didn't care. It didn't matter. He still wanted her. He always would.

The knowledge gave him a warm sensation, just above his heart. As if he had come home.

"Vivianna!" Oliver moved to take her into his arms.

But Vivianna had other ideas. She stepped behind the children, using them like a shield. The orphans gazed up at him with interest. Strangely, they appeared to have cobwebs decorating their hair.

"Lord Montegomery, I am sure you remember Eddie and Ellen?"

He looked into her eyes, trying to read them. There was tension in her, as if she were holding her emotions on a tight rein. He understood that. She must have had a dreadful shock. But he was here now. She was safe.

He wished she would cast herself into his arms like any other woman, but he supposed that was out of the question. She must still hate his guts, and he knew she had every right to.

Oliver turned to the children and tried not to show his agitation. "Of course I remember Eddie and Ellen."

They reached out and clung to his hands. In fact, once they had hold of him, they didn't want to let him go.

"I've sent word to the police," Oliver said. "They should be here soon. Where's Lawson?"

"Inside." She gave him a smug little smile. "He can't get out, don't worry."

"Will you give us a reward?" Ellen's soft voice interrupted.

"A reward?" Oliver looked back at Vivianna.

"Lord Montegomery, the children have something for you." Vivianna tapped Eddie on the shoulder. He dragged a bundle from inside his jacket and held it out to Oliver. "Here you go, mister," he said with a grin from ear to ear. "What do you think the reward'll be on this?"

For a moment Oliver could not move, and then he reached out a hand that didn't seem to belong to him, and his fingers closed over the bundle of letters tied with black ribbon.

He felt emotion well up inside him. Anthony had hidden these the night he died. Had he thought of Oliver then, had he believed that somehow Oliver would find them? Oliver hoped so. He hoped that his brother had forgiven him and trusted in him before he died.

The writing on the envelopes was in black ink; strong, sloping writing that he recognized at once as belonging to Lawson. It was the actual address that sent a tingle of amazement through him, and of comprehension. Even without reading the letters he now understood Lawson's single-minded intent to retrieve what was his. But still, he drew one out, unfolded it, and cast his eye over the contents.

It was worse than he had thought.

"Mister?"

He glanced down and saw Eddie's freckled face gazing up at him. The little boy was watching him with slight impatience.

"Yes, Eddie?" he said.

"The reward. Miss Greentree said as there'd be a reward."

Oliver smiled and rested his hand gently on Eddie's head. "And so there will be. I will open an account at my bank and place two amounts in it, one for you, Eddie, and one for Ellen, and when you are twenty-one, the money will—"

"Aw, mister." Eddie's face scrunched up alarmingly. "I don't want no bank account. I wanna go to the zoo! Will you take us to the zoo?"

"I want to go for a ride in a carriage," Ellen whispered. "A proper carriage with four white horses."

At a loss, Oliver met Vivianna's eyes over their heads. "Perhaps you can have both," she said tentatively. "If Lord Montegomery is willing, of course."

Oliver didn't even hesitate. "Zoo it is, then, and carriage as well!"

"Good," sighed Vivianna, "that's settled. Now, children, perhaps you could wait here on the steps for the policemen. Will you do that for me, Eddie? Ellen?"

Eddie and Ellen were agreeable, and Vivianna left them there and led the way inside.

"I did not even know they were here," she told

Oliver as she walked. "I thought they had gone with the others to Bethnal Green. The little scamps must have hidden and decided to explore instead."

"Vivianna—"

"I'm glad they found the letters," she said quickly. "I really am. That will be the end of it, then, won't it? You can bring Lawson to justice?"

Oliver nodded and placed the letters carefully into his jacket pocket. "Yes."

"I saw the address on them," Vivianna added. "I expect that means . . ."

"Yes, Lawson has finally overreached himself."

They had come to a bolted door. She turned and met his eyes, and her own were large and bright. And frightened. Vivianna was frightened.

"Tell me," he demanded. "How did you capture Lawson?"

She told him.

As she spoke, Oliver could feel fury tightening every sinew in his body. Lawson had dared to come to Candlewood after Oliver had done all in his power to keep her safe. If she had not taken him prisoner, he might have harmed her. Or worse. Oliver had expected his own life to be in danger—he had accepted it as part of the plan he was executing. But for Lawson to threaten Vivianna . . .

"Did he hurt you?" he demanded.

Vivianna blinked, startled by what she saw in his face. "No. He noticed that the door to the secret chamber was open and he went down into it. I was going to go with him, to stop him from taking the letters. And then Eddie came, and Ellen. But Lawson had seen the children—I knew he would come after them. And I . . . I couldn't let him free to do that."

"Vivianna," he groaned, "do you know how dangerous he is?"

She bit her lip. "Yes," she whispered, "I do."

She would have gone into danger for the letters? For him? Suddenly Oliver could not bear it anymore. Anthony and his death had been the most important thing in his world for so long, and now, suddenly, he realized it no longer was. He wanted a future. He wanted to live again.

He wanted Vivianna.

Oliver reached out, wanting to hold her, needing to feel her, but she stepped back again. Away from him.

"I'm perfectly all right," she said.

But he felt sick with rage and fear. "I wish I had been here to protect you," he began urgently. "This was never meant to happen."

It was the wrong thing to say. Vivianna's brows rose. "I don't need your protection," she retorted stiffly. "We did very well on our own, the children and I."

Oliver tried again.

"Vivianna, I never meant to involve you," he insisted. "I tried to keep you out of Lawson's way."

"Yes," she said, "you tried very hard to keep me completely out of the way. I'm sorry you had to bother with me at all. How boring it must have been for you, wasting your time seducing me when you had Lawson to catch."

"Is that what you think?" he demanded incredulously. But of course she would think that. He had wanted her to, so that she would be safe. "Vivianna, I made you hate me that night on purpose, to keep you away from me, to keep you out of danger. I could have made you hate me before we went to the Anchor, but I was too selfish for that. You asked for a night with the rake, and because I wanted you, I said yes. A night to remember, before I sent you away." His laugh was bitter. "Believe me, I haven't felt whole since."

"So now you would have me believe that, too, was part of the game you were playing? I'm confused, Oliver. How many lies have you told me during our brief acquaintance?"

She sounded furious, but there were tears in her eyes.

Before he could answer, Vivianna unbolted the door and flung it open. A long, cold room stretched before them. Murals on the ceiling, a colonnade, unfinished statues and moldings. Oliver glanced at her, wanting to continue their conversation, but she clearly expected him to precede her into the gallery.

"The door is over here," she said matter-of-factly. Vivianna led him toward a statue of a lion with a raised front paw. "The lion actually moves to one side, and there are stairs leading to an underground chamber."

Oliver stared at where she was pointing. "And Lawson is down there?"

"Yes."

"Alone in the dark?"

"Yes."

"Good."

Chapter 20

Vivianna should not have been surprised by the savage note in his voice. But she was. He was a stranger to her, this man. No longer Oliver the rake, the gentleman in need of redemption.

Not this new man. He didn't need saving. He was Oliver the avenger, and he was cold and focused and very self-contained. He no more needed Vivianna's help than did Lawson.

Vivianna knew it was stupid, ridiculous, but she preferred the rake. She wanted the man who had kissed her and made her come alive in his arms, the man who had made love to her in the most inappropriate places. She had always known he was completely unsuitable, that she could never ever marry him, and yet his charm, mixed with a touch of vulnerability, had appealed to her. She had fallen in love with him.

She missed him.

Vivianna swallowed her own grief, and found that Oliver was watching her again. But now there was no lurking smile in his eyes, no teasing light to make her heart pitter-patter. He was withdrawn, suspicious. He would use her if he could for his own ends and then discard her, just as he had after the night at the Anchor. Oh yes, this man was indeed a stranger.

And that was how she must treat him.

"You may have heard that I have been named heir to Angus Fraser's fortune."

Oliver frowned at her cool, polite tone.

"I won't go into details," Vivianna went on, as if this were an ordinary conversation in the most ordinary of circumstances. "Suffice it to say that I will soon have more than enough money to make you an offer for Candlewood. I assume you will not need to demolish it now?"

Oliver felt disoriented. Did she know what she was saying? And disappointed. She had given him the letters, placed herself in danger, and now he learned it had all been for the blasted house after all. Candlewood. Everything she did was for Candlewood.

Nothing had changed.

He turned away, so she wouldn't see how much the realization had affected him. He might be a fool, but he didn't want her to know it.

"My aunt called to tell me about your father," he said, as if it mattered to him not at all. "Should I congratulate you? He is very wealthy, isn't he? More money for your orphans."

"He is very wealthy, and there will be more money for my orphans. More money for houses and hospitals, too. I will be quite unstoppable now."

He laughed, but there was that note of bitterness in it.

"I expect Lady Marsh forbade you to see me again," she went on, and seated herself upon the lion's back.

Oliver eyed her uneasily. This was becoming more

bizarre by the moment. "Actually," he said, "my aunt is not easily shocked."

"Does she know that my mother is Aphrodite?" Vivianna asked woodenly. "She and Fraser were lovers and she had his child. I was taken away from her when I was six, and Lady Greentree found me."

Aphrodite!

He opened his mouth, closed it again. He had a feeling she was watching him very closely and anything he said may be misconstrued. It was wiser, he felt, to say nothing.

Her eyes blurred with tears.

Oliver cursed silently. Maybe there was something he could say after all. "Vivianna, let me help you. The Montegomeries are an old and distinguished family. I can help you weather this storm. Surely it would be better than running back to Yorkshire and hiding on the moors? I'm sure Lady Marsh would be more than happy to champion your cause, and I . . ."

But already Vivianna's face had grown cold and distant, and her eyes hard. "I'm sure the blue-blooded Montegomery family would welcome the child of a courtesan and a brewery owner. I am not a fool, Oliver, although you continually seem to think me one."

"I never thought that," he insisted earnestly. "Far from it. I admire you, Vivianna. You are the woman of my dreams. Let me help you, I want to."

The woman of his dreams? Vivianna stared. He seemed to be sincere. Was it possible he was telling her the truth? Had it all been a ploy to keep her safe from Lawson? Had he agreed to the night at the Anchor because he wanted her as much as she wanted him?

It would explain so much.

And yet, Vivianna did not dare trust him.

"Do you know," she burst out, "I much preferred you when you were a rake! Everything was so much simpler then. Now, will you just answer my question?"

"Question?" He felt utterly baffled. She preferred him when he was a *rake*? What in God's name did she mean by that? After she had lectured and harassed him for his lack of compassion, now she wanted that man back again? Or . . . Oliver frowned. Was it his physical attentions she was missing?

Was she missing him with the same sort of desperate *need* as he was missing her? He only had to remember her body naked before him on the bed at the Anchor, her mouth open in a little "Oh" of surprise, as he pulled her toward him and slid himself inside her. Seeing his body entering hers had given him a primitive thrill he had never felt before. *You are mine!* The words had rung in his head. They still did.

"Oliver?" She was peering impatiently into his face. "Oliver, did you hear me? I said, will you sell me Candlewood?"

He laughed, and this time it was with relief. "No," he said.

He had surprised her—he had surprised himself. Suddenly he did not feel nearly so confused. She wanted him. She had been angry after the night at the Anchor. Because he had deceived her? Yes. But also because she believed he had been playacting all along, that he had not really wanted her as desperately, as madly, as he said he did. She was an innocent—another, more experienced woman would have realized he was not pretending. But Oliver had convinced her too well, and she truly believed their kisses and all that followed had been a lie. Time to set her straight.

"Why won't you sell Candlewood?" she demanded.

She was pursing her lips. He felt the stirring heat in his groin.

"Some things aren't for sale for money, and Candlewood is one of them."

"But you don't want it!"

"Don't I?"

Vivianna stared at him wildly. "I don't understand. Perhaps you don't realize how wealthy Fraser is. He could buy and sell your aunt three times over."

Oliver grinned. "Are you boasting about the amount of blunt your father has, Vivianna? Hardly the behavior of a reformer, is it?"

"I'm not boasting! Name your price."

He gave her a lazy smile. Her eyes narrowed, suddenly suspicious, but he noticed she no longer looked quite as comfortable with the situation as she had. Good.

"Name my price? Is that what you said?"

"Yes." Vivianna bit her lip.

"Then I want you. *You* are my price."

Vivianna knew she was staring at him. She couldn't help it. The room was swirling about her, or maybe she was dreaming. He wanted her? How was that so? She had believed he would look at her offer from a purely financial view—this was the new Oliver and he would be as cold and pitiless as he had been after they left the Anchor. But he wasn't. He was looking at her in that particular manner.

Like the rake.

Despite her confusion, and her need to be cautious, Vivianna felt a treacherous shiver run down her spine. Desire curled in her stomach, and her breath quickened.

"Well, Vivianna, I'm waiting. What is your answer?

You for Candlewood. That was the deal you wanted to do with me at the opera. I must admit I was rather put out at the time—my feelings were hurt—but I've finally come 'round to it. I've decided I'll have you at any price, even if that means giving you Candlewood."

"No. My answer is no. Of course it's no."

"Why not? You know I need an heir, and I think we would make a very nice heir together. I would have to marry you, of course, but I wouldn't mind that. I quite like having you about, when you're not lecturing me."

"Oliver," she gasped, and her face twisted as if she were in pain. "Stop it. You know I can't . . . can't marry you. Apart from the fact that you lied to me, and humiliated me. I am—"

"I lied to you to protect you. I'm sorry if I humiliated you. I didn't mean to. I was worried Lawson would see how much you meant to me and hurt you just to hurt me. Vivianna, this sounds bloody stupid now, but I lied to you because I love you."

She was staring at him, the color rising in her cheeks, her eyes dark and bewildered. She didn't believe him completely, but she was beginning to. In a moment he would have won her back.

"Oliver—"

Beneath them came a loud, echoing thud.

Vivianna jumped and Oliver cursed. Then, seeing Vivianna's shocked face, he reached out and took her hand in his, his fingers strong and warm.

"He can't get out," he said quietly.

"What if he does?" she whispered, and realized she was shaking. "He'll be so angry. I don't think I can face him again."

"If he does, then I'll deal with him. It's the least I can do after what you did for me." Oliver put his arms around her, and despite herself Vivianna relaxed against him. He felt so good.

"Maybe I didn't express myself quite as I should have when I first arrived," he said against her hair. "I should have said you were the bravest, most wonderful woman I know. And that in capturing Lawson and finding those letters I owe you a lifetime of thank-you's."

"Eddie found the letters," she reminded him, her breath warm against his neck. "And Ellen."

"I'll thank them, too."

He leaned back, gazing down into her eyes. His mouth was so close; and then he smiled. Suddenly there he was. Oliver, the man who had turned her into a passionate and loving woman. The man who had set the seductress in her free.

Her Oliver.

Blindly, Vivianna lifted her lips to his.

The door at the end of the gallery banged open. "Miss! Miss!" Eddie's voice echoed wildly all around them. "The bobbies are here!"

After that there was no time for kisses. Oliver seemed to know one of the policemen—Sergeant Ackroyd—and he showed him the letters. Vivianna saw his expression twist in disgust. Then the lion was rolled back and Lawson, gray-faced, eyes watchful, was helped out.

"This man," he said in a shaking but authorative voice, "kept me prisoner. You know who I am. Arrest him!"

Oliver shook his head. "It's no use, Lawson. They know. We all know. Even if you manage to convince them they've arrested the wrong man, it can't be for long. Soon everyone will know. Even Queen Victoria . . . especially the queen."

Lawson's mouth turned down. "Ancient history," he retorted angrily, but it was a bluff.

"I hardly think she will view it in that way. That you wrote to Sir John Conroy, offering him your support in his efforts to bully the queen? That you were prepared to help him rule the country from behind the throne after her coronation? You even put yourself forward as prime minister. From memory I think your words were, 'I know how to handle spoilt bitches. I have a kennel full at home.' "

"Old news," Lawson cut through his words, the desperation more audible. "Folly, I agree, but why should a man's reputation be damned for something that happened so many years ago?"

Oliver could not help but be amazed by him. Lawson stood tall and intimidating, looking half crazed with self-righteousness. He could not believe he had done wrong; he would not believe it. There was no repentance in him. Everything must be sacrificed to the altar of his own ego—Anthony, Oliver, even the queen herself.

"How did you get the letters back from Conroy?" Oliver asked him, stepping closer.

Lawson flashed him a vicious look. For a moment it seemed as if he would not answer, and then anger tightened his jaw. "I paid him for them. I had to buy them back. He agreed and I thought it was all over, and then they happened to be delivered to my house when Anthony was there, waiting for me, alone."

"And he noticed the address and the handwriting and he could not help himself. He read them."

Lawson shrugged. "If you say so."

"I do say so, my lord. He found you out. He was cleverer than you. He was a *better* man than you."

"Stubborn and stupid." Lawson dismissed his oldest and dearest friend.

Oliver nodded to Sergeant Ackroyd, and two of the constables came forward and planted large hands on Lawson's shoulders. "You are going to be taken to see the queen, Lawson," he said softly. "You can explain it to her. And then I want to know all about how you murdered Anthony."

Lawson stiffened. "You can prove nothing."

"Perhaps. But I mean to try."

For a moment it seemed as if Lawson would refuse to go, and then his face went slack and he shook his head. "To be locked up by a scatterbrained woman and two grubby brats," he said, as if he couldn't believe his ill fortune.

"You should never underestimate the power of a woman," Vivianna declared, thinking of the queen.

Lawson cast up his eyes. "Take me away, gentlemen, I beg you."

Oliver barely had time to smile at her as he followed them out.

Vivianna hurried after them, but Oliver was all business now. He was accompanying the policemen and Lawson back to London. Vivianna stood on the front steps of Candlewood and watched while he drove away and the two children waved frantically at the departing vehicles.

Then she sat down on the stairs.

He had asked her to marry him. He had said he loved her. The confusion and joy that had first washed over her when he spoke those words had receded. Vivianna Greentree, who had always declared she paid no heed to society's rules and strictures, who believed that people should be judged on what they did rather than who they were, had come to a painful realization.

She could not possibly marry Oliver Montegomery.

Not if she wanted to be happy, and to make him happy.

He was a Montegomery, a member of a proud and ancient aristocratic family. Whatever he might say to the contrary, that heritage clung to him and had formed him into what he was. Lawson had been right in that, if nothing else. Oliver would be expected to marry the daughter of an earl at the very least.

Vivianna, the bastard daughter of Aphrodite and Fraser, was barred from polite society. She had been sneered at, stared at askance, and her family was ostracized and ridiculed. She might ignore all that and still insist on marrying him, but it would be a cruel and selfish act.

If Oliver really loved her—and who knew whether or not he really did?—he might pretend it didn't matter. But it did matter. It would matter to him, eventually. He would come to hate her.

Better not to put either of them in such an uncomfortable and ultimately disastrous position.

Despite how much she longed to.

Chapter 21

"I want ye to come and live here, lass."

Fraser looked thinner than ever, his hands like claws upon the covers. The big tabby cat had curled up on his bed today, comfortably within stroking distance, and with one eye on Vivianna.

"Alone?" she said. "My family would not approve."

"*Yer family,*" he muttered. "I am yer family!"

"But I have only just met you, Fraser."

"My blood runs in yer veins!" he shouted, and then he began to cough. Vivianna found him water, and helped him lift his head to sip.

Vivianna supposed that no matter how rude and nasty Fraser could be, he was her father, and soon he would be gone. She, who had always been weighed down by her sense of responsibility where others were concerned, found herself caught between the need to be a daughter to him and the wish that her father was someone else altogether.

She could not like him, and she knew he did not like her.

They were bound together by the ties of a kinship that exhilarated neither of them. And that made her sad.

At one time Vivianna had believed that finding her parents would make her the happiest woman in England, but it wasn't so. She had always had contentment—her life at Greentree Manor and her work with children. But a full and boundless happiness, what was that? Those fleeting moments with Oliver? The time she had spent in his arms, talking with him, sparring with him? But that, she reminded herself, had been an illusion. That man wasn't the real Oliver . . . was it?

He hadn't called upon her since Lawson's arrest. Of course, he had been busy. Word had got about that Lord Lawson was under close arrest for the murder of Anthony, although he had yet to formally confess. It was whispered that Lawson was enjoying the notoriety, and there were rumors of further unsavory matters perpetrated by him in the course of his long career. Bribery and threats, beatings and disappearances. According to the newspapers, Oliver was the hero of the hour. Lord Montegomery was no longer a scoundrel and a rake, but the nation's savior. It had a fine ring to it.

And he would see justice done eventually, Vivianna was certain of it.

Marry me. I love you.

Perhaps she should have gone to him, but she had been afraid. Vivianna, the fearless reformer, was suddenly shy of him. Besides, what would she say? She was the bastard daughter of a courtesan and her lover; Oliver was the last of a proud and aristocratic family. And now she had finally realized just how big a chasm there was between them, and it frightened her.

A tear leaked beneath her lashes and ran down her

cheek. She missed him. She missed everything about him. Her life was empty without him.

"Lass?" Fraser's thin, clawlike hand reached out and brushed her skin, capturing the tear. His hazel eyes were uncertain, a little dismayed. "Why do ye weep?" he demanded. "There's nothing to greet for. I dinna mind dying. I am old and my life is lived. Ye are young and yers is still to come."

"There was a man . . ."

Fraser snorted. "A man," he said in disgust. "Now ye can have any man ye want, girl! Have a dozen if ye so wish."

Vivianna couldn't help but laugh. "A dozen may be a little much for me, Fraser, but I will keep it in mind."

"And dinna choose one who will hurt you, lass," he added, eyeing her seriously. "I willna have my girl hurt by any man, woman, or child."

"I will be careful, Fraser. Thank you," she added, touched almost beyond words.

He nodded, and then sighed and closed his eyes. "I am tired now. Go away and leave me alone."

Vivianna crept to the door, but she was smiling. Perhaps there was more to Fraser than met the eye. Perhaps, somewhere in that tough and prickly heart, there was a small, warm patch with her name on it. Perhaps there was something in him to like, after all.

A liveried servant showed Oliver into a sitting room at Buckingham Palace and closed the door. The royal couple stood together, he tall and handsome, she shorter and plumper. Both men bowed deeply. It was the queen who spoke first, her slightly protrudent eyes fixed on Oliver.

"I believe you have done us a great service, Montegomery."

Oliver stepped forward to take the queen's outstretched hand and sketch a kiss upon it. "Your Majesty, it was my pleasure."

"A most unpleasant business," Prince Albert said with his thick German accent, shaking his head gloomily. "I believe you have given up a year of your life to find the perpetrator of your brother's death."

"My brother was murdered, Your Royal Highness. I always knew he had uncovered a secret concerning Lord Lawson—he had hinted as much to me. I . . . Unfortunately he never had a chance to tell me exactly what that secret was. But I knew he had found some letters, personal letters, incriminating letters. It was only a matter of finding them."

"We have seen the letters you found hidden at Candlewood." Victoria pursed her lips. "What took you so long to find them?"

"I did not know of my grandfather's secret hiding place, Ma'am, although my brother did. At first I believed the entire house would have to be taken down to find them, but fortunately that will no longer be necessary."

"I can hardly believe it," the queen said in a bewildered voice. "I know that Sir John had plans to run the country through me, and for years he tried to dominate me and intimidate me. However, I was made of stronger stuff, and when I came to the throne I threw off his attempts, and now he is banished. But Lawson, too? Once he was prime minister, did he mean to bully me, just as Sir John Conroy bullied me and my mother?"

Albert patted her hand comfortingly.

"I *liked* him, Albert, almost as much as I like Lord Melbourne."

"Never mind. I am sure, in time, you will grow to like Sir Robert Peel, too."

The queen looked unconvinced.

Albert gave her a fondly exasperated look, and then turned to Oliver. "You have done Her Majesty a great service. It doesn't bear thinking that a man such as Lord Lawson might have remained unmasked and eventually have become prime minister. A man who would kill another to prevent a scandal. You have our deepest gratitude, but tell me, is there something you would like in return? Some service we can render you, my lord?"

Oliver tried to clear his thoughts. He had avenged Anthony's murder, brought to justice the creature whose hunger for personal glory and ambition was so great that he would have done anything to feed it. And yet there was someone else. Someone who very much needed the assistance of the Queen of England and her consort, Prince Albert.

Oliver told them what was in his mind.

The royal couple exchanged a glance. "A very odd request," Victoria said primly, her eyes flashing with disapproval—she was clearly not amused.

"We owe Montegomery a great deal," Albert reminded her.

Victoria sighed, and bowed her head regally. "Very well, then. It shall be done."

Vivianna looked down at her hands in their long white gloves, clasped in front of her white satin gown. Her chestnut hair was dressed in ringlets with ribbons, and Lady Greentree had given her a string of pearls to wear about her neck for this most auspicious occasion.

She knew she looked as unlike Vivianna Greentree from Yorkshire as she had ever looked. She felt like a stranger, too. It did not seem real, any of it.

Who could have imagined that she would be introduced to the queen? By particular invitation? It was almost the same as being presented at one of the queen's drawing rooms.

"Better," Lady Greentree had informed her, "because you will not have a lot of other hopefuls pushing and shoving. There will be just you, Vivianna. Oh, I am so glad! Do you realize what this means? All the gossips, all the people who have cut us, will be silenced. If the queen will accept you, then so must everyone else!"

Once Vivianna would have declared that they must take her as she was, and she still might have, but not when her family had suffered so for her sake.

She wondered if she would forget her name or trip on her hem. It was such a great honor for a girl of her dubious background, and she did not want to spoil it.

Fraser was aware of that, too. He had insisted on seeing her in the gown Elena had made for her. He had been propped up in his bed, the big tabby cat sitting beside him. Both pairs of eyes had watched Vivianna cross the room. Fraser had nodded, his lined and yellowy face suddenly almost benevolent as he had smiled. "Aye, ye'll do," he had said with quiet pride. "Ye'll do, daughter. . . ."

Vivianna, who had thought herself prepared, found that when she arrived at Buckingham Palace she was woefully nervous. She was led into an elegant anteroom, and there waited for half an hour before she was taken to the drawing room where the royal couple were awaiting her.

She came forward, as she had been instructed, trying to remember the intricacies of the curtsy. She seemed to get through it without too many wobbles.

"Miss Greentree." The queen was small and plump, with a round face and large eyes. Recognizing her from the opera, Vivianna thought she was prettier close up. It was a pity she towered over her so.

"Your Majesty." She managed the words above the frightened thumping of her heart.

The queen spoke firmly. "Miss Greentree, I do not approve of you, but that is not why you are here today. I have been prevailed upon, by someone who has done me a great service, to give you the gloss of my approval. You can be sure that after this visit no one will snub you. No one will dare. Albert?"

The prince, handsome in a blue jacket and buff trousers, gave his wife an amused glance. "Her Majesty is very conscious of her debts, Miss Greentree, and she owes your sponsor a great deal."

"My sponsor, Your Royal Highness?" Vivianna managed. "I have a sponsor?"

The royal couple exchanged a glance. Prince Albert smiled.

"Yes, Miss Greentree," he said in his heavy German accent, "you do have a sponsor. It is Lord Montegomery, and believe me, he has your welfare in the forefront of his mind."

"He does?" Vivianna managed. "Sir," she added belatedly.

Prince Albert nodded. "Indeed he has. He did not tell you, then? Ah, perhaps it was meant to be a surprise. You see he was very much afraid you would feel the displeasure of London society because of your father and your mother, and he did not think it just. I myself am a great believer in marriage and the vows made before God, but I can see that your parentage is no fault of your own."

"Thank you, Sir."

His gaze fixed upon hers with an intensity that was rather startling. "I believe you work hard for the poor, Miss Greentree. I find such selfless service admirable. I, too, would like to see the many wrongs in this country righted."

Vivianna smiled with sheer joy. Here was a man after her own heart, an ally, and unlike herself, he was in a position to make a great deal of difference to the wrongs he spoke of. And it had been Oliver who brought her to his attention, Oliver who made it possible for her to meet him.

"I am very glad to hear you say so, Sir," she said. "I am very glad indeed."

"Lord Montegomery is very handsome," the queen said, with a sideways glance at her husband. "Do you not agree, Miss Greentree?"

Vivianna wondered what she should say. In the end she told the truth. "Yes, Ma'am, he is very handsome."

The queen nodded, but there was a twinkle in her eye. "You must visit us again, Miss Greentree. Come to one of my drawing rooms before your wedding."

Wedding?

"I . . . of course, Ma'am."

It was over. She was dismissed. Vivianna curtsied once more, and exited from the room backward, and the attendant closed the door.

Lady Greentree was waiting for her, her eyes shining with curiosity. "Well?" she demanded.

"They are almost like ordinary people," Vivianna said, still a little shaken. "Almost."

Lady Greentree laughed and hugged her. "You are a very fortunate young lady. You will see. This will make a very great difference to your life in London from now on."

"Mama," Vivianna whispered, "it was Oliver. He did this for me. He . . . he sponsored me."

Lady Greentree's brow wrinkled, her pale eyes quizzical. "Are you sure, Vivianna? Oliver Montegomery?"

"Yes, Oliver. He did it for me. To please me."

She felt her heart swell within her, and such happiness that she could hardly stop smiling. The savior of the nation really did love her, after all.

The following morning there were dozens of invitations to sit upon the mantel at Queen's Square—Vivianna Greentree, social pariah, was an overnight success.

"Vivianna, you are so lucky!" cried Marietta, her eyes wide. "I am so jealous. Why can I not meet our mother? I want to ask her so many questions."

Vivianna smiled at her younger sister. "That is exactly why you cannot meet her. Not yet."

"The Beatty sisters are here to see you, Miss Vivianna." Lil was at the door of the sitting room, her eyes sparkling.

"Thank you, Lil, I'll come and . . ."

But it was too late. Miss Susan and Miss Greta were inside the room, clasping her hands, their faces radiating happiness, their eyes teary with joy. They began to speak, their voices a confusion of intermingling words, but somehow Vivianna made sense of it.

"Miss Greentree! Lord Montegomery has given

Candlewood to us. Given it to us, as a gift! He will make repairs at once, he says, while we are at Bethnal Green. He will sign Candlewood over to the shelter in perpetuity!"

Vivianna could not speak. After a moment she managed an "Oh," and a tear ran down her cheek.

Oliver had done this? For the children?

But in her heart Vivianna knew he had not done it for the children, not wholly.

He had done it for her.

And the time had come to beard the monster in his den.

"Miss Greentree is here to see you, my lord."

Hodge looked disapproving, as always, but Oliver wasn't deceived. The butler had been looking out for Vivianna every day. And she had come. At last. He could understand she had been busy: By all accounts she was a success. With her passionate views and her way of saying exactly what she meant, Vivianna would be considered fresh and original. Her parentage would never be truly forgotten, and there would always be those who held it against her, but there were many more who were willing to overlook it and like her for herself.

Yes, she had no doubt been busy, but, truth be told, he could not have waited much longer.

"Show her in, Hodge."

Oliver wondered what she would look like this afternoon. Severe in one of her Yorkshire gowns, feminine with ribbons and bows, or with the queenly elegance of the woman she had been at the opera. But she surprised him yet again. She was wearing white silk, striped in cherry red, that rustled when she moved and gleamed in the light from the windows.

Her hair was coiled about her head in braids, and more were looped at the sides. And, most surprising of all, she carried with her a basket in which reposed a large, yellow-eyed tabby cat. It looked heavy.

"Lord Montegomery," she said, and set the cat down with some relief upon the Turkish rug.

"Miss Greentree," Oliver said, coming closer. "You never fail to astonish me." He eyed the cat cautiously. "Who is this?"

"This is Fraser's cat. I was visiting him before I came here, and Fraser asked me to take care of the cat for him. He tried to make me believe that he does not want him anymore, but what he really wants is to be certain he has gone to a good home, before he dies. Otherwise he will fret, you see. Fraser, I mean, not the cat."

Oliver thought about this. "What's his name?"

"Robbie Burns."

"Of course."

A tap on the door, and Hodge entered. He was carrying a saucer of milk. "Miss Greentree asked me to bring this, my lord."

"For Robbie Burns?"

"The poet, my lord?"

"No, the cat, Hodge!"

The saucer was duly placed down on the rug, and Hodge retreated. The cat, in its basket, looked at Oliver, and Oliver looked at Robbie Burns. He sighed. "I know what you want," he said. "You want me to take the cat. Is that it?"

Vivianna bit her lip, her eyes wide and very green. "I would not ask, but Mama has Krispen at home in Yorkshire, and Krispen can be very jealous. Robbie Burns is a very nice cat, and I am sure he will be no trouble, but he is a man's cat. He does not take to women."

"Vivianna, Vivianna," Oliver murmured, "what more must I do? I have arranged to restore your reputation, I have given Candlewood to your children, and now I must take your father's cat. Where will it end?"

"I didn't know it was you who arranged for my reputation to be restored," she said in a small voice. "You should have told me."

He glanced at her. "I would have, but you didn't ask. Your reputation didn't matter a jot to me, but I could see it might be awkward for you and your family. Prince Albert said you were charming, by the way, and will make me a very obedient wife."

Vivianna blinked. "Oh."

"He cannot know you very well, can he, if he thinks you will be obedient?"

She ignored that. "Did my reputation really not matter a jot to you?"

Oliver smiled to himself, and reached down to unfasten the basket. The tabby cat stepped out onto the rug and began to wash himself, as if he had expected nothing less than a new home in Berkeley Square.

"It really didn't. You are far more to me than who or what your parents might be or have done."

"Oh."

"Vivianna, before you came into my life, all I thought about was my brother and avenging his death. I didn't dream of the future; I didn't imagine I might have a life after Lawson was punished. But you changed that. Suddenly I could see that I did have a future, and I wanted it with all my heart, because you were in it."

Vivianna stepped closer. "But you are a hero now," she said quietly. "The newspapers admire your dreadful waistcoats—they have become quite the fashion. Women swoon in the street whenever they see you."

He laughed. "The only woman I want to swoon when she sees me prefers to lecture me instead."

"Oliver . . ."

"I hope you're not going to abandon me now you are a wealthy heiress," he went on, and his gaze was dark and sensuous. "I still need you. Maybe you don't realize it, but I have always considered myself the black sheep of the Montegomery family. You have to save me from my sins, Vivianna. I desperately need the sort of redemption only you can give me."

Vivianna caught her breath. "I would have thought you had become a golden sheep now," she replied, eyes bright. "Rescuing the nation from the greedy hands of Lord Lawson, handing over Candlewood to the Shelter for Poor Orphans, saving Robbie Burns from a life on the streets!"

Oliver smiled.

"Giving me a truly remarkable night of passion," she added softly.

His gaze sharpened. "Did I?"

"Oh yes." She shivered at the memory, hugging herself. "I wake up from sleep and I'm remembering it so clearly. My body is alive with your touch, aching for you to be there in the bed beside me. But I'm alone, Oliver. I don't want to be alone anymore."

"Marry me, then, and we'll have a night of passion every night for the rest of our lives."

Vivianna smiled. "Yes, please. I love the rake in you, Oliver. . . ."

Oliver's heart sank. She loved the rake; he knew that. But there was more to him than the rake. He had hopes and dreams and ambitions that Oliver the rake could never imagine. Couldn't she see that?

"I love the rake," Vivianna said, and she was standing before him, gazing up into his eyes, "but I love *you* more."

His lips curled into a lazy smile. "I'm going to kiss every inch of you," he drawled.

Vivianna's legs trembled, and with a laugh she flung herself into his arms. "Oh, Oliver," she breathed, feeling his warmth, his strength, the wonderful sensation of being held by the man she loved.

He looked down at her as if she were the only woman in the world for him. "I can't live without you, you know that, don't you? I crave lectures like other men crave strong drink."

"As long as you don't mind about Aphrodite."

"Hmm," he said with a wicked smile.

"Don't you dare say it!" Vivianna declared.

His mouth brushed hers, then stilled, and now they were both shaking. "Say what?" he whispered.

"Like mother, like daughter."

"Promise me something, Vivianna," he said, his breath warm against her lips. "That you will always be *my* courtesan. Mine alone."

"I promise, as long as you will be *my* very own rake."

He grinned, and kissed her, and they sealed their promises as passionately as they knew how.

Epilogue

"I received a letter from Mama today," Vivianna said, setting down her soup spoon. A servant came to remove her plate, while Hodge stood, supercilious, his eye upon the room.

"Lady Greentree?"

"Yes, Oliver. You know she is my mama. I call Aphrodite 'Aphrodite,' or it becomes too confusing."

"Of course, my sweet."

The next course was served.

"She says that Marietta is longing to return to London, but Mama thinks it would be best to wait. She knows about Aphrodite, of course, but she won't meet her yet. And Francesca, how will Francesca cope with the news that she is the daughter of a famous courtesan?"

"How indeed." Oliver gave her his lazy, charming smile. Beneath the dining table, Robbie Burns brushed against his legs, purring monotonously. He slipped a piece of roasted fowl beneath the board and was rewarded as it was snatched unceremoniously from his fingers.

"I sometimes think Aphrodite and Dobson are fonder of each other than they let on," Vivianna was saying. "I must ask if she has written any more in her diary."

Oliver had his own thoughts on Aphrodite and Dobson. It wasn't the ideal setup, having a wife who was the daughter of a famous courtesan, but it didn't particularly bother him. Nor did it seem to bother Lady Marsh, who stated herself more than content with Vivianna as Oliver's wife.

Hodge sent a servant to clear the meal. Vivianna caught his eye, and then rose gracefully to her feet.

"I must instruct the chef with regard to dessert," she said. "It's something very special tonight. I'll only be a moment, Oliver."

He nodded, absently stroking the cat beneath the table. Married life suited Oliver. He had never realized before just how restful it could be, married to a woman one loved as much as he loved Vivianna. They had their disagreements, but it didn't seem to matter, because they shared such a deep and abiding commitment to each other. There was something very wonderful in waking up in the night and finding Vivianna by his side. . . .

The door opened and Hodge appeared. Behind him, upon a sturdy trolley with wheels, was a very large serving plate with a cover concealing whatever was upon it. Under Hodge's instructions, a pair of servants wheeled the contraption into the dining room and then, with a nod from Hodge, lifted the covered plate and placed it carefully upon the dining table. Before Oliver.

He sat up straighter and looked inquiringly at Hodge.

Hodge's face was inscrutable. "Lady Montegomery's instructions. Dessert, my lord," he said. He nodded at the servants and, with one on either side of the cover, they lifted the cover off the dish and carried it swiftly from the room. Hodge followed, and closed the door behind him.

Oliver couldn't think of anything to say. His mind had gone numb, even as other parts of him had come very much to life.

Before him, prettily posed upon the serving plate, knelt Vivianna. She was completely naked, apart from some cream decoration. Rosettes covered her nipples, and swirls meandered across her belly, ending in a rather large dollop of cream at the juncture of her thighs. Swags of flowers had been placed upon her flanks, and the rounded cheeks of her bottom were patterned with green cream leaves and what looked like reproductions of cherries.

Oliver met her eyes.

She looked a little uncertain. As if it had seemed a good idea at the time, but now that she had actually gone and done it she wasn't quite sure how he would react.

Oliver stood up. He climbed onto the chair and onto the table, divesting himself of his jacket and cravat as he went. Reassured, Vivianna's mouth curved into one of her most seductive smiles. She gave her head a little shake and her hair, knotted at her nape, came tumbling wildly about her.

Oliver tore off his shirt.

And then his mouth closed on hers, and he felt as if he were going to explode right there, with just their lips touching. His hands hovered over her, frightened to touch, not wanting to spoil . . . anything. He bent and licked the rosette off one of her breasts, and then the other. His palms closed possessively over the cherries and the leaves. Her fingers were on his trousers, hurriedly unbuttoning them, as he returned to her mouth.

"I hope you don't mind," Vivianna said between licks and kisses. "Aphrodite told me about a dinner she once held, and I've been wanting to replicate it ever since."

"Mind?" he groaned.

He pulled her into his arms and she straddled his thighs, knocking a bowl and some silver cutlery to the floor. Then Vivianna suddenly stilled, held his face in her palms, and gazed into his eyes with perfect trust and perfect love.

"Oliver," she said, rubbing her cheek against his and smearing him liberally with cream. "Let's eat dessert."